Praise for
THE EXCALIBUR MURDERS

"This obviously is a different take on Camelot as it is a country filled with intrigue, double crossing, betrayals, and ambitious people who believe they are more deserving than their liege to rule . . . It is a more realistic place populated with individuals who seem genuine and not the archetype goodness fantasy of the myths . . . Using Camelot as a backdrop, J.M.C. Blair provides a great historical mystery."
—*Genre Go Round Reviews*

"If you are a fan of the Malloryesque mediaeval dream world approach to the Arthurian cycle and enjoy whodunits, then here is a new series that is aimed straight at you . . . Mr. Blair has obviously been reading Mark Twain and T. H. White with his semihumorous but pessimistic view of a boisterous but disillusioned King Arthur, wicked Morgan, scheming Guenevere, and brainless Lancelot. Having the court as pagans is an interesting twist, as are the murders themselves."
—*Crime Thru Time*

"Though Merlin has no magical powers, he is as brilliant as Sherlock . . . A fascinating vision. I frankly loved this book and want to read more of the author and the series."
—*Huntress Reviews*

"The setting is well developed, the characters are generally quite interesting, and the mystery is good enough to carry the story to its conclusion . . . I wish the series well."
—*Don D'Ammassa*

THE
LANCELOT
MURDERS

A MERLIN INVESTIGATION

J.M.C. BLAIR

BERKLEY PRIME CRIME, NEW YORK

THE BERKLEY PUBLISHING GROUP
Published by the Penguin Group
Penguin Group (USA) Inc.
375 Hudson Street, New York, New York 10014, USA

Penguin Group (Canada), 90 Eglinton Avenue East, Suite 700, Toronto, Ontario M4P 2Y3, Canada
(a division of Pearson Penguin Canada Inc.)
Penguin Books Ltd., 80 Strand, London WC2R 0RL, England
Penguin Group Ireland, 25 St. Stephen's Green, Dublin 2, Ireland (a division of Penguin Books Ltd.)
Penguin Group (Australia), 250 Camberwell Road, Camberwell, Victoria 3124, Australia
(a division of Pearson Australia Group Pty. Ltd.)
Penguin Books India Pvt. Ltd., 11 Community Centre, Panchsheel Park, New Delhi—110 017, India
Penguin Group (NZ), 67 Apollo Drive, Rosedale, North Shore 0632, New Zealand
(a division of Pearson New Zealand Ltd.)
Penguin Books (South Africa) (Pty.) Ltd., 24 Sturdee Avenue, Rosebank, Johannesburg 2196,
South Africa

Penguin Books Ltd., Registered Offices: 80 Strand, London WC2R 0RL, England

This is a work of fiction. Names, characters, places, and incidents either are the product of the author's imagination or are used fictitiously, and any resemblance to actual persons, living or dead, business establishments, events, or locales is entirely coincidental. The publisher does not have any control over and does not assume any responsibility for author or third-party websites or their content.

THE LANCELOT MURDERS

A Berkley Prime Crime Book / published by arrangement with the author

PRINTING HISTORY
Berkley Prime Crime mass-market edition / May 2009

Copyright © 2009 by John Curlovich.
Cover illustration by Dan Craig.
Cover design by Annette Fiore Defex.
Interior text design by Kristin del Rosario.

ISBN: 978-0-425-22813-5

BERKLEY® PRIME CRIME
Berkley Prime Crime Books are published by The Berkley Publishing Group,
a division of Penguin Group (USA) Inc.,
375 Hudson Street, New York, New York 10014.
BERKLEY® PRIME CRIME and the PRIME CRIME logo are trademarks of Penguin Group (USA) Inc.

PRINTED IN THE UNITED STATES OF AMERICA

10 9 8 7 6 5 4 3 2 1

ONE

Evening at Camelot; late May

The sun sat precisely on the horizon, and its last brilliant reds, yellows, oranges colored the sky. In the east the sky had darkened and there were a thousand stars and an enormous moon. Among the trees owls were calling softly to one another. The creeks, rills and rivulets that made the countryside fertile were flowing softly and gently. To all appearances England was at peace.

Merlin was in his laboratory, one level below his living quarters in what everyone at Camelot, to his constant annoyance, called "Wizard's Tower." In front of him on the lab table was a glass blank; he poured a fine abrasive on it and ground it slowly, carefully, with a gentle circular motion. His raven, Roc, perched serenely on his shoulder and watched what he was doing, puzzled in a disinterested way. Merlin himself found the activity relaxing; he was lost in idle thought.

When the lens seemed to be finished he took it to the

window and held it at arm's length while with his other hand he held a second one close to his eye.

The bird on his shoulder nuzzled his cheek.

"Look, Roc. See the beauty of the world. See the peace." Yet something nagged at him. Everything was too calm, too lovely, and much too serene. "So why do I find that peace so ominous?" he whispered. "Why is calm always shattered? Why is that so eerily predictable?"

The bird squawked.

"It is my race, Roc. It is humanity. We see a sweet thing and feel the urge to destroy it. What unnatural creatures we are."

Then there came a knock at the door. Greffys, King Arthur's squire, opened it and put his head in. "Excuse me, sir. The king wants you."

"What is it this time?" The interruption wasn't welcome. He returned to his worktable and placed the lenses carefully on it. Roc squawked shrilly and flew out the window.

"I don't know, sir. A courier just arrived with some mail, and Britomart brought it directly to the king. I heard her say something about an 'intelligence report.'"

"Intelligence? Britomart runs the military."

"I know that, sir. The king read the dispatch and his mood darkened. He fell silent for a long time. Britomart tried talking to him, but he just stared into space and wouldn't respond. Then he came around and told me to fetch you."

Merlin narrowed his eyes suspiciously. "It is midevening. Shouldn't you be doing your lessons?"

"Not when the king requires my service, sir." He shifted his weight awkwardly. "Do you . . . do you think it might be another traitor? Or war, maybe?" The latter prospect seemed to excite Greffys.

"It took me months to persuade the king to let me open a school for the squires and the pages. It will do no good if you ignore your studies."

"We have duties, sir. More immediate ones than learning

about Roman comedy and the metaphysics of Aristotle. What do you think this intelligence might be about?"

"How could I possibly know? Something foul." He felt a twinge of pain and leaned on the table. "Hand me my cane, will you?"

Greffys stared at his equipment with undisguised curiosity. "May I ask what you are doing, sir?"

Merlin was annoyed at being interrupted, but the teacher in him could not be repressed. "Here, come and see. I am grinding this piece of glass into a lens. Look." He took the lens and held it above his left hand; the fingers were magnified. Greffys watched, fascinated. "That's remarkable, sir. I've never seen anything like it."

"You remember the lenses you and Petronus used to focus the torchlight on the night we exposed Mark's villainy?"

The boy held his own fingers under the lens and wiggled them. "Yes, I do. But . . . but what is this all for?"

"The theory underlying optics goes back to the Greeks." He said this pointedly, to remind the boy of the importance of his lessons.

"But what exactly are you doing, sir? And why?"

"I have been experimenting with them. I find that if I grind them differently, they produce different effects. Some make distant objects appear closer. Others magnify whatever is held under them. And I am finding that combining them in various ways can produce the most remarkable effects. Come and look."

He led Greffys to the window and showed him how to hold the two lenses. "Look through them at that tower on top of the hill there."

"The one off on the horizon, with the lights?"

"Exactly."

"But . . . it's too far away."

"Do it anyway, Greffys."

The boy did as he was told. It took him a moment to find

the correct distance between the lenses, and he seemed to have trouble holding them steady. "I can see it! I can see the windows clearly enough to count them."

"Precisely. I still don't know how to grind the lenses perfectly. There must be a formula for it, but so far I have to trust my hands, their experience, and hope for the best. About a quarter of the lenses I grind turn out useless. But other combinations magnify very small objects to enormous size."

"And you say you're not a wizard."

Merlin glared. "This is science, not sorcery. I am determined—Arthur would say mad—to see everything in the world as it actually is. If my lenses can help me do it . . ."

Greffys was lost. "How else can we see it?"

He took a deep breath. "Look at Arthur, for instance. He takes nearly everything and everyone at face value. If a knight pledges loyalty, in Arthur's mind he must be loyal. If another country promises peace, he sees peace. But look below the surface and you see the world of men quite differently."

"And so you magnify your fingers?" The boy couldn't hide his befuddlement.

"Let us just say that trying to see things properly is a hard habit to break. Look out there. See how beautiful the world appears? But I tell you, Greffys, as sure as anything, there are forces out there that will lead to bloodshed and death. There always are. The stars are beautiful, but they are indifferent. They shine on killers and victims alike. But enough of that. Look over here. I have been studying the properties of the substance called phosphorus. It is quite fascinating. Under the right conditions, it glows."

"But, sir, Arthur wants you. Another time, perhaps. We should be going."

Merlin snorted at the boy. "Would you hand me my cane, please?"

Advancing arthritis in his right hip had brought about a rolling limp and made it necessary for Merlin to walk on a cane. Greffys looked around the room and saw it resting against the hearth. It was of dark wood, highly polished, carved elaborately with figures of mythical beasts—dragons, unicorns, griffins. A fantastical snake ran the length of it, down one side and up the other with the tip of its tail in its mouth. The boy took it up, ran his fingers along the carved surface, then handed it to Merlin. "This is really beautiful, sir."

"I agree. But I wish I did not need it." Merlin frowned. "It was a gift from King Pellenore. He actually believes in these preposterous animals."

"So did most of your Greeks, sir."

"Be quiet and hand me my stick."

"Oh." Greffys seemed uncertain how to react. "Pellenore?"

"Yes," Merlin grumped. "Pellenore. The mad old man. The craziest man in Camelot—or the sanest. Do you know what this serpent represents?"

It was clear Greffys had no idea what he meant. Blankfaced, he stammered, "It's a snake. The king said to have you hurry, sir."

"Kings always say that." He sighed. "It would do Arthur good to have to wait a few minutes. But let's go."

Wizard's Tower was a hundred feet tall; only the tower where the king lived was taller. A stone staircase wound down the inside to the main floor of the castle. Merlin moved down it slowly, steadying himself against the wall and leaning heavily on his cane. Greffys offered a hand to help him.

"I've been working on a scheme," Merlin told the boy, "for a mechanical lift with cables, pulleys and counterweights. It is based on an invention of Hero of Alexandria. If I can get it to work, I'll never have to negotiate these stairs again."

"But if this device should fail . . ." The boy sounded dubious.

"Then I would fall to my death. What would be so terrible about that? No more traitors, no more wars, no more 'come at once.'"

"Have you thought about moving to another part of the castle, sir?"

"Where could I move that would suit me better? Besides, all the bedrooms are on upper floors. My tower keeps me away from other people. That solitude is quite precious to me. It makes study possible. It makes life bearable."

"Oh." Again the boy was puzzled. Uncertainly, he asked, "Er . . . this is arthritis?"

Merlin nodded.

"Can't you heal yourself?"

"Medical science has limits, Greffys."

"But you're a sorcerer."

Merlin glared at him and stopped moving. "I am," he said slowly and heavily, "no such thing. I am a scholar and a sometime physician. There is no such thing as magic and you ought to know it. You helped me stage the 'miracle' that exposed Mark of Cornwall. Remember?"

"Uh . . . yes, sir."

Once they reached the foot of the staircase Merlin was able to move more quickly. The main part of Camelot was busy with servants coming and going, knights clanking about in their armor and dozens of other inhabitants less easy to classify. The household staff were busy lighting torches in all the hallways.

Merlin noticed a large brown spider in a crack in the wall. "Look. Predators conceal themselves everywhere. Someone ought to do something about that."

Greffys held out a thumb and squashed the spider. "There."

"You'll be a good knight. You've already lost every trace of subtlety."

"I beg your pardon, sir?"

"Nothing."

They moved on and in a few moments they reached the foot of the King's Tower. Merlin regarded another spiral staircase and sighed. "I was not made for an age like this. The world was a better place before large-scale building. People were content in one-room houses made of mud brick."

"You lived in Egypt. You always tell us what wonders the Pyramids are."

"The Pyramids are tombs, not houses."

"I can't imagine you in a mud-brick hut, sir. Where would you keep your books and your laboratory things?"

"I suppose a tomb would be as good a place as any. Learning *is* dead."

"King Arthur says you complain too much."

"Be quiet and help me up these stairs."

A guard was posted at the bottom of the staircase; it led to the king's quarters, after all. The guard extended a hand to help Merlin up the first few steps. But just as Merlin was about to go up, he saw his assistant, Nimue, in her customary disguise as the young man called Colin, farther along the hallway. "Colin!"

She rushed to meet him. "Merlin. Have you had dinner yet? They have the most succulent ham in the refectory, glazed with honey."

"I thought there was eel on the menu."

"I had the ham and it was wonderful."

"Well, good for you. But I want you to come up to Arthur's quarters with me. There is something afoot."

"Something?"

"That is as much as I know. Come on."

The three of them climbed the stairs, with Merlin leaning on his cane and "Colin" for support. Greffys scrambled ahead. Merlin stumbled once and winced with the pain. But they made good time and reached the top level of the tower fairly quickly.

Another guard was posted there. He saluted them and waved them past, looking suspiciously at Colin. "Did the king summon you?"

Merlin got between them. "Colin is my assistant. I asked him to come along."

"Oh. Yes, sir."

The king's rooms were bright with torchlight, brighter than anyplace else in the castle. Through the windows shone the last orange-purple glow of sunset.

Almost at once they encountered Arthur; he was pacing the corridor that connected his suite of rooms. His clothes were disarrayed and his thick blond hair was unkempt. He looked angry, or perhaps lost in unpleasant thought. Britomart stood at the far end of the hall, watching him and looking concerned. When she saw Merlin she waved and called to him. "Merlin! Come here."

Merlin looked at the king, who seemed not to have noticed them. "Arthur?"

The king stopped his pacing but stared blankly into space.

"Arthur!" Merlin took his arm and shook it.

He snapped out of his reverie. "Oh. Oh, Merlin. I'm glad you've come."

"What is wrong? You look awful."

"Thank you so much. We appear to have a crisis."

"We're the government. We always have a crisis."

"Not like this. Come along. I'll let Brit explain it all to you."

"But—"

"Come along, Merlin."

They moved to the study at the end of the hallway, where Britomart was waiting. Merlin kept plying Arthur with questions, to no avail. They shook hands all around and Brit said, "I knew you could bring Arthur out of it. You have such an unsettling effect on people."

"I choose to take that as a compliment."

She grinned. "It is. In a way."

Arthur harrumphed. "Go ahead and talk about me as if I weren't here."

"Sorry, Your Majesty." Brit looked properly abashed.

"Let's sit and talk about this situation and have some wine."

"What situation?" Merlin asked loudly.

Instead of answering, Arthur gestured at the table.

They arranged themselves around it and Greffys poured cups for each of them. The wine was sweet and full-bodied. Merlin tasted it and liked it. "Our vintners are getting better."

"It's Italian."

"Oh. Sorry. Anyway, what is this all about? Brit?"

She took a long drink, sighed deeply and produced a large sheet of parchment. "This. This is an intelligence report from Guenevere's castle at Corfe. It was sent by Captain John Dalley, who you'll remember is the commander of our garrison at Corfe."

"Intelligence report? Do you mean to say you've set up spies there?"

"There and other places. Soon we'll have them all over the country." Brit was pleased with herself. "After the last treason, I convinced Arthur it is necessary."

Merlin didn't like the sound of this, and he didn't try to hide it. "Spies. Informers. They corrupt everyone and everything they touch. That is the sort of thing I'd expect at the Byzantine court, not Camelot. Nero used spies, and Caligula, the two worst tyrants of ancient Rome."

Nimue smiled. "So did Augustus and Hadrian, the two best."

"Be quiet, Colin." Merlin looked to Arthur for a response but the king's face was stone.

"The country is in a fragile state of balance, Merlin." Brit looked at the parchment scroll, not at him. "If we're to remain in power, we must maintain that balance."

"I'm not at all certain the only way to do that is with informers and spies making people fearful and turning them against one another. And I'm certain that is not the best way."

Arthur spoke. "We have enemies. You know that as well as anyone here. You helped me become king, Merlin. Surely you don't object to my *remaining* king."

Merlin looked to Brit. "And you've even managed to get people inside Corfe Castle?"

"The Spider's House. That is what the residents of Corfe call it." She nodded, grinning. "Captain Dalley managed it. He suggested to Guenevere that he should post a military attaché in her castle, for convenience of communication or some such. Naturally she suspected the attaché would be a spy, so she rejected the proposal. With her distracted by that, Dalley was able to get a real spy into the castle with no trouble."

"Who?"

"That is a secret."

"I'm the king's first counselor. Tell me."

Britomart fell silent and looked at Arthur. Softly, the king said, "In good time, Merlin. When you need to know."

Merlin sighed exaggeratedly. "Just so . . . And so now Guenevere is planning another insurrection, with her parents' help, no doubt. Is that it?"

"Guenevere," Arthur said slowly and sadly, "my lady wife, who has never been much of a wife to me . . ." He paused and looked around the room. It was clear that the news in the intelligence report, whatever it was, had upset him deeply.

"Yes, Arthur?"

"She has gotten married."

For a moment everyone fell silent. No one even blinked for what seemed a terribly long time. Then Merlin said softly, "What did you say, Arthur?"

"Married." The king looked away. "My wife has shattered her wedding vows and married that French knight she bellies with."

Brit unrolled the parchment on the table. "It's all here. Three weeks ago, she announced that she was dissolving her marriage to Arthur, and she and Lancelot went though a formal wedding ceremony. They exchanged vows, exchanged rings, exchanged gifts, even shared a huge cake with the people of the court. Their gifts to one another were ceremonial golden daggers with elaborately carved ivory handles, imported from France. Apparently they were provided by Queen Leonilla."

"That was all? Those are paltry gifts for a royal wedding."

She looked up. "There is no record of what else they might have given each other. But if I know Lancelot, his to her was something cheap."

"Not in that family," Arthur said ruefully. "I imagine they value murder weapons above anything else."

"This is treason indeed," Merlin said, turning it over in his mind. "In a messy sort of way. But surely only the king can grant a divorce in a case like this."

"Obviously."

Merlin smiled a rueful smile. "Most women are miserable enough with one husband. If there is a woman alive who deserves two, it is Guenevere." He made a sour face. "Unless it is that horrible mother of hers."

"Leonilla? My sweet bitch of a mother-in-law?" Arthur took a deep drink. "She rules her husband Leodegrance the way he rules his province—sternly and resolutely. Whatever else she is, Guenevere is her mother's daughter. But I'm glad you find the situation so amusing."

"I don't. But it is so unexpected . . . it is difficult to know how to react. Why would she have done such a thing?"

"Why, to hurt me, of course. She never stops finding new ways. Other women do needlework; Guenevere spouts venom."

Merlin took a deep breath and sat back in his chair. "The queen is capable of vindictiveness, to be sure. But she is first and foremost a political creature. She would not have done this unless she stood to gain by it. The question is, what exactly could such an act gain her?"

"Wounding me. Making me more miserable than she already has."

"It is not that simple, Arthur, and I think you know it."

Brit spoke up. "This is the grossest kind of lèse-majesté. Arrest her. Send me to Corfe with a column of soldiers and we'll take them both. And put them on trial."

"And execute them?" Merlin took the report and perused it.

"If need be, yes."

"Think for a moment, both of you." Merlin spoke with force. "Guenevere did this for a reason. A concrete political reason. We all know her. She is as shrewd and calculating as any queen in Europe. What she does, she does for advantage." He sipped his wine pensively. "Guenevere is not the kind of woman to go off the deep end and marry a knight out of untrammeled passion. Especially not a knight like Lancelot, with no political connections other than her herself. There is more going on here than a defiant wedding. We need to understand what."

"Whatever she is up to," Nimue said, "surely arresting her would put a stop to it."

"That assumes she is the only one involved. These plots are never simple. Her parents must know about it—they've been involved in all of her treasons—and possibly some of their allies in France or elsewhere on the Continent, and heaven knows who else. The French have had their eyes on England for as long as anyone can remember."

"But Guenevere is the key to whatever they may be plotting, Merlin." Nimue pressed her case. "She must be. If we seize her—"

"That is too simple by half, Colin."

"I know this is going to sound odd." Arthur drained his cup and held it out for Greffys to refill. "But I don't much want to dungeon up my wife. Or burn her at the stake." He kept his eyes focused on the cup. "Or torture her. That is not the kind of England I've wanted to build."

"Treacherous queens are as old as civilization itself, Arthur." Brit was growing vehement. "The history books are full of them. Augustus's wife Livia. Ahab and Jezebel. Jason and Medea. And kings who do not move to counter them always pay the price."

"Even so, Brit. Say I seal her in a prison cell for the rest of her life. Say I torture her till she confesses responsibility for every tragedy since the fall of Troy. What would that do to all Merlin's fine diplomatic efforts to persuade Europe to take England seriously as a modern power? How barbaric would it make me look?"

"Like a king." Brit spoke emphatically. "Justinian tortures his enemies, and look at him. He is the strongest emperor since Augustus."

"No. No, I think Merlin is right. There is something more going on than we know about."

"Arthur, strike." Britomart's tone was beginning to grow heated.

Calmly, Merlin got between them. "Think for a moment, Brit. Guenevere is already in jail, effectively at least. Corfe is a place of self-imposed exile from Arthur's court. She needs money. And she needs people as well—her courtiers keep abandoning her. Your own squire Petronus defected from her court, remember? None of that has stopped her plotting."

"She can't plot much in a jail cell."

He sighed loudly. "Do you think you're the only one with secret agents? We have no idea who might be working for her." He snorted derisively and looked away. "Government. Politics. I swear, as long as I live I'll never understand all the games people play in the name of power."

Arthur smiled a rueful smile. "Are you saying you no longer want to be my minister?"

"Of course not, but—"

"Merlin is right, Brit." Oddly the king was grinning like a schoolboy. "Guenevere can't do much on her own. Her army, such as it is, is too small, and technically the soldiers are mine anyway. She has fewer troops of her own than the king of Latvia. She needs allies. We must find out who they are."

"But, Arthur—"

"No, Merlin has the right idea. We must watch her and wait till we know more. Are your spies at Corfe reliable?"

"Yes, of course. I'm quite sure of them."

"And can you manage to get more inside the castle there?"

"I think so. As Merlin said, she needs people. She can't be too choosy. I'll have Captain Dalley do it as quickly as he can."

"Do it, then. And suggest to Captain Dalley that he post a cordon of, er, 'observers' around the castle. Not too close, not too obvious. But I want her watched."

Merlin interrupted. "I can send Dalley some of my lenses. They will make it possible to watch the castle from a considerable distance, without anyone ever suspecting they are under surveillance. The trick, you see, is to use convex lenses. If you mount them in a framework—"

"Excellent, Merlin." The king rubbed his hands together. "I want to know who comes and who goes, who might be up to no good. There is something happening, and my dear, loving, bigamous wife is at the center of it. And whatever it

is, it will certainly end in death. We need to learn what is
going on—and who else is involved. Let us hope it is not
more of our own people. Mark's treason hurt me. Deeply. I
don't want that to happen again."

On that uneasy note the meeting ended. No one talked
much as they left.

Merlin asked Nimue to wait for him a moment. Then he
collared Brit at the foot of the tower stairs. "You are assembling a spy network? Why wasn't I told?"

"Arthur wants security."

"I am his prime counselor."

"Even so."

"What else do I not know about?"

"How can I know what you don't know, Merlin?" She
grinned and walked off breezily.

"Brit!"

But she kept going. Merlin looked to Nimue and sighed.
"I should have stayed in Egypt. I was happy when I lived
there."

"Do you seriously expect me to believe that everyone in
Egypt is devoted to learning? That there are no politicians
there?"

Unexpectedly, Arthur ran lightly down the steps and
joined them. "I always wonder how a man as learned as
you can be so naïve, Merlin."

"You were eavesdropping." It was an accusation.

"How could I not? Some voices carry. Besides, Brit
wants me to master the art of espionage. I believe in starting small." He grinned his boyish grin.

But Merlin was in no mood for this. "I am not naïve."
His voice was firm. "Whatever I am, I am not that."

"Power is a drug, Merlin. Like sex, it is satisfying for itself. People—some people—lust for it the way boys chase
after butterflies. For no other reason than that to have it is
satisfying. You've never understood that. You're too besot-
ted with books."

"Is this a confession, Arthur? Are you admitting that you are addicted to power?"

"No." The king became distant. "I want power for the good it can do. But Guenevere . . . she wants it for itself, the way her dumb consort Lancelot pursues sex with scullery maids. Understand that, Merlin. It is government."

"You are too cynical, Arthur."

"Wearing the crown makes a man a cynic. Let's go to the dining hall. I haven't eaten, and I hear they have some good ham."

"I will follow in a moment, if you do not mind. I want to have a word with Colin."

Arthur headed off to dinner. Merlin turned to Nimue. "Thank you for waiting."

She smiled. "I've already eaten, remember?"

"Probably too much, as usual. You should exercise more."

"Are you trying to hold me to the standard for women, Merlin? Or, a man named Colin, remember?"

"While you can get away with it. People are gossiping. I've overheard two different conversations among servants who think you odd, who think you are hiding something."

"Servants gossip. What of it?"

"If they are talking about you, other people may be as well."

She exhaled deeply. "And if they are?"

"Think. You adopted this male disguise for a reason. If Morgan should even suspect you are living here as Colin, you will suffer the consequences. At the very least, she would demand you be returned to her court. She might force you to go through with that marriage to her son. And those are the benign possibilities. If she feels vengeful . . . You know as well as I do how vindictive she can be. Remember the chest of poisons she keeps."

"What do you want me to do?"

"Just be careful how you present yourself, in public. You

are the best assistant I could want. And for that matter you are a good friend. I hardly want to lose you."

So everyone at Camelot watched and waited. And two weeks later more intelligence arrived from Captain Dalley at Corfe. Merlin, Brit and the king sat in the king's study and went over this new report.

Things had been unsettled at the queen's castle. Guenevere and Lancelot, though married, maintained separate apartments. They did not often dine together. Lancelot insisted on this, apparently so he could continue his infidelities with every woman who gave him the opportunity. Guenevere was oblivious to this, or she simply did not care. Still, publicly they were happily married royal newlyweds, and the court functionaries worked diligently to quash any gossip that suggested otherwise.

Arthur listened, smiling grimly. "Good old Lancelot. Deny him what you will, he is consistent. And what about visitors? Has anyone suspicious come or gone?"

Brit scanned the remainder of the report. "Apparently not. A pair of French trading ships docked in the harbor but unloaded their cargo and left within a day. That is all."

"We need a navy. The French use our ports at their convenience, and we can never do much about it."

"Can we afford one?" Merlin asked. "Ships are expensive. Sailors expect to be paid, and we have none with any real experience. And heaven only knows where we'd find a naval architect in England."

"We have tin and silver mines, remember?" the king said. "If need be we can raise our prices. And sailors can be found. Europe is full of them. We're an island nation, Merlin. We need a fleet."

For a moment everyone fell silent. Merlin scanned the report and smiled a satisfied smile. "So there is trouble in paradise. Does it occur to you that we may not have to act at all?"

Arthur took the report and stared at it. "What do you mean?"

"She couldn't keep up her marriage to you. What makes you think this one will last?"

"She is still my wife, repudiate me though she may. And she is laughing at me, she and her whole court. I know it. And when word of what she's done spreads through Europe—"

"Let her laugh. She is still isolated. She still needs money. So she has exchanged vows with the man she has been fornicating with for years anyway. Not much has changed that I can see. Let us bide our time."

Brit snorted derisively. "She's still a traitor. So her treason is weak. What of that? I still say we should have imprisoned her the moment we got the news."

But Arthur, following Merlin's counsel, was still reluctant to move against her.

Several days later a huge storm blew up from the south Atlantic and strafed England with ferocious winds, drenching downpours and even hail. The entire country came to a full stop for days before the storm finally moved on to ravage the Continent.

Camelot leaked in enough places to cause mild alarm; the household staff were kept busy placing pails and pans to catch the water. Arthur's majordomo, Simon, a Yorkshireman, said he was worried that parts of the castle might actually collapse; but he was an alarmist and no one took him seriously. Once the storm passed it took nearly a week for the country to recover and for the flood waters to recede.

Just as things were returning to normal at Camelot a soldier arrived from the coastal fort at Dover. He had ridden nonstop to reach the castle, and he was taken directly to report to Britomart. She in turn decided the news he brought was important enough for the king.

And so Arthur, Merlin and Brit gathered still again in the king's study. Because of all the damp weather Merlin's arthritis was bothering him. "I hope this is important. Those damned stairs . . ."

"You won't be disappointed." She smiled. "I think we may have the information we need."

"About Guenevere?"

"Quite possibly."

Arthur had been in a quiet mood, but this perked him up. "We know what she's up to?"

"We have a good idea now."

The soldier, whose name was Martin of Cokesbury, made his report, prompted now and then by Brit. "Martin, will you please tell King Arthur and Merlin what you told me?"

"Well." He drew himself up as tall as he could, hoping it would make him seem authoritative. "You know this storm we just had."

"Yes, of course." Merlin was impatient. "What of it?"

"The storm wreaked havoc on the Dover coast. Fishing boats were lost. Houses and other small buildings were toppled by the wind. And several ships ran aground.

"One of them was foreign—like nothing any of us had seen. So Commander Larkin sent some of us out to investigate.

"Most of the ship's crew had been washed overboard and presumably drowned. The ones who were still alive spoke some gibberish none of us knew. But after a long while of interrogating them, Commander Larkin found one who speaks French. And it turns out that the ship is from Byzantium."

Merlin sat up. "Byzantium? It was one of Justinian's ships? They don't trade here, except for occasional tin purchases. And then their ships dock at Cornwall."

"Yes, sir. Exactly."

"Did he say what they were doing in our waters?"

"No, sir. But the sailor seemed to think being from the emperor should give them diplomatic immunity or some such. Commander Larkin wasn't at all sure how to proceed, so he sent me here."

Arthur spoke. "That is a wise move. It will take months for Justinian to realize there's something wrong and to make a protest. But I wish you had been able to get more out of them."

"Sorry, Your Highness. All we were able to do was confiscate all the documents in the captain's cabin."

Merlin leaned forward. "What do they say? About Guenevere?"

Martin produced a sheaf of documents from his pack and laid them on the table. "Most of these are in French. The rest—well, they are in a foreign code or something. At any rate, none of us can read them."

"Let me see." Merlin took the documents and riffled through them, squinting; then he took a magnifying lens from his pocket and examined them more closely. "Greek. These are in Greek." He looked at the king. "You know, Arthur—the language you keep telling me I shouldn't be teaching to the young men of the court? The one you say is a waste of time?"

"Save your sarcasm, Merlin, and tell us what they say."

From the stack he pulled a large parchment with what appeared to be an imperial seal attached to it. "I imagine this is the important one." He narrowed his eyes, adjusted his lens and read it.

"For heaven's sake, Merlin, what does it say?"

He translated:

To our royal cousins Lancelot and Guenevere of Britain. Greetings.

Know by these presents that we are most pleased at the invitation to the celebration of the queen's birthday. And we are most delighted that the occasion will also observe and honor the royal wedding.

The court of the Eastern Roman Empire is most anxious to establish harmonious relations with Britain, and our Ambassador Plenipotentiary, Podarthes, shall attend in our name.

May the festivities be joyous. And may the relations established be felicitous for both our courts.

Justinian

Having finished, Merlin put the document on the table and looked at his companions to see how they were reacting. None of them said a word.

"So." He looked again from one to the next. "Guenevere and Lancelot are presenting themselves as the legitimate rulers of England and attempting to conduct diplomatic negotiations with Byzantium. And Byzantium is complicit with them. Justinian addresses them as his 'royal cousins.'"

Arthur was quite immobile. Brit squirmed in her chair. "If she can actually make an ally of Justinian it will strengthen her hand immeasurably. He commands the greatest army in Europe."

"But if she believes she can do that," Merlin said softly, "she is being incredibly foolish. The Byzantine army swallows up cities and provinces the way a swarm of ants swallows vegetation. Justinian's general, Belisarius, is relentless."

Arthur spoke again, sounding even more tired than he had a moment earlier. "We've been trying to open diplomatic relations with Justinian for years. And we've always been rebuffed. He may see Guenevere—a weak monarch, to say the least—as his entrée to England. A simple way to gain access without encountering resistance. And Guenevere just might be desperate enough to permit that.

She would be Justinian's puppet, but with his support she would be a ruler."

"We need to think," Merlin said. "To examine this from every possible angle. Who else might she have invited to this birthday celebration? Who else might she be enlisting as an ally, or trying to?"

"Her father and some of his French allies, presumably. But the French want England for themselves. They can't be happy about Byzantine involvement." Brit leaned back in her chair and put her feet up on the table. "With Justinian behind her, who else would she need?"

Merlin didn't respond; it was clear he was thinking furiously. "Suppose this. Suppose we let this 'invitation' stand. Then when this Podarthes arrives for his piece of birthday cake, suppose he finds us securely in charge. Any plans Justinian might have for an easy takeover of England would be brought to a quick halt."

"And if Podarthes lands with an army?" Arthur asked.

"Why would he come with an army when he has a compliant Guenevere ready to hand him the country in return for his recognition of her right to rule?"

"If that is what is really happening here." Brit sounded skeptical. "The Byzantines are too devious for such a straightforward plan."

"Are they?" Arthur stood and began pacing the room. "I say we should act now. We have waited long enough. We wanted better insight into what Guenevere is up to. Now we have it."

"I agree." Merlin took a long drink of wine. "The time has come to arrest Guenevere and Lancelot on charges of treason. Have them brought here so we can interrogate them. The threat of imprisonment—or worse—will make them back away from this plan."

"And if it doesn't?" Brit swirled the wine in her cup.

"Then we make certain that imprisonment is more than a threat." Arthur sounded resolute for the first time. "If I know my loving helpmate, the mere suggestion that we might torture her or burn her at the stake will do the trick. Not that I would actually do those things," he added weakly. "But Guenevere has always laughed at my hope to build a more just society.

"So, Brit, assemble a detachment of soldiers. Make sure they are all loyal beyond question. Do not use anyone who might have the remotest interest in seeing Guenevere on the throne of England. Get to Corfe as quickly as possible."

"A forced march, Arthur?"

"No. But *move*, and do it fast. Bring the traitors here under heavy guard. Imprison them in the North Tower. We'll let them stew there awhile."

Merlin turned to Martin. "You still have all of the Byzantines in custody?"

"Yes, sir, of course."

"Excellent. Once we've dealt with Guenevere and Lancelot, we can release them. But first let them 'overhear' that Guenevere has arranged their release. That should reassure Justinian that things here are as he believes them to be, or wants them to be."

They looked at one another blankly.

"And before you let them go, interrogate them further. Some reliable intelligence would be helpful."

"I'll have our agents at Corfe find out what they can." Brit drained her wine cup. "I'll send word that we want to know about any mention of Justinian or the Byzantine Empire."

"Excellent. Meanwhile, we need to give some serious thought to other people we might invite to Guenevere's birthday celebration, potential allies if worse comes to worst. The Byzantines are strong but they are not invincible."

They all stood to go. But just as Merlin was about to leave, he paused. "Arthur, Brit, I have to ask something."

The both looked at him, puzzled. "Yes?"

"How secure are we here? I mean, really?"

"Camelot is the best-defended castle in England. You know that." Arthur seemed annoyed at the question "I want my wife in jail. Her army can't possibly be strong enough to make much trouble."

"That is not what I mean."

"Then . . . ?"

"We have spies out there. We can't be the only ones. Justinian's network of spies and informers is notorious throughout Europe. How likely is it we can do anything without him knowing?"

Arthur sulked. Britomart bristled.

"We all know Justinian's reputation," Merlin continued. "His court is the most ruthless there is. They are not above using murder—er, assassination—to further their ends. We must all give more thought to security, and not merely while they are in the country. Taking them on, even indirectly, puts us all at risk for premature death. Add to that Guenevere's venomous nature . . ."

And on that grim note the council ended.

TWO

It took Britomart three days to assemble the legion she wanted for her mission to the Spider's House. In another four days they were there. She had moved so fast that even if Guenevere had spies—which seemed likely—and knew what to expect, she could hardly have prepared adequately. Brit's soldiers, supplemented by Captain Dalley's men from the Corfe garrison, surrounded the castle quickly and efficiently, and Guenevere and Lancelot were taken without putting up a fight.

She and Lancelot surrendered quietly, all the while professing ignorance of any treasonous plot and insisting that Arthur's intelligence must be mistaken. Her soldiers, badly outnumbered and taken quite by surprise, watched, unable to help her. There was rain on the journey back to Camelot so it took an extra two days. But the party finally reached their destination amid brilliant sunshine.

Arthur was in the castle courtyard, exercising with some of his knights, when they arrived. Merlin, Nimue and

Simon of York were watching and chatting about castle affairs. No carriage had been provided for the queen and her illicit consort; they rode horses like the others in the party, and they were heavily shackled. Guenevere did not attempt to disguise her displeasure at the affront to her royal dignity

Arthur left his companions and approached her, the very picture of heartiness, accompanied by a half dozen of his knights. "Why, Guenevere, you've come to visit."

She glared. "Do not waste your irony on me, Arthur. Why have we been brought here?"

"Goodness, is it so odd for a man to want to see his wife now and then?"

"Arthur." She had not climbed down from her horse. "I want to know why I—we—have been arrested."

"Arrested? Why, Guenevere, whatever do you mean? You used to have a pet ape. Didn't you bring it along? Or have you replaced it? Hello, Lancelot." He held out a hand to help Guenevere dismount, but she pulled back from him.

"I can get down without your help." She jumped to the ground. "In fact, you would be amazed what I can do without your help."

He put on a wide grin. "As long as you have Daddy?"

"Arthur, I'm warning you—"

"Yes?"

His knights drew their swords. Glumly she said, "Never mind."

"I'm sorry, Guenevere, I think I must have missed something. I had the impression you were about to make a threat of some sort."

"No." She said it softly.

Arthur looked around the courtyard and signaled to Simon, the majordomo. "What precisely is the nature of your warning, then? Are you going to have your soldiers, the ones who couldn't prevent your capture, come rescue you? Will that awful mother of yours turn me to stone with one of her withering looks? Will your new husband here, or should I say your fellow prisoner, manage to save you somehow?"

She glared. "I am a queen, Arthur. You would do well to remember it."

"A queen by virtue of your marriage—which you have dissolved." He couldn't resist adding, "In favor of this lump."

Lancelot growled like an angry dog and lunged at Arthur but four knights caught him and restrained him.

To Simon, Arthur said, "Install them in the North Tower. See that they're kept there, under tight guard." He smiled a cordial smile. "Until I want them."

"Yes, sir."

Simon clapped his hands loudly and a group of attendants ushered Guenevere and Lancelot inside the castle at swordpoint.

Merlin joined Arthur. "Your loving wife. When she was still a girl in her teens they used to call her the She-Wolf of France. Yet you let yourself fall in love with her."

"Don't remind me."

"Why did you ever marry her? I've never understood it."

"I was young. She was beautiful. I thought she loved me." He shrugged, then glanced at Merlin and looked quickly away. "And I thought she'd give me an entrée to France. You always told me to expand my kingdom when I could."

"I meant solidify your position here in Britain, not across the Channel. And I certainly never advised you to marry the daughter of a minor French king to do it. One of Guenevere's uncles or one of the petty warlords will inherit the province, not her. Let us hope it takes years to sort out. Marriage is about politics and strategy, Arthur, not love or beauty."

"Is it? Aren't they the same thing, sometimes?"

"For heaven's sake, Arthur, have I taught you nothing? You still talk like a green schoolboy at times. You've seen her mother, Leonilla. A face like a rusty axe and a personality to match. But she was a princess, heiress to a small yet mildly desirable French province. So Leodegrance gritted his teeth and married her. It was politics—it was power. Not love."

"And he's been miserable ever since, the poor oaf." Arthur laughed. "Are you telling me I should have wanted a wife and a marriage like that?"

Merlin made a vague gesture at the door the queen had been taken through. "You got her daughter. And you got such a marriage anyway. Has Guenevere stopped plotting against you for even a minute since the day you married her? She wants to deliver England into her father's hands. Or to hold it in her own."

"At least Guenevere is beautiful. Was. When I looked at her in bed beside me, at least I didn't shudder."

"At least."

"Shut up, Merlin. Let's go and have some lunch."

For a full week Geuenvere and Lancelot stewed in their confinement while Arthur and his advisors tried to decide what to do with her.

"Arthur, you should let her out," Simon of York advised him. "At least give her the freedom of the castle. She is a queen, after all."

"Don't remind me, Simon. And don't stand on protocol."

"She is entitled to consideration. She is not a common criminal."

"No, she is quite uncommon. Nevertheless, she will remain confined where she is."

Simon let out a sigh. "At least move her to a more livable part of the castle, sir."

"So she can contact whatever spies or agents she's planted here? No, Simon, we're all safer with her in the North Tower. It leaks and there are terrible drafts." He smiled, pleased at the thought. "But I like her there."

"Have you talked to her?"

"Good God no. What would I ask her? 'How does your new husband measure up in bed?' "

"You shouldn't be so bitter, sir."

"Find yourself a wife like Geuenvere, then come back and tell me that. Why don't you go and count the silverware or something?"

Meanwhile, Merlin and Brit had conferred privately about the situation. When they were satisfied they had arrived at a good plan they approached Arthur in his study. Greffys, as always, was in attendance and made certain the wine kept flowing. Merlin brought "Colin" to take notes.

"Arthur, we've decided the best course of action would be to send her back to Corfe."

The king slammed his goblet on the table. "What?! You're the ones who told me to have her brought here in the first place."

"Calm down, Arthur. We didn't say you should release her. Keep her here for a little while, so we can interrogate her and her French clod. *Then* send them back—under heavy guard. Keep them imprisoned in their own castle."

"The Spider's House? I've always thought it perfectly appropriate that of all the castles in England, she chose the one with that name."

Brit spoke up. "We have more than enough troops to control Corfe Castle—or the Spider's House, if you prefer—and everything that happens in it. Keep the two of them there."

"Why? What on earth will that gain me?"

"The upper hand, Arthur." Merlin spoke softly and calmly. "I've suggested it before. Proceed with this damned foolish birthday celebration for her. Proclaim it throughout

England and announce it to the rest of Europe. Invite delegates from every civilized European court, and even some from Asia and Africa if possible. They will arrive here to find an England in peace and prosperity, with no dissension and with you firmly in charge. Guenevere's little diplomatic coup will become yours."

The king looked from one to the other. "What about this Byzantine, Podarthes? Do we know anything about him?"

"I knew him when I visited Byzantium," Merlin said. "He was not much more than an acquaintance, but—"

"Is there anyplace you haven't lived?"

"Very few, and none of them are in any way interesting or desirable. Podarthes was a minor court functionary when I knew him. He seems to have climbed the Byzantine political ladder very nicely."

"Is he honest? Is he trustworthy? Can we count on him to support us, or at least to keep his word?"

Brit laughed. "Arthur, he's a diplomat. And a Byzantine diplomat, at that."

"Point taken. One more thing occurs to me."

"Yes?" Merlin was pleased the king seemed to be taking their suggestion seriously.

"When Guenevere was a schoolgirl, she lived in Byzantium. Or Constantinople, as they call it now. Her mother sent her there to be schooled. Suppose she has ties there we know nothing about?"

Merlin consulted some notes. "She was there for two years from the time she was twelve. Not even a woman as devious as Guenevere could have been hatching plots at that age."

Arthur fell into silence, mulling over the idea they'd suggested. Finally he asked, "Who should we invite, then?"

Merlin produced a sheet of paper covered with written notes. "Brit and I have discussed that. We have a few suggestions. We would advise not inviting your knights and nobles. You know how they babble, especially when they've been drinking. One of them would almost certainly spill a few inconvenient beans."

"Obviously. Who, then?"

"Well . . . I was thinking you ought to invite the Pope to send someone."

Arthur blinked. "Pope? What the devil is a pope?"

"I've told you about him," Merlin said patiently. "Pope Honorius. He is the bishop of Rome."

"If you don't stop talking in riddles . . . So the Pope is a bishop. Fine. What on earth is a bishop?"

"Arthur, I've explained this all before. I wish you didn't drink so much."

"Don't nag me. I'm the king."

"Fine. The Pope is emerging as the leader of the Christians. They've been squabbling among themselves for generations, bickering for precedence, and Rome seems to have taken the most influential position. Europe is leaving the old gods, country by country, and adopting this new Christian one. And the Pope is the leader of it all. As with all religious matters, it involves politics. International politics. Guenevere's parents are both nominally Christians, and—"

"That is not exactly an endorsement."

"—and if you recall, she herself claimed to be one till she came here and married you. A delegate from the Pope might carry considerable influence with the three of them."

"It's difficult to believe any religion could turn that family decent. But fine, go ahead and write to this—this—"

"Pope Honorius. The head of the Christian Church. Even Justinian is Christian. As I am certain you must know." He said this with a tone of heavy irony. "If we can win Honorius to our side, he may even be able to restrain Justinian. I wish you'd pay more attention."

"Stop talking to me as if I were still a schoolboy. I'm a king, damn it. I'm old enough to have a treacherous wife."

Brit added, "Having a Christian leader here will certainly annoy your sister, Morgan le Fay, Arthur. You know how devoted she is to traditional religion."

He beamed at the thought. "Good."

Ignoring this, Merlin went on. "I think it would also be useful to have someone else from the Byzantine administration here, to counter any plots Podarthes may hatch. They never stop working against one another. I'd like to invite my old friend Germanicus Genentius."

Arthur had been drinking steadily. His attention was beginning to drift. "You knew this man in Byzantium, too?"

"I first met him there, yes. And he and Podarthes were—what is the polite term?—rivals. But I really got to know him when I lived in Egypt. He was adjutant to the imperial governor. Now he is governor himself."

"Merlin and I talked about this man," Brit said. "I'm not sure I agree that having another Byzantine official here would help us in any way. They all reek of murder and treachery."

"Brit," Merlin said patiently, "he is one of Justinian's officials, yes. But as I've explained to you, he is not quite the same kind of careerist as Podarthes. He fosters the arts and learning. The Library at Alexandria has flourished under his rule, and so have the scholars who work there. Germanicus and I speak the same language. He could be very helpful to us."

"But can we invite him here without going through Justinian?" Arthur did not like the sound of it. "And Podarthes?"

"As I said, Germanicus is an old friend. If I write to him informally, and if he decides he misses me and wants to pay his old companion a visit . . ." He grinned and spread his hands apart as if to say *voilà*. "Justinian is crafty. We must be, too."

"Fine. Write to him."

Merlin beamed. "As for the rest of Europe . . . I'm not at all certain. We should definitely avoid any of the other French kings. They would likely as not support Guenevere."

"Agreed."

For the first time Nimue spoke up. "What about Leodegrance and Leonilla? It would look odd to everyone if they weren't invited to their daughter's big party."

"Agreed again. I'd be surprised if Guenevere hadn't alerted them already. I can't imagine them missing this for anything." Arthur's speech was becoming slurred. "Especially if it involves plots against me."

Merlin decided the meeting had gone on too long; it was time to end it.

"That only leaves one issue to be dealt with," Arthur said softly.

"And what is that?"

"Guenevere."

"Oh."

"Yes. Oh."

The king furrowed his brow, trying to concentrate through the fog of wine. "How can we persuade her to go along with this?"

"Persuade, Arthur? I would use the word *compel*." Brit was emphatic.

The king pounded the table. "No torture. I've told you that time and again."

"No, Arthur, of course not. We wouldn't want to damage that beautiful olive skin of hers. But there are other threats. She is already bristling at her confinement. The suggestion that it might become permanent . . ." She smiled.

Arthur sighed. "We are constructing a nest of vipers, all of them seething with venom. Why does kingship have to be so interesting?"

"You wanted it, Arthur." Merlin was serene.

"Don't remind me."

"Pellenore."

The mad old king, who had been conquered by Arthur and whose castle Arthur now occupied, was galloping along a corridor on an imaginary horse. When he saw his friend Merlin he reined it in. "Merlin. Hello, Merlin. There is a troll loose in the castle. Help me find it."

"Wouldn't you rather hunt down a venomous serpent?"

Pellenore seemed to forget his pretend horse and imaginary quarry almost at once. "What do you mean?"

"You know all the passages that riddle Camelot. I've tried to have other people find them, but . . ." He spread his hands in a gesture of futility. "I need your help."

"I'll do anything I can for you, Merlin. You're the only one who ever takes my quests seriously. There are monsters."

"Believe me, I know it. And none of them are so awful as the human ones. What hidden passageways are there in the North Tower?"

"Not many. It's the oldest part of Camelot. But there are a few."

"Will you show them to me?"

"Of course."

Within moments they were inside the castle walls, moving toward the north wing, lighting their way with torches. Dust and cobwebs covered everything, and the floor was littered with all kinds of objects from scraps of cloth to old rusted swords and armor. "Be careful not to stray from this passage," Pellenore said at one point. "You will find the remains of the dead." Unwilling to pursue this topic, Merlin pressed on. Then the corridor began to ascend. Soon they were in the wall behind Guenevere's rooms.

There were enough chinks in the masonry to permit

sound to carry quite clearly and even to permit limited views of the rooms. Merlin pressed his eye to one of the cracks.

Lancelot and Guenevere were on the bed, locked in one another's arms. Merlin watched, intrigued. "It is like watching the mating dance of Egyptian cobras," he whispered.

In the bedroom, Guenevere pushed her man impatiently away. "Not now, Lancelot. This isn't the time. We have to think."

"I'm no good at planning. You always say so."

"Then leave the thinking to me, but don't distract me."

"We're in jail. What do we have to think about?"

"Getting out." She got to her feet, pulled on a robe and began to pace. "I wish I could know how Arthur learned, or guessed, what we were up to. I wish I could know what he'll do with us."

"We've been caught committing treason. I told you it was a mistake to have a public wedding. But you wanted to rub his nose in it. I guess he'll have us killed. I had such a promising future once, and now—"

"He may have us killed for the affront to his dignity, perhaps. Not for treason. No, Arthur can't possibly know anything." She was trying to convince herself, not Lancelot. "Besides, we were plotting to take what should be rightfully mine."

"Rights are a matter of power. Arthur has us. Come over here and make love to me."

She sneered at him. "It was going so smoothly. We would have staged my 'birthday' celebration and invited him. And he wouldn't have been able to resist coming, if only to pry. Once we had him at Corfe—there are a hundred possibilities: poison, a knife in the dark . . ."

"Instead we now have to worry about the headsman's axe in broad daylight. I want to make love to you. It may be the last time."

"Be quiet, Lancelot. What will he do? Arthur would

merely have us killed, yes—if he was left to his own instincts. But he's advised by that foul old bastard Merlin. Merlin is far too subtle for a simple execution. He'll have some plan, and it will be devious. I've never trusted him, not even back when Arthur and I were on good terms."

"As long ago as that?"

"Be quiet."

The "foul old bastard" listened, fascinated. So they had in fact been planning to remove Arthur. It only made sense. Someone planning treason would find the living king inconvenient, to say the least.

Lancelot crossed to her and threw his arms around her, and this time she did not resist. He began kissing her, fondling her. She moaned softly. "Does the approach of death make love more exciting?"

Merlin pulled away from his spy hole. Pellenore took his place there and looked. "Don't you want to see more? They're getting undressed."

"Spare me, Pellenore. I once sat quietly on the bank of the Nile and watched a pair of crocodiles make love. The sight of this would be redundant."

"I want to see."

"Come back later, then. If Lancelot's reputation is to be believed, they'll still be at it. But I want to get out of here."

Glumly the old king gestured back the way they'd come. "All right, let's go. Maybe we'll encounter that troll."

"More redundancy."

"Can I be there when you interrogate her, Merlin?"

Nimue sat with Merlin in his study, sharing a plate of venison and a skin of wine. His mood was blue, and she was trying to shake him out of it.

"I don't think so, no. I don't think Arthur wants anyone there who doesn't have to be. Would you parade your spouse's infidelity in front of an audience?"

"I suppose not. But even with the secrecy . . . well, word is spreading about what Guenevere has done, or tried to do."

"Even so. He hasn't many crutches left to lean on where she is concerned. Let us not deprive him of that one."

"Do you think she would really have given the country to the Byzantines?"

"Between her hatred for Arthur and her lust for power, it is not hard to imagine. And given her sense of self-importance, I doubt if it would have occurred to her she was being used. It is such a typical plan for the Byzantines. Why bother invading England when you can sweet-talk the king's wife into handing it to you? They would have given her enough freedom, or autonomy, to feel that she had accomplished what she wanted—at first. Justinian has vassal kings all over the map. Then, slowly, inch by inch, they would have taken it away until even Guenevere would have realized what a fool she had been. But by then, of course, it would have been too late for all of us."

"We would have known Byzantine prosperity, wouldn't we? Wouldn't England have flourished under them?"

"It is far more likely we would have known Byzantine cruelty before we ever saw any benefits. Do you know about some of the tortures they have devised? They do things to the human body that would have given pause to Caligula."

They fell into silence for a while and ate and drank. Finally Nimue asked, "But if they really want England, won't they come and take it anyway?"

"Perhaps. Perhaps not. Justinian's great general, Belisarius, might die. People do. Or he might plan to try to seize the throne for himself. Generals have been known to do that." He sighed deeply. "I can't tell you how tired I am of the human race. The things, the awful things we do to each other . . . they are so . . . so . . ."

"Cheer up. You're an old man, Merlin. You won't have to see much more of it."

"If you mean that as a joke—"

"I don't."

"I can't tell you how I hope you are right."

"Let Guenevere go free and we'll see."

"Unfortunately the king is devoted to his kingship. It is not as if I have any real choice."

After a long pause Nimue asked, "What was he like?"

"Who? Arthur?"

"Yes. When he was young, I mean. Before he took the throne."

"Do young men differ very much? He was a scrawny boy with big dreams and bigger ambitions. His father, Uther, was a minor warlord who ignored his son completely. Arthur had potential, but he was painfully trusting, not to mention naïve. And I am afraid he has never quite reconciled himself to the fact that other people's plans might cross his."

"What will he do to Guenevere?"

"Do you care, Nimue?"

"I care because she is a woman. So few of us ever approach so near to power."

"Maybe someday you will."

"Don't humor me. Arthur will do what you counsel him to do. What will it be?"

"You overestimate my influence. Sometimes I have to shake him by the shoulders, at least figuratively, to get him to see the simple truth."

"And what is the truth, Merlin?"

He glanced at her sideways. "I don't know. I wish I did. Would *you* like to shake *me*?"

The following morning, before dawn, Guenevere was brought to Arthur's chambers in chains by a half dozen soldiers under Britomart. Only two torches burned in the room; the corners were in deep shadow. The queen wore

plain clothing made of dyed homespun, no embroidery—
not exactly a prisoner's clothes but not much better.

They made her sit on a low, rough wooden stool.
Torchlight shined directly into her eyes. Arthur and
Merlin sat waiting. She entered the study proudly, head
unbowed. But she looked drawn and frightened, and despite her best efforts, she could not hide it. Merlin wondered if it was Arthur or Lancelot who was wearing her
down.

Arthur leaned close to Merlin. "I've never seen her like
this."

"Don't lose your resolve, Arthur."

"I know that I can't afford that."

"Then remember your duty to yourself. If that does not
carry enough weight, remember your duty to England, to
give us a stable monarchy. Do you want to see her on the
throne?"

"Of course not. England would be a French province in
no time. Or a Byzantine one. I can't tell you how I hate
politics."

"Then you must put an end to this scheme now, and for
good."

Arthur turned to his chained wife. "Guenevere. We
found this dagger among your things." He produced a
golden knife with an elaborately carved ivory handle. "It's
quite a beautiful piece. Wherever did you get it? Was it a
gift, perhaps?"

She did not respond, did not even move.

"From Lancelot, perhaps? On what occasion might he
have given you such a thing?"

"So you've finally noticed me. I thought your fascinating conversation with Merlin would distract you all day."

"There is no point to sarcasm, Guenevere. It will hardly
help your case."

"There is every point to it, Arthur. As a wise man once
observed, there is no fate that cannot be surmounted by

scorn. And scorn is what I feel for you and your 'chief minister.' Scorn in abundance."

Merlin decided it would be a mistake to let this go on. He leaned forward in his seat and announced, "Guenevere of Camelliard, you are charged with treason against the crown of England."

"And what," she said softly in a flat tone, "is the nature of this supposed treason?"

"You have conspired to replace your husband at the head of the government of England. You have conspired to assassinate him. And, unwilling even to wait for his death, you have married bigamously your coconspirator."

She stared at them wordlessly.

After what seemed an eternity of silence Arthur burst out, "Say something. Have you no defense?"

Calmly Guenevere lowered her eyes. "You cannot possibly have evidence of any of this, for the simple reason that the charges are false."

Merlin produced several documents. "This," he intoned, "is an eyewitness account of your marriage to Lancelot du Lac. And this letter was intercepted on a ship from Byzantium. You have been carrying on diplomatic negotiations with Justinian. Or trying to. We have his letter to you as evidence of it."

"I invited them to my birthday celebration, that is all." She looked at the king. "It was your idea, Arthur, remember? Months ago you suggested to me that we make my birthday a national event and use it to increase England's prestige internationally."

"I never authorized you to do this." He took the letter and shook it in her direction.

"And at any rate," Merlin interjected, "are you going to suggest that it was also Arthur's idea for you to murder him?"

"I have contemplated nothing of the sort."

"I heard you myself, only yesterday. 'Poison, a knife in the dark.'" He picked up the ivory-handled dagger. "This knife, perhaps?"

Her eyelid fluttered slightly; otherwise she showed no reaction. "How ironic, Merlin. For years you have urged Arthur not to turn England into a society dominated by informers, gossips and spies. Now you have become one yourself."

"Merlin is not the one on trial here." Arthur raised his voice.

"Is that what this is? A trial? Where is the jury, then? Where is the judge? As trials go this is most irregular."

"I am the king of England. The final judge."

She smiled. "So I am to be executed." Almost as if it were an afterthought, she added, "And Lancelot, too, I imagine. In this fair England of yours, this land of justice and equality."

Arthur sat back and crossed his legs casually. "No."

For the first time Guenevere reacted with something like genuine emotion. "What did you say?"

"I said," he told her with a grin, "no. I could easily consign you to the flames or the chopping block. But that would be too easy, don't you think? Or, let us say, too convenient."

"Do it then, and get this over with. I would never wish to inconvenience you."

"No, it would be much too simple. Merlin?"

The king put his feet up on the table and leaned back; he avoided looking directly at his wife. Merlin spoke for him.

"You are to be taken to Corfe Castle under guard. Both you and Lancelot, that is. There you will be confined but have the freedom of the castle. Any attempt to escape will result in you being transported separately to other castles and imprisoned there for the rest of your lives."

Guenevere smiled. "Or the rest of Arthur's reign, which is likely to be of much shorter duration."

Merlin ignored this and went on. "In November your birthday celebration will occur exactly as planned—with additional guests invited by Arthur."

"May I ask whom?"

"You may not. When the guests arrive you will make a show of supporting Arthur in whatever diplomatic negotiations he conducts. Once again, failure to do so will result in announcement of your indisposition, and you will be promptly jailed. Once the event has ended, you will remain in Corfe Castle under strict and permanent house arrest. Lancelot will be taken elsewhere."

Guenevere might have been made of granite. She spoke to Arthur, not Merlin. "I have been living in virtual confinement at Corfe for years now. Do you honestly believe that the threat of further confinement will intimidate me?"

Arthur glared at her. "For as long as I can remember you have flouted your marriage vows—one of which was an oath of loyalty to England. If this is what it takes to enforce them, so be it. I am not the one who brought us to this pass, Guenevere."

"No. Of course not. Very well, send us back, then."

"Not right away." Merlin folded the Byzantine letter and put it back in his pocket. "Britomart has arrangements to prepare. Your soldiers—the ones who serve and protect you at Corfe—are technically members of the English army. They are to be posted to the most far-flung parts of the country, to Scotland and Wales. New troops—or should I say guards—will be provided to look after you, ones whose loyalty to Arthur is beyond question. Captain John Dalley from the king's garrison at Corfe will be posted at your castle to command them."

Guinevere lowered her eyes and softened her voice. "Arthur, please don't do this. I'm begging." Tenderly she whispered, "I still love you."

Arthur laughed at her. "You do? So, was your 'marriage' to Lancelot actually a ritual renewal of our wedding vows, with him standing in for me?" He gestured to Britomart. "Take her away."

Guenevere sprang to her feet. "No! I will not be led in chains like a criminal."

"'Please don't put a saddle on me. Not on *me*. I am a horse.'" Merlin laughed and shifted his weight, prepared to turn away from her. "Brit."

Seemingly from nowhere Guenevere produced a knife, a small silver one whose blade gleamed in the torchlight. She made a move toward Arthur. But Britomart overpowered her and the knife clattered to the floor. Merlin called for soldiers.

"So help me, Arthur, you will pay for this." She struggled as Brit coiled another length of chain around her; she spit in Brit's face. Brit smiled and pulled the chains tighter. Then two of the soldiers took her by her arms and led her from the room as she struggled vainly against their grasp.

When they were gone Merlin turned to Arthur. "So help me, you have the strangest taste in women."

"I was a boy when we met. She seduced me. I fell in love. Don't make this harder for me than it is."

"Sorry, Arthur. I've suspected for a long time that you still love her."

"Forgive me, Merlin, for being such an irrational creature."

"Forgive you for being human?"

Suddenly Arthur peered at him. "Does anyone have a secret from you, Merlin? I thought I was being very close with my emotions."

"Perhaps I know you too well. How long has it been? Twenty years? More?"

"Brit plants her spies here, there and everywhere, yet she only knows half of what goes on. You, Merlin—you stay in your tower with your ravens and your lenses and your medicines, and you read us as clearly as you do those books that line your walls."

"Comedies, mostly."

"Don't be flippant."

"Sorry, Arthur. But it really isn't hard to understand people. Most of them do the obvious thing from the obvious motive. Only the Byzantines have learned to be consistently more subtle. That is why the prospect of having them here chills me so."

"What is it you said once? We are stepping into a viper's nest of our own construction. When all their subtle devices fail, they murder."

"Let us hope we can defang these vipers before they strike."

"Let us hope they never strike at all."

"To hope for that would be to deny the viper's nature. But we must be permanently watchful, Arthur. We have no choice but to go ahead with the birthday nonsense. If we back away from it, I am afraid Justinian would see us as weak. And he would strike—invade. But while we are reveling and eating Guenevere's birthday cake and drinking toasts to one another's good health, let us remember to voice a hope that everyone will emerge from this alive."

Arthur was drunk. Fully, completely, numbly drunk. His wife's perfidy was not forgotten, exactly, but it didn't seem to matter.

It was the dark middle of the night, and three candles burned low in his bedroom; they did not give much light at all. The king lay in bed. Four empty wineskins sat on the floor beside him. The room spun around him, and he found it reassuring. No one could penetrate that kind of moving room, not Guenevere, not Lancelot, not Justinian.

Slowly, groggily, he climbed out of bed and reeled toward the door, holding on to this piece of furniture or that for support. A part of his mind understood that it was not the room that was reeling but himself. He laughed, quite loudly.

At the door the guard had been nodding off. He was only half awake when Arthur staggered past him. "Sir— Your Majesty!"

"I'm going to the privy, Walter."

"Let me help you."

"You want to help me take a piss?"

"Let me help you get there and back. The stairs are steep, and you are—you may need someone to steady you."

"I'll be fine. Stay here."

"But—"

"Stay."

"Yes, sir."

Arthur took a candle from a wall sconce and lurched forward. And lost his balance, slamming into the wall. The guard Walter moved to help him, but Arthur glanced back over his shoulder with a look that warned him to keep his distance. "I'll be fine, Walter."

"Yes, sir. But I—"

"Stay!" He roared it.

Walter, quite uncertainly, resumed his post. Arthur staggered on.

The stairs were in fact steep and he had to steady himself against the wall as he descended. The castle was dark; absolutely no one was awake at that hour and in that deep, deep night. Wax from his candle dripped onto Arthur's hand, burning it, but he didn't mind and kept going.

Finally he reached the privy. The blackness was Stygian; he had that thought, then decided to leave the Styx to Merlin's classical library and laughed to himself. The candle he was carrying barely cut the darkness; but the privy was familiar and he found his way to the seat without much trouble. And he plopped himself down quite heavily. Then after a few moments he lowered his head and drowsed off, thinking that he wished he'd brought a skin of wine with him.

Suddenly there was an explosion of pain, like a lightning bolt striking his shoulder. He opened his eyes and looked around. There was someone there in the dark room. He reached for the man, missed and fell to the floor. The candle fell and went out. "Help! Murder! Help!" As the last echoes of his voice died off he could hear his assailant's footsteps as he—or she?—ran away in the dark. Then, unconsciousness took him.

When he woke he was on a bed in Merlin's surgery. Merlin was rubbing a salve on the knife wound in his shoulder; Nimue was behind Merlin, preparing bandages.

"It is not too bad, Arthur. At least it is not too deep. I think the attacker wanted to stab you in the neck. But in that darkness . . ." He smiled.

"An assassin has struck and you find it amusing."

"I was thinking that I have lectured you about your drinking often enough. I will not do it again."

"For this relief, much thanks."

"Did you see who it was?"

Arthur tried to shift his weight and winced in pain. "Drunk, in the darkest part of the night, in a privy with nothing but a candle?"

"Britomart wants to talk to you. She will ask."

"Let her."

"She will press you to remember harder than I would."

"Women."

"Silly woman—she wants to keep you alive." Merlin grinned again. "Which seems to be more than you do."

"Don't nag." Arthur sat up on the bed, winced again and buried his face in his hands. "Guenevere. She is behind this. She must be."

"Or Justinian, or Leodegrance, or someone else we don't even know about."

Arthur tried to stand up and winced with pain. "You said this wasn't bad."

"I said it is not *too* bad."

"It hurts like hell." Slowly he stood, steadying himself against the bed. Then he looked Merlin in the eyes. "I hate this, Merlin. I hate a world where people do things like this."

"You wanted the throne."

"Stop saying that all the time."

"Sorry, Arthur. But this is the world you wanted. You could have been a jolly farmer, plowing fields and hoping the brood sow will drop healthy piglets."

"Stop it, Merlin. My sweet loving wife has tried to have me murdered. What did I ever do to her—what could I possibly have done—to make her hate me so?"

"Simple. You got between her and her ambition. Brit is planning to take personal charge of your security now. This will not happen again."

"Not now, it won't. But what will happen when we all gather at Corfe?"

"We will all get fat on birthday cake."

"If it isn't poisoned." He started to pull his shirt on and winced again. "Give me a drug to kill the pain, will you?"

THREE

Arthur's wounds healed well but slowly. He complained to Merlin about it. "When I was a boy I used to heal so quickly. Maybe you should try another ointment."

"You are not a boy anymore, Arthur. No physician, not Hippocrates himself, has an ointment that could reverse aging. You need to take better care of yourself. And drink less."

"Somewhere there must be court physicians who don't nag."

"There were, Arthur, but all their kings are dead."

"Be quiet."

Britomart doubled the number of guards assigned to protect Arthur and gave them emphatic orders to be especially vigilant when he was "vulnerable"; they all understood that she meant "when he has too much to drink." Arthur bristled at it, but Brit and Merlin insisted strongly enough and vehemently enough that they finally wore him down; he was resigned to constant attention, which he had never wanted.

Merlin drafted letters of invitation to all the courts they

had discussed. He was careful to mention that Podarthes would be coming, representing Justinian; most of the lesser rulers would be anxious to curry favor. Then he took them to Arthur for approval. Liking the tone of what he read, he signed them with a flourish, *Arturus Rex*. "These are perfect, Merlin. They strike the precise tone between humility, diplomacy and royal majesty. I'll dispatch couriers to the various courts to deliver them first thing in the morning."

"Choose your couriers carefully, Arthur. Remember the image we wish to project. The whole idea is to persuade Europe to take us seriously. Sending a drunken lout—no, that would not do at all."

"Some of the younger knights, perhaps," the king mused. "And some of the older squires—the ones you've been teaching. Perhaps we might delay their leaving for a few days while you school them in the ways of diplomacy."

"Turning a lump of coal into a gemstone takes more than a few days, Arthur."

"Even so. It will help. Select the ones you think are most promising for a mission like this."

"I'll give it some thought."

"Excellent. Merlin, where would I be without you?"

He pretended to think about this. "In Guenevere's dungeon?"

"Stop it."

Merlin began to gather up the letters and put them in his pouch.

Arthur had another thought. "Let's consult Brit about who to send. They may be able to gather intelligence for her while they're on their travels."

"In that case, we must really select them carefully. Having the more loutish ones tip their hands could be disastrous." He stood to go.

"Merlin?"

"Yes, Arthur?"

"Where is this going to end? Where will this all lead?"

"If you want divination, send for your sister, Morgan. I have enough duties."

"Always difficult, aren't you?" He paused for a moment. "Merlin, I've never been involved in a situation like this. I want to establish England as a power on the map of Europe; I want the world's respect. But I'm a bit frightened. Overwhelmed,"

"That is understandable. But which situation are you talking about? A huge diplomatic effort, or treason on the scale Guenevere may be planning?"

"Is there a difference?"

He shrugged. "Probably not. I have been meaning to ask a favor of you."

"Ask. Anything."

"Colin has been helping me with the boys' education. In fact, he has shouldered most of the work. So he doesn't really have time to assist me in my other duties as he used to. Might you assign me another assistant?"

Arthur rubbed his chin. "Hmm . . . what do you think of young Petronus?"

"A bright boy. Solid, reliable, conscientious. But he's Brit's squire."

"I've been thinking that she's so busy with the army she doesn't really have time to train him properly. And, quite honestly, he isn't a very good athlete. He might make a good assistant for you, don't you think?"

"Yes, but . . ."

"But?"

"He wants to be a knight, doesn't he? He might find working with me a disappointment."

"I'll have to talk to him about it."

"Of course . . ." Merlin put on a show of thoughtfulness for the king's benefit.

"Yes?"

"Has it ever occurred to you that military service is not the only way of being useful to the court and the country?"

"What do you mean?"

"Suppose—when the time comes— you award Petronus a knighthood for scholarship and for assisting in the formulation of policy?"

"A knighthood for something other than military training? That's unheard of. No king in Europe has done such a thing."

"Be the first. Start a vogue. It might even catch on everywhere."

"But—but—I mean, where would that end? Sooner or later I might even have to make knights of poets and actors." He made a sour face to show what he thought of the prospect.

"There are many ways to serve England, Arthur."

"And I suppose you'd want a knighthood for yourself, too?"

"It has never occurred to me. But there are so many others who—"

"I wish you didn't have so many damned ideas, Merlin. Why can't I have counselors who are less clever? All this original thinking." He grumped for a moment. "I'll think about it, all right?"

"Fine, Arthur. That is all I am asking."

"Good. Keep it that way."

Meanwhile Britomart assembled the military escort and returned Guenevere and Lancelot to Corfe. Once again no carriage was provided; the prisoners had to ride on horseback, and the queen made no secret how unhappy she was. When she complained Brit told her, "Be grateful Arthur isn't making you walk." There was not much conversation on the journey, not even between the treacherous lovers.

But at one point Geuenvere reined her horse next to Brit's. "You are loyal to your monarch, Britomart. That is an admirable trait."

Brit smiled sardonically. "Admirable enough for you not to want to subvert it?"

"What a blunt woman you are."

"I'm a plain-talking military commander. And I am no one's fool. Least of all a prisoner's."

"We have allies, Britomart, powerful allies. If you come to our side, your future would be ensured."

"Thank you for the offer, but I don't much fancy a future of imprisonment in Corfe Castle. Not that the company would be unpleasant." She smiled sarcastically.

Guenevere glared. "Arthur is not fit to rule. My erstwhile husband has always been a wittering, half-drunken dolt. And an easy target for any assassin." She hesitated, realizing she might have said something ill-advised. "What is it about him that inspires such ill-placed loyalty?"

"If you've never understood that, Guenevere, you are the fool, not Arthur."

"Do you mean to tell me people take seriously all his nonsense about justice and freedom and the rest?"

"They are ideas worth taking seriously."

"To a philosopher, perhaps—to someone like that old fool Merlin. But you are a soldier. Look at the world, Britomart. Look at Justinian's rule. Do you know the exquisite tortures his people have devised? Do you know what they do to their prisoners' genitals, for instance?"

"Then shouldn't you be happy that Arthur listens to someone like 'that old fool'?"

Guenevere began to lose her temper. "Look at the facts, for God's sake. And there is only one fact that matters in the world—power. Justinian has assembled the most powerful empire in half a millennium. Arthur sits in a stolen castle built by a madman and drinks while his prime minister plays with ravens. We are going to win, Britomart. The idea of rulership, the idea that some are born to rule and others to serve and to follow—that is one of the cornerstones of civilization. Destroy it and you destroy everything."

"Justinian may win—someday. I wouldn't be too quick to include myself in his plans, if I were you."

"Suppose they are my plans?"

"Does that make a difference?"

Guenevere was rapidly losing patience; she was not used to being spoken to this way, and it showed. She forced herself to speak calmly. "I was born to rule. Royal blood flows in my veins. Arthur was the unwanted son of a mud-soaked warlord; open his veins and you'd find hayseeds and alcohol. My parents raised me and schooled me to be a ruler. Arthur . . . Arthur is no one. If you want a strong, stable England, join me."

"So all of this is about your feeling that you married beneath your station?"

"If you want to put it that way. You know it is true."

"A strong, stable England is what we have. There is only one person working to destabilize it, and that is you, Guenevere. Besides, do you seriously expect me to believe that Lancelot was born to rule, too? I shudder to think what flows in his veins. Sap, maybe."

"He is my husband."

"Not under the law. He is handsomer than Arthur, that I'll grant you. But a mind for governance?"

"He has me to advise him. I would be the real power, not him. You do see the advantage of having a woman rule England, don't you?"

"That would depend on the woman. Is it true that when you were still a girl people called you the She-Wolf of France?"

"Wolves eat what they please. Join us. Release us. Help me to assemble the army I need. Trust me to rule England as it should be ruled."

Brit reined her horse around a pothole in the road. "Arthur trusted you. In fact, I believe he genuinely loved you. Look what it's gotten him."

That ended the conversation. Guenevere rode her horse

back to Lancelot and the two rode side by side without talking much.

Corfe Castle was one of the oldest in the country, if not the oldest—so old it did not have a protective outer "curtain" wall. The central keep, an octagonal structure of heavy stone, was rumored to have been built by the Romans, though no one knew for certain, and it did not resemble other Roman architecture in England.

From each of its eight facets a long "arm" stretched hundreds of feet; several of them had fallen into disrepair. The underlying strategic concept seemed to be that anyone attacking the keep would have to advance between two of these "legs" and was therefore vulnerable; this was not a building plan that had been repeated anywhere in the country. Yet, apparently, it had stood for centuries, guarding a strategic port. And for as long as anyone could remember, this odd, eight-branched building had been known as the Spider's House.

Brit installed her two prisoners there under tight guard. Then she went directly to meet with the commander, Captain John Dalley, who had moved from the royal garrison in the town of Corfe to the castle to oversee security there.

Dalley had arranged a full military parade in Brit's honor. Once the pageantry was over, the two of them retired to his office.

"You have brought them?" he asked.

"Yes, the royal spider and her mate are back at home, presumably producing more venom."

Dalley was unaware of the diplomatic plot Guenevere had hatched—he only knew about the marriage—and so Brit explained it. He listened carefully and whistled softly when she'd finished. "I've been here for years, watching the pair of them. And I've always thought this a thankless post. But now! I mean, I've always assumed she was scheming. But I never envisioned anything on this scale."

"I don't think any of us have. Her sheer audacity would have protected her if that Byzantine ship hadn't run aground in the storm."

"A good military lesson: Never underestimate your opponent."

"Indeed. But I'd like to meet Petronilla while I'm here."

"You don't know her?"

"I've read her intelligence reports, of course. But we've never met face-to-face."

"She's probably busy with Guenevere—getting her reinstalled here and helping her adjust to her life under lock and key. She functions as Guenevere's secretary, you know. But I'll arrange for her to meet with us in town this evening. If we do it here, she'd almost certainly be seen. That would be the end of her work for us."

"Excellent."

And so after dinner Brit and Dalley walked into Corfe, to the garrison where they could meet in relative security. Later, under cover of night, wrapped in a black cloak, Petronilla arrived and was admitted through a side gate. A guard ushered her quickly to Dalley's office.

Dalley introduced the two of them and they sat. "So." Brit smiled conspiratorially. "You are our agent at Corfe Castle."

Petronilla was a young woman in her early twenties. She had dark hair and bright blue eyes, and she spoke with a strong French accent. "And you are the commander of Arthur's army. I'm pleased to meet you."

"Your reports have been quite invaluable."

"Thank you. But gathering intelligence at Guenevere's court isn't exactly hard. She is quite sure of herself. Except for that correspondence with Byzantium, everything she's done has been done in the open. I try to tell myself it is not because of her sex, but every plot she hatches, she babbles about—to me, to her knights, to anyone who will listen. She actually thought of sending heralds into town here to announce her foolish wedding. I persuaded her not to."

"And she thinks she's fit to play diplomatic games with the Byzantines. The arrogance of power." Brit laughed. "Except that poor Guenevere doesn't actually have much power."

"She thinks that will change."

"She can reign over the mice in her prison cell, then. But she trusts you, Petronilla?"

"Yes. I've never been certain why, except that she seems impressed by a woman with a formal education."

Brit smiled. "We are rare, aren't we?"

A kitchen servant came and Dalley ordered meat and wine for the three of them. "Brit, did you know that you have a connection to Petronilla?"

Brit's puzzlement was obvious.

"My little brat of a brother," Petronilla said with a grin. "I hear he has become your squire."

"Petronus is your brother?"

She nodded. "I can't imagine he's much of a squire, though. He's never been good for a thing."

"He's a bright boy. He's been a lot of help to me and to Merlin. You heard about Mark of Cornwall and how we caught him?"

"Petronus was involved in that? Maybe I've underestimated him. Anyway, when he defected to Arthur's court, my mother forced me to come here to take his place. Mother and Guenevere are old friends; they grew up together. But once I realized the situation here, I understood Petronus had made the right decision. And so I followed suit. I want to be of use to Arthur."

"Believe me, you have been. But . . . Petronus has never mentioned you. Does he know you're here?"

"We're not close, I'm afraid. Not the way a brother and sister should be."

"Oh."

"He used to ridicule me for wanting to learn to read. Said I should be content doing needlework."

"Men." Brit glanced sideways at Dalley and was relieved that he seemed to take it as a joke. "But he's busy learning things himself, now. He heads the class in Merlin's school for the squires and pages."

"You're joking. I really have thought too little of him."

The servant brought wine and told them their venison would be ready shortly. Brit leaned back in her chair, looked from Dalley to Petronilla and sipped her claret. "So how do the two of you work?"

"Mostly," Petronilla told her, "it's been a matter of me slipping notes to Captain Dalley or one of his aides, furtively, whenever the chance presents itself. When we pass each other in town, or when Captain Dalley visits the castle. This is the first time I've actually come to the garrison."

"But now that I'm stationed at the castle," Dalley added, "things will be a lot easier."

The three of them chatted for a while about various topics of small talk—Arthur, Petronus, politics. Then when the hour began to grow late Brit suggested they return to the castle, one by one. "You are performing a great service for England, Petronilla. Please believe that our gratitude will be made concrete when the time comes. In the meanwhile, you must be careful. Guenevere has always been a dangerous woman. She has conducted more treasons against Arthur than anyone sane could. The idea of rule seems to have made her mad. And now, caged, she will be even more dangerous. She is not above murder."

"I will be as careful as I can."

"Excellent. I hope when your undercover work is finished we can get to know each other."

"I hope so, too, Britomart."

And so things in England began to settle, at least on the surface.

Guenevere and Lancelot, resigned to their confinement—at least for the time being—gave no signs of making more trouble. Captain Dalley, with covert assistance from Petronilla, monitored all their correspondence. He suspected they must have plans, at least tentative, hopeful ones, but there was never any evidence.

As the summer went on, Lancelot made several attempts to escape his confinement—interestingly, without his "wife"—but was always captured and returned. On one occasion they even caught him dressed as a woman, trying to buy passage on a ship to France.

Guenevere, on the other hand, seemed serenely resigned to life as a prisoner in Corfe Castle. To appearances, at least, she hatched no plots, schemed no schemes; she was a compliant and obedient prisoner.

She made a point of trying to befriend Dalley. "You are an efficient, resourceful officer, John." She flirted; she flattered. And she was dismayed when he remained aloof, a professional jailor.

"You aren't being used well," she told him once. "You are a military leader, not a warden."

"I still command the Corfe garrison—plus all the soldiers assigned here to the castle. And there will be more of them when the conference happens. My status has actually increased."

"You are being wasted. A wiser monarch than Arthur would recognize your abilities and put them to better use."

"I know of no wiser monarch than Arthur. He has Merlin to advise him."

"You haven't traveled much, have you?"

He laughed.

"You are a handsome man, Captain. How is it that you have no wife?"

"Don't waste your time trying to seduce me, Guenevere. I have no ambition to become a prisoner instead of a jailor."

"But Captain—"

"You already have two husbands, Guenevere. A third would be laughably redundant to everyone, even to the two you already possess."

"Believe me, Captain Dalley, someday soon it will be my face on England's coinage, not Arthur's."

"Then I must handle my money well, mustn't I?"

She snorted to show her contempt for him and stormed out of the room. But she never let up, apparently convinced that her charms would win him over sooner or later.

Meanwhile Petronilla kept giving him reports of the queen's other activities, very few of which came to anything. But Dalley sent them all dutifully to Brit, along with his own reports on Guenevere's failed flirtations.

And Brit dutifully read them and forwarded them to Arthur. With each one Arthur seemed to become sadder and more detached.

Britomart never mentioned to Petronus that his sister had left France and was living in England, much less that she was living at Corfe Castle and was secretly in Arthur's service. He seemed to have no idea of either fact; as Petronilla had said, they weren't close. But Brit did not raise the least objection when Arthur detached the boy from her service and assigned him as an assistant to Merlin.

Then, late one night, in the smallest hours of the morning, Merlin awoke. Restless, he walked to the window. Two of his ravens were sleeping there. They stirred and looked at him groggily, then closed their eyes again.

He looked out across the main courtyard to see Arthur's rooms in the king's tower ablaze with light. It was unusual; given Arthur's mood—mad drinking—of late, he had been sleeping heavily and late, most mornings. Merlin even found lights mildly alarming. He got his cane and took the stairs down one level to Petronus's room, entered and shook the boy out of a sound sleep. "Petronus, I need you."

Half-awake, the boy gaped at him. "Hmm? What time is it?"

"Late. Late enough that everyone should be asleep. Except— Get up, will you?"

Rubbing his eyes, Petronus did so. He had been sleeping under a down-filled comforter; he was in his underclothes. "I'm sorry. What's wrong?"

"I need you to go to the King's Tower. Arthur is awake. Find out if he is all right. Or if he needs me."

"Yes, sir." He climbed into a pair of trousers and a shirt and pulled his boots on.

The two of them stepped out onto the landing. Just as Petronus was about to leave, Merlin saw someone coming up the spiral stairs with a torch. After a moment he realized who it was. "Arthur!" he called.

The king continued his ascent without answering.

"Arthur. Where are your bodyguards?"

Arthur shrugged, then laughed. Finally he reached them, paused, looked around and walked into Petronus's room without saying a word.

Petronus looked at Merlin. "He's been drinking," he whispered.

"Wait here."

Merlin followed the king inside and closed the door. Arthur was sitting on the bed with his face buried in his hands. Without looking up he said, "Merlin, I want this to be over."

"It will be, Arthur. Sooner or later."

"I still love her. Do you understand that? She still owns my love."

Softly Merlin replied, "I know it. I can't imagine why."

He looked up. "You don't think she still loves me?"

"The word in that that gives me trouble is *still*."

Arthur looked away from him. "It's late spring, almost

summer. I used to love this time of year. Birds, butterflies, flowers, refreshing rains. Now it all looks more foul to me than I can say. You remember, Merlin. I met Guenevere when I was twenty. Still green, still a boy. She seemed the most magically beautiful, sophisticated woman I'd ever seen. And she said she loved me. *Me*."

"Love, even when it is not an illusion, rarely lasts. Arthur, you are a king, but you are not exempt from human behavior." He lowered his voice a bit. "Or human suffering."

"She's going to kill. There will be death. I know it. Not everyone will survive this year alive."

"We don't know for certain that she was behind the attempt on you. It seems likely, but—"

"She was. You know it. We both do."

Merlin sat beside him and put an arm around him. "You need sleep. Let me have Petronus take you back to your tower."

Arthur pulled away from him quite violently. "Did you hear what I said? This year will bring death."

"Every year does. Arthur, come along."

"No. Leave me alone."

"When you were a boy, Arthur, you begged me to teach you how to be a king. Show me that you learned your lessons well. It is time."

Outside the door Petronus listened to all this, fascinated. When, finally, ten minutes later, Merlin called him and asked him to get the king back to his rooms, he was wide awake and ready.

But the next morning he knocked softly on Merlin's door. Merlin was grinding another one of his lenses.

"Sir?"

"Yes. Come in, Petronus. Thank you for your help last night. I hope you will keep what you saw to yourself."

"Yes, sir, of course. But . . ."

"Hmm?"

"I don't understand. When I was very small my mother used to tell me I'd understand things better when I grew older. I don't. Even Arthur doesn't."

Merlin sighed and sat down. "Can I tell you a secret? No one does. We all improvise our way through life, missing cues, mistaking motives, trusting the wrong people. Reason and logic—clear vision, to the extent it's possible—is our only hope."

"I don't understand."

"I told you. No one does."

Petronus was lost. "I—I— Is Guenevere real y likely to murder someone? Does she have other—doe. she have agents here?"

"Quite possibly. Maybe even probably. I don't know. I don't see how anyone can know. Brit is investigating, but— Do you not understand what I've been telling you?"

"No."

"Well, you are young. It might make sense to you some-day. Then again, it might not. It comes down to this: Nothing human is calculable. I wish I could be more helpful to you. I am not really much of a teacher, am I?"

"You do your best, sir."

"Thank you. But there are times when I think that any-one's best can never be good enough."

Clearly bewildered, the boy left.

Merlin watched him go. The boy had started to ask whether Guenevere had *other* agents at Camelot, then caught himself. He had defected from Guenevere and Lan-celot. But was his defection real? He would have to be watched.

Merlin, as Arthur's chief minister, was de facto in charge of diplomacy. Not that that was much of a job. England's status as an island, and its relative isolation from the rest of Europe, meant that diplomacy had never been much more than a cottage industry there. Arthur had posted a few ambassadors here and there, but most of the important European courts had rebuffed his overtures.

Guenevere's birthday celebration was changing that, and changing it rapidly. Diplomatic correspondence arrived at Camelot almost daily. And most of it had to do with the birthday observance; one court after another accepted Arthur's invitation. And they had sense enough to advise the court of England quite specifically how many would be in their representatives' parties and what they would require. "They do not seem to trust us to know how to treat them," Merlin complained to Nimue.

Those communiqués began arriving in early summer, and they came in a steady stream. Nimue, as "Colin," took charge of all the diplomatic communication; she sorted it, filed it, drafted routine replies for Arthur's signature and brought the important matters to Merlin's or Arthur's attention. Aside from policy concerns, there were practical matters to take care of—lodging for emissaries, and so on. She happily took charge of that, also.

One afternoon in early July she approached Merlin, who, uncharacteristically, was relaxing. No books, no lenses, no phosphorus, no medicines. "Merlin, I'm beginning to feel out of my depth."

"You have taken on a great many duties. Teaching the squires, managing the foreign ministry—such as it is. I should have been more attentive."

"It appears we will have emissaries from at least fifteen European courts, possibly more. Even the king of Armenia, wherever that is, is sending someone. I'm not certain Corfe Castle can accommodate them all, not in proper fashion. I have the sense that their egos can be sensitive. One after another demands to be lodged either next to the Byzantines or as far away from them as possible. They can't all be made happy."

"Do your best and try not to worry. Diplomats can be so

undiplomatic. If I am correct, this is only the first evidence of their various rivalries and intrigues. Still, if we are to make the impression Arthur wants, we must arrange this event properly. When will the first of them arrive?"

"The first week in November. Most of them should be arriving in quick succession."

"We can't simply assign them quarters on a first-come, first-served basis. The more important ambassadors will have to be assigned the most impressive rooms."

"If memory serves, Corfe Castle doesn't have that many good rooms. Except for the Great Hall and the refectory, most of the rooms don't even have doors, just curtains hanging at the threshold. You recall? Three of the eight 'arms' are in poor repair. We should have thought twice before we went ahead with an event like this in a place like that."

"You are right. I'll talk to Arthur. We can send as many workmen as we need to renovate. There will not be time to fix up the entire castle, but we can always close off the wings that have not been fixed. We can claim it is a security matter or some such. Why don't you make a quick trip to Corfe and see what needs to be done? We should be able to make at least one of those three arms livable."

"I'll leave first thing in the morning."

"Excellent. And I will have that talk with Arthur. He is quite committed to this event. I can't imagine he'll want to stint on the preparations."

She stood to go. "Merlin, are we out of our depth, here?"

"Everyone is always out of his depth, one way or another. It is a rule of life."

"Don't be glib. I'm asking seriously."

He considered for a moment. "We can do this. We can bring it off."

"You do realize the downside, don't you?"

"Downside?"

"If all these emissaries, legates, ambassadors and so on arrive and find Corfe Castle in good shape, won't that enhance Guenevere's prestige, not Arthur's?"

"Let us hope not. We will make a point of emphasizing to them that Guenevere lives on Arthur's largesse. But that is far from my biggest worry."

She stopped at the door. "What do you mean?"

"Let us hope they leave their poisons, daggers, garrotes and such at home, where they belong. And let us hope, if they do bring them, they do not use them. All we need is a well-placed knife in the dark to turn this affair into a catastrophe. A strategically done political murder would undermine our cause more effectively than anything I can think of."

Her face was immobile. "You're serious, aren't you?"

"Never more so."

"They really are that savage? I mean, England has the reputation for being the barbaric place in Europe."

"When we kill, we do it with a grimace instead of a nice, sweet diplomatic smile. That, apparently, makes all the difference. In Byzantium there are apothecary shops on every corner, making fine profits vending poisons. They dispense them with a pleasant smile. We would be fools to think Podarthes's people might not bring some with them. Who knows how well they get along with the Armenians or whoever? Or whether they might simply want them out of the way, for profit, for territory, for any of a dozen reasons I can think of."

"Should we worry much about the Armenians, or the Libyans or the Romans or any of the others? Surely our own people are the ones we must be concerned for."

Merlin raised an eyebrow. "Why should they want to kill any of us?"

"With Arthur out of the way they could carry on their negotiations with Guenevere, couldn't they? At least some of them are already committed to that."

He narrowed his eyes and peered at her. "You are getting

the hang of international relations far too quickly. It be-speaks a bad character."

"You are teaching me."

"Why—I ask myself a thousand times a day—why do human beings have to be so clever?"

"But at least we have one comfort, Merlin."

Suspecting some sarcasm was in the air, he asked her suspiciously, "What is that?"

"You." She grinned.

"What the devil do you mean by that?"

"You are a master detective. If something bad should happen, you will get to the bottom of it."

"Don't be foolish, Nimue."

"I mean it. Amid all the confusing evidence, you uncov-ered the last treason that was hatched here. If there should be more murder . . ."

"That is hardly a thing to dwell on. It would be better to be preparing yourself mentally for all the tensions that might erupt. If we anticipate them, we will be able to deal with them when they arise. After the fact . . . Clever assas-sins do not leave clues. They strike in the dead of night, in darkened bedchambers or in privies, at victims too drunk to notice or remember anything. Brit has investigated, and we still don't have a clue who struck at Arthur that night."

"Can murder—even diplomatic murder—ever really be anticipated?"

"Yes. I anticipate I will wring your neck if you don't stop harping on this and get back to work."

Late summer night. Well after midnight. Everyone in Came-lot, except for the guards at their posts, was asleep. Like everyone else, Merlin was deep in slumber. Three of his pet ravens perched on the edge of his worktable, also lost in repose; his favorite bird, Roc, slept at the head of his bed.

Then something woke Merlin and Roc almost simultaneously. The other birds remained asleep. But there had been some noise in the night, loud enough to waken Merlin, vague enough not to be identifiable.

He climbed from his bed and into a robe. Softly he called, "Who is there?"

There was no answer, not to his surprise. The fire was burning low; he put two small logs on it. Then he got his cane and climbed slowly down the stone stairs to the level where Nimue and Petronus had their rooms. He knocked gently at her door. "Colin?" From inside he heard the sound of snoring. Crossing to Petronus's room he knocked a bit more loudly. "Petronus?" But the boy did not answer.

Something was wrong in Camelot; his every instinct told him so. Slowly, heavily, he descended to the castle's main floor. He had not thought to bring a light; dim torches at wide intervals along the walls gave the only illumination.

Then ahead of him he saw someone approaching, carrying a brightly blazing torch. And it was Arthur. He was staggering—drunk as nearly always at night.

"Arthur."

The king stopped. Swaying, he steadied himself against the wall and asked, "Who's there?"

"It's me, Arthur, Merlin."

"Oh. What are you doing up?"

"I heard something, or I think I did. Where are your guards?"

"I gave them the slip. They always follow me on these late-night walkabouts, and I hate it. I need to be alone to think."

"You are in no condition to think."

"You sound like Britomart."

"She is right, then. Did that attempt on your life teach you nothing?"

He lowered his torch; his face was in shadow. "I don't much care if I'm killed. I don't want to be alive."

"Stop talking like that."

"It's true. Merlin, if someone were to kill me, I would die happy, knowing that the end had come and that I am through with the human race."

"I sympathize with your view. But what advantage do you see in expressing it at this hour?"

Footsteps clattered up the hall behind Arthur. Two of his guards. "Your Majesty, come with us, back to your tower."

"No. Leave me alone."

"Britomart told us to keep watch on you. She'll demote us if she knows you got away from us."

"Get away from me."

"Please, sir. We have wives and children. We can't afford to be demoted."

Merlin spoke up. "You both know me?"

"Yes, sir," they said in unison.

"Good. Then I want you to take the king back to his rooms. Do not worry, there will be no trouble. I will take the responsibility."

"Yes, sir."

"Use force on him if you must."

They took Arthur by the arms and began to push him back in the direction he'd come from. He fought for a moment then resigned himself to it.

"Good night, men. Good night, Arthur."

"Merlin," Arthur cried, "I've always loved you. When I was a boy you seemed the wisest man possible. I revered you. I think you know that I still do. Please, tell them to release me."

"Then you must know that I love you, too, Arthur. I love you much too much to leave you open to another attack, even if you lack that much sense yourself. Go to bed, Arthur. And, for heaven's sake, don't drink anymore. We will talk in the morning."

Arthur, deflated, stopped resisting his guards. Merlin watched them go, then went back to his own tower and began slowly to climb the steps.

When he reached his room he noticed that the ravens were gone. That was not unusual; they often came and went all night long. But then . . .

There was something on the hearth. He went and looked. And it was two of his birds. They had been beheaded; their severed heads lay near their bodies, facing grotesquely backward.

"No," he whispered. "No, not this."

Their bodies were still warm. He wrapped the corpses in soft cloth; in the morning he would bury them.

There came a knock at the door. "Yes?"

It was one of Arthur's guards. "Something . . . strange has happened, sir."

He was holding the cloth with the corpses of his pets. "What? What else?"

"Else, sir?"

"What happened?"

"We got the king back to his bedchamber. He insisted on undressing himself. When we went back a few moments later to put him to bed, I pulled back the covers. And there in the bed was a bloody knife. Bloody and with . . . with . . . well, I know it sounds odd, sir, but . . ."

"Get to the point, will you?"

"Well . . . there were black feathers sticking to the blade."

It was a warning; Merlin knew it. But a warning to who—to him, or to Arthur? Or both? He thanked the guard and sent him back to the king's tower. Then he crawled into bed.

But sleep would not come. After a time he sat up and cradled the dead birds in his arms. And softly he murmured over and over again, "I must think. I must think."

Summer stretched on, and as fall approached the preparations for the queen's birthday became more and more intense, more and more focused.

No one had seen anyone awake and moving about the castle the night the birds were killed. The killer might have been anyone. Brit increased Arthur's security again and assigned a bodyguard to Merlin as well. Arthur remembered nothing of that night, nothing at all.

It was the warmest, loveliest summer anyone could remember. Crops were abundant; the grape harvest was the largest ever, with the plumpest, sweetest grapes on record; beehives overflowed with honey. Even the fishing fleets at Corfe and Dover reported larger than average catches. The assembled diplomats would not want for good food and drink.

Nimue made frequent trips between Camelot and Corfe, overseeing the repair work, making certain sufficient stores were laid in for the event, monitoring the activities of Guenevere and Lancelot, and coordinating everything with Captain Dalley, who had proved resourceful and efficient. Britomart was there frequently, too, planning security and meeting secretly with Dalley and Petronilla.

The would-be royal couple had been complacent, for the most part, except for Lancelot's halfhearted attempts at escape and a few peculiar letters to Guenevere's parents in France. Once Lancelot tried to sneak out of the castle in the cart of a fishmonger, under a load of mackerel that had been rejected by the castle cook. He was caught at the front gate of the castle by one of Captain Dalley's guards, who noticed that the dead fish seemed to be moving. The jokes at the French knight's expense didn't let up for weeks.

At Camelot Merlin took over the diplomatic end of things as the conference drew closer and the various matters became more pressing. Assisted by Nimue, he kept up an active correspondence with the various courts who were sending legates. As the event began to draw near, their demands became more and more supercilious. This king demanded fresh bottles of wine for his people every second hour; that petty ruler wanted chambermaids with blond hair; and on and on. Merlin handled it all as delicately as he could without making any promises. Everyone, he assured them, would be treated with due deference, dignity and respect.

From Byzantium and Podarthes there had been no further correspondence directed to Guenevere at Corfe. No one knew what to make of that. Was it possible Justinian had learned somehow that she and Lancelot had been jailed? It seemed the likeliest explanation; Byzantine spies were everywhere.

All of this happened despite Arthur, who was drinking regularly and heavily. He kept late hours and often woke this courtier or that one in the middle of the night to be reassured that he was a good king, that his polices were just, that he was loved by all his people if not by his wife. Merlin tried repeatedly to talk to him about what he was doing to himself—not to mention the court and the country—without much success.

He complained about it privately to Nimue. "Our king," he said heavily, "is a lovesick schoolboy. What can I do with him?"

"Make him stay after class. Spank him. Paddle him. Send him to bed without his dessert."

"You make my mouth water. If only it were that simple."

Then in mid-October a dispatch arrived from Captain Dalley at Corfe. "King Leodegrance and Queen Leonilla are here. Come at once."

FOUR

And so Merlin and Nimue, accompanied by a long line of soldiers, made the ride from Camelot to Corfe. Arthur was to follow in a few days' time, with Britomart, Simon of York, Petronus and others who would be needed. They avoided the main roads and took a more direct route, which involved using a combination of cow paths, footpaths and paths that were so vague they barely existed and defied simple categorization. "No sense making ourselves too easy for assassins to find," Brit said ruefully.

"I've never met Leodegrance and Leonilla." Nimue kept her eyes on the road.

"You're young, Colin." Merlin laughed. "You've never met anyone of any real note. But the king and queen are in their seventies. They rule one of the poorest of the French provinces, Camelliard, in the foothills of the Pyrenees. And they have been scheming to increase their territory and their power for as long as anyone can remember, without much success. Leodegrance is ruthless and Leonilla more so; but as political strategists they have always been ineffectual. They arranged Guenevere's marriage to Arthur in hopes that it would give them a foothold in England. Of course, we had our eyes on France, as well. So at best they had created a stalemate."

"Arthur fell for that?" Nimue sounded genuinely startled. "I mean, you permitted Arthur to fall for that?"

"He was young and in love. They seemed relatively harmless, as the French go. Not strong enough to make real trouble."

" 'Seemed.' " Her tone was heavily ironic. "How many times has Leodegrance been in and out of England— always unofficially, of course—trying to move his daughter to treason?"

"It appears he was finally successful in an undeniable way."

Nimue asked, "What about his wife?"

"I hardly know her. When our king and queen became betrothed Arthur asked me to handle all the negotiations with Leonilla, but that is my only experience with her. The marriage was a diplomatic event. So I shuttled back and forth across the Channel, negotiating, treating, bargaining. Of course it was all for nothing. Each side knew the other's ambition. We were very frank about it all.

"Poor Arthur. He actually believed it was a love match. He actually thought a royal wedding could be made out of affection and not political ambition."

"What is Leonilla like?"

"In Egypt, you know, they dry out the bodies of the dead, wrap them with spices and keep them lying around. Leonilla looks more like a living mummy than anyone I have ever seen. Or she did back then, and that was ten years ago. I cannot imagine the passage of time has helped. But do not be fooled by her frail appearance. Leodegrance rules Camelliard, but Leonilla rules him. Anyone who gets in her way dies mysteriously. She does not even use poison, like a good English queen. Her enemies die the most horrible deaths."

"But—aren't they Christians? I thought their religion taught—"

"Don't be naïve, Colin. No god and no religion—not Apollo, not Isis, not the god of the Christians—has ever turned politicians into decent human beings, or ever could. If there actually *are* any gods, they are quite derelict in their duty."

Nimue thought for a moment. "No wonder Arthur is dragging his feet. He should be with us."

"He will come, Colin. I've managed for Brit to sober him up and persuade him it was time to behave royally. And he knows that anyway. But you know how drinkers come to love their wine . . . I've set Petronus to keep an eye on him and to travel down here with him."

"Petronus is coming to Corfe?" Nimue couldn't hide her concern.

"Yes. Is that a problem for some reason?"

"Of course not. I just— Will Arthur listen to a boy his age?"

"Not likely. But Brit is there, too, and at least we will have someone to let us know what he is up to."

She lapsed into silence.

"What is wrong, Colin?"

"Nothing, really."

"I know you better than that. Tell me."

"Well, it's only that . . ." She glanced at him then looked quickly away. "It's only that . . . Do you trust Petronus?"

He narrowed his eyes. "Why would you ask that?"

"Do you know where he was the night the ravens were killed?"

"Asleep in his room." He added with emphasis, "Like you."

"Do you know that for a fact?"

"I wasn't in bed with him. What are you suggesting?"

"Petronus came to us from Guenevere's court."

There was a long, awkward pause. "You are suggesting that his defection was a ruse? A way to plant an agent among us? They tried to kill him, remember? He was badly injured."

"More deception?"

"It seems a terribly elaborate way to plant a spy. Guenevere and Lancelot have been to Camelot often enough. And agents representing them even more frequently. They would have had every opportunity to bribe someone—or blackmail someone—into acting for them. A plot like the one you're suggesting . . . it is too complex to be believable. For that matter, it is too subtle for Guenevere. Her coat of arms should feature a sledgehammer." He laughed. "And it is certainly too subtle for Lancelot."

"I wish I could believe that."

"Well, I will write Brit and tell her to keep an eye on him, if it will make you feel better."

"It will, Merlin. Petronus is there with Arthur, after all. And whoever their spy is has already made one attempt on the king's life."

"Brit will watch him. Don't worry."

"I'm in the diplomatic service now. It's my job to worry."

"If it is any solace, you are doing a first-rate job of it."

The Spider's House was looking good. Workmen had given it a fresh coat of whitewash; it gleamed and caught the eye from a great distance. And they had made enough cosmetic repairs so that the disrepair on the older wings was not noticeable. The visiting dignitaries would, for all they knew, be visiting a first-rate piece of real estate.

Sentries were posted everywhere around the castle. Captain Dalley had arranged for three rings of them, one just outside the building, one in the middle distance and one still father away. The most distant of them was equipped with Merlin's "long-distance viewing lenses" mounted in wooden frameworks. The chance that either Lancelot or Guenevere might escape, or foreign agents penetrate the castle undetected, was remote.

Dalley greeted Merlin and "Colin" at the main entrance. "It's good to see the two of you again. I hope you've traveled well."

"Yes, thank you. How are things here?"

"The queen fumes and tries to act regal and commanding. Lancelot keeps making these absurd attempts at escape."

"But is he attempting to escape from our guards or from his new wife?"

Dalley shrugged. "Everything is as usual."

"Excellent."

Some servants helped Merlin and Nimue settle in to adjoining rooms in the best wing of the castle; Arthur would be housed nearby when he arrived. They had a light meal, then Merlin took a short nap. When he was up again he asked a servant, "Where is the queen?"

"The—the queen, sir? She is in the Great Hall."

"Fine. Thank you. I must go and have a talk with her."

The Great Hall was in the octagonal keep at the heart of the castle. Merlin headed directly for it. Servants, soldiers, the dozens of people that keep a castle alive, all seemed to recognize him and clear the way for him; some even bowed, which made him feel odd. Then he reached the hall.

The heavy oak doors were closed. Inside, it was nearly pitch black. The only light came from two torches that burned fiercely at either side of the queen's throne. She sat there, barely moving, dressed in heavy black robes. The scene was odd; there were only two servants, or retainers or whoever, in attendance on her. For a moment he was not sure it was Guenevere; she looked small, frail.

Merlin stepped into the hall. In the vast space his foot-steps echoed. From the direction of the queen's throne came a soft voice, which despite its low tone echoed even more clearly. "Merlin. You may approach." There was the faintest French accent.

Softly he laughed. "I may approach? Exactly whose prisoner do you think you are?"

"Prisoner? You mistake me, Councilor. Typical English dullness."

The voice was not Guenevere's, despite its French accent. He moved toward the throne and realized it was Leonilla seated there. There was about her the oddest still-ness. Behind her, in the near-darkness, servants moved. "Queen Leonilla. You must excuse me. With two queens in residence, mix-ups are bound to occur."

"Not too close. Do you want to be dazzled by my enor-mous beauty?"

"Your beauty," he told her in an ironic tone, "is being heavily cloaked by this thick darkness you have arranged. Shall I have some servants bring more lights?"

"No." The word hung in the air as if it was made of granite. "All queens are beautiful, regardless of age or the light. It is a matter of definition."

"Naturally." He continued his approach. "Age does not touch royalty. Everyone knows that."

"Do not come any closer."

He kept walking.

"Stop, I say!"

But he did not stop till he was five feet from her. Ironi-cally, with a sarcastic flourish, he bowed. "Welcome to England, Your Majesty."

Leonilla held her hands up and spread her fingers so he couldn't see her face. The gesture was so much like what he'd expect from a shy young girl he found himself mildly startled. Yet despite her demure gesture he was able to get a good glimpse. And despite her coyness she looked more like a living Egyptian mummy than he would have thought possible. The effect was more than mildly unsettling.

"I would advise you to take me more seriously, Merlin. You must remember me. At any rate, you must know my reputation."

"If you plan on killing everyone who notices your age, Leonilla, you will not have many followers left."

"People die anyway. The tactful ones will remain."

"Spoken like a true French queen."

For the first time she moved, inclining her head slightly toward him. The gesture seemed, odd, disjointed, unnatural, like a movement by a marionette. "I remember your impertinence from our meetings a decade ago. I should have had you murdered then. It would have saved so much trouble with my idiot son-in-law. I had a first-rate strangler in my employ, one of the *hashishin* from Aleppo."

"Had? What happened to him?"

"Someone strangled him."

He paused; he could not let her take control of their conversation. "You are sitting on Guenevere's throne."

"Your jailers have confined her to her rooms. The throne was not being used. It seemed a waste."

"You always were ambitious. It is a pity you did not marry better."

"Leodegrance has been a disappointment, yes. But he has had his uses and will again."

"They say you were a great beauty when you were young. You still are, of course. But you could have had any throne you wanted. Alexandria, Rome, Byzantium even— they were yours for the asking. Yet you chose Leodegrance, the ruler of a backward French province. What could have possessed you?"

Softly she laughed. "Love, shall we say?"

"If Your Majesty chooses." Merlin made himself smile. "But love is no rival for ambition. You had most of France and all of England in your sights."

"You are suggesting that I have political designs? A simple woman like me? I weave homespun and do embroidery. I cook and bake and polish my husband's silver. I am the picture of a dutiful wife."

Merlin laughed. "And how *is* King Leodegrance?"

"Asleep. Nursing his royal arthritis. He is aging badly."

He had to work not to smile at the irony of this. "I trust your crossing was good?"

"As well as can be expected, given the Channel's treacherous winds and currents. We used a Byzantine ship." She smiled faintly to make certain the point wasn't lost on him.

But he refused to be intimidated. "Your own navy is in such disrepair?"

"Surely you know better than that. The dimmest spy in Europe could have told you otherwise. Do you remember our meetings ten years ago?"

"With the greatest pleasure, Leonilla."

"You recall that one of your servants had an accident in our stables?"

"He was kicked by a poorly trained horse, as I remember."

Leonilla did not speak for a long moment, did not even move. "It was a warning to you. After all this time you have still not taken it."

"You are confessing?"

"Can you believe it?" She looked slightly away from him. "All these years I have maintained my reputation chaste, intact. I have been suspected of this and that, but there has never been any proof. Suddenly I feel as if I've disrobed."

Grateful she had done no such thing, and hoping to see something like life in her from a better angle, he took a step to one side. "I am an old man, Leonilla. And you have a generation on me. Surely it is time for you to stop this kind of scheming. It seems so . . ."

"Unqueenly?"

"Let us say unseemly. Undignified. One reaches a station in life where all the games that mattered in youth seem foolish, to say the least."

"You think power is a game? You think the will to rule is foolish, as if it were better to be ruled? That is dangerously close to blasphemy."

"Then call me infidel."

"My royal husband has never been—how would you say?—never been much of a husband to me. But I have had my crown for comfort. If it is not as great as the one I might have had . . . well, what is size?"

Merlin glanced at the servant who stood behind her on the right. For a startled moment he thought it was Nimue, dressed in a gleaming suite of ceremonial armor. Then he realized it was a strikingly handsome young man. Despite himself, Merlin found himself wondering . . . But no, surely even Leonilla must be past that.

"That is my servant, Jean-Michel." Oddly, she grinned. "Also lurking back there is my maid, Marthe. You may ignore them both."

"I fully plan to do so. But you . . . Are you planning to sit here in the dark all day long?"

"It is the only throne in the castle. And I am the only queen."

"Guenevere might not agree."

"My daughter, like her father, has been a disappointment to me in so many ways."

"As I'm sure you have been to her. You promised her England, and look what she has come to. None of your promises to her were worth the air it took to speak them." He made a sweeping gesture that seemed to emphasize the room's gloom and emptiness. "We have dinner at six. I will see you then."

"I have not dismissed you."

"And I have not asked you to. The birthday celebration

does not begin for two and a half weeks. It is unfortunate that you chose to arrive so early. But I hope you enjoy your stay, Leonilla."

"Leave my presence."

Not hiding his amusement, he went.

From behind him, he heard her voice. "Jean-Michel. My shoulders are sore. Rub them for me."

Just as he left the Great Hall, Merlin spotted an old man coming down the corridor toward him. For a moment he thought it must be a stranger, perhaps one of the townsmen hired for the celebration. Then with a start he realized who it was. "King Leodegrance—Your Majesty."

The man was alone and unattended. He shuffled toward Merlin as rapidly as his apparent infirmity would allow. Merlin made a slight bow; Leodegrance was the true power, after all, at least officially.

"I imagined you would be here, Merlin."

Uncertain what to say to the old man, Merlin repeated, "Leodegrance."

The king narrowed his eyes. "You didn't recognize me. It's all right, Merlin. Time has not been kind. I know that. Would you believe I'm six years younger than my wife?"

"Leonilla is not exactly ripe for plucking, herself." Merlin looked back over his shoulder into the Great Hall, hoping she hadn't heard.

"Except perhaps by the Grim Reaper. Be grateful you don't have to see her in her bath." The king paused and looked into the dark hall. "She is in there?"

Merlin nodded. "Seated on her daughter's throne."

"My poor wife. The trappings of power are all that is left to her."

"And to you, Leodegrance? You keep letting her concoct these absurd plots against Arthur."

"They are my plots as well, but never mind. Plotting is what kings do. Arthur should expect it. In Persia they play a game called chess, in which little imitation knights and nobles try to topple the opposing king. We play the same game, only for real. My wife sent for me. She wants to see me."

"She told me she had one of my grooms murdered ten years ago."

"Grooms?"

"When I was at your court, making plans for the royal wedding."

"Grooms? What do I know about grooms? They hardly matter."

"This one was a fine young man, tall, handsome and strong. I have always heard that Leonilla had a habit of killing her lovers, tossing them away like leftover scraps of food. Do you suppose that was the motive here?"

The king hardened. "I'm afraid I have no such recollection, Merlin."

"I see. Perhaps you should go in and attend your lady wife."

"Yes. She wants me. She sent for me."

"You said. Go, then."

And so they parted ways. Merlin told Nimue about his encounters later, over dinner. "And soon enough the entire castle will be filled with people like them. It is going to be such an interesting birthday party."

"Appropriate for Guenevere, would you say?"

"Appropriate for the Spider's House, at any rate."

Three days later Arthur arrived, attended by his squire Greffys, Britomart, Petronus and Simon of York. They all had a quick meal, and Merlin made it a point to sit with Brit. In a low voice he asked, "How is he?"

"Sober, thank god. He says he knows it is time for him to act responsibly. But he is still melancholy. Sometimes his mood is so dark it frightens me."

"I'll find some pretext to talk with him and see if I cannot help, somehow."

Later they all gathered around a table in Arthur's quarters for a conference. Merlin brought them all up to date on developments at the Spider's House, as he insisted on calling it.

Then Brit explained to him and "Colin" what had been happening at Camelot. "There have been a few more letters from the various courts. Routine things. We handled them ourselves—there didn't seem to be a need to consult with you."

"Everything is happening as it should, then?" Merlin asked.

"The Armenian legate wants rose water for his bath. Your friend Germanicus requested that books from the royal library be made available to him. And there's more in that vein. Easy requests—nothing of any moment. But—" She paused dramatically and took a deep breath. "There has been another incident. Another bloody dagger found on Arthur's pillow."

"Are my ravens all right? What was killed this time?" Merlin didn't try to hide his alarm.

"As near as we can tell, nothing and no one. We haven't been able to find out where the blood came from."

Nimue asked, "You're certain it was blood, then, and not—I don't know—cider or something?"

"It looked and smelled like blood. That's as much as we know."

"And when did this happen, Brit?"

"Two nights ago."

Merlin said, "I wish I had been there. I might have noticed something no one else did."

Arthur hadn't said a word, just listened and frowned at it all. But now for the first time he showed signs of animation. "Merlin, the great detective."

"This is not a thing to joke about, Arthur. Your life is being threatened, quite clearly. Someone who could sneak a bloodstained knife into your bed could just as easily use it on you."

"I'm not worried, Merlin. Don't you be, either. If the villain wanted to hurt me, he would have done so by now."

"He has, once. Have you forgotten?"

Nimue leaned forward. "Has it occurred to anyone but me that these incidents—call them threats or whatever—must have been done by someone in the inner circle at Camelot? Someone with easy access to the King's Tower?" She glanced quite pointedly at Petronus. And the boy slumped down in his chair and looked away.

Just then there was a knock at the door and a young woman came in. Seeing her, Petronus's eyes widened and he jumped to his feet. "Petronilla!"

She smiled at everyone around the table. "Good afternoon, everyone. For those of you who don't know me, I am, as my brother so abruptly announced, Petronilla, secretary to Queen Guenevere."

Petronus could not hide his astonishment. "Her secretary?"

"You must all excuse my younger brother. He has always been slow to pick up on obvious points."

"But—but—" the boy sputtered. "You're all right. I mean, what are you doing here?"

"Later, brother." To the rest of them, she said, "The queen welcomes you to Corfe Castle and hopes that your stay here, in observance of her birthday, will be pleasant."

Arthur sat up. "You may tell the queen that we are pleased that she seems to be content at our generosity in providing her this castle."

"Might I suggest, with respect, Your Majesty, that you have one of your own people convey that message to her?"

"Are you afraid of her, then?"

"Let us say that I know her moods. And I am not a brave woman."

At this Petronus laughed out loud. "No, not brave, only brazen."

Merlin interrupted this. "You may tell Guenevere that we are all here, safe and sound. No more."

Petronilla smiled. "I will certainly do so, sir. Is there anything else any of you require for the moment?"

They looked at one another and said nothing. Merlin told her, "I think we are all quite fine, thank you."

Petronilla made a slight bow, turned and left. Everyone in the room turned to Petronus.

"I—I didn't know she was here, like this" he stammered. "Honestly."

"We believe you." Merlin made his voice reassuring, glanced quickly at Nimue and said, "But we could not escape the conviction that you are not exactly close. Would you prefer to return to Camelot?"

"N-no, sir. I don't want to miss all the grand delegates and all the ceremonies. And the performers. Please let me stay."

Softly and gravely Arthur asked, "What kind of woman is your sister? What should we know about her?"

"Well, sir . . ."

"Yes?"

"She's . . . she's a bitch. From my earliest memories she has hated me. I've never understood why."

"I see. We shall have to keep you away from her then."

"But . . . but can I stay?"

"Yes, I think so. But stay out of trouble. And stay out of Petronilla's way."

"Yes, sir. You can count on it."

Simon of York busied himself training all the new staff that had been hired from Corfe, in their duties and, more importantly, in protocol. They were instructed when to speak, when not to, when to bow, how to enter and leave a room properly, which title to use with which diplomat, and on and on. To his dismay, most of them seemed not to take it very seriously.

Two weeks later the delegates began to arrive. Some came singly; some had traveled together. Most brought aides and attendants. The Armenian was a short, plump man who wore bright red silk trousers and wore them ostentatiously. His name was Phenobarbus. There were legates from Spain, Morocco, Libya, Sweden, Castile, Salesi, from every conceivable quarter of the Mediterranean world, even a place called Flausenthurm, a region Nimue could not find on any map. Merlin's friend Germanicus Genentius arrived with four young boys as his body servants. Even though most of these people were technically vassals of Justinian, they presented themselves as representative of sovereign, independent courts. Of Podarthes there was no sign as of yet.

Merlin and Germanicus got reacquainted over a noon-day meal. "I hope you traveled well."

"The sea was most cooperative."

Germanicus could not hide his interest in the castle's curious architectural plan. Merlin explained the building's history. "As far as I am aware, neither the Romans nor anyone else ever repeated the experiment."

"Our Roman forebears were not always as wise as we like to imagine."

"They were geniuses, Germanicus. Their aqueducts still water a great many of our cities. Their roads cover Europe and are still in use."

"And so are the tortures they devised. There's no need to lecture me, Merlin. I know all that. But have you ever seen the ruins of Nero's Golden House? The word *folly* hardly seems adequate."

"Nero was mad."

"Can you think of an emperor who wasn't?"

Merlin laughed. "Be grateful Podarthes is not here yet."

"I know him. I am."

The delegates' self-importance was a source of constant

amusement to the Englishmen. The Roman pope sent a priest named Gildas, who announced to a startled court that he had been appointed Bishop of England. He was tall, parched, unnaturally thin; he looked as if he hadn't enjoyed anything since before puberty. "It is the will of Honorius," he proclaimed serenely, "that I serve here."

"Do you mean to say you will be staying?" Merlin didn't try to hide his shock at this arrogant breach of protocol. "Remind me—when did we request a bishop of our very own? There are no Christians here for you to preside over."

"That unfortunate fact will be corrected in good time. I intend to prepare you all for your meeting with the Almighty in Paradise in the next life."

"Excellent," Nimue told him. "Now may we move your luggage out of the hallway?"

All in all, and given their pretensions, they were not a promising lot. Merlin complained about it to Germanicus, who was unmoved. "What did you expect? You've visited most of these courts and you must have at least secondhand knowledge of the rest. Petty nabobs and ambitious nobodies, starting wars for their own personal gain or amusement, jockeying for position with Justinian . . . You know international diplomacy well enough to have known it all and expected it."

"I often accuse Arthur of naïveté. I suppose I am guilty of the same thing myself, in my old-fashioned way. And yet Arthur thinks me a cynic."

"You are a cynic, Merlin. In the high old sense, in the sense the Greeks meant. 'The Cynic questions everything in order to learn what is true.'"

"And what did Zeno's cynicism get him? He is quite as dead as the Epicureans and the Stoics."

"So you think the point of intellectual inquiry is immortality? A good cynic could tear that proposition to shreds."

"Be quiet, Germanicus."

"I'd like to get some exercise. Is it possible for me to work out with some of the knights?"

"I'll arrange it."

Over the following days more and more delegates arrived. Before long the harbor at Corfe was crowded with their ships.

Nimue served as official greeter when Merlin was occupied with other business. She saw to their comfort, explained when the ceremonies would begin and what they would consist of. Then they went their own ways, conspiring together, plotting against mutual enemies and friends, trying tirelessly to find ways to use the gathering to their advantage. Both Merlin and Nimue tired of them quickly; when they were alone together they expended a great deal of wit at their guests' expense.

One bright, cool afternoon Germanicus took advantage of the chance to exercise with the knights and squires. Petronus and Greffys were among them. They were in a paved courtyard between two of the castle's arms. Some wrestled, some ran footraces, several of them practiced with their longbows. Lancelot, under heavy guard, was permitted to practice with the bowmen. Germanicus joined them.

Nearby, Arthur, Merlin and Nimue strolled, chatting about the coming events, making minor corrections to the plans. Suddenly, as if from nowhere, an arrow whizzed past Arthur's head, missing him by barely a few inches, and drove itself into the stone castle wall.

Immediately knights surrounded the king, swords, spears and other weapons at the ready. Others surrounded and seized Lancelot. Greffys wrested the bow from his hands. Once he was certain the king was unharmed, Merlin rushed to join the knights.

"He did it, sir," Petronus told him, pointing to Lancelot.

"He shot the arrow at the king. I saw it." Several of the knights backed him up.

Merlin turned to Lancelot. "Is this true?"

"It was an accident, Merlin," the French knight said. "My hand slipped. One of the others—this boy, in fact— jostled me as I was about to shoot."

"Jostled you? The targets are thirty feet from where Arthur was standing. That would take a lot of jostling."

He fought against the men who were restraining him. "It's the truth. Ask any of them."

Merlin was skeptical and said so.

"For heaven's sake, Merlin, I'm already a prisoner. What would I gain by killing my jailer?"

Merlin's face broke out in a sardonic smile. "Revenge?" To the knights he said, "Take him away. Not to the rooms where we have been keeping him. Find the deepest, darkest dungeon and lock him there."

They led him away; he did not stop fighting them for a moment. Everyone else in the courtyard had watched what happened, riveted. The various delegates were already separating into little groups to gossip about it.

Germanicus crossed to Merlin. "He's telling the truth, you know. I saw it. One of the young men bumped into him and threw his aim off."

"I do not doubt that that happened, Germanicus. But I do not doubt that Lancelot would have taken advantage of such an accident to provide cover. It hasn't been noised about, but Arthur is holding Guenevere and Lancelot prisoners here." He lowered his voice. "They've been conspiring against him."

"I know that. Everybody knows that. Still—"

"You do?"

"Of course." He put on a smug little grin. "You know how news travels. Especially bad news."

Merlin put an arm around Germanicus and led him back

inside. "We were so certain we were in control of the situation."

"This is Europe, Merlin. *Modern* Europe. No one is ever in control of any situation. Not even Justinian. The world has become too complex and chaotic for that. Justinian steals, he plunders, he sends out Belisarius with an army large enough to take what he wants. But not even he has found a way to stop gossip and rumor and innuendo. They're the lifeblood of governments."

Merlin sighed heavily. "I do not know much about the religion of the Christians, but I know about their monasteries. Men go there and forget about the world, and they live lives of quiet and contemplation. They never even talk to anyone, not even each other. I would be so happy for a life like that."

"You're an old fraud, Merlin. You—live in silence? Within five minutes you'd be bursting with news about some new lens you'd ground, or a new insight into Plato."

"You are right." Merlin exhaled deeply again. "We haven't seen each other for years. How can you know me so well?"

Germanicus shrugged and laughed. "You have become like the books you love—open and waiting to be read."

"Don't be rude, Germanicus. Here—come up to my chambers and let's drink some wine and talk."

"We'll have to talk softly. There are no doors to these rooms. What's wrong with you English?"

More and more delegates arrived. Of Podarthes there was still no news, neither where he was nor when he might arrive. It was not even known how he was traveling.

But nearly everyone else who was expected had arrived, and Corfe Castle was bursting with activity. The legates and their retinues filled the halls and chambers, prying gently, trying to find out everything about everyone. Word about the attempt on Arthur's life spread quickly; opinion was divided on whether it had really been an accident. People who knew Lancelot insisted it must have been deliberate; he was too skilled an athlete for it to have been anything else. Others were more inclined to give him the benefit of the doubt, choosing to accept Germanicus's account.

The only ones in the castle who remained silent and avoided speculation were Guenevere, Leonilla and Leodegrance.

Then the next morning Guenevere, attended by Petronilla, burst into Arthur's chambers. A meeting was in progress. Arthur, with Merlin, Nimue, Simon and Britomart, was going over all the plans for the celebration. Suddenly the door-curtain flew wide open. Brit jumped to her feet at once and drew her sword. Guenevere stood at the threshold, tall and imperious, attended by Petronilla; beyond them in the corridor outside two of Arthur's soldiers waited, looking concerned. Arthur waved at them to let them know this was all right. Slowly the queen took a step into the room.

"Guenevere." Brit took a step toward her.

But the queen ignored her and spoke to Arthur. "Release Lancelot."

Arthur looked to Merlin, who in turn looked at Guenevere. "Is this sort of behavior supposed to convince us that what happened really was an accident? Might you not at least have had yourself announced first?"

Guenevere ignored Merlin. Her eyes were fixed on the king. Slowly, more loudly and with emphasis she repeated, "Release Lancelot."

Once the startling effect of her entrance died down, Arthur relaxed and put on a slight smile. "I beg your pardon? Did you say something?"

"You heard me perfectly clearly. Set him free."

"It would be an odd monarch who let assassins loose."

"Monarchs don't come any odder than you, Arthur."

"So you think insulting me will help your case."

Merlin leaned forward in his seat. "I believe His Majesty is wondering why you think he would do such a thing."

"Because I have commanded it." Suddenly her manner softened and she added, "And because Lancelot is innocent and I think you all know it."

She looked around the room. Neither Arthur nor any of his councilors said a word.

Brit spoke up. "His Majesty is also wondering how you managed to escape your guards."

"Shall we say they were . . . indisposed by some bad wine they drank?" Realizing that she was making no progress, she changed tactics. "Once you have caught a venomous snake and bottled it up, Arthur, you have the knotty problem of what to do with it, haven't you?"

Merlin decided he was in no mood for this. "I'm afraid we don't follow you, Guenevere."

"Lancelot and I are already your prisoners. Release him from that horrible dungeon, or—"

It was clear from Petronilla's attitude that she had no idea what the queen was about to say. She listened intently and made mental notes on the exchange. Merlin glanced at Britomart as if to ask, *Are we certain we can trust this woman?*

Guenevere went on. "We are at the start of the largest, most important diplomatic event England has ever witnessed. You expect to make great gains here with the nations of Europe. But if the serpent you are holding bares its fangs . . ."

"Just what we need," Arthur told her. "A serpent, or a pair of them, slithering loose in Corfe Castle right now. I can always put the serpents, both of them, into an even more secure bottle. This castle's dungeons are deep and secure. And I have other castles."

"Jailing your wife in the midst of this conference? Yes, that will certainly increase England's prestige across Europe. Do it."

"Be serious, Guenevere." Merlin adopted a tone of cold authority. "These are diplomats. They understand treason. Besides, you are in no position to be making demands. To be perfectly frank, you should count yourself lucky you still have your head."

"I swear to you, Arthur, I will disrupt this conference and your plans for it any way I can. The least hint of trouble will interfere with what you are hoping to accomplish. And if you jail me, there are enough people here with at least some loyalty to me who will gladly do it on my behalf."

Merlin waited till she finished, then sat back in his seat and put on a warm smile. "Who exactly do you think you might influence? Your would-be allies the Byzantines have not appeared yet. And we have managed to acquire no intelligence about where they might be. Do you think the Moroccans and the Latvians care about you and Lancelot?"

"Lancelot and I are not the issue. You want to impress the Mediterranean world. Will anyone be impressed once rumors start circulating about the disarray here?"

"If the source of those rumors is in jail, they might be."

Finally Arthur got between them. "I think Guenevere has a point, Merlin. A small one but a valid one. We should have moved this gathering to Camelot or to one of our other castles. Keeping it here has given my wife a stronger hand than she could have ever had otherwise."

Then he turned to Guenevere. "There is enough doubt to call into question whether Lancelot was actually attempting to harm anyone. But I can hardly return him to the suite of rooms you were sharing, not after what you've just said." He smiled the least sincere smile he could manage. "He will be moved to rooms of his own, in another wing of the castle. Both he and you will be under constant guard, and it will be heavier than anything you have known till now. Be advised, wife. If anything remotely untoward occurs involving the two of you, you will be moved immediately to the deepest, coldest dungeon in Scotland, birthday or no birthday. And after that . . . we shall consider what your prospects are." With a mordant grin he added, "Not good, I would think."

Guenevere's attitude changed. She softened; she looked almost girlish. Her voice turned sweet. "Arthur. Arthur, you wouldn't do that to me. I thought you loved me."

"You married Lancelot, remember? Should I love another man's wife, then? The two of you have already been more trouble than I ever should have permitted. I should have had your heads the first time I caught you plotting against me. Be grateful the love I used to have for you lasted as long as it did."

It was almost possible to see Guenevere's mind racing, turning over the options and strategies. But she clearly realized her hand was not as strong as she'd thought. She smiled a gentle smile and asked, "You will release Lancelot, then?"

"Release? Within the confines of his rooms, yes."

Conflict showed in her face. What she was about to say was plainly difficult for her. In a low voice, slowly, she said, "Thank you."

Arthur signaled to a pair of his guards and told them, "Take the queen back to her suite. And this time see that she stays there."

Brit got to her feet. "Wait—I'll come along. I want to see what happened to those guards. They should never have taken wine from Guenevere."

"Wine." Arthur broke into an enormous grin. "I knew there was something missing from this meeting. Simon, send for some."

"Yes, Your Majesty."

Merlin rolled his eyes and leaned his head back. Britomart had managed to sober the king up; one encounter with his wife and he was drinking again.

The remaining delegates arrived—minus Podarthes, of whom there was still no news. A Turk in enormous baglike trousers came, attended by a dozen boys, in whom he had a fairly over erotic interest.

There was a legate from somewhere in Eastern Europe; at any rate that was the best guess anyone could make—he spoke a language like nothing anyone at court had ever heard. Even the other delegates were at a loss to fathom the things he said. But he carried an invitation, one addressed to the warlord of Estonia.

Merlin and Nimue were quite certain they had not invited him. But they made him welcome. They had sent out pro forma invitations to a great number of minor countries, and they assumed one of them must have found its way to him somehow. Nimue identified herself to him and asked him to follow her to his rooms. "You are from Estonia, then?"

"Lithuania," he replied, beaming enormously. *"Ningaturkman holo duk."*

"Oh. Of course."

She tried Latin, Greek and French, but he just kept repeating, *"Flausenthum."*

Britomart was concerned that admitting someone who had, apparently, not been invited, constituted a breach of security. But Merlin was not so certain. "Suppose he turned out to be important? I know how improbable it sounds, but . . . Let us admit him and keep an extra careful watch on him."

Brit's expression as he said this was half smirk, half scowl. "Lithuania."

"Look at him, Brit. He could not appear more harm-less."

"Of course. Today, Lithuania; tomorrow, the world."

Late in the afternoon on the day before the queen's birth-day, with the castle abuzz with activity, and with heavy autumn rain falling, an enormous black carriage was seen approaching in the distance. It was pulled by four jet-black horses, and the coachmen wore black livery trimmed with sable. Greffys ran to summon Arthur and Merlin. "She's here."

"God, I was hoping she wouldn't come." Arthur moaned.

"I'm afraid she has, sir."

The carriage pulled into the courtyard and came to a halt precisely two feet from the main entrance. Its occu-pant could step directly indoors and never feel the rain. Slowly a footman pulled open the door. A tall, pale woman wrapped in black fur stepped down and strode into the castle as if she owned it. A pack of servants ap-proached her, obediently asking if she required anything. Merlin and Arthur were still halfway to the entrance; they scrambled to follow.

"Morgan." Arthur called to her.

Grandly she turned to face him. Huge sleeves billowed as she spread her arms. "Brother."

"You've come. We weren't certain you would." They embraced.

"In fact," Merlin added, "we were just about to give your rooms to one of the delegates."

"You have so little faith in me. You always have. Where are my rooms?"

"Someone will show you directly. You look fit, Morgan."

"As do you. Both of you." She nodded condescendingly.

"But—fit for what, precisely? I understand there is an up-start here. A—what is the word?—'bishop' or some such, I believe he calls himself."

"Yes." Merlin was in his element. "A legate from the head of the Christian religion in Rome."

"What business could such a creature have in England? Here, we worship the true gods. We have since the beginning of time, and the gods have served us well."

"He says he wants to prepare us to meet his god in the afterlife."

She glared at him. "When we die, if we have lived good lives, we go to the Hall of Heroes." Then she smiled in a conciliatory wau. "That is key to our worship."

"When we worship at all," Arthur muttered.

And Merlin added, "He is a diplomat, Morgan, here on a diplomatic mission. Nothing more."

She turned icy. "You are quite certain? No one at court is contemplating—what is the term they use?—*converting* to this absurd faith? The man may find himself approaching the next life sooner than he thinks."

"No one, Morgan, is converting to anything." Arthur was resolute. "Now, I expect you to behave yourself. The last thing I need right now is you making trouble. You are a member of the royal family, after all, and we have important aims here. Thank heaven you left your chest of poisons at home."

"I have a stripped-down version for travel. But you speak as if *I* were the usurper. I am devoted to England and its gods and traditions. If I use unorthodox means against our enemies now and then, it is in the service of my country."

"Now, stop it, Morgan. I told you, Gildas is here as a diplomat, no more. He is not an enemy in any sense." Arthur hoped he sounded convincing.

"Excellent. He will present no difficulty then. Have one of your men fetch my luggage. Then have someone bring me food. If you kept the royal roads in better repair, travel could be so much pleasanter."

Wanting to change the subject, Arthur asked about her son, Mordred.

"He has chosen to remain at home. He expressed distaste for the scheming and plotting that would certainly occur here."

Merlin leaned close to Arthur and whispered, "He grew up in his mother's house. Who could know scheming and plotting better?"

They watched her go, more than mildly startled at her overbearing entrance.

"My sister has always been a bitch. Age isn't helping."

"If you kept the royal roads in better repair, you could send her home much more easily."

"Suddenly I feel like a young gazelle in a savage jungle."

"That is all any of us ever are, Arthur. I keep telling you."

"Try to keep your cynicism in check this week, will you? It's the last thing I need to hear right now."

"Sorry."

"And send a servant to tell Nimue I want Morgan installed next to that man from Lithuania. They'll make good company for one another."

The next day was officially Guenevere's birthday. First thing that morning, Merlin had his people spread word that something special was planned for that evening, for the opening ceremony of the conference. Naturally the castle was humming with speculation as to what it might be.

When everyone gathered in the dining hall for their morning meal, the general air was one of conviviality. People ate, drank, socialized, table-hopped, whispered together. At the head table Arthur and Merlin watched it all, pleased.

"Look at them," Arthur chuckled. "You'd never know what vicious rivals some of them are."

"Unless you looked under their robes and found the knives and the poisons."

"Be quiet, Merlin."

Morgan entered the room and moved directly to Gildas's table. Within moments they were arguing, loudly, with violent gestures. Arthur rushed to the table and did what he could to calm things down. Finally he was compelled to ask Morgan to sit at a table on the opposite side of the room.

The servants brought breakfast. At a cue from Merlin, two musicians played a loud trumpet fanfare, the room quieted and Arthur made a welcoming speech. "We greet you on behalf of England and its people, this land of harmony and peace."

Several delegates whispered to one another about the long series of bloody wars Arthur had fought to take control and unify the country, but they were all too discreet to say so aloud.

Once everything had settled down and people were busy with their meals, Britomart came in with a soldier; they went directly to Arthur. "This man is from our post on the Isle of Gibraltar."

"The Pillars of Hercules," Merlin corrected him, pleased with the chance to inject the classics into the morning's affairs.

"Be quiet, Merlin. Save your academic quibbling for some other time." Brit turned to the soldier. "Go ahead, Stephen."

"Well, Your Majesty, no Byzantine ships have passed through the—" He glanced warily at Merlin. "—through the Pillars. There has been no sign of Podarthes."

"Perhaps," Arthur mused, "he traveled overland. Or hired a ship from another country. The Byzantines have enough vassal states—er, excuse me, allies."

Merlin added, "Perhaps he has been captured by Italian banditti and is being held for ransom."

"Merlin," Brit scolded, "he is too important for that attitude. If he doesn't come, half of the point of this affair will be lost."

"We have people on the Continent. Send to see if any of them has news of him traveling overland. And tell them he travels swiftly; he may have been detained. I hear there were heavy storms in the Balkans. Someone somewhere must know something."

"Will they be back before the conference ends?"

"No, of course not. But we will *know*."

Arthur invited Britomart and the soldier Stephen to eat with them. They finished the meal, avoiding anything like official conversation. Gossip and chitchat seemed more in order. Brit and her soldier chatted about mutual acquaintances in the army.

After a few minutes Simon of York came rushing into the dining hall and went straight to the king. In a loud whisper, he said, "Your Majesty, Lancelot has shaken his guards."

"No!"

Brit had overheard. "It's not likely he escaped from the castle. We have too many sentries posted outside."

"Double the ones on duty indoors." Arthur's fist was clenched. "Scour the castle. Find him."

Merlin had listened to all this. "How did he escape the guards?"

"It isn't clear, sir. There hasn't really been time to question anyone."

"I see. Well, all of us must smile and pretend there is nothing wrong. We have a refectory full of guests we must play happy hosts for."

Arthur whispered a few more orders to Simon, who bowed and left. Then, following Merlin's lead, they all smiled and acted as affable as they could.

At length the meal ended and all the delegates left the dining hall and headed their various ways. In a startlingly short time the hall was empty of breakfasters except for Arthur, Merlin, Brit and Stephen. Servants cleared the tables, swept the floor, sneaked leftovers into their pockets.

"Brit, I want you to go and take charge of the search. I want him found."

"Captain Dalley is overseeing everything. He is—"

"Do it."

"Yes, Arthur." She left hurriedly.

After a few minutes had passed, quite suddenly, from somewhere indeterminate, an ear-piercing scream shattered the peace. It was a male voice, and it seemed to echo through the castle's hallways forever. An instant later came a woman's voice, screaming even more loudly and more hysterically.

The three of them—Arthur, Stephen and Merlin, with Merlin lagging behind on his cane—rushed out to the main corridor and looked around, trying to see where the noise had come from. Other people in the hallway also stopped. By the time Merlin caught up, it was clear that no one knew where the scream had originated.

Britomart and two soldiers came rushing around the corner and straight to the king. "You heard it?"

Arthur nodded. "I wish sound didn't travel so efficiently in these damn buildings."

"I think it came from someplace near Guenevere's rooms. Come on."

They all followed Britomart. She led them back the way she had come, then at the end of the corridor turned in the opposite direction from the one she had come from. A fair number of people—legates, soldiers, servants—followed along.

They turned another corner, into the hallway that led to the queen's rooms. And there, lying on the floor with an ivory-handled dagger plunged into his throat, lay King

Leodegrance. Blood spurted from the wound, covering the floor.

Standing over the fallen king's body, gaping down at it but doing nothing to help the man, stood Lancelot. Just behind him was Petronilla, crying, sobbing hysterically.

FIVE

"Guenevere is behind it. She must be."

It was late, past midnight. Throughout the castle everyone was asleep but the guards, Arthur and Merlin. The festivities were to have begun that night, but Arthur had seen that every delegate present got word that because of the day's tragedy, everything on the agenda would be postponed by one day. A few protested, claiming they were on tight schedules, but there was nothing to be done. The rain that had begun earlier had worsened; it was now a thundering downpour and showed no sign of letting up.

The two of them were in Arthur's study, talking over the day's events, trying to make sense of it all. The king had been drinking, but he was not really drunk. He had had just enough to be morose.

Merlin watched Arthur. "How can you be so certain it was Guenevere? We're in a house with dozens of politicians and their minions. And all of them have knives."

"I've been married to her for ten years. Well, more or less married."

"You think she plotted the death of her own father? Why would she—even she—do such a thing?"

"Merlin, she would cut out her own liver if she thought it would hurt me. What is the life of one old man to a creature like her? You saw her at dinner tonight. Smiling, chatting, laughing. She could barely contain the glee. Arthur's big diplomatic moment, his entrance onto the stage of international politics, has fallen apart. Half the delegates want to leave; the rest are insisting on armed guards round the clock."

"Give them guards. It won't make them any safer, not from a really determined assassin, but it cannot hurt."

Arthur looked into his cup. "And if another of them is killed? What on earth would we tell his king?"

"That, Arthur, is quite simple. Hand over the assassin to his justice. That would satisfy any monarch alive."

He swirled the drink in his cup. "I don't like mead. So help me, I don't. But until the Cornish started making wine it was the only beverage we English were any good at. Even our beer tastes like vinegar. So I drink. I am the ultimate civic booster."

"Arthur, will you try to stick to the subject at hand?"

"Why? Honestly, Merlin, I don't even remember why I wanted . . . this. Any of it. When I was a boy, ignored by my father and with no prospects at all, and you found me and took me under your wing and promised to engineer a throne for me, it sounded like the most wonderful thing imaginable. I think I thought I wanted it. But I was a fool. I'd have been happier growing beans or herding sheep."

"Of course, of course. How many times have you cried on my shoulder this way?"

"I mean it, Merlin. I can't tell you how tempted I am to give the whole bloody mess to Guenevere. She deserves it."

"You would never do such a thing."

"Would I not? She deserves these headaches, not me. In ancient Judea there was a king named Herod. He had eight wives— Or was it nine? Memory fails. And he had them all killed. Each in turn. One by one they went to meet the gods. Wise king. Beside him I look like a fool. I'm only grateful we have no sons. If she had a son to scheme for, and not just herself . . ."

Merlin had had enough of the king's self-pity. "You asked me to come here and tell you what we've learned, remember?"

"It makes no difference to me. I want to go and raise beans."

"Arthur."

Suddenly the king was deflated. He put on a sardonic grin. "Oh, all right. Tell me. But make it good, will you? And make my wife the villain."

"One way or another, she is involved, if only by being the victim's daughter. Isn't that enough?"

Wider grin. "You said you have information."

"Honestly, Arthur. If you don't like mead, why not stop drinking now?"

Arthur slammed his cup onto the table. Mead splashed over everything on it. "There. Is that what you want?"

"I'm not going to argue with you, Arthur. I only want to tell you what we—"

"Tell me, then."

He sighed. "First, per your instructions, Britomart has had her soldiers establish a tight, secure cordon around the castle, and Captain Dalley's men have tightened security inside. No one may enter or leave without permission from you. The delegates do not seem to have realized this yet, but they will. When one or more of them tries to leave to-morrow, they will realize, and they will raise the devil."

"Let them."

"Next, I examined Leodegrance's body. He was stabbed not once but a great many times. The killer must have stood over him and quite deliberately plunged the knife into his throat more than enough times to do him in. Quite horribly cold-blooded. The right side of his neck was cut through altogether. I think it must have been someone he knew, otherwise he would not have let the killer get so close without crying out. And there were no signs that he fought—no cuts on his arms or hands. It was someone he knew, I am certain of it."

"Like a daughter?"

"Possibly, but—"

"Guenevere killed him. She evaded her guards somehow. She closed her eyes and imagined he was me, and the knife went in."

"You have evidence of this, of course."

"The feeling in my gut is evidence enough for me. I'm the king, damn it!" He pounded the table and his cup fell over, spilling the rest of its contents.

Merlin scrambled to gather up his papers. "The world will be watching us, Arthur. They may not find your gut sufficient evidence of a capital crime."

"The world will be impressed by the swiftness and severity of my justice."

"And if Guenevere is not the killer? And if we cannot even prove that she was the one behind Lancelot? There may be someone else. Do you want a vicious killer running loose among the delegates?"

"Stop it, will you, Merlin? I'm going to the privy."

Merlin paused and leaned back in his chair. "Alone?"

"Why? What did you have in mind?"

"Stop it, Arthur, for god's sake. There is a killer on the loose. Whether today's villain is the same one who attacked you before, we do not know. But you mustn't go walking about on your own after dark."

"I'm only going to empty my bladder. Don't you trust the king's security?"

"I'll walk along with you just the same."

As they were leaving Arthur's rooms something stirred in a dark corner. Someone dashed out from behind a tapestry and away into the darkened hallway. It was the figure of a small man dressed in dark clothing. Merlin cried out for the guards and they appeared almost at once. But when they started to search, it became clear that whoever it was had gotten away. Merlin looked at Arthur and cooed, "The king's security."

"He's gone." Arthur growled. "How does he keep getting away?"

"Obviously one of our own people has changed his—or her—allegiance."

"Why would anyone do that?" He sounded genuinely puzzled.

Merlin shrugged. "Money. Blackmail. Sheer inexplicable madness. I can think of a dozen reasons without really trying. How much do we know about the private lives of the people here? Colin even suggested the villain might be Petronus."

"That's not possible. He's a good boy. I know him."

"So do I. And I don't think he is the culprit. But, Arthur, anything is possible. And nothing human is reliable or calculable. We must never forget that."

When the tension had died down and the soldiers finished their search, Arthur said, "Come on. I really have to take a leak."

"We're bringing the guards.."

The king sighed. "If we must. But now. And quickly, or I'll do it here."

At the privy Merlin insisted the guards go in first to make certain there was no one there. Then Arthur finally got to relieve himself.

But it did not seem to improve his humor. When he came out again his manner was brusque. "Merlin, I want you to find me the proof that Guenevere is behind her father's murder. Do it."

"But, Arthur—"

"Do it, will you?"

"I will investigate. I will follow the trail—wherever it leads."

"Good. It will lead to my wife. There is no doubt in my mind."

"Well, that makes one of us. Colin retrieved that knife from the murder scene. It matches the description of the ones Lancelot and Guenevere exchanged at their 'wedding.' I have not had the chance yet to verify that, but Petronilla will know."

"There, you see? Guenevere's knife. She is the villain."

"More likely it is Lancelot's. He is the obvious suspect. After all, he was found standing over the body. Once again, when I interview Petronilla tomorrow—"

"We. We will interview her."

"Listen to me, Arthur. This will require clear thinking. Our object is to find the killer, assuming it is not Lancelot. Your determination to blame everything on Guenevere will not be helpful."

"I'm the king, damn it. Everything I do is helpful by definition."

Exasperated, Merlin left him and headed for bed and for a long night of restless sleep. The absence of the door on his room meant that sounds from the corridor—servants cleaning, guards patrolling—kept disturbing him. He muttered to his pillow, "Damned Roman architects."

First thing the next morning Arthur sent word to Queen Leonilla that he and Merlin wished to pay their respects. She sent the reply that she would be in her daughter's throne room. The household staff reported that, except for a few hours' sleep, she had been there since word of the killing reached her. Nothing but the call of nature had moved her.

So, not long after dawn, the two of them went to her, heavily guarded at Merlin's insistence and to Arthur's annoyance.

"You can't think I'm going to take this many men with me everywhere I go."

"You can and you will. The king is the state. It is his first duty to protect himself and by so doing to protect the stability of government."

"You told me that when I was fourteen. In exactly those words, as I recall."

"Clearly I didn't teach you well enough."

Arthur grumped and kept walking. But Merlin was determined to shake him out of his mood. "Leonilla seems to be quite fond of sitting on thrones. The throne room is where I met her when she first arrived."

"She has always admired the trappings of power. The way snakes love holes."

"Try to be a bit more sympathetic, will you? Her husband of half a century has been horribly murdered."

"Have you considered the possibility that she might have done it?"

"Last night you said it was Guenevere."

"Guenevere, Leonilla, this one, that one." Arthur stopped walking and looked at Merlin. "Why have all the women in my life been monsters? My wife, my sister, my mother-in-law . . . Are they the Furies, punishing me for my ambition?"

"Surely the number of mistresses you have taken must make up for that. Here we are, Arthur. Try to remember, we are here for condolence, not confrontation."

"Perhaps you should remind *her* of that."

"Come on. She's waiting."

As on the day of her arrival, Leonilla had ordered the throne room kept dark but for a few widely spaced torches. She sat in a pool of light surrounded by deepest gloom. Merlin wondered whether her preference for darkness was out of vanity or deteriorating eyesight. He and Arthur stepped into the room, then stopped to let their own eyes adjust to the dim light.

Leonilla sat on the throne, perfectly upright, perfectly motionless. Except for the flickering of the flames, not a thing in the room moved. A servant, that same strikingly handsome young man who had attended her that first day, stood to attention just behind her on her right. Her maid, Marthe, stood on the left. Both of them wore black clothing; the boy's armor sat in a neat pile not far away, gleaming in the torchlight.

Merlin whispered to Arthur, "You have never been to Alexandria. But there you may see the body of Alexander, embalmed in honey, propped upright in a glass coffin. Leonilla makes much the same effect."

"I thought you wanted me to be positive," he whispered to Merlin. "Leonilla!" Arthur called. His voice reverberated off the eight stone walls.

The old queen sat motionless, not replying, not even turning her head in their direction. But her young servant did look at them. He held a finger to his lips and said softly, "Her Majesty is in mourning."

Arthur took a few steps toward the throne. "So are we all. The loss of Leodegrance has touched us deeply." Merlin noted with satisfaction that the king actually sounded as if he meant it.

Arthur continued his advance; Merlin lagged behind, watching the scene. Slowly the old queen inclined her head in Arthur's direction. In a low, hoarse voice she asked, "Have you come to imprison me? To place me somewhere out of sight like the old, useless thing I am?"

"Leonilla, I have come to offer my sympathy. That Leodegrance was murdered in my realm, in one of my castles, is a source of deep shame."

"A king who is capable of shame." Her eyelids fluttered.

"Even at my age I find novelties in the world. Whoever would have thought?"

Slowly Leonilla raised her right hand and extended it toward Arthur. It struck Merlin as an odd gesture; then he realized she expected Arthur to kiss it. But Arthur was either oblivious to her intention or quick to realize it. He took her hand in his and shook it; then he held it for a long moment, as if offering condolence. "Leonilla," he intoned, "if there is anything I can do to make your grief more bearable, you need only to ask."

She ignored him and turned to her young man. "Jean-Michel, I want wine."

The youth sprang to action. From behind the throne he produced a wineskin and a goblet. He filled the cup, ostentatiously tasted its contents, then handed it to the queen. She took a long, deep drink then fixed her eyes on Arthur once again. "What solace can you give me that the wine cannot?"

Merlin had listened long enough. Leaning on his cane, he advanced and joined them. "Among other things, Leonilla, we were wondering about plans for your husband's funeral. What preparations should we make?"

"You may do as you like. Ask my daughter. Embalm him and ship him back to France. Burn him. Dump his body in the Channel, for all I care."

"Leonilla!" Arthur was genuinely shocked.

"Leodegrance is dead, son-in-law. All the pomp and ceremony you can arrange will not change that. Soon enough, I'll be gone, too. Why should I care what you do with him? He was never much of a husband anyway, if you take my meaning."

Merlin looked at her servant Jean-Michel and understood what she meant. Guenevere was not the first queen of her line to take a young, handsome "servant."

Arthur cleared his throat. "Perhaps we should consult

Bishop Gildas. I'm afraid a funeral for a Christian king, or even the preparations for one, are not really—"

"What are you going to do with Lancelot?"

Her abruptness startled him. "Try him. Punish him."

"And execute him? I have always found public executions very exciting." She reached out and took Jean-Michel's hand.

"We do not," Merlin said with emphasis, "execute anyone in England for the pleasure of onlookers."

"Pity. At least Lancelot's death would have more use than his life. Why, of all the knights in France, my daughter chose him . . . They were lovers even before she came here to marry you, you know. But Guenevere has always been a contrarian. She sneers at conventional wisdom as being too conventional and not very wise."

"Yet we know that you encouraged her bigamous marriage to him." Merlin made himself sound official. "It was Leodegrance who opposed it."

For the first time an expression crept into her face; she smiled. "Why, Merlin, is it possible you have hit upon a motive for Lancelot's crime?"

"It would serve as an equally clear motive for Guenevere. Or you, for that matter."

"Don't be absurd. Leodegrance has been dying a slow death for years. His exit was only a matter of time. As is mine. Why would I waste my energy plotting his death? Besides, aren't you forgetting that Lancelot was found over my husband's corpse?"

"No, Leonilla, we are not forgetting that."

"Excellent. You have dungeoned him up?"

"Yes."

"Securely, where he can talk to no one?"

Merlin was fidgeting restlessly. "Your interest in our penal system is touching, Leonilla. The trial should begin in several weeks. Will you remain here and attend?"

"Perhaps. You may deal with the cur as you like. He was

going to make Guenevere the sole monarch here. Did you know that?"

"We had our suspicions, yes."

"He was going to make all of southeast England a gift to France. It would have increased our treasure vastly. And Leodegrance opposed that. The men in my life have all been fools. All of them, always. Can you grasp what that means?" She sighed. "If only it were possible to know in advance what they will be like." She glanced pointedly at Jean-Michel.

"In fact," Arthur said, "I expressed a similar thought only last night." His tone was impatient; the old queen was beginning to bore him, or to grate on him—or both.

Merlin sensed it and moved to end the interview. "You must excuse us, Leonilla, but we must be off about our business. English courts are rather more rigorous than the ones in France. We shall have to gather irrefutable evidence, and we must do so while the crime is still fresh."

Leonilla chuckled. The sound was like parchment being wrinkled. "Fresh. Is that a word apt for describing death?"

"For death, I am afraid, almost any adjective will do. Fresh, stale, horrible, tender, shocking, amusing . . ."

"I do not wish to know which one you would choose for my husband's demise. Or for my own, for that matter. I have no doubt you anticipate it keenly." She turned to Jean-Michel, took his hand again and pulled him down so his face was close to her own. Then suddenly, forcefully she kissed him, and he kissed back. When they were done she looked Arthur directly in the face for the first time. "There. That should suggest plenty of adjectives for the two of you. You may vilify me with any of them you choose."

"Thank you for the exhibition, mother-in-law." Arthur turned to go. "Will we see you at lunch today?"

Instead of answering she chuckled again, more loudly than before.

Merlin made a slight bow and the two men walked side by side out of the queen's less-than-august presence.

"So much," he said to Arthur, "for grief."

"I hope, when I am gone, I will be mourned with more conviction."

"Are you suggesting that courtiers might be insincere?"

"Shut up. Let's get some breakfast."

After they had a light meal Arthur had two guards bring Petronilla to his study. She looked terrible, as if she hadn't slept for weeks—eyes puffed-out, skin waxy and pale. Her clothing was disheveled; the bodice of her gown was not laced up properly.

Merlin smiled as cordial a smile as he could manage and gestured to her to sit at the table with them. "Good morning, Petronilla. I hope you are feeling well."

She bowed to Arthur, then Merlin, and took her seat without responding.

"Would you like something to drink? There is some warmed wine."

"No, thank you, sir."

"Well, if you change your mind, you need only ask. We know the last twenty-four hours have been difficult for you."

"Difficult would be the word, sir, yes." Her French accent sounded particularly strong to Merlin's ear.

Arthur spoke up. "We appreciate your cooperation in our investigation, Petronilla, as we have appreciated your help previously."

"It has been my—no, sir, I could not say this has been a pleasure, not at all. When I started mixing in intrigue, I never thought that . . ."

"You have given us invaluable intelligence. We will not forget that."

She lowered her eyes. "Thank you."

"You understand, Petronilla," Merlin said gently, "you are the only witness to a horrible crime. As such, your account of what happened will be indispensable."

"Yes, sir."

"And we will need you to testify at the trial."

"Of course, sir. When—do you know when it will be?"

"As soon as possible. To delay justice is tantamount to denying it. We need to assemble as many facts as we can. The king's verdict is final, so we must be as certain as possible."

"Yes, sir, I understand."

"Excellent. Can you describe what happened, please?"

She looked from one of them to the other, then glanced away. "I was in Guenevere's study, putting some papers in order. I realized it was later than I'd thought, so I left to get some breakfast before the kitchen staff stopped serving. Just as I was leaving the study I met Lancelot. It startled me; I knew he was under house arrest, but there he was, walking about quite alone. I knew him—knew his moods— so I was careful to make neutral conversation, nothing that might annoy him.

"He said he was looking for Guenevere, that he needed her help to escape the castle. He wanted money, to bribe the guards at the gate. What little he had went to buy the cooperation of the guards on his room.

"We were still talking when King Leodegrance appeared in the corridor. He knew both of us, of course, and he wished us both a pleasant day. It did not seem to strike him as odd that Lancelot was unguarded. He was looking for Guenevere, and I told him she had already gone down to breakfast."

Merlin was taking notes. "He seemed sound and healthy?"

"Yes. I had never seen him looking so well."

"I see. What happened then?"

"Suddenly Lancelot raised his voice to the king. 'You

opposed my marriage to Guenevere,' he said. And he demanded to know why."

"Leodegrance explained calmly that such a marriage, though it might be desirable politically, would be bigamous. He said something about the Church. And he added that there were better, more subtle ways to accomplish France's aims in England. But before he could say more, Lancelot flew into a rage and caught him by the shoulders and began to shake him. Leodegrance was not the strongest of men, far from it, and I was afraid he might be hurt. I tried to get between them, to calm things down, but Lancelot pushed me away.

"Before I quite realized it was happening, he had drawn his dagger and—" She buried her face in her hands.

"There, there." Arthur tried to be consoling. "We know what you saw must have been awful."

"Quite terrible, in fact," Merlin added. "But are you certain you were the only ones there? Might someone else have—?"

She looked up, and her face was covered in tears. "I saw him stab the king. Kill him. I saw the blood, all the blood. What more can I say?" Her crying became nearly uncontrollable.

Arthur handed her a kerchief. "Please, Petronilla, try to stay calm."

She looked from one of them to the other, as if it were the strangest thing she'd ever heard.

But Merlin pressed ahead. "You recognized the knife he used?"

She tried to focus her thoughts. The effort seemed to calm her more than all the reassuring words. "It was—it was the golden knife Guenevere had given him on the day they went through their marriage ceremony. They are quite distinctive, with beautiful ivory handles. The ivory is carved into spirals, and their initials, G and L, are cut into the blades."

"I see. There is no doubt, then, that it was Lancelot's knife."

"No, sir."

"And can you remember anything else we should know?"

"Well . . ."

"Yes?"

"Leodegrance and Lancelot had never liked one another. It was part of a larger tension at court. I mean . . . you know that Leodegrance had designs on English territory."

"Yes, of course. Everyone knows that."

"Well, there were always discussions about how to accomplish that. Leodegrance wanted Guenevere to act as a covert agent, subverting the English government from within, weakening it. He always said it was a slow strategy but it was certain to work.

"But Leonilla pushed Guenevere to be as confrontational as possible, to provoke the king, to stir up trouble every way she could. This marriage was part of that. Leonilla always argued that if King Arthur was provoked enough, he would make a blunder and England would fall into the lap of the French." She made a slight bow to the king and lowered her eyes. "Sorry, Your Majesty."

"It is quite all right, Petronilla. I have always been aware of Leonilla's attitude toward me."

"Most of the court disagreed, Your Majesty. If that matters."

He smiled. "It is nice to hear, I suppose."

Merlin asked her, "What was the attitude of the French court toward Lancelot?"

"They found him . . . useful. He was a good knight, a first-rate athlete. I suppose, if it comes to it, that he was not the most thoughtful man at court, but as I said, he was an athlete. And Leonilla was always aware that Guenevere found him attractive. She encouraged that. So he became a pawn in the struggle between the countries."

"Were they lovers before she came to England?" The king looked away from her as he asked it.

"I don't know, Your Majesty. That was before my time. But for as long as I can remember, they were . . . were . . ."

"Yes. They were."

Merlin looked quickly through his notes. "I think that is all we need from you for now. Thank you very much, Petronilla. You will of course repeat all this at trial?"

"I . . . I . . . Yes, of course."

"And you need not worry. Leonilla and Guenevere will be furious at your testimony, but we will give you ample protection from them and their agents. They have tried to assassinate Arthur, with no success. Your things will be moved to another wing promptly."

"Assassinate?" Alarm showed in her face. "They have agents here?" She said it as if it were a new realization, though she must have known it before.

But Arthur reassured her. "Every court has agents in every other court. It is a game monarchs play."

They made a few more minutes of casual chat, and when she was calm they gave Petronilla leave to go.

Then Merlin turned to Arthur. "It all seems simple enough. There had been long-standing hostility between Lancelot and Leodegrance. What else should we need to know?"

"There doesn't seem to be another thing, Merlin. We could have no better evidence than the eyewitness account of one of our own agents. Which is just as well. At dinner tonight we can announce that the killer has definitely been caught and will be tried and executed in short order. The assorted dignitaries, though they have scant dignity, will be reassured, the damage will be repaired and with luck we can get this damn fool conference back on track and maybe even get some good out of it. We were better off when we were a diplomatic backwater."

"Aren't we still?"

"Be quiet."

"One question occurs to me, though."

"And that is . . . ? Trust you to complicate matters."

"Why would Lancelot be walking around with a ceremonial dagger? And one that was a wedding gift, at that."

"He was escaping. He needed a knife. Perhaps it was the only one at hand."

"Perhaps. I wish it did not keep nagging at me."

"Merlin. Thank you so much for coming."

It was mid-morning. The rain pounded the castle relentlessly. It was no simple rainstorm; it was an early winter storm. Wind rattled the windowpanes in Guenevere's sitting room.

The bigamous queen sat on a small chair fashioned like a miniature throne. Apparently she had not slept. She looked drawn; her eyes were sunken and her skin unhealthily pale. She glanced at the rattling windows then looked back at her visitor. Weakly, Guenevere smiled.

Merlin found her manner as odd as her appearance. To see her, he would never have guessed that her lover had murdered her father. "Good morning, Guenevere. It seems we're to be visited with awful weather."

"We already have been." There was no trace of irony in her voice.

Merlin stood at the far side of the room from her. "Are you speaking in metaphors? It is not at all like you. The one thing I can usually count on with you is your literal-mindedness."

Her eyelid fluttered; she showed no other reaction. "Please, sit. I can have the servants bring you cushions if you like."

"Thank you, no. I prefer to stand. Arthur has asked me to keep an eye on the storm."

"I see. And how is my—how is Arthur today?"

"Still alive. It seems mildly miraculous, doesn't it?"

"Please, Merlin, I didn't ask you here to spar with you. Far from it."

"They say a two-headed calf was born in Kent last week. The world is full of novelties." He glanced at an ottoman near where he was standing, paused for a moment to consider, then sat down.

"I deserve your sarcasm, for once." She exhaled slowly and deeply; it was the saddest sound Merlin had heard in a long time. If it had been anyone but Guenevere he would have been moved.

"First metaphors, now humility. Guenevere, you are a changed woman."

A goblet rested on a table beside her. She picked it up, started to drink, then thought better of it and returned it to its place. "I hope I *have* changed, at least enough to touch you."

He narrowed his eyes. "Touch me how? With what?"

"Merlin, I must ask a favor of you. A large one."

"If you are attempting to be comical, Guenevere, I'm afraid the humor is lost on me."

"I am asking seriously."

"Fine, I shall try to restrain my penchant for being a smart aleck. Tell me what you want."

"I want . . ." Something seemed to choke her. "I want to ask . . ."

"Yes?"

"Merlin, I love Lancelot."

"I should hope so. Two loveless marriages, both deliberate, would be rather a lot, don't you think?"

She brushed this aside. "I love him. And he is innocent."

For a long moment the words hung between them. Merlin blinked, not certain he was hearing correctly. "Your loyalty to him is touching, if misplaced. He was found over the body. The murder weapon was his. You should know; you gave it to him. An eyewitness—your own secretary—saw the crime. What more could anyone need to know?"

"He is innocent." She said it with such serene self-assurance that Merlin was a bit unsettled. It was like hearing a madwoman deny gravity.

"He is? Then how do you account for—?"

"That was not his knife. It was mine. I kept it in a silk-lined casket on my dressing table. Someone took it."

"And you are going to ask me to examine the empty casket, correct? All that would prove is that you've hidden your knife in a desperate attempt to confuse the plain facts."

"The two knives were marked distinctively by the jeweler. *G to L* and *L to G*, etched in very small letters on the blade just below the haft. Use one of your famous magnifying lenses, Merlin. You will see that the knife you have is not marked *G to L* but rather the reverse. Father was killed with my knife, not Lancelot's, and it was stolen from me. The girl is lying."

"Petronilla? She is— I have made inquiries. She has a good reputation for honesty and reliability. Why would you have made her your secretary if you did not know it?"

"I needed a secretary. She was the daughter of my mother's old friend, she could read and write and she was there."

"Nevertheless, she has no motive for lying."

"Everyone has a motive for lying." She was beginning to lose her composure; he could hear it in her voice.

"Perhaps in your court. Really, Guenevere, if this is all you want, I will be going. You will be permitted to tell your story at Lancelot's trial, if you so choose. But you should not permit yourself to hope anyone will believe it."

She stood and rushed across the room to him. She caught him by the sleeve and said, "Please, Merlin. Tell me what you want. Name the act—I'll do it. But you must prove that Lancelot is innocent. He did not kill my father."

He glared at her and she removed her hand. "All this would be easier for me to believe, Guenevere, if not for the inconvenient fact that Lancelot tried to kill Arthur, too, mere days ago. Regicide appears to be second nature to him."

"That was an accident and you know it. Investigate for me. For him. For *us*."

"This is perfectly grotesque, Guenevere. You and Lancelot have done everything you could, for years, to bring down Arthur and his court. Evidence aside, do you honestly think I would help you go on with your assorted treasons?"

"Is that it, then? I can promise you there will be no more."

"The serpent promises not to bite. Do not be absurd, Guenevere."

"I swear it. I give you my solemn vow, Lancelot and I will never plot against you and Arthur again. Prove his innocence."

Slowly he stood and walked to the nearest window. Heavy rain was falling; streams were cascading from the roof; wind was bending the trees. "Once in the stoa at Athens I listened to a clever philosopher prove that black was white. Like everyone else in the crowd, I was dazzled by his sophistry. But when he finished I still knew the obvious difference between the two. Now you want me to play that same kind of mental game, expecting it to change . . . what, precisely?"

"Please, Merlin. Do I have to beg the man who claims to love justice? Shall I get on my knees? My knife was stolen. Find who did it. The girl is lying. Discover why. Free Lancelot and anything you want will be yours."

Softly he chuckled. "Suppose what I want is you and your lover in chains? I already have half of that. Will you give me the other half?"

"I'll do anything. Write a confession; I'll sign it."

"And then tear it up at the first chance you have. Honestly, do you think you are dealing with a gullible Corfe fishmonger?"

"I'll sign it in my blood."

"I am afraid the paper would rot."

"For God's sake, Merlin, do you want to see an innocent man punished for someone else's crime?"

"Lancelot is an innocent man? Perhaps that Greek was right after all and black really is the color of snow."

"A treaty. A concordat. An act of submission. I'll sign anything, do anything. But you must help me."

He could not resist grinning at her. "I am afraid I am enjoying this much too much. Would Bishop Gildas tell me it is a sin?"

"Punishing Lancelot for someone else's crime would be a sin."

"Well, I will promise you this. I will discuss the matter with Arthur. If he thinks your signature has any worth, I will proceed."

She had been tense; her body now loosened up quite visibly. "Thank you. Thank you, Merlin."

"It will be Arthur you must thank."

She clenched her jaw. "If it comes to that, I will do it. On my knees or prostrate before him, if need be."

"There, there, Guenevere. It won't hurt too much."

"You will talk to Arthur, then?" She let a hopeful note creep into her voice.

"For what it may be worth, I will. But you must not expect too much. A wronged husband can hardly be blamed for—"

"Go to him now. Please."

He took a step toward the door. "I must confess, you have managed to surprise me. I was expecting more grief. I thought you might want me to arrange a meeting with your mother."

"Mother does not need my sympathy. Besides, she has already been here."

He raised an eyebrow.

"She goes walking about the castle, late at night. She is half-senile, you know."

"Ah, a daughter's love."

She ignored this. "You will keep your word? You will talk with Arthur for me?"

He nodded. "As I promised."

They exchanged a bit of small talk and he left.

"She wants *what*? You must be joking." Arthur strode about his study like a caged animal trying to decide if it was hungry or furious.

"No. I am afraid not." Merlin looked from the king to Britomart. "It seems incredible, given her general heartlessness, but I think she may actually be in love."

"With that lump Lancelot." Brit was deadpan.

"Yes."

"Well, there are women who keep goats." She was wry. "I suppose this isn't all that different."

Arthur went on pacing. "You realize what this means? She's exposed her weak spot to us. Shown her underside, like a pig wallowing on its back in the mud. Which is what you will be doing, more or less, if I permit you to help her."

"I daresay she is pretty well finished one way or the other." Merlin smiled at the king's metaphor. "You won't let her loose again, will you? She'd be at work raising an army in a matter of weeks."

Brit snickered. "Let's hope for her sake it's better than the last one she raised. Boys, old men and dozens of priests each claming his own god could bring victory. I think the Christians may have the right idea. With only one god, when things go wrong . . ." She shrugged. ". . . they know exactly who to blame."

"It isn't the gods I'm worried about, Brit. It's the French." Arthur sat and put a boot up on the conference table. "If Guenevere can do what her father never managed to accomplish—unite all those damn French kingdoms and provinces into a coherent force—we could never hope to win a war against them. With Leodegrance out of the way, it might actually be possible.

"She could sign a hundred acts of submission, and none of them would be worth the parchment it's scrawled on. And besides, even if Lancelot really is innocent of killing Leodegrance, he is guilty of so many other crimes. And any number of those were capital offenses. Executing him now would be justice delayed, but I can't imagine he'd complain about the extra time he's been given. I say we let Guenevere stew for a few days, then hand her a resounding *no* to her request."

Merlin turned thoughtful. "But suppose she is right? Suppose her paramour really is a poor innocent, unjustly accused? We want a just England. And then . . ."

The king took his foot down and sat bolt upright. "What are you getting at?"

"Well, for one thing, there is no real evidence of anything Guenevere suggested, except for one thing. I have examined the murder weapon, and it is indeed her knife, not Lancelot's. The inscription *L to G* is quite clear under a magnifying lens, etched into the blade just below the handle. And I have had Lancelot's rooms searched, and there is no sign of his own dagger—which likely means that he, or she, or one of their people threw it down a well or some such.

"Nevertheless, an investigation should hardly take very long. And if he is innocent and we are the ones to prove it, well . . . freeing your wife's lover in the name of justice is precisely the kind of thing that could give your reputation a huge boost across Europe. Your justice will be known to everyone here. And that is exactly what we were hoping to achieve with this conference."

"Believe me, Merlin, rendering any assistance at all to my wife is the last thing I was hoping to achieve. Besides, it might enhance my reputation for justice, yes—but it might equally well make me a laughingstock."

Brit was catching Merlin's drift. "No, Arthur, think. How many treaties has Guenevere broken? Suppose we take a page from her book."

"I don't follow."

"And you haven't even been drinking." Merlin folded his hands in a gesture of complete serenity. With Brit's backing, he thought he could persuade Arthur to a course of action that would benefit England enormously.

"Be quiet, Merlin. What are you suggesting, Brit?"

"Simply this. Suppose you accept Guenevere's act of submission or whatever she wants to call it—and publicize it to everyone here. Have her swear it in front of all the delegates. And assume Merlin can actually prove Lancelot's innocence. Who's to say you really have to free him? Keep him in a nice, cool dungeon for a few years, on some other charge; there are enough for us to choose from. Hell, he tried to kill *you* two days ago. After all, you would only have promised Guenevere you would let Merlin investigate; no one has said a word about releasing him. And if she complains, you still have both her written oath of allegiance *and* her boyfriend. That would give you leverage if she ever tries another double-cross. Or should I say *when*?"

"I like the sound of this."

"The diplomatic end of it will have to be handled delicately, and with discretion." Merlin yawned. "I mean, if it looks like we're actually setting her up—"

"But we are, Merlin."

"Of course we are. That is what diplomacy is: maneuvering the other fellow into an untenable position, then striking. Everyone will realize that is what we are doing. But if you advertise the fact, you give away the game. In

Asia it is considered a sign of intelligence never to be forth-right about one's motives, and never to answer any question directly. Let us become more Asian."

Arthur spent a long, silent moment considering all this. Then, unexpectedly, he broke into laughter. "I like it. And I love you, Merlin. For all your talk about honesty, truth and justice, you're as devious as anyone on earth."

"I choose to take that as a compliment."

"Do. It is."

Suddenly, Simon of York entered in an unaccustomed rush. "Excuse me, Your Majesty. My apologies for inter-rupting, but I'm afraid we have trouble brewing."

"Par for the course, Simon. What is it now?"

"It's the delegates, sir. They are beginning to realize there is a security cordon around the castle, and they are unhappy about it. In fact, some of them are perfectly furi-ous."

"Damn. They know there was a regicide yesterday. Would it make them feel better if I let everyone move about freely?"

"They seem to think their diplomatic status should ex-empt them from any security measures. They have selected a committee of three to make a formal protest."

Merlin asked, "Which three?"

"Bishop Gildas, Count Andrea of Salesi and that man from Flausenthurm or whoever he is."

"Him? He can't speak an intelligible word."

Arthur and Britomart watched Merlin for a reaction. Re-alizing it, he explained, "You both know Gildas. Since he claims to be the Bishop of England, I can't imagine why he would bristle at having to stay here. Andrea of Salesi is something of a question mark. In fact, I am not quite cer-tain why we even invited him, except that we wanted a good turnout so we cast our nets wide. Our agents have no intelligence on him. I think we somehow got the idea that he is more important than he has turned out to be." He looked from one of them to the other. "To be quite truthful, I am not even certain where Salesi is."

"I believe," Brit interrupted him, "it's a minor Italian city-state. Down near the toe of the boot, across the strait from Sicily. They have a small army and a large treasury. Rumor has it they found the hidden treasure Spartacus was going to use to finance his fanciful revolt."

"Thank you. But that does not explain what he is doing here. I have checked with Colin, and we have absolutely no memory of why we invited him."

"Diplomacy." Arthur snorted. "And what about this Lithuanian?"

"An enigma wrapped in a mystery. You've seen him, surely. Short, plump, alarmingly pale and fair-haired, excitable. He seems to speak no known language. He is not even making the effort. Latin is the language of diplomacy, but when I speak Latin to him he looks baffled and jabbers on in whatever tongue he speaks."

"Why on earth did we invite him? Or did we?"

"We sent pro forma letters to the states around the Baltic. Who could have guessed they would come? The Finns and Estonians had sense enough to realize they would be out of their league and stayed home. Then again, he was overheard mentioning Albania, or something that sounds like it, so he may actually be from somewhere in the Balkans. It is anyone's guess."

"But why one earth would they have chosen him to represent their grievance?"

"Perhaps they thought it would rattle us."

Arthur turned to Simon. "Is this committee of three here now?"

"Yes, Your Majesty."

"How undiplomatic. But I suppose we ought to see them. It appears we have the chance to be more Asiatic already. Usher them in." Simon turned to go.

"No, wait." Merlin help up a hand. "Give us a few moments to go over the intelligence reports on them. Such as they are."

"Yes, sir."

"And have three stools arranged here. Put plush cushions on them."

"Yes, sir."

Brit sent for the files; a clerk hurried to fetch them.

As it turned out, there was nothing much in them they did not already know. After twenty minutes Simon came back in. "Your Majesty, they are fuming. Gildas says it is unheard of for men of their stature to be kept waiting."

"It is standard practice to keep diplomats cooling their heels. They showed up with no appointment, after all. If they are angry, it gives us an edge."

Arthur handed the intelligence reports to Brit, who folded them and put them where they couldn't be seen. Then he told Simon to arrange the three stools and show the gentlemen in. And, plainly peeved and not trying to disguise it, they entered. Gildas appeared even taller, thinner and more emaciated than he had on his arrival at Corfe. He glared at Arthur, Merlin and Brit in turn and sat grandly down on the center stool.

The Lithuanian—no one in the castle seemed to know his name; Brit wondered if people even had names in his country—entered second. Everything about him was in constant motion, his limbs, his facial features, his eyes. He walked to the stool on Gildas's right and made to sit down. But he almost missed. Gildas caught him by the arm and steadied him.

"Garjentamius," said the man from Lithuania.

Andrea of Salesi entered last. He was young for a diplomat, and darkly handsome, as the expression has it. He was also obviously fit; it was possible to see how muscular he was through his clothing.

The three of them made an odd trio: thin, fat and in the middle. If Andrea had not been so good-looking the scene would have been quite comic.

"Welcome. You know my advisors, Merlin and Britomart." Arthur played the hearty ruler. "We understand you have a grievance. I hope your accommodations are satisfactory."

Andrea started to speak but Gildas cut him off. "They are quite satisfactory, King Arthur. But they could not possibly be satisfactory enough. We appear to be confined to them."

"Surely not." Arthur pretended surprise and turned to Merlin. "Can this be true, Merlin?"

"Certainly not, Your Majesty." Merlin arranged his robes. "We have taken certain security measures, in light of yesterday's tragic occurrence. And of course there is this storm. There have been reports of flash floods. We could hardly permit our guests to put themselves in danger by wandering about the countryside." He turned to the three. "You must all understand that we have to be certain of the castle's security—your security and that of your colleagues."

The Lithuanian began to babble something rapidly. Andrea interrupted. "One of my men wished to go into town earlier, to buy some provisions."

"Provisions?" Brit interrupted him. "What could you possibly need that we cannot supply? Besides, as Merlin has noted, it's pouring down rain."

But Andrea ignored her and went on. "He was stopped by your soldiers. Forced to return. Are we to be your prisoners, then? Is that England's idea of diplomacy? Hostage taking?"

"No one is a hostage." Arthur spoke firmly. "You are our honored guests. You would not wish for the assassin of Leodegrance to escape and run free?"

"Of course not. But—"

"Or to strike again?"

Gildas jumped to his feet. "Given a preference we would rather have him outside of the castle. That, apparently, is not to be permitted." He smiled sarcastically. "Besides, do you not already have him in custody?"

"He will not escape," Arthur said firmly. "But we do not know that he acted alone. We must maintain security until we are certain everyone—including all of you—is perfectly safe."

"But, Your Majesty. The killer is Sir Lancelot. Everyone knows it. Most of us witnessed his apprehension. What need could there be for further security?"

The Flausenthurmian stood up and began shouting incomprehensibly and waving his arms wildly. *"Gedjia deebok Lithuania!"* Gildas put a hand on his shoulder and pushed him firmly back to his seat. From between them, a knife clattered to the floor. Gildas jumped back and away from it, then looked at the king, plainly abashed, and bent to pick it up. But Brit lunged for it and took the weapon before he could.

Arthur put on a wicked grin. "You see, Bishop? Knives appear out of thin air and nearly injure you. And you thought we should relax our security."

They bickered for several minutes more, with Gildas and Andrea insisting security be relaxed and Arthur holding his ground. Finally Merlin took the king aside and whispered something in his ear. Arthur smiled, nodded and returned to his seat. "I am afraid it is not possible for us to relax our security measures. But we are most sensitive to your needs and requirements. Therefore we will assign a member of our household staff to each of you, personally, to see that all your needs are met. There should be no more necessity to leave Corfe Castle for provisions of any kind." He smiled at them in what he hoped was a conciliatory way.

They grumbled; they protested about constraints on their

movements; they asked whether these "members of the household staff" would be in fact anything but spies. But Arthur refused to be moved. "You are guests in our country and in our castle. We must do what we feel is right to protect you. We regret that you mistrust our motives, but we simply must do what seems right and proper to us."

Amid more protests the three of them finally took their leave, plainly unhappy. Even the Lithuanian seemed to have sensed somehow that they had been rebuffed. As they left they began to bicker among themselves—at least Andrea and Gildas did; the Lithuanian burbled more of whatever he had been burbling all along and was roundly ignored by his colleagues.

Once they were out of sight, Arthur, Merlin and Brit relaxed. Arthur called for wine and asked Merlin, "You're sure you don't mind suspending school for a few days?"

"The squires and pages have been working hard at their lessons. Well, most of them have. The more athletically inclined among them have no use for actual learning. But I think a break will do them all good. And I daresay most of them will be happy for this chance to play at being secret agents. We can call them 'diplomatic actors' or some such."

Brit asked, "Are they really bright enough to do this? I mean, do they have enough on the ball, or do they only have jousting and wrestling on their minds?"

"The majority of them will be fine. Once you and I have taught them how to behave and the kind of things to look for, I am fairly certain they will do a good job for us. The duller ones among them can be assigned to the less important delegates. That peculiar man from Lithuania, for instance."

"How can we know how important he actually is?"

Merlin shrugged. "Or how unimportant. But I am beginning to be suspicious of him. How odd is it that the delegates would have selected him, of all people, as one of their spokesmen?"

Arthur gaped at him. "What on earth do you mean?"

"Well, have we had any word yet about Podarthes?"

"You think that he might be—?"

Again Merlin shrugged; then he noticed something from the corner of his eye. He got to his feet and began to amble about the room in an uncharacteristic way. "There is no way to know, is there? But it would explain his presence here, despite his plain inability to interact with us, diplomatically or otherwise. And it would explain why at least some of the others wanted him to represent them—if they know who he really is, I mean. At any rate, we will have to choose one of the brighter squires to keep watch on him."

Merlin was now standing near a tapestry. Suddenly he pulled it back. "This squire, for instance." Standing behind it, clearly eavesdropping, was the boy Petronus. When he realized he had been exposed, he gaped wide-eyed at Merlin, then at the king. And he drew a dagger and bolted, ran away so fast Merlin was a bit startled. Brit lunged and grabbed for him but he was too quick.

Merlin shouted, "Walter!" A guard just outside the room planted himself squarely in the doorway. Petronus tried to push past him, but Walter was too big and too strong. He caught the boy, confiscated his knife and dragged him, struggling wildly, back before the king.

"Well, well, well." Britomart's tone was strongly ironic. "We seem to have caught ourselves a would-be assassin."

SIX

An hour later the three of them—Arthur, Merlin and Britomart—headed resolutely down to the dungeons, accompanied by two soldiers. Brit had suggested putting Petronus in the same cell as Lancelot, whose squire he had been before he defected to Arthur's court. "Then we must place someone to eavesdrop on them. With luck they'll say something incriminating and save us the trouble of probing for the facts."

Merlin liked the idea but said, "I wish we were at Camelot. Pellenore knows all the hidden passages there. Nothing happens at Camelot that he does not know about."

"Perhaps we can ask Petronilla. She may know about the castle's hidden places. I think she would be delighted to incriminate her brother."

They had decided to let Petronus and Lancelot keep company for an hour before confronting the boy. Then the time approached.

The jailor told them that he had been listening carefully,

but neither of the prisoners had said much. He unlocked the cell door and the three of them went in, followed by the two guards in case either prisoner made a break for it or tried to overpower them.

The cell was dark; it might have been midnight there. Two torches, one at either end, gave the only light, and they barely seemed to penetrate the gloom. Lancelot was pacing angrily. Petronus was sitting on the stone floor, back to the wall, looking worried, as well he might. He was also shivering; the cell was icy. And dribbles of cold rainwater poured in through cracks in the wall. He looked as if he might have been crying.

But before any of them could address Petronus, Lancelot planted himself squarely before them. "You've come to talk."

"Yes, Lancelot." The king was sanguine. "But not to you."

"You have to talk to me. I have rights. That is one of the hallmarks of your England, isn't it? I have the right to be heard."

"There will be a trial soon enough." Arthur signaled to the soldiers to move him out of the way.

Merlin smiled what he hoped was a warm smile and took a step forward. "Petronus."

"You sound surprised to find me here." The boy sulked. "You did put me here, remember? I'm cold. I can't stop shaking."

"Now, now, Petronus. That is no way to talk."

"How would you talk, in my situation?"

"I would cooperate with my captors in hopes of bettering my circumstances."

"Of course."

Brit advanced a few steps toward him. "I must say I'm grateful for one thing, Petronus. You are no longer my squire. To have you do this while you were in my service would have been a considerable disgrace."

The boy started to say something, but Merlin cut him off. "Instead you did it in mine. I wish I knew what to think. I have always liked you, Petronus, ever since we first met, in this very castle. And all of us have been good to you—welcoming and kind. How could you have betrayed us like this?"

Petronus looked at Lancelot, who glowered at him. The boy was clearly frightened of him. Merlin whispered to Arthur, "Perhaps this was not the best idea. He will not tell us anything with Lancelot present."

Arthur thought for a moment, then nodded.

"Petronus," Merlin said, "we have decided to move you to a warmer place. Just so you will understand we mean you nothing ill, if you will only talk. Who put you up to this?"

Abruptly Lancelot exploded. "And what about me? You will give this rat a more comfortable prison, but I have to stay here in this icy hole?"

Arthur smiled at him. "And you are still on your honeymoon. Life can be terrible, can't it?"

At Arthur's signal the guards took Petronus and led him from the cell. Arthur, Merlin and Brit saluted Lancelot with mock-cordiality and followed them. To the guards Arthur said, "Take him to my study for now. But keep close watch on him. He's quick."

On their way back up to the king's rooms, they discussed what to do. Merlin noted that there certainly seemed to be something between Lancelot and Petronus, but it had the air of distrust and intimidation more than conspiracy. "Let me interrogate him. I've been working with the squires in school; I think I've learned how to talk to them."

"The young are always alien." Arthur sounded resigned to the sad fact.

In the king's study, Petronus was sitting at the conference table, the guards just behind him. He was apparently fighting back tears, and he looked terrified. Two more soldiers stood at either side of the room's entrance, watching him. When he heard the three of them enter he looked up, wide-eyed. "Are you— You're going to torture me, aren't you?"

They took seats around the other three sides of the table. Merlin smiled gently. "Of course not. But we must know why you did what you did. We have been so kind to you since you came here. This hardly seems the way to repay us."

"I—I'm sorry. I'm so ashamed. They made me—they told me—"

"Who are they? Lancelot and Guenevere?"

The boy nodded. Then he turned and looked directly at Arthur. "I'm sorry, Your Majesty. I'm so sorry. I never meant to—"

"What did they threaten you with?" Merlin interrupted.

"They—they said—I—"

"Calm yourself, Petronus. If you did what you did under coercion, we will certainly take that into account. But tell us."

"They said—they—they told me they had my sister. They said they would torture her, even kill her if I didn't do what they wanted. They sent me a lock of her hair and a brooch, a family heirloom, as proof that they had her."

Brit spoke up. "But you and Petronilla don't even like each other."

"Even so, she is my sister. I couldn't just let them . . . do those things. A squire has a code of honor. Protecting his own family is one of the cornerstones."

Merlin shot Brit a glance as if to say, *See what comes of your so-called chivalry?* Then he turned back to the boy. "And what did they require you to do?"

Softly, so softly it was almost a whisper, he said, "Spy for them. And kill the king."

There was a long silence. His words seemed to hang in the air around them. Finally Petronus lost control and began to cry, to sob loudly. "They fooled me. She was with them, she was all right, she wasn't their prisoner at all. I'm so stupid. I'm so ashamed."

"There was no way you could know. But why didn't you come to us? Why didn't you tell us what they were doing?"

"So you could do what? What could you have done? Would you have raided Corfe to rescue her? A French girl you didn't even know? Would you have risked civil war over that? I —I felt trapped. But—but I tried to— I never really told them anything important."

"You attacked me. In the dark. It was you." Arthur raised his voice menacingly and pointed an accusing finger at the boy.

"I didn't want to hurt you, Your Majesty. I tried not to. But it was dark, and you fought. I . . . I never really would have . . . I had other chances . . . and I . . . I thought if they thought I was trying, that would make them leave me alone. Please believe me. I didn't want to hurt you. Or anyone. I had my knife, and I thought if I could maybe nick you with it, they would hear and think I was trying to do what they wanted. But you fell against me, and . . ." He finally broke down completely and sobbed like an injured animal. "I'm so ashamed. I'm so sorry. Please believe me. They made a fool of me, an evil fool."

"Folly is always evil." Merlin made his voice gentle. "Look at me, Petronus."

Slowly the boy raised his head and looked Merlin in the eye.

"You said it yourself. They deceived you."

"You believe me?"

"Let us say your story seems plausible. And perfectly in character for Lancelot and Guenevere. But there is one thing we need to know."

"Yes?"

"How did they do this? How did they contact you?"

"There's . . . there's a Frenchwoman, a laundress, who comes to Camelot now and then. She is their agent. You must know the one I mean. A large woman, fat, dresses like a man."

Merlin exchanged glances with Brit. "Yes, I think I know her."

"She started talking to me not long after I came to Camelot. Then she started trying to get me to spy. And then . . ." He lowered his head again and raised a hand to wipe his eyes.

Merlon asked him, "Are you willing to repeat all of this in court? Under oath?"

Petronus nodded.

"We will have to do what we can to verify all this, Petronus. In the meantime, we must keep you in custody."

"With Lancelot? Please, I'm afraid of him. He—"

"I think we can arrange for you to be held someplace else. Perhaps even in your own rooms next to mine. Under guard, of course." He looked to Brit. "The soldiers you have posted to guard me can keep an eye on him, too, don't you think?"

Relief showed in the boy's face. "Thank you, sir, thank you."

"But I must warn you. Be very careful what you say and do. If you give us any reason at all to doubt what you have told us, it will not go well for you."

"I will give you none. Trust me."

"If we could trust you, Petronus, none of this would be necessary. See to it that we have no cause to doubt you further."

The guards took the boy away, with instructions to place him in his room near Merlin's. Brit wanted him kept in one of the dungeon cells, but Merlin and Arthur overruled her.

When he was gone the three of them looked at one another and sighed. Merlin began the discussion. "It sounds plausible. It sounds perfectly in character for Guenevere."

Brit was doubtful. "Yes, but it leaves the question of who to believe."

"What do you mean?"

"Petronilla has been our agent. And a good one. Every piece of information she's given us has been reliable. If she cooperated with this scheme of theirs, to the point of giving them some of her hair and that brooch . . . What does that suggest about her true loyalties?"

Merlin disliked the sound of this. "But—"

"Yes, Merlin?"

"But her testimony is the principal evidence against Lancelot in the murder of the French king. If she is loyal to Guenevere, why would she do such a thing?"

For a moment the three of them looked at one another in silence. Since neither Arthur nor Brit had a response, Merlin went on. "For the first time we have reason to doubt her account of the murder. Or at least to doubt her motives."

"She is French." Brit made a sour face. "Why should we trust anything any of them tell us?"

"Well, either Petronus is telling us the truth or his sister is. That seems inescapable."

Arthur clenched his fist. For a moment it appeared he was going to pound the table as he often did when he was angry. "Damn the French. Damn all of this—damn all of Europe. We should never have gone forward with this damned birthday celebration. Anything with Guenevere in it was bound to be poisonous."

All day long the rain came more and more heavily. Brooks and rivulets swelled and overflowed their banks; the countryside was ravaged by flash floods. And there was wind, ferocious and unrelenting. Vicious waves lashed Corfe harbor. All the ships docked there rocked wildly in it. At one point two of them collided; one was damaged heavily and sank in a matter of minutes. It effectively blocked a good bit of the harbor. The delegates were trapped at Corfe whether they liked it or not.

Realizing this, Britomart ordered a relaxing of the security cordon around the castle. "Who would have thought that winter would be a friend to us?"

"Early winter. It is still November." Merlin watched out of his window. The storm showed no sign of abating. He, Brit and Nimue were in his study, going over the preparations for that night's opening ceremony. He turned to face them. "Let us hope the actual season, when it comes, will be less fierce."

Brit leaned back in her chair. "Or more. If we still have these diplomats on our hands, it would make them much easier to, er, to monitor."

Nimue watched Merlin watching the weather. "I hate winter. I always have," she said. "It is the season of death."

"Haven't you noticed, Colin? Every season is the season of death."

"You're in one of your pessimistic moods, Merlin."

"You have read Marcus Aurelius, haven't you? He comments on the surprising fact that human deceit and treachery always surprise us. They are constant, and they are everywhere, but every time they crop up, we are caught off guard."

"Roman emperors had good reason to distrust everyone around them."

"Everyone has, Colin. Husbands cheat on wives and wives on husbands, mothers kill their infants, brothers and sisters learn to loathe each other, children steal from their mothers' purses. Loving, faithful dogs are beaten . . . There is no bottom to human evil."

Britomart got to her feet. "Really, Merlin, we can't afford the luxury of this kind of talk. There are things to do."

"What? Everything seems on track for the opening festivities tonight. The kitchen has more food than it needs, and they've baked hundreds of those honey cakes Arthur loves so. The actors and jugglers and musicians and so on are all rehearsed. Arthur's speech is written, and he's actually practicing it—would you believe it? Unless we have another murder—"

"And what makes you think we won't, amid all this human evil?"

He sighed. "Anything is possible. But let us hope that for once evil will not show its hideous face."

There came a knock at the door and a moment later Simon of York came in, followed by one of the squires. "Excuse me, all of you. I hope I'm not interrupting anything important."

"Not at all," Nimue said cheerfully. "Only one of Merlin's lectures on perfidious human nature."

"Merlin has a point, young man." He turned to Merlin. "You all know Andrew of Okun?"

They said hello to the young man.

"Andrew, you may recall, is the squire who was assigned to that peculiar Lithuanian."

"Or whatever he is." Andrew smiled. "I'm still not certain."

"You have a handful." Brit laughed and offered him a cup of wine.

"In a way, it's not too bad. The other squires are going mad trying to decode all the diplomatic double-talk they're overhearing. I mean, the delegates aren't stupid. Well, most of them aren't. They certainly realize we've been attached to them not simply for security but for intelligence. So they're all being especially cryptic, and I'm sure it's for our sake. All of them except my man, that is."

Merlin thought for a moment. "Have you had any indication that he speaks anything other than . . . whatever it is that he speaks? Does he know English or Latin, perhaps? Or Greek?"

Andrew shook his head. "You know that he only brought one aide with him. They talk in their own language, and that is that."

"Do they seem to pay attention to other people's conversations?"

"No, not at all. But I took a chance and searched their packs when they were eating this morning. And I found something quite suspicious."

Nimue sat up. "Like what?"

"Like this." From his sleeve, he produced a knife. It was golden, gleaming, evidently new, and it had a carved ivory handle. "Lancelot's, I think."

Merlin took it and examined it. Then he rushed to a worktable and got a lens. "Yes, this is Lancelot's. *G to L* is etched into it quite clearly."

"I knew you'd want to see it."

"Yes, of course. Thank you, Andrew."

The young man bowed, glanced at Simon and left.

Merlin placed the knife at the center of the table. Nimue picked it up and examined it. "This doesn't make sense. Is the Lithuanian involved in the murder, then? What possible motive could he have?"

"With politicians, you never know, Colin," Brit said. "They talk in code, all of them. Most of them are so devious they can't ask for lunch when they're hungry. Politics is little more than an organization of sociopaths."

Brit laughed. "You mean international politics, don't you? Surely you would never suggest such a thing about our English lords?"

Merlin brushed her little joke aside. "On the subject at hand, we must consider the Lithuanian a suspect and watch him carefully. I will have a word with young Andrew later. Of course, the knife might have been planted among his things. But we cannot take the chance of operating on the assumption."

"Should we arrest the Lithuanian, then?" Nimue asked.

"Not yet. But he must be watched, and carefully."

Simon interrupted the exchange. "Excuse me, Merlin, but there is another problem."

"Splendid. What?"

"Gildas, that bishop person, is demanding an audience with the king."

"Gildas? What on earth does he want?"

"It seems he has learned that Morgan le Fay is to speak the invocation at tonight's ceremony. He is demanding to take part. Since most of the delegates are Christian, he reasons that the opening blessing should be Christian."

Merlin looked at Brit then back at Simon. "You may remind the 'Bishop of England' that this is not a Christian country. We honor the gods here—those of us so inclined do, at least—and we must honor them properly."

"He won't be happy."

"What politician ever is?"

A short while later Merlin sent for Andrew of Okun again.

"During the ceremony tonight, I would like you to search the Lithuanian's rooms again. See if you can find anything else suspicious or incriminating. Or anything else that might indicate who he is and what he is up to."

"Yes, sir."

"But first you must make certain that both he and his aide are in the Great Hall. I want you to take no unnecessary chances."

"I can handle them, sir. Either or both of them."

"Spoken like a fighter. Unfortunately, a fighter is not exactly what we need right now. Be subtle. Use your wits. Try to act as if all the lessons Colin and I have given you actually penetrated. The last thing we need now is another death."

"I'll do my best, sir. But we are not trained in subtlety."

"Try it. You might even find that you enjoy it. Battering something is not always the best way to get results."

As it happened, the French laundress who had been spying for Guenevere was in the castle, among the numerous locals who had been hired to help deal with all the visiting diplomats. Brit's men found her and arrested her. Protesting loudly her innocence—of everything—she was taken to a dungeon.

Merlin rushed to interrogate her. She drew a hard line with him, but he bluffed her with a threat of torture and the possibility of losing a finger or two, and she opened up and burbled a confirmation of Petronus's story, point for point.

The boy was still guilty of attacking the king and of espionage, though it seemed likely he was being truthful when he swore he had given no important information to his blackmailers. Merlin interviewed him a second time.

"I'm sorry, sir. Please believe me. I have been a complete fool. I let them turn me into a villain."

Merlin assured him things would not go too hard on him and left him in his room, under guard. He was grateful the boy's story had been confirmed so quickly and easily. The last thing he wanted to do was perform still another investigation. This was all a distraction for Merlin. His mind was on that night's ceremony and the numerous opportunities it offered for more violence and death.

SEVEN

All day long the strength of the storm increased. Ferocious winds, driving rain and lightning lashed the southern coast of England. Ships moored in Corfe harbor rocked violently.

Late in the afternoon a ship was spotted in the distance; its apparent intention was to dock but it was physically impossible. People in the town and at the castle watched as it neared the shore then was driven out to sea again, repeatedly. Even if it had managed to reach land, it likely would have been dashed to pieces.

In time it was blown back out to sea once and for all. Observers were astonished at how rapidly it disappeared from sight. By the time word about it reached the king, everyone was abuzz with speculation it might have been Podarthes's ship.

In the castle Captain Dalley's men kept up their security watch even though it was clear no one could leave. There was some talk of relaxing their watchfulness, but in the end it was decided to maintain vigilance. Delegates and their aides watched the weather carefully; they were trapped, and the fact was inescapable. Reports began to arrive of sudden, devastating floods around the countryside.

Among Arthur's people, preparations continued for the opening ceremony. Thrones were set up in the Great Hall for Arthur, Guenevere and Leonilla, though no one was certain she would attend. Since her husband's death she had taken to drifting aimlessly about the castle, at all hours of day and night, in a kind of daze. She would suddenly come to her senses, not knowing where she was or why she was there. Her man, Jean-Michel, tried to follow her, but she was too quick-witted for him and kept losing him, hiding in crowds, concealing herself in nooks, distracting him and then walking quickly around convenient corners. Brit assigned a small group of soldiers to guard her, which proved difficult; she was evasive in unexpected ways and shook her guards time after time.

The kitchen was alive with activity. And the squires and pages kept up their surveillance of the delegates on the flimsy pretense of protecting and assisting them.

Merlin took Andrew of Okun aside. "Have you seen anything else suspicious?"

"No, sir." He hesitated. "Except that . . ."

"Yes?"

"I keep hearing one syllable again and again in his speech. Are you certain he is a Flausenthurmian?"

"To be honest, Andrew, I do not even know what a Lithuanian is. About him, I am certain of nothing. Why? What have you heard?"

"Well . . . I keep hearing . . . I think he may be a Turk."

"A Turk? He does not dress like one."

Andrew shrugged. "I keep hearing that, or what sounds like it. It seemed worth mentioning."

"Good observation. But during tonight's festivities, when you slip away and search all of their effects, do it thoroughly. Anything out of the ordinary—the least thing, however trivial it might seem to you—should be noted and reported to either me or Britomart. Certainly inform us of anything that might lend substance to your guess about him being a Turk. And if you can find any writing— even if you cannot decipher it—if the language is the least bit recognizable, for heaven's sake, tell one of us. Better yet, make a copy of it if there is time. Do you understand?"

"Yes, sir. But—but I can barely read English. You know that from school."

"Do your best, Andrew."

"And suppose they catch me? I mean, I'm training to become a knight, not a spy."

"I will have someone stationed to watch them in the Great Hall. If either of them moves to leave, I will have one of the younger boys run and alert you."

"Petronus is the fastest runner among us. You should use him."

"Not Petronus, Andrew. No, not him. But there are other good runners. Britomart will know the right one to use."

Andrew sounded uncertain as he said, "Yes, sir."

Just as they were finishing this exchange, Merlin noticed a pair of people coming down the hall. It was Leonilla and her serving-man, Jean-Michel. She was dressed in her usual black; he was in brightly colored clothing. For once she appeared to be in her right senses.

As they approached, Merlin bowed to the old queen. "Good afternoon, Leonilla. How you are today?"

"I am old. What else?"

"A condition we share. And may I ask, will you be attending tonight's festivities?"

"Festivities? With my husband dead?"

"You would not be the first widow to behave in such a way. After all, you are a grieving widow, but you are also a queen, with a queen's responsibilities."

"Rubbish. But there are rumors, Merlin, about what will happen tonight. They say Guenevere is going to formally submit herself to Arthur's authority."

"I have no information on that."

"Don't play games with me. I was playing and winning them when you were in diapers. I want to know."

"I swear to you, I have no definite information. Arthur and Guenevere have reached an understanding. But I have no idea why she would submit to him now, of all times." He hoped that lie sounded convincing.

But she was relentless. "It is true, then. My husband's death has undermined my daughter." She smiled and chuckled softly.

"Your grief is rather peculiar, Leonilla."

She leaned very close to him. "Let me tell you a secret, Merlin."

"Yes?" He made his tone conspiratorial.

"I do not like my daughter."

"You startle me. Then tell me, will you, why you have actively promoted her plans for greatness here in England."

Bitter laugh. "England? What on earth is England? It is nothing. So tell me—will she submit to him?"

Cautiously he said, "Believe me, Leonilla, there is not a thing I can tell you. You will have to attend tonight if you want to know."

"Why are the English such stubborn fools?"

"We have learned the necessity of it from centuries of dealing with the French."

Again she chuckled, and she and her young man walked off down the hall. An image flashed into Merlin's mind of their flesh—his young and fresh, hers old and wrinkled—commingled. He forced himself not to think about it. But she seemed to be showing signs of recovering from her mad grief; that, at least, was a relief.

And so after a huge feast in the refectory, all the delegates began to gather in the Great Hall. In total there were nineteen of them: Frenchmen, Greeks, Egyptians, Northern Europeans of various descriptions, and the increasingly suspicious Lithuanian. They and their retinues, which ranged in size from one aide for the Lithuanian to eight or more for some of the others, ate, drank, gossiped, met furtively, schemed more or less openly, and generally made themselves a burden. Merlin found himself hoping, more than once, that putting up with their presence would prove worthwhile.

He spent some time moving from one group to the next, playing the gracious host, inquiring whether everything was to their satisfaction. And one visitor after another asked whether he was going to perform any of the sorcery he was famous for. He explained patiently that he was not a magician and had no idea how that reputation had arisen.

When he finally grew tired of this, he sought out Nimuc's company to complain. "There is a line in the Christian holy book, penned by one of their prophets," he commented dryly to her. " 'They toil not, neither do they spin.' It does not become you and me to sneer at the Christian prophets."

In one area of the octagonal hall a platform had been set up for musicians. They practiced and tuned their instruments, adding to the cacophony of dozens of voices, then began playing lively tunes when enough people had arrived to make a proper audience. Servants passed among the crowd with trays of food, and minstrels and jugglers performed. Despite the death of Leodegrance, everyone seemed to be in a cheerful mood.

Gildas made his way through the crowd to Merlin. He was dressed in robes the color of blood; the effect would have been somber except for the abundant gold jewelry. Uniquely among the assembled legates, he seemed not to be enjoying himself. "Merlin, this is genuinely outrageous. These good Christian men are to be subjected to pagan prayers."

"I suspect they won't mind too much, Bishop. In my experience, politicians believe only in politics, and that only when it is to their benefit."

Gildas harrumphed and stalked away, following a waiter with cakes and ale.

Through the crowd Merlin noticed Andrew of Okun, dutifully attending his Lithuanian charge, who was engaged in lively conversation with his aide. They were both plainly excited—by the crowd? the event?—and gestured vividly with their hands as they talked their gibberish. Andrew caught Merlin's eye and winked.

Nimue flagged down a servant and took several honey cakes; she gave signs of enjoying the evening. "All the work we did to prepare the way for this night, Merlin, and now it's happening."

"You have done an excellent job preparing this, Colin. Certainly you deserve the lion's share of credit. I could hardly have done better myself."

"That's a mighty sunny sentiment for you, Merlin. Shouldn't you be worrying and hoping the evening will come off without any unpleasantness?"

"With this many politicians here, that would be an unreasonable hope. I will be happy if we get through the night without another murder."

"Now that sounds like the Merlin I know." She looked around for another waiter. "When is Arthur coming?"

"Shortly. I sent a page to tell him everyone was here." He lowered his voice. "You ought to go easy on those cakes. You have a figure to maintain."

"Men don't worry about things like that. And I am Colin, remember? Disregard for my personal appearance is one of the advantages of this disguise."

Guenevere entered the hall. The musicians struck up a fanfare and she progressed in a slow, stately march to her throne, followed by Petronilla and two handsome young male attendants. Merlin found himself wondering whether she was taking a page from her mother's book. Her manner was quite regal; she nodded to friends here and there in the crowd but never wavered from her progress. The fact that she was attended by such a small retinue made her demeanor look faintly foolish, to Merlin's eye.

Once she reached her throne he made his way through the crowd to her. "Good evening, Guenevere."

"Merlin. What have you discovered?"

"There is some slight doubt about your father's murder. About the murder weapon, specifically. It was your knife, not Lancelot's."

She smiled a queenly smile and watched the crowd, not him. "As I told you."

"I am not at all certain why you seem so pleased. Your father was killed with your dagger. And the only witnesses to the crime were your lover and your secretary. A wiser queen might be worried."

"Investigate. Neither Lancelot nor I had a thing to do with it. You will see." She waved and smiled at Gildas, who made a half-bow to her.

A moment later the musicians struck up a second fanfare, a slow, dolorous one. They played it noticeably louder than they had Guenevere's. Everyone stopped talking and looked to the door for Arthur's entrance.

But instead of the king it was Leonilla who entered. She was dressed in her usual black robes, now doubling as widow's weeds. Beside her was her servant and constant companion, Jean-Michel, dressed in gleaming ceremonial armor. She rested a hand on his arm and they moved through the Great Hall. Leonilla looked ahead majestically, never to either side, as if to suggest these nonroyals were not worth her notice. Once she seemed to stumble slightly, as if her legs were failing her, and Jean-Michel caught her by the elbow and steadied her.

Her throne had been set up in another corner of the hall, away from Guenevere. Merlin whispered to Nimue, "Come, let us greet Her Majesty."

They reached the old queen's throne just as she was seating herself in it. "Queen Leonilla. Good evening."

"Good evening, Merlin."

He presented "Colin" and expressed mild surprise that Leonilla had come, since she had indicated earlier that she wouldn't. "I am not at all certain of the protocol for royal mourning, but surely—"

"I mourned for my husband when he was alive. For his failed ambitions, his dwindling power, his absurd pretense of political influence. Mourning his shriveled corpse now would be slightly redundant, wouldn't you say? I found I could not stay away."

"Not even death penetrates your character, does it, Leonilla? I must confess a certain grudging admiration. But how far will you carry this? You are not going to kiss your young man here, are you?"

For the first time she looked directly at Merlin. "The whims of a queen are notoriously difficult to anticipate."

"For heaven's sake, Leonilla. Try to remember who you are. And where. And what happened only yesterday."

Her face was granite. "You seem to have forgotten. My daughter's lover murdered my husband. She herself most likely engineered it. Yet she sits in a place of honor at her 'husband's' side." She leaned heavily and ironically on the word *husband*.

"Before the evening is over, you will see her position clearly enough, as will everyone here." He winked at her.

"So she will do it, then. I am quite looking forward to it. Jean-Michel." She turned to her young man.

"Yes, Your Majesty?"

"A pillow for my back."

"Yes, Your Majesty."

He got one and arranged it for her. She smiled and closed her eyes like a contented cat.

Merlin and Nimue moved on into the crowd. Nimue expressed surprise and mild shock that the widowed queen was in attendance. "I never thought she would come. I had a throne set up for her just in case. It's lucky I did."

Merlin whispered to her, "She wants to see her daughter humiliated. I infer there is more rivalry between them than we ever suspected. I will tell you about it tomorrow."

Through the crowd Merlin spotted his friend Germanicus. He excused himself to Nimue and moved to join the man.

Germanicus had been drinking and it showed. He grinned an enormous grin, took Merlin by the arm and said, "All these diplomats, all these grandees, all of them here to work—to the extent that what they do can be called work. I seem to be the only one here with no agenda but to eat and drink. Thank you for inviting me." He beamed.

"You have a brief as well," Merlin said softly. "I need intelligence about these people. You are the only one who can give it to me."

"Ah, so."

"That Lithuanian, for instance—or whatever he is. What do you know about him?"

"He can only speak his own language, apparently. That makes him less than useful as a diplomat, wouldn't you say?"

"There is a suspicion among some people that he might really be Podarthes, here incognito."

"I know Podarthes. Believe me, he is nothing like that

man. Not only would you be able to understand him, you would never be able to shut him up."

"Splendid. And I was thinking it was too bad he hadn't come."

"The last I heard, he was on his way. I've been quietly hoping he was waylaid by Italian bandits or African pirates." He smiled. "I've never much liked him."

Suddenly more servants entered the hall with blazing torches and the music blared still more loudly. The musicians played a royal fanfare and Arthur entered, wearing Excalibur at his side, attended by his squire Greffys and a dozen servants carrying still more lights, walking in two files, one on either side of him. He progressed to his throne, on the same platform as Guenevere's, without acknowledging the assembled legates, bowed slightly to Guenevere and took his seat.

"Arthur has been studying Justinian." Germanicus sounded half disapproving, half pleased. "Justinian can retain his imperial detachment from us mortals for hours on end. He is capable of standing or sitting enthroned all evening without ever acknowledging that there might be any lesser mortals present."

"It sounds remarkably dull."

"The emperor is the personal representative of God. How could he behave otherwise? Personally, I like the homey old Egyptian gods—but don't tell anyone I said so."

"So the pinnacle of imperial behavior is to become a statue? Most rulers are content to leave that for after their deaths."

"With the love of the Lord there is no death."

"Of course."

Unexpectedly the musicians continued their fanfare. A moment later Morgan le Fay entered, dressed in magnificent flowing sable robes trimmed with silver. A file of pages preceded her. And behind her came another page carrying on a black velvet cushion the Stone of Bran, the polished crystal skull reputed to be a powerful mystical object.

"Good heavens, she has trotted out that absurd relic." Merlin's eyes widened. "I expected to see a good bit of nonsense tonight. I did not think it would come from our own court."

Germanicus watched the procession. "What on earth is it? Something to do with the god of death?"

"A fraud, as all these 'sacred relics' are. I will tell you about it later."

Morgan's procession headed directly for Arthur, and she took her place at his right hand, with the boy holding the relic behind him on his left.

Merlin crossed to Nimue. "Why did you not tell me they would be doing this?"

She laughed. "Morgan insisted. Arthur didn't seem to have the energy to argue."

"But—but—everyone at court knows what a sham the thing is. Even Arthur has admitted it. How could he—?"

"It will impress the visitors, or so she claims."

"You think all these learned men will be impressed by a lump of glass?"

"You always refuse to get involved in discussions of court ceremony, Merlin. You say you have more important things to concern yourself with. Then, when you don't like what happens, you complain."

Abruptly the music stopped. Arthur stood. Everyone in the hall bowed to him.

"Friends, welcome visitors to our court, we greet you warmly and cordially. And we trust that our hospitality has been pleasing to you. We are here to celebrate the birthday of our beloved wife, Queen Guenevere."

The crowd applauded politely as if on cue—and as if they meant it.

"And we are gratified at your attendance upon her on this happy occasion. By honoring her, you honor England."

So he made the salient diplomatic point. No one in the crowd seemed convinced that either she or England merited such honor, but being diplomats they smiled and applauded again.

Arthur was about to go on when the sound of a loud sneeze filled the hall. Everyone looked around. The Lithuanian was wiping his nose on a lace handkerchief and blushing. He said something incomprehensible, presumably an apology.

Bishop Gildas intoned, loudly and importantly, "God bless you."

The Lithuanian ignored him, grinned at the crowd and repeated whatever it was that he had said.

Merlin leaned close to Nimue and whispered, "I am beginning to like that man more and more."

"Why, for heaven's sake? You can't understand a word he says."

"Precisely. He has that advantage over all the others."

"Really, Merlin."

"Andrew of Okun thinks he may be a Turk."

"Shush."

Unflapped by the interruption, Arthur went on with his speech. He welcomed all the delegates, naming the important ones specifically. He praised Europe as the cradle of civilization and enlightenment. And even though no one from Byzantium had appeared, he praised Justinian's empire as the stalwart defender and propagator of that civilization.

He went on for long minutes. Impatience began to become apparent in some of the crowd. Then Merlin realized that another interruption was occurring, though what it was was not immediately clear. The members of the audience closest to the door were ignoring the king and watching someone or something there.

Gradually more and more people became aware of what was happening; in a short time nearly everyone was pretending to listen to Arthur but actually watching the doorway.

Finally Merlin saw: A short man in magnificent apparel was standing there, flanked by half a dozen attendants. And then even Arthur noticed this overdressed stranger.

The man's cloak was, or seemed to be, spun gold. Three heavy golden chains hung around his neck; each of them bore a magnificent ruby. His cap was silver, and he doffed it with a grand, dramatic gesture. His hair was brilliant red, his skin as pale as seafoam and even at a distance it was possible to see that his eyes were the brightest green.

Merlin moved toward the man, whoever he was. From his platform Arthur glared at the man. He stopped speaking and peered at him, disapprovingly but with undisguised curiosity. "And who, may I inquire, are you, sir?"

"I am," the man announced in an unexpectedly big voice, "Podarthes, Ambassador Plenipotentiary of His Christian Majesty, Emperor Justinian." He produced an ornate envelope bearing what was presumably the imperial seal. "These are my credentials. I have come to treat with Queen Guenevere, the divinely ordained ruler of Britain."

In a low, flat voice, Arthur asked, "Ordained by which divinity, precisely?" He froze even more completely than he had when he was trying to appear regal. On her throne Guenevere broke into a wide smile; she did not even attempt to hide it. Across the room, Leonilla did not react; did not so much as narrow her eyes slightly.

Merlin rushed to Arthur's side and whispered, "Tell him you are pleased he has arrived at long last but that you will not talk with him until after he has been installed in his quarters. Stall. Simon will know what to do—he can find a dozen excuses. The rooms aren't ready. Unexpected arrival. Short staff, overworked. We can put him off till we have the chance to talk this over. Whatever you do, do not give him an opening."

Arthur took the cue; he welcomed Podarthes at consid-

erable length and with florid language. To Merlin's relief he
said exactly the correct thing. "We welcome you to our
court, Podarthes. And we are gratified at your devotion to
our loyal vassal and wife, Queen Guenevere."

For a brief instant a look of concern crossed Podarthes's
face. The word *vassal* had had the desired effect. Then he
recovered himself and replaced it with a diplomat's smile.
He bowed to Arthur, quite ostentatiously.

Meanwhile Merlin found Simon and made certain he
understood the situation. Simon reassured him. "Don't
worry. Just give me time to make the proper arrangements."

"You know the diplomatic service, Simon. Stalling is
what we do best."

On the dais, Arthur announced that his loving wife,
Queen Guenevere, was about to mark her birthday by re-
newing on Excalibur her vow of fealty to him as well as, by
implication, her marriage vow. There was a buzz among the
delegates; they all certainly knew what she and Lancelot
had done. If they hadn't known before they arrived, they
certainly picked up the gossip at Corfe Castle.

The musicians began playing a composition heavy with
pomp and majesty. The queen stood and slowly walked to
Arthur. He in his turn drew Excalibur from its sheath. It
seemed to more than one person in the audience that she
was shaking as she stood before him. With anger? Humilia-
tion?

Slowly she got to her knees. She bent to kiss the hem of
his garment, then Excalibur. And she recited in a loud,
clear, expressionless voice the words of the oath Merlin had
written for her, acknowledging Arthur as the rightful king
of England and her rightful husband, swearing lifelong
allegiance and fidelity, pledging her blood and her life to
his service and to the interests of his England, and on
and on.

No one in the audience seemed to know what to make of

the scene. Podarthes was frozen to immobility. Except for the queen's voice there was not a sound in the Great Hall.

Arthur announced that he was touched and quite pleased by her assertion of loyalty. He bade her rise and return to her throne.

When the scene finally ended, Simon approached Podarthes. "If you will follow me, sir, I will see that you are installed comfortably in a suitable suite."

Podarthes smiled, and his green eyes seemed to flash even more brightly, and it all seemed completely artificial. "With pleasure. And you are—?"

Simon introduced himself. A moment later Merlin joined the two of them and did likewise.

"Ah, Merlin." Podarthes beamed. "The famous sorcerer and King Arthur's chief counselor." He looked around the hall. "Arthur is fortunate to have you. It will take a great magician indeed to deal with all of this." He gestured vaguely at the crowd in the hall.

"I am afraid," Merlin said, trying to disguise his annoyance, "that my reputation for wizardry is rather wildly exaggerated. I am merely a humble scholar, and King Arthur's servant and advisor. At any rate, I am afraid your arrival was somewhat abrupt, sir, and quite unexpected at this late moment. Simon will see that you are comfortable and have the opportunity to dine and rest. There will be plenty of time for us to talk afterward. I must tell you, though, that your understanding of the political situation in England may not be quite up to date."

"So I gathered, and as the king seems to have indicated. I am quite famished. Your hospitality is most welcome. But perhaps you misunderstand. We have been in your country for weeks, traveling about, meeting people, learning everything we could." He smiled. "We would have been here days ago but for all this rain. I cannot recall a less hospitable climate."

"You have been here all this time? Without notifying us?

That is most irregular, Podarthes, as I am certain you must know."

"We were lost." He tossed off the lie as if it didn't really matter. "But about dinner . . . ?"

Merlin gestured to Simon, who took immediate charge.

On the dais Arthur had been watching all of this, plainly concerned. When he saw Podarthes smiling, his concern turned to mild alarm. He made a few more quick remarks to the crowd, then clapped his hands grandly and the various entertainers began circulating about the Great Hall, performing their tricks, singing, plying groups of men with riddles and whatnot.

Arthur climbed down from the stage and made his way through the crowd, acknowledging this delegate and that, till he finally reached Merlin. They stepped apart from the crowd into a small side room. "So he's here." The king frowned. "What on earth are we to do with him?"

"That is easy. Keep him waiting. That is diplomacy at its purest."

"Don't be glib, Merlin. If we do anything he regards as a slight, it could have terrible consequences."

Merlin was breezy. "We have more pressing things to concern ourselves with."

"More pressing? Be serious, Merlin. Wars have been started over such things."

"Podarthes's presence makes it that much more urgent that we get to the bottom of the murder of Leodegrance. If we can prove that Guenevere was involved, it will pull the rug quite completely out from under his intention to treat with her."

Arthur was deflated. "You're right. What do we do?"

"I think," Merlin said softly and slowly, "Lancelot has stewed in his cell long enough. It is time we interviewed him."

EIGHT

"So you have come to question me. It is about time." Lancelot was sitting on a stone ledge in his cell, which was darker and colder than Merlin remembered from his interview with Petronus.

Merlin and Arthur stood in the doorway of the cell, each holding a torch. Just behind them the jailor and two guards watched, making certain they were safe and Lancelot did not have the opportunity to attack them.

"You must give us a moment, Lancelot. The dungeons here are so much darker than the ones at Camelot. Are we actually underground, do you imagine?"

"Move me to Camelot if it troubles you."

The king brushed this aside. "We have so many castles in England—all with dungeons. Would you like to have your choice?"

"No doubt you will choose the one with the most efficient torture chamber."

Merlin laughed softly. "You always did have a flair for

the dramatic. Why else choose a lover as . . . as problematic as Guenevere?" The two of them swept into the chamber, trying to display the confidence of men with the upper hand, and stood over him.

"Wife." Lancelot got to his feet.

"I beg your pardon?" A note of menace crept into Arthur's voice.

"You said lover. She is my wife."

"Under what law, Frenchman? The Christian Church, as I take it, considers your marriage bigamous. Not even your partisan Gildas has said a word to defend it. And under English law you are both guilty of high treason." Almost as an afterthought he added with a grin, "A capital offense."

The interrogation was not off to a promising start. Merlin decided to try a more conciliatory approach. "We have come to hear your account of the killing of Leodegrance. Surely you do not want to antagonize us and miss the opportunity."

"As if you'd believe what I told you."

"Merlin is investigating." The king followed his counselor's lead. "We intend to determine the facts, whatever they may be and wherever they may lead."

Lancelot sat again and glared up at them. "Facts? What would you know about facts? We heard about you in France years before I ever came here. How Merlin rigged that stunt with the sword in the stone to convince the gullible you were destined to be king. Could a king whose reign is based on such fraud be concerned with facts?"

"None of this," Merlin said firmly, "is helping your case. Would you like to tell us what happened that day? Better yet, would you like to confess to the French king's murder?"

"I didn't kill him," Lancelot muttered. "And I think you both know it. There is nothing I could tell you that would make a difference. I half suspect you had him killed yourselves, so you could blame it on me."

"The facts would make that difference, if they can be verified."

"Facts?" He seemed genuinely puzzled by the word. "Kings manufacture facts to suit their whims. The things called facts are nothing but political tools."

"Yes, facts." Merlin repeated the word with emphasis.

"You're French, Lancelot," Arthur added, "but even so you should be able to understand what facts are."

"I didn't kill the damned old fool. That is the only fact."

"Then who did, do you suppose?"

"Kings have enemies. Old, vulnerable kings have more."

"What enemies?"

The French knight glared. "You think I'm going to answer that?"

"I think you want to save yourself from hanging."

He fell silent.

"Come now, Lancelot." Merlin was the soul of patience for the prisoner's benefit. "All we want is to hear your account of what happened that morning. Where is the harm in that? It might do you a world of good."

"And it might not." He sulked. "But . . ."

"Yes?"

"Nothing. Never mind."

Arthur was beginning to lose patience. "Look, you do understand your situation, don't you? We have a witness who says you stabbed him. A trusted witness. And the murder weapon was yours, or rather your wife's. My wife's."

"Witness? What witness could you possibly have?"

"Why, Petronilla, of course. She was there with you. She saw the whole horrible affair, and she is prepared to testify to it in court."

"Petronilla! That bitch!"

"The queen's private secretary. Who could be more reliable?"

"Almost anyone could. That lying bitch."

"You are repeating yourself, Lancelot. Why should we believe she would lie about this? What would it gain her?"

"Revenge," he said softly.

Arthur smirked and stepped back a few paces to lean against the opposite wall. Merlin pressed on. "Revenge? For what? You and Guenevere took her into your household and gave her a privileged position. Are we to believe she wanted revenge for that?"

He looked up at Merlin as if he were the dumbest man on earth. "She wanted me to marry her."

"She—! What?"

"She was—is—in love with me."

"For heaven's sake, Lancelot. She had only just seen you marry the queen. How could she expect—?"

"She expected it because I told her I would, that's why."

"You—?"

"Or at least I told her I loved her." He looked from Merlin to Arthur, then stared down at the cell floor. "We were having an . . . I was . . . we were sleeping together."

"On your honeymoon." Arthur's voice dripped with sarcasm.

"She is young and pretty. She was willing. And Guenevere . . . well, let's just say the fires of love don't burn bright in her."

"You're telling me that?"

Lancelot laughed bitterly. "I thought she would be different with me. When we were courting, she . . . you know."

"Yes, I know only too well. But Guenevere is not like other women. Ambition flows in her veins, not blood. Copulation for her is a political tactic to be used like any other. Once she has a man, she sees no need to do it anymore."

"Don't remind me. I was a fool. We were both her fools. I love her, I really do. But I need sex, like any other man."

The interrogation was getting far off track. Merlin decided to take charge. "And so you began an affair with her secretary."

"Yes." He was glum.

"And promised to leave Guenevere for her."

"Yes."

"You French are supposed to be such skilled lovers. Couldn't you have come up with something more original?"

"I'm a knight, not a troubadour."

"So, you are telling us that Petronilla is lying about what happened, to revenge herself on you for, shall we say, toying with her?"

"Yes. Or maybe she's just crazy. Either way, I did not kill Leodegrance."

"You had a motive. He opposed your 'marriage' to Guenevere."

"That was a done fact. His opposition never counted for much. Leonilla was the real power in Camelliard, and she wanted us married."

Arthur snorted. "Mothers-in-law."

Merlin ignored the interruption. "So tell us what happened."

Lancelot paused and took a deep breath, as if remembering, or concentrating, was difficult for him. "Well . . . we had slept late. We were late for breakfast."

"She spent the night with you?"

The knight nodded.

"Guenevere has her spies, as you well know. Wasn't that risky?"

"Of course. But Petronilla was quartered close to me. In the room next to mine, in fact. It was easy enough for us to visit each other in the night. When we woke that morning, she began pressing me again. When would I tell Guenevere? When would I leave her? When would we be married? As if any man in his right mind would leave a queen for a servant. I put her off, as I had a dozen times before, but she wouldn't let up."

Arthur interjected, "A good warrior should admire such relentlessness."

Lancelot glanced at him but decided to ignore the jab. "When we finally dressed and headed for the refectory, she kept at it. I told her to be quiet, someone might hear, but she wouldn't stop. So I put on speed and moved ahead of her. There was nothing else to do. She was wearing one of those heavy beaded gowns and couldn't keep up with me.

"When I turned the corner into the main corridor leading to the dining hall, there was Leodegrance. Already dead, or nearly so. He was on the floor, and the knife was stuck in his throat. Blood was everywhere. His body was convulsing. I took a few steps toward him, but he stopped moving."

"That is all?"

Lancelot nodded.

"And you did not see anyone else?"

He thought; he tried to focus. "There was someone down the corridor ahead of me. I couldn't see clearly. In an instant she was gone."

"She?"

"He, then."

"You are not suggesting Petronilla did the murder?"

"No, of course not. She was behind me, not ahead."

"But Lancelot, why did you say *she*?"

"Whoever it was was wearing a gown."

"A gown?" For the first time Merlin's attention was up. "Are you certain? Could it have been a man's robe of some description? Half the legates here wear them, especially in a castle as drafty as this one."

He shrugged. "They might have been robes. As I told you, I got only the briefest glimpse. The next thing I knew, Petronilla had caught up with me. When she saw what had happened she began shrieking like a madwoman, and a moment later everyone came."

"And Petronilla accused you."

"Yes. She was angry, furious. The bishops always say that hell has no fury like a discarded woman."

Arthur stepped away from the wall he'd been leaning against and stood next to Merlin. "Petronilla is nothing in the fury department. Wait until Guenevere hears your story. She seethes with rage even when she hasn't been misused."

"Queens are difficult. Her mother—"

"Guenevere is so much like her mother it frightens me."

"Anyway, she loves me. She will forgive me. When I fall into her arms and do my 'I'm an impulsive little boy' act, she melts. It has never failed." He sounded quite pleased with himself.

"She has caught you being unfaithful before this? And forgiven you?" Arthur sounded amazed. "This side of her is one I've never seen before."

"She knew that I had tupped a few scullery maids and so on."

"Screwing her personal secretary may seem different to her. I'd be careful, if I were you. Impulsive little boys can only get away with so much."

"You think she might divorce me?" He sounded alarmed.

"You'd be lucky if that's all she did."

"But—but—I've never cheated on her before. Not with anyone of consequence."

Both Arthur and Merlin burst out laughing. "Save the innocent act for her, will you? Your womanizing is legendary across half of Western Europe. What is the name of that bastard son you have in France? Gilead or something, isn't it?"

"Galahad." He sulked. "A horrible kid. Completely insufferable. I'm ashamed that he's mine. He takes what the priests teach seriously. Goes around boasting about how pure he is. No one can stand him." Then he realized what Arthur had said. He blinked. "But you have better intelligence than I thought, I'm impressed."

"You should be impressed by more than my espionage network. Guenevere has begged us to free you and find what she calls the real murderer. Presumably the owner of those robes you saw vanish around the corner."

"Guenevere? Begged?" He couldn't hide his astonishment.

Arthur nodded, smiling. "She has not forgotten who the real power is in England. Neither should you. We have enough evidence to convict you at trial, Lancelot. You know what that will mean."

"Yes." He turned glum. "My head."

"Is there anything else you can tell Merlin and me that might help your case?"

Sullenly he shook his head.

"We'll just be going, then."

Lancelot sprang to his feet. "Arthur, please. I've served you ill. I've never been loyal to you, not since I arrived in England. But I know you. You believe in justice, in fairness. Do not execute me for a crime you know I didn't commit."

"I know you *say* you didn't commit it. That is not quite the same thing. Every murderer on record—"

"I wouldn't lie to you, not about this."

Arthur paused and smiled. "I know. You're just an impulsive little boy."

Lancelot's features froze. "I suppose I deserve that."

"Of course you do. But what else do you deserve? That is the real question here, isn't it?"

Merlin also paused in the doorway. "Oh, and by the way . . ."

"Yes? What else?"

"We've uncovered the agent you sent to assassinate Arthur. I hope you were not counting on him to do his job. You will have to pin your hopes on something else, I fear."

"That little rat Petronus. What has he told you?"

"A great deal." Merlin grinned. "Thank you for the verification."

A moment later the king and his advisor left their prisoner to sulk and wonder how badly he had hurt his case. Arthur had found the interview highly satisfactory; Merlin had his doubts.

"What on earth do you make of that?" Arthur walked briskly back to his rooms.

"Lies. Or so I would guess. Lancelot is the only logical suspect. Who else could have done the killing?"

Arthur shrugged. "We have a castle full of men with ulterior motives. England should have stayed a backwater. You will question Petronilla again?"

"Do you really think it would accomplish anything, Arthur?"

"It might make Lancelot's story more plausible."

Merlin sighed. "And this was looking so neat."

"Do you want neatness, or do you want the truth?"

"That is a question you should ask yourself, Arthur. You have Guenevere's pledge of loyalty. You have her 'husband' in jail. You have gained the recognition—at least some recognition—of the international community. Why upset the applecart?"

"Question Petronilla again. Better yet, search her room. She may have been foolish enough to keep a diary or something."

Merlin made an ostentatious bow. "As you wish, Your Majesty."

"And don't be a smartass."

"Your wife is . . . a prisoner?" Podarthes smiled at Arthur and adopted the faux-humble demeanor of a professional courtier.

The king, Merlin and Britomart were receiving him privately. He seemed mildly put off by it; Byzantine grandees were used to attention and considered it their due. Nimue was in attendance, taking notes, and four guards were stationed at the corners of the room. Podarthes was dressed, rather pointedly, much more magnificently than anyone else present. His golden cloak shimmered in torchlight. Nimue found the ostentation amusing.

Arthur frowned at the ambassador. "My wife is, shall we say, indisposed. But it is not her wish that we discuss the reasons."

"I see. Perhaps it is merely her time of the month, then? But I am quite at your service, Your Majesty. On what subject may I enlighten you?"

"You may," Merlin interjected, "explain why you have been in England for nearly a month without presenting yourself. You must certainly be aware of how . . . irregular that is. We have already drafted a letter to Justinian protesting formally."

"Our ship was blown off course. We landed somewhere to the north. The country was unfamiliar to us, and so . . ." Podarthes smiled; he didn't expect them to believe a word of it.

"Mightn't you have asked for directions? And why would you have come here so early—a month before the queen's birthday?"

"Surely it is not unusual for a ship to be blown off course here. English weather is notorious everywhere. This storm that is raging outside now, for instance. Do you think it will let up anytime soon?"

Arthur smiled. "There has been only one report of a vessel being blown astray by this wind. And that was one of yours, en route to France. And now your ship . . . You are pinning a great deal on the wind. Or perhaps you ought to find better navigators."

"Just so, Your Majesty. But I was under the impression you wished to open diplomatic talks."

Britomart was in an impatient mood. "That is exactly

what we're trying to do, Podarthes. What have you been doing here? And how did you escape the notice of our agents for all that time?"

"The emperor has carried on a lively correspondence with Queen Guenevere, under the reasonable impression she is the reigning monarch in England. Imagine our surprise when we learned it to be otherwise."

"So you were gathering intelligence?"

Merlin decided to get between them, and to take a shot in the dark. "Surely your agent here—the one who pretends to be a Lithuanian—could have told you what you needed to know."

Podarthes's eyes widened. "Lithuanian?"

"He is your agent, is he not? I have suspected as much all along. There was no other plausible explanation for his presence here. Tell us the truth, Podarthes. He speaks perfect English, Greek and Latin, does he not?"

"I have," the ambassador said slowly and carefully, "no knowledge of the man. I am as bewildered by his language as anyone."

"That hardly answers the question."

"At any rate," Arthur said firmly, "you now have a correct understanding of the political situation here. The queen is not the one you must treat with."

"Yes, of course, Your Majesty. But you understand, I must contact Byzantium before I can proceed at all. This altered political situation . . ." He smiled feebly.

"Go and write, then. I will have a special courier take your letter there as rapidly as possible."

"With respect, Your Majesty, I should prefer to send one of my own men."

"We will take that under consideration. But you do understand the situation, do you not?"

His face was blank. "Situation?"

Merlin spoke. "We are investigating the assassination of King Leodegrance. Your earlier absence made it out of the question to suspect you. Now that we know you were here in England all along . . . You do see the question that raises?"

"Neither I nor any of my people had anything to do with that crime. Besides, you are certainly aware that I have immunity from prosecution." He smiled wickedly. "As a diplomat."

"And you are certainly aware," Merlin said smiling back at him, "that we do not have formal diplomatic relations with Byzantium. A claim of immunity would carry no weight."

"But . . . you certainly have the killer in custody already."

"As the king said, we are investigating. There are unanswered questions." Merlin glanced at Arthur, who nodded slightly. "I believe that is all for now, Podarthes. You may go."

Clearly unhappy with the way the meeting had gone, Podarthes stood to go, bowed and walked out of the room. These English were better at the game than he'd expected.

When he had gone, Arthur sat back in his chair and relaxed. "Evidently the Byzantines aren't quite as clever as their reputation would indicate."

"Or they are more so." Brit was still bristling. "Can we believe anything he said? Anything at all?"

"Justinian loves spies and spying." Merlin adopted his best schoolteacher tone. "He spies on his own subjects ceaselessly. It is not out of character for him to send his people here early and place them undercover. We must send riders out to our own people across the countryside and see if we might learn—or guess—what Podarthes has been up to."

Brit jumped to her feet. "I'll send men out right away."

"Excellent, Brit. But now it is time for us to, er, to have a talk with Petronus. Do you wish to remain for that?"

"God, no."

He turned to Nimue. "I would like you to leave as well, Colin. This may prove delicate, and I want him as much at ease as possible."

A moment later they were gone and the boy was ushered in under heavy guard. The head guard whispered a quick exchange with Arthur, who told him to have his men wait outside. Petronus sat on a low stool, facing the king and Merlin; he was clearly worried about what was going to happen.

Once the guards had left the room, Merlin turned to him and smiled his best schoolteacher smile. "Petronus. Hello, Petronus."

"You sound surprised to see me here."

He chuckled. "Not at all, I am merely trying to make you feel welcome, to put you at ease."

"Why?"

"Now, do not take that attitude. We have taken you from prison and let you stay in your own room, Surely that should demonstrate our goodwill."

"Well . . ." He sulked. "I guess so."

"Excellent."

"What did Lancelot and Guenevere tell you? About me, I mean."

"Lancelot made some comments that seem to support your story, at least in part. But we have more to learn. In the meantime—"

"What more could you need to know?"

"Please, Petronus. A great deal has been happening in the Spider's House. I will tell you frankly that there are more mysteries than we bargained for. Unless we get to the bottom of them . . ." He spread his hands in a gesture of helplessness and put on a sadder-but-wiser expression.

"People always say you learned to act from Samuel Gall, that actor friend of yours. And that you've outclassed him as an actor."

"People at court always love nasty gossip. Courts thrive on it."

"It is true, though, isn't it?"

"Listen, Petronus. Your guards have told us you have been exceptionally well-behaved. Do you really want to turn this meeting into an adversarial one?"

"No, sir, I guess not. But I—"

Arthur interrupted. "Petronus, we want to know about your sister."

"I—" It had caught him off guard and it showed. "Petronilla?"

"Exactly."

"What could you possibly want to know about her? She is Guenevere's secretary. And she's a lying scheming bitch. She always has been."

"Yes." Merlin smiled again. "So you've told us. But there must be more to her than just that. What about love, for instance?"

"Love? Petronilla?! You can't be serious."

"I an afraid we are. Did she have affairs before she came to England? Did she take lovers?"

The boy was lost; his face made it clear. "She—she lived in a nunnery at Lyons from her early teens. I was eight when she left, and it was as if my world had suddenly been flooded with sunlight. Then when I was fourteen she came home. She claimed she had left the convent voluntarily. But there were rumors she had had an affair with one of the priests. The abbot's secretary, in fact. I think our parents knew the details, but they would never discuss them with me."

"But you heard? And you guessed?"

"Well . . . yes."

"And?"

"They were only rumors. I don't actually know."

Sternly Arthur said, "Stop this shilly-shallying. Tell us what you heard."

"Well, Your Majesty. they said she was madly in love with this priest of hers. Desperate to marry him. But his vows . . . he wanted no part of that. You know how ambitious they can be. Petronilla was nothing to him but a bedmate."

"No, we don't know a thing about priests and their ambitions. This is England, not France. Go on."

"Well, what I heard was . . . was . . . that she had tried to poison him. The one she said she loved. How's that for an older sister to look up to?"

"And do you believe it?"

"That she . . . ?"

"Yes. Did she do it, do you think?"

"Well, they never found any real evidence. There were just lots of suspicions. But she was driven out of the convent and came home to us. The poor priest was left feeble-minded by whatever she had done."

"You believe she did it, then?" Arthur raised his voice. "If you do, just say so."

And Petronus cowered a bit. "All I can say, Your Majesty, is that it seems in character for her, as I've always known her. Petty, vindictive, self-centered, grasping . . . She is a complete horror of a woman. I have to think my parents sent her to England to be rid of her."

Arthur and Merlin exchanged glances. Merlin looked at the boy, not smiling for once. "So Petronilla is capable of trying to eliminate a lover she is not happy with."

"That was the rumor, sir, yes."

"And were there any other lovers who ended unhappily?"

"None that I know of. But Petronilla and I have never been close. When I was a child she used to torment me. Stick needles into me. I . . . It's a terrible thing to say, but I hate her."

"Yours is not the first family to spawn such a creature, Petronus." Merlin's tone was fatherly, or as close to it as he could manage. "Or such feelings. Go back to your rooms, now, and behave yourself. This birthday gathering will be over soon enough. Or it will be if this bloody storm ever lets up."

"But, sir, if I may ask, what is this all about? I thought you'd want to talk about the charges against me. I—"

"Go to your rooms. We will talk further, I am certain. Perhaps not till the delegates are gone, but you may count on it."

Without saying a word, and with an unmistakable look of confusion on his face, the boy left. Merlin heard the guards form up and take him away.

"What on earth are we to make of that?" Arthur stared at the stool where the boy had sat.

"If he is telling the truth, Arthur, it tells us a great deal about Petronilla's character, does it not? For the first time I find myself seriously considering the suggestion that Lancelot might not be the murderer of Leodegrance. I will have the girl's rooms searched. It is too much to think that she might have kept a diary or any such thing, but we can hope. And we must have our agents in France find out what they can about her."

"A teenage girl in a nunnery? Who would ever have noticed her? Why would they?"

"True, Arthur. But if she is lying to incriminate another lover . . . Why kill Lancelot herself when she can have us do it for her?"

"There are moments, Merlin, when your dark view of human nature makes sense to me."

"I wish it did not seem quite so reasonable."

Not having his accustomed tower at Camelot for solitude, Merlin had chosen to occupy rooms at the far end of the longest of the spider's legs. He headed there now, walking slowly along the corridor, lost in his thoughts. Some time alone . . . perhaps a bit of reading . . . maybe even a good long nap . . . That would be so sweet.

A young guard hurried up behind him. "Merlin, sir."

His spirits fell. He paused and turned slowly to face the man. "What is it?"

"I'm sorry to bother you with this, sir, but it didn't seem quite important enough for the king, and—"

He resumed walking. "If it is unimportant, by all means, tell me about it."

"I didn't mean to imply that—"

"No, no, and I did not take it that way. I am so tired of dealing with important matters. A small one will make a nice change."

"Well, sir," he said uncertainly, "it is not exactly trivial. It's the queen."

"Do you mean Guenevere, or Leonilla? Leonilla is more and more distracted. She keeps going on these little walk-abouts of hers at the strangest hours, and to the strangest places."

"No, sir. It is Her Majesty, Queen Guenevere. She wants to receive visitors."

Merlin stopped walking. "Visitors? She is a prisoner and she knows it. Refuse her." After the briefest instant he found himself wondering who she might want to receive.

"The Byzantine, sir. Podarthes."

"Oh." He took a deep breath and exhaled it slowly. "Tell her no. Tell him no. She is to have no 'guests.' And inform Podarthes that any diplomatic business is to be presented to the king."

"We've told her all that, but she is being very insistent."

"Damn. Very well. I will deal with her."

A few minutes later he was at Guenevere's rooms. "Good morning, Guenevere."

"Merlin." She smiled a tight smile. "How very nice of *you* to visit me, at least."

"I hope my humble company will be sufficient for you."

"Why, whatever do you mean? And how is the conference proceeding?"

"The delegates have been meeting, with Arthur and with one another. And getting nowhere, mostly, like carts stuck in the mud. If anything substantial has developed, I am not aware of it. But then, this is much more a social gathering than an official one. And I have not been actively involved. There is a murderer to capture."

"You are working on the case, then." She smiled.

"Indeed. If only because we do not want any more . . . untoward incidents. I hope to know the killer's identity by the start of tonight's plenary session."

With a touch of wistful sadness, she told him, "I wish I could be part of it all. Being confined here is so . . . inconvenient."

He sighed and sat down. "You fascinate me, Guenevere. Do you think we do not know about your attempt to set young Petronus to kill Arthur? And that you have been trying to arrange for 'visitors'? You really do never tire of this."

Her face betrayed nothing. "You mean Podarthes, don't you?"

He nodded slightly but said nothing.

"Podarthes and I are old friends. Surely you know that when I was a girl, Mother sent me to Constantinople to be educated. I have known him since that time. Why on earth do you think a man as important as he came to England?"

He had known about her time in Constantinople but had never made the connection. But it made perfect sense. He hoped his surprise was not apparent to her. "There is a kind of spider in living in the Egyptian desert. A large brown thing, covered with thick hair, quite repulsive."

"You came to give me a lesson in natural history?"

He ignored this and went on. "It never ceases spinning webs, and its territory can cover a startling amount of desert land. Prey is scarce, you see, and it must spin or capture no food. When it entraps some insect or small reptile or whatever, it eats voraciously."

Guenevere sat at her dressing table and began to brush her hair. She smiled at him. "I hope you don't mind. I think it is important to maintain one's appearance."

He brushed this aside. "The peculiar thing is, this creature seems unable to stop eating. On the rare occasions when it manages to capture more prey than it actually needs, it keeps eating till its sides swell and burst. Its own gluttonous nature results in its death."

She brushed her hair vigorously and studied her appearance in the mirror. "Is this supposed to be of any interest to me? The eating habits of spiders are hardly—"

"Other spiders, when there is an abundance of food, use it to feed their newly hatched young. Not this one. They are the first things she devours. Even then, she keeps right on feeding. As repulsive as it is, it is quite fascinating to watch. Done in by her own appetite."

"It you have a point, Merlin, make it and go. I am expecting someone."

"No, you are not." He spoke slowly and heavily.

"I beg your pardon?"

"Let me be more precise. You may be expecting someone. That does not mean he will arrive."

"Why do courtiers all talk like that? My father had a—"

"I realize that the oath you took to Arthur only last night must not mean much to you. Oaths never do to your sort. But you cannot seriously believe that taking it would free you to carry on with life as you lived it before."

She carefully placed her hairbrush on the table and turned to face him. "You are trying to tell me what, precisely?"

"Have you forgotten? Lancelot is still in jail. You are not exactly behaving like a woman who wants to see her boyfriend free."

"Husband. Oh, how I enjoy saying that. You are not going to renege on our agreement, are you?" A faint note of alarm crept into her voice. "Lancelot is innocent."

"How can you know that so confidently unless you also know the identity of the actual assassin?"

"Merlin, I—"

"No negotiations. No diplomatic maneuvering. None. Do you understand? There will be none. Do not even make the attempt, not if you want to see your lover vindicated. Arthur does not know about this—yet. But I promise you he would not receive the news graciously."

The queen's face froze. After a moment she said, "Why, what can you be talking about? Diplomatic maneuvering? I? I am a humble servant of King Arthur, as you are yourself."

"Podarthes is being informed that you are indisposed and are at any rate not receiving visitors. Any further attempt at communication between the two of you will result in the immediate trial and execution of Lancelot."

"But he is innocent!"

"Innocence be damned. Lancelot is guilty of more treasons than most culprits ever dream of. As are you. This rubbish with Petronus, for example. Thank heaven the boy has a conscience." He said this last in the most pointed tone. "Did you really think taking that oath of fealty would give you free rein to resume your plots and schemes? Since you are lonely for company, I am having your guard doubled. I hope that will satisfy your need for society."

The queen's eyes widened, which was as close as she would permit herself to get to showing rage. "Let me talk to Arthur."

"Guenevere, there is no point. He will only reinforce what I have told you. And he might possibly do much worse to you. Do you really want to give him that opening? Be a good queen and stay here with your prayer books and your needlework."

"Merlin, I am warning you—"

"Warn all you like. Unless you are prepared to brain me on the spot with one of your hymnals, nothing will come of it. Those Egyptian spiders keep fighting even after they have ruptured their own bodies, spitting venom even as the desert birds descend and tear them to pieces. But in the end they expire." He put on a sardonic grin. "And in the end it is their own doing."

For a long moment she did not move. Then slowly she picked up her hairbrush again; it was obvious she was working to appear casual. "Have you found that other knife yet? Lancelot's?"

"Yes. Never mind where. We have yours—which we know was the murder weapon. Oh yes, and Lancelot thinks he saw a woman rushing away from the scene."

"La—" For an instant a flash of anger showed in her eyes. Then she caught herself and broke off what she had been about to say. "You are trying to set us against one another."

"You are married. Why should we need to?" Merlin shrugged. "That is his claim. A woman, at the scene of the murder. He will repeat it in court, under oath, no doubt. Not that oaths seem to mean much to the two of you."

"I know you, Merlin. If Lancelot said such a thing, it can only be because you led him to say it. You may even have gotten him to believe it. But you love the truth. I know that. You must exonerate him. That knife will tell the tale."

"To what end? If it went missing, it is because someone stole it for its beauty or its value. Or because you yourself hid it to confuse the investigation. What possible relevance can the fact that he lost it have when it was not involved in the crime?"

"It is relevant because its theft shows that there is someone at work, for some unknown motive, trying to incriminate him."

He smiled beatifically. "Or not. Lancelot had every reason to resent Leodegrance. He had every opportunity to do the murder—and we have a witness who will swear she saw him do it. What could the other knife prove?"

"We had a bargain, damn you, Merlin. I expect you to live up to it."

"I will, Guenevere. Just as faithfully as you have. Oh—" He pretended an afterthought had occurred to him. "They were lovers. Did you know that?"

"Lovers? Who?"

"Lancelot and Petronilla."

"No!" She shrieked the word.

"Yes. At least, according to him. Have a nice day, Guenevere."

He left her still fuming. It had been a productive meeting, he thought, and he smiled to himself.

A few minutes later Nimue joined him in his chambers, to all appearances in a bright mood. "It's noon. Aren't you hungry? They have roast beef."

Merlin stood at the window, feeding breadcrumbs to his ravens. There were more of them than usual; the storm had driven them indoors for shelter. "Remarkable birds, these. Somehow they knew I had left Camelot and come here. And they followed."

One by one, like little soldiers, they lined up and waited patiently for their food. Without looking at her, he said, "I prefer my ravens to human company. They are hungry, they are greedy for food, but at least they do not try to hide the fact. The only honest human beings are the ones who claim to despise all the other ones."

"You're in a mood. Every time there's trouble you get like this."

"Is there some reason why I should not? A boy walks through a peaceful forest, cheerful, optimistic. Birds sing, squirrels play, rabbits scamper about. To all appearances the world is a harmonious place. And then he idly picks up a stick and probes a hole. And a snake or a toad strikes at him. Moments later he is dead. What would you say? Was his optimism justified?"

"Not being a boy with a stick, I couldn't guess."

"A thousand years ago, more or less, at the height of the Peloponnesian War, and seemingly from out of nowhere, a plague ravaged Athens. Thousands died."

"I know that, Merlin. I've read my Thucydides."

He ignored her interruption. "We know the disease. That is, we know its pathology. The historian himself suffered from it but happily recovered, so we can trust his account of its progress. And the symptoms correspond to no known illness. Do you understand that?"

Despite herself Nimue was curious where he was going. "Of course. It's a simple enough fact."

"The question then becomes, *what was it*? And even more to the point, *where is it*? This unknown disease, this slaughterer of thousands, what has become of it? Is it possible it has simply . . . vanished, ceased to be? Do diseases do such things? Or is it out there in the world somewhere, lurking, waiting for its opportunity to strike again, to ravage another city and reduce its population?

"No one thinks about it. It struck Athens and went away, that is all. Why should the rest of us worry, a millennium later? But it is there, Nimue, waiting. Sooner or later, it will strike. And it will conquer again."

Listening to him, she ambled about the room. The largest of the ravens went to her and she stroked its head. "Why all this plague talk? I'd have thought you had more than enough on your mind."

"It seems relevant, that is all."

"Plague in Athens." She was deadpan.

"Yes. Or . . . you have read enough history. Pick a city; disease has erupted and crippled it, always at a time when everything seemed prosperous. Name a king, he has been weakened by something he could not fathom. Name a family, no matter how happy and prosperous, and vice has crept in. Arthur and Guenevere are the world in small scale. And evil is everywhere. We all fall victim to it in the end. If there was only some way we could know, we would see that the nature of the universe is corruption. If we could only see it, we would know that even the stars die."

Nimue crossed to the window with the raven on her arm. Outside, the rain was pouring down torrentially. It was possible to see distant brooks and rivulets, swelled beyond their banks, flooding the landscape. The world was alive with rushing floodwater and, it appeared, with nothing else. "You are confusing human evil with accidental processes in the natural world. You should know better than to lapse into such a fallacy."

Merlin turned to face her. "You are a good young woman, Nimue. Or should I say a good young *man*, Colin? But they are one and the same. Human nature is a reflection of the nature of the universe of which it is a part."

"Grasshoppers disguise themselves as sticks. Does that make them evil, then, or merely clever?"

For a moment he fell silent and watched the raging storm. Lightning flashed in the distance. "There is a legend of a king called Lear. He had three daughters, only one of whom loved him. And of the three, she was the one he destroyed."

"Lear was mad."

"And is madness not a kind of evil? The worst kind? Those grasshoppers eat their own young."

She took a few steps away from him, trying to appear casual. "I can't stand it when you get into one of these moods. And this is the worst I've ever seen."

He shrugged. "I've just been with the queen."

"Oh." She stroked the bird's head and it cooed softly with pleasure.

"You should be flattered. He does not normally let anyone touch him but me."

She looked directly at Merlin. "We searched Petronilla's room."

For a moment he seemed lost in his dark thoughts. Then, softly, he asked, "And what did you find?"

"Nothing. Nothing incriminating, at any rate. But she does carry a small portrait of Lancelot in her luggage. At least, we think it's Lancelot. You know those French portrait painters."

"It is not labeled?"

"Only with *mon cher*. There is no way to know whether he gave it to her or she had it painted herself. Or even whether it is really him."

"No. Of course not. We can't very well question every miniaturist in France. Not that anyone in his right mind would want to. If there is a human being more lunatic than a French artist . . . Did you find anything else?"

"Clothes, books—prayer books—some letters from Leonilla."

"I see. I shall have to question Petronilla a second time. There seems no way of escaping it."

"You sound as if it will be a burden."

"Have you not been listening to me, Nimue?" Uncharacteristically, he raised his voice. "The soul of the human race—its genius, if we could but see it—is as black as a moonless midnight. And the human soul is a reflection of the universe. Plants grow full of poison. The smallest toads are filled with deadly venom. Rain pours from the sky, brooks flood and babies drown. How could we be other than we are?"

She was beginning to become alarmed. "The king is drinking again, I think. And you are raging with melancholy. No one is in charge here."

"No one is ever truly in charge anywhere. Do you not understand that?"

"The gods—"

"Are myths. Children's stories, spun out and made

elaborate for adult minds. You grew up in Morgan's court.
You hide from her vengeance by pretending to be something you are not. You must know that as well as anyone."

"If belief leads to stability, then shouldn't we foster
belief?"

"What do you think the lion believes in when it is de-
vouring the young of the antelope? What creed spurs the
formation of poison in the viper? The world is what it is."
Suddenly he seemed to lose all his energy. Sadly, he added,
"And I have not been getting much sleep. That must be at
the bottom of this mood I am in."

"I thought you'd never realize it."

"Let me sleep for an hour or two. I'll be better then."

"Petronilla—"

"Keep her in her room. Find some pretext. Don't let her
know we have doubts about her." Suddenly, he yawned. "I
am old, Nimue. And getting older. Each day takes me one
step closer to the sepulcher. Sleep is a foreshadowing."

"Get some anyway. You'll find that sepulcher retreating
into the distance."

He leaned forward and kissed her gently on the fore-
head. "You know I have never married. I do not regret that.
But it has always been a wish of mine to have a daughter.
Perhaps that wish, at least, has been granted."

"I believe Lear once said much the same thing."

"I express one faint hopeful thought, and you puncture
it. You are my daughter indeed. Amid the floods and the
poisons, there is that. Go and see to Petronilla."

"I think I want to return to Egypt with you, Germanicus. I
was happy there, as I have never been in any other place."

Merlin and his friend walked the less-frequented corridors of Corfe Castle, lost in idle conversation. Merlin's
cane tapped softly on the stones as they walked, giving
their talk a rhythm.

"This is getting to me." He avoided looking his friend in the eye. "All this murder, vice, duplicity . . . I have never much liked the human race. It has been my misfortune to fall into a profession that brings me face-to-face with its most repellent qualities."

Germanicus smiled at him. "You're a fine one to talk about human duplicity."

"What on earth do you mean?" Merlin stopped walking for a moment, then went on.

"I mean you invited me here for precisely this reason— so you could return to Egypt with me. Or at any rate to luxuriate in the thought of it."

After a long moment Merlin said, "You are probably right. No, I confess it—you are perfectly right. I have used you ill, not like a true friend."

"Merlin, don't give it a thought. I have spent my life in politics. *Byzantine* politics. Everyone uses everyone else, not always in obvious ways. In Byzantine terms, everyone in England is an amateur."

"When I was young," Merlin went on, "I traveled everywhere I could, eagerly. As if gadding from one place to the next could make life more bearable. Now it is time for me to retire, to know peace or what passes for it in human existence."

Germanicus listened to him, smiling faintly. "You were not in our country very long, Merlin. Was it even two years? It must be easy for you to think of it as a kind of paradise. But believe me, it is not. We have factions, both political and religious. Christians poison pagans and vice versa. Partisans of one party in Byzantium jockey for advantage over the others. And you should see how vicious the various parties in the Hippodrome can be. Nothing erodes the human character faster than sports.

"It only seems different to you in Egypt because of all the ancient monuments. Their timelessness makes all the squabbling seem small. But even they have a negative effect. Every crackpot in the Mediterranean world comes to Egypt, looking for the supposed wisdom of the ancients. As if stones could be wise."

"Perhaps the men who placed them were."

"That is rubbish and you know it. They were stone-masons, nothing more."

Merlin sighed. "I say again, when I lived in Egypt I was happy. I was free to study at the great library in Alexandria. There is nothing to study here but fog and rain. This damned murder . . . Why did Leodegrance not stay at home?"

"Murder and politics can teach you at least as much as piles of old stones." He sighed in frustration. "Look at what you've accomplished here, you and Arthur. You have built, or are building, a society based on fairness and justice for everyone, not just a handful of nobles. All across the Mediterranean world, people talk about it."

"Gossips."

"Nonsense. You are refusing to acknowledge what is happening here. Not since Athens in its glory days has there been such a society. You are working wonders here, genuine wonders as impressive as the Pyramids."

"Then why does it all seem so futile?" Merlin brushed aside a piece of rubble with the tip of his cane. "If I could peel away one thin sliver of the world's evil, how much would still remain?"

"Stop talking like that. You are doing some good, even if it seems minimal to you. Other people will do the same, in time. You are showing them the way."

A serving woman rushed past them, carrying a bundle of something; it was impossible to tell what. She barely acknowledged them as she hurried past.

"This current business—the murder of Leodegrance— that is what is weighing me down. For as long as I can remember he has been part of our world, and now . . . I need to go someplace where I will never have to deal with such affairs again."

"The North Pole?"

"Stop it, Germanicus. I am serious."

"So am I. The only place you can find no problems is a place where there are no human beings. Personally, I relish all the problems. They keep my mind fresh; they keep me alive."

"You are a politician. I am a scholar, or try to be. That is the difference."

"You are precisely right, Merlin. All the squabbles and infights, all the plots and schemes, even the occasional murder—they excite me. I am engaged with humanity in a very vital way. I would never trade that for a stack of books."

"People have been having this discussion since before the time of Homer. And it keeps resurfacing, like the plague."

"Like the—? I don't follow you."

"Never mind. Your colleague Podarthes has more or less admitted to us that the peculiar Lithuanian man is in his service, by the way."

"Really? I tried to engage the man in conversation last night. But it was no use. Greek, Latin, English, French—he was impervious to them all."

"Your Byzantine court is not capable of directness. You must be aware that 'Byzantine' is becoming a watchword for complex deviousness. He has been here, pretending to understand nothing but doubtless taking in everything that is said in his earshot. I think some of the other delegates must have known, or suspected. I can only imagine what intelligence he must have been able to give to Podarthes. Germanicus, I want you to understand that I am serious. I want to go back to Egypt, to live the rest of my life there in quiet contemplation. Take me back with you."

"My old minister, Cathacticus, died last month. I haven't found anyone to replace him. Do you want the job? I may have to require that you accept it."

"You would do that?"

"You are too intelligent, too resourceful, to be permitted to retire from pubic service."

Merlin stopped walking and leaned against a wall. "There is never any rest, is there?"

"Of course not."

"So that I might help you remain engaged with humanity, I must do the same."

Germanicus thought for a moment. "I'm not certain I'd phrase it that way, but yes."

Softly Merlin said, "I need to be alone. Do you mind?"

"I don't like seeing you in this kind of mood."

"You are the second person who has said that to me today. Leave me alone, will you please? The mood will pass."

Looking concerned, Germanicus headed off to the refectory.

Wanting solitude, Merlin made his way to one of the castle's ruined "arms" and proceeded to walk along it. A guard was posted to keep delegates from drifting into the ruin by mistake. There was no one else in sight, which pleased him. The guard saluted him and he walked past the man without saying a word.

Almost at once he felt like he was in another place, another world, quiet and empty. The floor was littered with scraps of stone which had evidently flaked off the walls and ceiling; there were cobwebs everywhere. From ahead of him came the sound of running water.

Halfway along, the roof had partially collapsed. Rainwater poured in, then vanished through cracks in the floor. Wind blew in and ruffled his clothing. He looked back over his shoulder. No, he could not go back and face more people.

Ahead of him, the roof was intact and no more rain and wind got in. He moved quickly past the gap in the stones, covering his face with his cloak to fend off the rainwater, then resumed a more leisurely pace.

At the end of each of the eight arms was a tower. They were octagonal in shape, like the heart of the castle itself, and narrow, unglazed windows looked out from them. This place was as far as he could get from the occupied part of the castle without actually going out into the storm. He headed directly to the window opposite the entrance and gazed out at the drowned world.

"You'd think the rain would come in, wouldn't you?"

The voice came from behind him. Merlin turned, alarmed, and thought it was Nimue. But it was a young man, standing in an angle of the walls. He was dressed in court finery and he was vaguely familiar, but it took Merlin a moment to place him. He was Jean-Michel, Leonilla's servant, or gigolo, or whatever he was.

"There are enough cracks. But somehow the elements stay out. The ancients knew more about building securely than we do." The young man smiled. "But then I'm no architect. Hello, Merlin."

"Jean-Claude," Merlin was not at all happy to find him there.

"Jean-Michel. You recognize me. At least somewhat."

"I came here to be alone." He said it pointedly, hoping the boy would take the cue and leave.

"So did I." Touché.

"Is it not your job to tend Leonilla? Frankly, she seems to need a lot of tending."

"She has disappeared on another of her little walk-abouts. There are a dozen servants looking for her. Marthe, the head maid, doesn't like me. I decided to come here instead."

"You sound as if you know this place. How did you get past the guard?"

"I've been coming here every day. Sometimes more than once a day. The guard knows me; I bring him sweets. It is so lovely to be away from people."

"You could be myself as a young man."

"I will take that as a compliment. And what is King Arthur's chief minister doing here, may I ask?"

"The same as you. Seeking solitude. If it were not for this bloody rain, I would be outside, walking in the woods, studying the trees and the animals."

"There we differ, then." Jean-Michel smiled. "I have nothing to learn from rabbits and badgers."

"But damp stones and drafty corridors can teach you what, exactly?"

"The sweet, sweet pleasure of solitude. Euripides abandoned Athens to live in a cave. I could happily do the same."

"Your mood echoes my own."

"Perhaps I should become a minister, then."

Merlin rested his cane against the wall. "Instead of what? What exactly are your duties?"

The young man laughed. "You want to know if I sleep with the queen?"

"She is old enough to be your grandmother. No, your great-grandmother."

"I love her."

"Er, yes. I suppose someone has to."

This puzzled the boy, and it showed.

"Leonilla is a formidable woman." Merlin adopted the tone of a lecturer. "People respect her, fear her. But I have never heard anyone mention her and love in the same sentence. Not even her daughter."

"She took me in when my parents died. I was twelve. You know what happens to orphans—nothing. No prospects, no future, none at all. Leonilla decided she liked me and raised me as her own."

"I don't recall seeing you at her court."

"I was there, keeping quietly to the background." He hesitated. "I know what people think of her. But she has been like a mother to me."

"A loving mother." Merlin's voice dripped with irony.

"We—yes. I—what would be the word?—I like older women. I have always beeen attracted to them. My earliest memory is of attraction to a schoolmistress. And Leonilla, I love. Is that a crime?"

"Flaunting your 'love' as you do is a lapse of taste, to say the least. And would be for even a more conventional couple. I would appreciate it if you would leave now, Jean-Louis. I want to be alone."

"Jean-Michel." He turned to go.

"No, wait. There is something I would like to ask you."

"Yes?"

Merlin took his cane and crossed the room to a stone bench. Sitting down heavily, he patted the seat beside him. "Sit here. Let us talk."

"Isn't that what we've been doing? But you want to be alone. I'll just go now."

In an instant Merlin turned from tired old man to royal minister. "Sit here. Let us talk."

Compliant, Jean-Michel sat.

"There is a young woman, Petronilla. You know her?"

"Yes, of course. Her mother is an intimate of the queen."

"Tell me about her."

Jean-Michel's eyes narrowed. "You think she was involved in the murder."

"No." Merlin hoped the lie was convincing.

"You think she was working secretly for Leonilla."

"That had not occurred to me. Thank you for the insight."

The young man jumped to his feet. "And you are investigating the murder. Why would Leonilla have her own husband killed? What would she gain?"

"I am only concerned with Petronilla, not with your . . . adoptive mother. Tell me about her."

"There is not much to tell, really." He shrugged and sat. "Her mother and Leonilla are old friends. There is a little brother, too, a boy named Petrus or something."

"Petronus."

"Yes, that's it. He was . . ." He groped for the memory. "He was sent here to Guenevere's court. Then he disappeared. Nobody seemed to care much. But if you're looking for a suspect, he would be a likely one." His eyes narrowed. "He is here, isn't he?"

"But the girl." Merlin was not about to be drawn from his inquiry.

He sighed. "She was groomed to be one of Leonilla's attendants when she came of age. Good education, every luxury . . ."

"What about lovers?"

"You do have a curious mind."

"It is my job."

Jean-Michel wrinkled his nose and went on. "There were stories. Gossip. People said she had a vindictive nature. She took lovers, then treated them horribly when they lost interest in her, or she in them. I never paid much attention."

"I see. Do you have any idea why she was sent to England?"

"To be Guinevere's secretary, I think. What is this in aid of?"

"Nothing. Just an old man's curiosity, no more."

Jean-Michel leaned back against the wall. "You expect me to believe that?"

"What you believe, Jean-Paul, is no concern of mine. But tell me about Leonilla and her marriage."

"Jean-Michel. I keep telling you. Is this some sort of official inquiry, then?"

"Let us say a friendly questioning. A murder has been

committed here, a royal one. You must understand that we cannot let it go uninvestigated—unsolved. You were one of Leodegrance's subjects. You must want justice at least as much as I do."

"People say you are a wizard. Why don't you just summon up a genie or a spirit or something and have it tell you who the killer is?"

"If a tenth of the things people say about me were true, I would be the most powerful man in Europe. The king—Leodegrance, I mean—opposed this absurd 'marriage' between Lancelot and Guenevere?"

"I think so, yes. But I never mixed in affairs like that. I told you, I always preferred to keep in the background."

"And Petronilla? Who did she side with?"

He shrugged. "I have no idea. But you're talking to me as if I might know something worth knowing."

"Do you not?"

"Most people at Camelliard would tell you no. In their minds, I am Leonilla's . . . boy, nothing more. The fact that I might love her and yet still have a sound mind never seems to occur to them. I am young and handsome, and I have the queen's favor, and so in their minds there can be nothing more to me."

"I try never to underestimate anyone. Anyone at all." Merlin took his cane and got to his feet. "Thank you very much for the information. It has been most enlightening."

"Really? I haven't told you much—certainly nothing but gossip you could get from any servant." Jean-Michel smiled at him. "If you want to know who killed Leodegrance, you should look to his daughter. She wanted to marry her knight; I have no idea why. Lancelot is not much more than a lump, a mass of muscle. But love is so strange."

"You would know that."

He bristled. "Leodegrance opposed the marriage quite vigorously. Guenevere hated him."

"Perhaps you are right. Our queen has committed so many villainies." Merlin sighed. "One more would hardly seem to make much difference. At least, I doubt it would, to her. But thank you for the information."

"I have given you so little."

"More than you think. You will keep this talk confidential, I trust."

"Who would I tell?"

"The queen—your lover."

"No. You've seen her, talked to her. You know about these odd walks she goes on, where no one can find her. Her mind is going. At her age . . ." He looked away from Merlin and lowered his voice. "I wish old age did not do that to us. It is so difficult to see her like this."

"Old age does its worst. I shudder to think what will happen to my mind in the coming years."

"A mind like yours will never decay. Not till your body does."

"It would be so nice to believe that. But I have never had that kind of luck."

"This reputation of yours—all these claims that you have magical powers—can it have survived if you did not work to promote it?"

"People still believe in dragons despite the fact that dragons do nothing to promote it."

It was a new thought to the young man; it showed in his face. "I . . . suppose so."

"Once, just once before I die, I would like to pass an entire day without having to explain to anyone that I am not a magician, wizard, mage, sorcerer, conjurer or any of the other species of that ilk. Such persons do not exist except in folktales."

"Folktales are all most people have to believe in."

"Believe me, I know it. Thank you again for the talk, Jean-Claude."

"Jean-Michel."

"Yes. Thank you."

"You might at least get my name right."

Merlin recounted his unexpected exchange with Jean-Michel to Nimue and Brit. "It seemed so obvious that Lancelot had done the murder, most likely at Guenevere's insistence. But now . . . Every time I question anyone the situation grows muddier. I suppose we should be grateful for this rainstorm. It is ravaging the country, but at least it is keeping all of the interested parties bottled up here."

"This strikes you as a good thing?" Brit sounded skeptical. "Doesn't it make more death inevitable?"

"Let us hope not."

"You have never struck anyone as a man for hope, Merlin. It's almost comical—the great man of reason, hoping for the best amid all this intrigue."

Nimue was listening carefully; she decided she didn't want the two of them bickering. "So what do we know? Who might have killed the king?"

"I think Lancelot and Guenevere are still the likeliest suspects. But there is Petronilla, hoping to pin the murder on her lover, Lancelot. There are all the other delegates. We have no certain way of knowing what plots they might be involved in. I must question the squires who are attached to them. And there are of course the Byzantines and that bloody man from Lithuania or . . . or wherever."

"What motive could they have?"

"They are Byzantines. Wheels within wheels, boxes within boxes. They never do what they do for clear, obvious reasons. If they thought killing Leodegrance would in some way help to topple another petty ruler at the far end of the empire, they would not hesitate. Look at the game they have been playing with us, with that Lithuanian fraud pretending not to understand any known language. It is so improbable, yet they expected us to believe it without question. Thank goodness young Andrew found that knife."

He paused and looked from one of them to the other. "And of course there are other, less expected suspects."

"Who?"

"Leonilla. And that absurd young lover of hers."

Nimue said, "It doesn't seem like he could be involved."

"What makes you say so?"

"I know him. I mean, not well, but we have struck up a kind of friendship. I mean, even the servants have noticed us together. They talk about him. Nothing substantial, only gossip. He seems genuine to me. At least, I think he is genuinely distressed by what happened to his king, not to mention Leonilla apparently coming unhinged."

Merlin raised an eyebrow. "Leodegrance and Leonilla had disagreed, I gather rather bitterly, about Guenevere's new marriage. Leonilla has a long record of disposing of her opponents. And it is difficult to imagine her stabbing the king herself. She would entrust that duty to someone younger and stronger. For that matter, no one has ever precisely accounted for all the deaths of her other rivals. Jean-Pierre could easily be her pet assassin as well as her pet."

"Jean-Michel. He's a nice young man." Nimue said it so forcefully it was almost shocking. "Or at least, he seems like it. It's hard to believe him capable of murder."

"A man may smile and smile and be a villain. But I am only speculating, you understand. There are twenty diplomats here, with their entourages, any one of whom is capable of devious plotting. It is what they do for a living, after all. We must not lose sight of any of the possibilities."

"Petronilla." Merlin smiled broadly. "Good afternoon."

She sat in her room doing needlework. "So you are behind this detention. I should have guessed. Every time I've tried to leave my room, I've been kept here on some pretext or other."

"My apologies for any inconvenience."

"It is more than inconvenience. It is insulting, Why am I being treated like a prisoner?"

"No such thing, Petronilla. The guards have perhaps been overzealous, that is all." He tried to make the lie sound as convincing as possible.

"Why do I have guards at all?"

"Why, Petronilla, you sound downright imperious. You have perhaps been with Guenevere too long."

She looked up from her needle. "Don't be funny with me, Merlin. I've been as forthright with you as I could be."

"There is a murderer on the loose. Do you really mind being protected from him?"

She glared. "You have the murderer. And I don't deserve to be treated like this."

He had had enough of trying to be pleasant. "What you deserve is for the king to decide. Besides, we are not at all certain Lancelot did the murder."

Her eyes widened but she said nothing, which pleased him. After a long pause he told her, "There have been rumors. Mildly disturbing ones. I have been trying to establish what truth there is to them—if any. That is all."

"About me? What rumors could there possibly be about me? I am the queen's secretary, no more. It is the dullest, least impressive job imaginable."

"I am afraid I even had to have your rooms searched." He made a vague gesture around the room they were in.

She paused, glared, pretended to return her attention back to her needlework. "Oh? And was that a valuable use of time?"

He decided to be direct. But he smiled a gentle smile as he said, "You and Lancelot were lovers."

She paused for a moment, then went on sewing. "What could have given you that idea?"

Slowly he produced the miniature portrait of him. "*Mon cher* does mean *my sweet*, does it not?"

She reached out and tried to take it from him, but he pulled back.

"Please, Merlin, that is personal. It isn't Lancelot. It is a portrait of a man I . . . fell in love with before I came here from France."

"The one you lied about to incriminate?"

"Give me that picture!"

She lunged for it but he moved it behind his back. The sound of her raised voice brought one of the guards into the room. Merlin handed him the portrait. "Everything is all right here," he said, "but I would appreciate it if you would stay close by awhile and hold this for me."

Petronilla's eyes flashed with anger.

"Why, Petronilla, this is a side of you we have not seen before."

"You haven't stolen my personal property before."

"I was told you have a vindictive nature. I am not certain I believed it till now."

She worked to compose herself, and the work showed. "I'm sorry, Merlin. It's just that . . . I love him, that's all."

"So it really does represent a French paramour?"

"Of course." She was trembling with anger and tried to hide it.

"That is interesting. When I first saw it I thought it might be Lancelot."

"No!"

"Well, you know how imprecise artists can be. Most of their work could represent almost anyone."

"Yes. But it is—"

"I am afraid your meals will be served to you here from now on." He smiled benevolently. "For your own protection, The king does not want you exposed to any danger."

"And will my meals consist of bread and water?"

"Now, now, Petronilla. You are a valuable witness. We

can hardly afford to have anything happen to you. If Lancelot should come to trial, we shall certainly require your testimony."

Finally she managed to compose herself. "You said you're not certain he is the killer. I told you what I saw. How could there be any doubt?"

"This is England, Petronilla. Arthur's England. You know the reputation we have for fairness and justice. If a man is accused of a crime, we go to every length to make absolutely positive he is guilty before we punish him. With a capital crime like this one . . ."

"I suppose that makes sense."

"It does. You know it. We are making a new kind of nation here. If we were not—if what we have built is arbitrary and can be set aside at the will of the monarch or on the word of a secretary—then it counts for nothing at all."

She pouted slightly. "Leonilla would have had his head by now."

"Leonilla is not Arthur. Her France, though it is only across the Channel, is a million miles from Arthur's England. Please, you must be patient. This confinement will end soon enough. I will have books brought. Or music. Whatever you want. I hardly want this to be unpleasant for you."

"He did it. He killed the king." She said it with perfect conviction.

"Of course he did. We will have proof of that—incontrovertible proof—soon enough."

"What? What proof?"

"In good time. More than just the world of one witness."

When he left her she seemed reassured. He hoped it was not another act of hers.

"So what have you discovered? And what do you suspect?" Arthur hooked a leg over the arm of his throne and drank wine, deeply.

"Frankly, Arthur, it is a tangle. There are several reasons to think Lancelot might not be guilty, and heaven knows there are enough other suspects. But . . ."

"Yes?"

"I want him to be the killer. Executing him would solve so many of our problems. Who knows—it might even tame Guenevere."

"My loving wife will not be broken so easily. She thrives on treachery the way mosquitoes thrive on blood."

"Apt metaphor."

"How could it not be? I'm married to the bitch."

"I believe," Merlin said slowly, "that is what is known as a diplomatic miscalculation. Not to mention a sexual one. There was actually a time when I thought her beautiful myself. That was before I saw the evil in her eyes. Can I have some of that wine?"

Surprise registered in the king's face. "You? You want a drink? Have you forgotten all your temperance lectures?"

"The last two days have been . . . tense. How is Colin coping with all the delegates?"

Arthur took up the skin and poured a cup for Merlin. "I feel a bit guilty putting all the burden on him. But he's doing a bang-up job. Keeping them all happy, or as happy as they are capable of being, making them feel important. I've had private audiences with most of them by now. They've even stopped complaining about the bloody rain."

"Good. Now if only the rain itself would stop. Half the country is flooded. We're getting reports from farther and farther north and west."

"Of course, that is not to say they are all happy, or even content." Arthur took a deep drink. "They never seem to stop squabbling, like a pack of old widows."

"You wanted England to be a player in Europe, not me. Left alone on our tight little island with its dreadful weather, we could have finished building the society we want."

"Don't start."

Merlin told him about Guenevere's attempt to meet with Podarthes. "She says they're old friends from Constantinople. She wants to catch up on his life, nothing more. She says."

"Good God, and she expected you to believe that?" Arthur put his cup down loudly, eyed it, then picked it up again. "She hasn't been there since she was sixteen, two or three thousand years ago. And even then, she was as unimportant as any of Justinian's 'guests.' Did you know, by the way, he's just issued an edict officially closing all the Athenian schools of philosophy?"

Merlin fell silent for a moment; distress showed in his face. "I hadn't heard, no. He is remaking the world as he wants it, and that is not good for the world. As long as surfaces are gilded, why worry that the wood underneath is rotting? But the Byzantines have always preferred style to substance. Court ceremonial matters to them more than political philosophy ever could. But suppose she was not?"

Arthur blinked. "Suppose who was not what?"

"Guenevere. Unimportant."

"What do you mean? A pubescent girl from a backward French province? It must have taken them months to get the mud off her, Merlin."

"No wonder you fell in love with her."

"If you have a point, Merlin, make it."

He took a deep draft of his wine. "Listen, we know well enough how the Byzantines operate. They spin webs—the more elaborate the better—and they wait. Like venomous spiders, they wait. Suppose they have always had their eye on France, or England. When this green princess fell into their lap, it was too good to be true. They nurtured her, coddled her, planned ways to use her. It occurs to me that your marriage may even have been their idea."

"No, alas, that was my own work."

"But you see what I am suggesting. Perhaps all these

years she has been their agent, waiting, plotting, hoping to deliver France or England—or both—into their hands. It would explain her secret correspondence with them, and their eagerness to recognize her as ruler of England, and if she knew or believed she had their backing, it would explain all the treasonous plots she has hatched."

Arthur leaned forward and peered at him. "And would it explain why she killed her father? You saw what he was like, Merlin. He would have been dead soon enough anyway."

"That is a problem for the theory, granted. We have other suspects, but none of them seems as likely as Guenevere. I want her to be the culprit—along with her pet knight."

Arthur slouched back and closed his eyes. "The webs are all around us. Keep working, keep untangling them. It would be nice to have something to announce to the delegates at the plenary meeting tonight. And you know tomorrow is the final session of our little diplomatic gathering. I don't suppose you could promise me to have the killer by then?"

"I wish it were possible."

"It is. It must be."

"You know I will do my best, Arthur."

"Of course. But try to do a little better than that, will you?"

Late afternoon. Nimue, in her guise as Colin, had just finished pouring water on another minor diplomatic fire. As she walked past the entrance to the refectory, she decided something sweet would make a nice little reward.

She caught the eye of a serving girl. "Are there any of those honey cakes Arthur always has you make for him?"

"Yes, sir. Shall I fetch some?"

"Please."

Waiting for the girl to return from the kitchen, she spotted Jean-Michel sitting alone in a corner, eating a bowl of soup. She put on a wide smile and crossed to him. "Hello. It's a bit early for dinner, isn't it?"

He looked up; the expression on his face and his body language both said he was tired. "Oh. It's—Colin, isn't it?"

She nodded. "You look like you haven't been getting much sleep. You could almost be one of my staff."

He yawned. "Sorry. I'm afraid the queen has been keeping me busy."

She narrowed her eyes. "So what they say about you and your . . . duties . . . is all true?"

"Leonilla is a queen. Rulers have favorites. I am hers."

"There are times I wish the world I move in was not quite so devoted to euphemism."

Jean-Michel laughed at this. Nimue found it odd; she hadn't meant it as a joke. "At least you only have one person to keep happy," Nimue said. "I've spent the last hour mediating a dispute between Morgan le Fay and Bishop Gildas. Neither of them is exactly filled with the milk of human kindness."

"They are rivals. If I were more cynical I would say business rivals."

"For the moment, Morgan holds the franchise. But the thought of a new religion taking root here clearly has her worried."

"As well she might be. But really, you would all be so much better off under the Christian Church. Have you looked into it?"

"I'm afraid I haven't." She resisted the temptation to make a wisecrack. "It hardly seems to have improved the morals of Guenevere."

"Love is love, Colin. She loves Lancelot."

"And an oath is an oath. She swore to love and obey Arthur. But her damned schemes never end. Even now, under heavy guard, she is trying to nurture her plots. Frankly I'm surprised she hasn't tried to meet with Leonilla."

He blinked. "You think she would do that?"

"If it were to her advantage, I think she would cut off her own leg."

"No, but I mean . . . You don't know about her and her mother? They are not exactly close."

"What do you mean? Leonilla has been behind most of her treachery since she came to England and married the king."

Jean-Michel sipped his soup. "They are rival queens, Colin. There is no love lost between them, none at all."

"They are rival *French* queens. It has never been much of a secret that they wanted to extend France's territory across the Channel, into the British Isles."

"That was the original plan, yes. But ever since Leonilla realized that would make her daughter more powerful than she is herself . . ." Suddenly he stammered and blushed. "I mean . . . I imagine . . . I mean . . . I'm sorry . . . I'm tired."

"I understand perfectly what you mean." She bit into her honey cake. "They're not making these as sweet as they used to. Honey is scarce this season."

"Nothing is as sweet as it used to be."

She laughed. "You sound like Merlin."

"I don't mean to. He was questioning me today and trying to sound like he wasn't. I hope I never become so obvious."

She refrained from commenting on this. "Merlin is quite a brilliant man in many ways. He has found some old plans drawn up by Hero of Alexandria. He thinks he may actually be able to build working models of his steam engines."

"Steam engines?" He made a sour face. "What on earth for?"

"Spoken like a member of the French court. Do you have any idea what will happen to Leonilla now? Does she still have enough influence to keep her throne?"

He smiled a wide smile. "I certainly hope so. Whatever would become of me if the nobles depose her?"

"There's always Guenevere." She said it without thinking.

"Guenevere is spoken for."

"Twice over." She grinned back at him. "If you get my drift."

Suddenly his own smile vanished. "When will Lancelot go to trial?"

"As quickly as possible. A matter of weeks, probably. It will involve assembling a jury of his peers. We are summoning a party of Arthur's knights from Camelot."

"Ah, the famous Knights of the Round Table."

"Yes, exactly. And preparing the case against him will take time. Merlin is to prosecute, and he won't be able to give it his full attention till the last of the delegates is gone."

"I should have thought the case was open-and-shut."

"There is some doubt whether Lancelot is the actual killer, it seems. Merlin wants an airtight case. But I shouldn't be talking about it."

"It is quite all right, Colin, You can trust me. So there are other suspects in the murder?"

"As I said, it isn't something I should discuss. Eat too much of that soup and you won't be hungry for supper."

"I'll eat light. I usually do. The queen likes me to stay trim."

"Oh, to have the problems of a queen."

"My queen, at least." He stood to go. "It would hardly be pleasant having Guenevere's problems, would it?"

Just as he reached the door she had a flash of insight. She asked him, "What exactly is your position at Leonilla's court, Jean-Michel?"

"I'm an ordinary courtier, nothing more. As lowly as they come."

She decided to take a chance and repeat one of the bits of gossip she's heard from the servants. "That's funny. I heard a rumor you were the court jeweler."

An expression of alarm crossed his face; he worked to conceal it. "Jeweler? Whoever could have told you such a thing?"

"I'm not sure I remember. It was just a shred of idle gossip, that's all. I'll see you tonight."

Looking concerned, he told her he'd make a point of looking for her.

Nimue brought Merlin and the king up to date on what she'd learned from Jean-Michel as the king was dressing for dinner. Greffys helped him into his ceremonial robes.

"We've always assumed Guenevere and Leonilla were working together. He says they're not, at least not recently."

Arthur gaped at her. "My lady wife is not the brightest of women. It's difficult to believe she has hatched all these plots on her own."

"She is an extraordinarily cunning woman, Arthur." Merlin, like the king, was puzzled by the news.

"Yes, Merlin, but cunning is not quite the same thing as intelligence, is it? A bigamous marriage to Lancelot was hardly a clever move."

"As you have pointed out yourself often enough, Arthur, Lancelot is not exactly an intellectual. He is handsome, to be sure, and he is a superb athlete, but that handsome face has never been clouded by thought."

Arthur was finished dressing. He sent Greffys away, then turned back to Merlin. "Can you imagine Guenevere conducting serious diplomatic relations with Justinian? It's not as if he needs her. He has inscrutable Lithuanians."

Merlin laughed and said, "I suppose you are right, Arthur. You usually are, when it comes to Guenevere."

"Besides, most of the evidence still points to Lancelot as the killer of Leodegrance."

Merlin leaned back in his chair and closed his eyes. "It

keeps coming back to the murder weapon, in my mind. It was not Lancelot's knife. But does that really mean so much? His knife and Guenevere's are identical but for tiny inscriptions. They could easily have switched them without realizing it. I had to use one of my lenses to be certain what the inscription said. Then there is our witness—if we can believe her."

Nimue looked at him and smiled. "By the way, I think—and this is only a guess—but I suspect Jean-Michel might be Leonilla's court jeweler."

Arthur grumped. "What of that?"

But Merlin caught her drift. "Do you suppose he might have made those knives?"

Arthur's shoulders slumped. "Fine. Another complication." He looked at Nimue. "How certain are you of this?"

"Not at all certain. But when I asked him he looked mildly frightened, as if some secret had gotten out, and he left at once."

"That's wonderful," Merlin said. "Just what I need is another wrinkle in this matter."

"You sound as if you want a simple case. It's too late for that."

"I suppose I do. There is too much evidence against Lancelot. Even without Petronilla's testimony. He was the only one there. It comes down to that simple fact, really—that and the knife." He shifted his weight and yawned. "I need to get more sleep."

"One more day of these people, then we can all get a good rest." Arthur put an ermine-trimmed cape around his shoulders.

"Let us hope the rain does not keep them here."

"All this polite diplomacy is wearing me down. Oh—I've canceled most of the formal agenda for tonight, all the speechmaking and such. There will be music, dancing, a little play and very little else. I'll announce it at dinner. We could all use a break from this damnable intrigue."

"Excellent idea, Arthur. Let us hope they all get good and drunk. Have you been outside lately?"

Arthur stared at him and blinked. "Of course not. I'm not an otter."

"The rain is slowing. If it keeps tailing off, it will be finished by morning."

"Excellent. These people can leave for sure, then."

"Once all these bloody flash floods subside. And we'll have to send someone down to the harbor to take toll of the damage done there. Let us hope all their ships are seaworthy."

Nimue said, "One sank, remember?"

Suddenly a guard entered. He was obviously nervous. He quickly saluted the king. "Your Majesty."

Arthur fussed with Excalibur. "What is it?"

"I regret to inform you, sire . . ."

"Yes? Out with it. Has one of the cooks stolen some eggs? Has my prize cow's milk gone dry?"

"None of that, Your Majesty."

"Get to the damned point, man."

The guard swallowed nervously. "It's . . . it's . . . Lancelot, Your Majesty. He has escaped."

Arthur grabbed him by the shoulder and shook him violently. "What?"

"Somehow—we don't know how—he got away from his guards."

Arthur let go of the guard and closed his eyes, obviously trying to contain his anger. "Guenevere bribed them somehow. Or he did himself. Or—"

Merlin got to his feet. "We must mobilize every guard in the castle. And I will have Brit tighten security outside. If there should be another incident . . ."

"Incident?" Arthur glared at him. "Is that really the word you want? Shouldn't you say murder?"

"Call it what you will, we cannot afford it." He took a step toward the door.

"And while you're at it have Captain Dalley double the guard on Guenevere. No, triple it. And make certain they're guards we can trust. If *both* of them should escape . . ."

"Not a pleasant prospect. I will see to it at once."

"And, for God's sake, make sure no one tells any of the delegates. I don't want them nervous. And I don't want them thinking we're so careless."

"Yes, Arthur."

Merlin left. After a moment Arthur asked the man, "How on earth did it happen?"

The guard shrugged. "Someone must have helped him, obviously."

"Obviously. But who? And how?"

"Should I investigate, sir?"

"No. Britomart will want to do that herself." He dismissed the guard and looked around for Greffys. Remembering he had sent the squire away, he found a wineskin and poured himself a large cup. The wine was sour; he made a face and spit it out.

The dining hall was crowded. A few of the delegates had noticed the rain easing off, and word spread among the rest of them quickly. As a result, spirits were sufficiently high enough that no one noticed or paid attention to the extra, eavesdropping servants circulating with more wine, ale and mead than usual.

Arthur entered and took his seat at the head table, flanked by Merlin and Britomart. At once the staff began to serve dinner—more roast beef, and it was particularly succulent that evening. After a few moments of waiting for what Brit described as "softening them up with food and drink," Arthur stood, the musicians played a fanfare and he began a short speech.

First he confirmed what they already knew, that the rainstorm was finally ending. He assured them that, as of the next morning, they would be more than welcome to come and go as they pleased, the only proviso being that there might still be minor flash floods in the region and that his soldiers would do reconnaissance before any of the visiting delegates would be permitted to travel anywhere but to the harbor.

Next he announced with apparent pleasure that there would be no formal agenda for that night's plenary meeting. "Minstrels and troubadors will entertain you, there will be more food and more wine, and you will experience British hospitality at its best."

Of Lancelot's escape he said nothing. There seemed no point alarming the assembled diplomats, and as he had noted, he wanted them to take home with them the most favorable impression of England possible.

While he was speaking Merlin surveyed the audience for reaction. He leaned behind Arthur and whispered to Brit, "Would you like to bet that Podarthes will not have anything favorable to report to his emperor? Look, he hasn't even bothered to come to dinner."

"He's a Byzantine, Merlin. English cooking is probably too simple for him."

Just at that moment one of Britomart's lieutenants entered the hall and hurried to her side. He whispered something in her ear, and her face turned to stone. She stood as unobtrusively as she could and moved to Merlin's side, where she repeated what her man had told her. A look of deep concern crossed his face, and he got to his feet, too.

A moment later they were outside in the main corridor, rushing to the wing where the Byzantines were quartered.

Podarthes's men were gathered in the hallway around the door to his suite. None of them seemed to be talking; the ones at the rear of the crowd were craning their necks to see inside. Merlin noticed Leonilla's maid, Marthe, among them.

Brit rushed ahead of Merlin and pushed through them.

At once she turned and shouted, "Merlin—quickly!" The men in the hall parted to let him through.

He was not prepared for what he saw. On the floor, in formal court dress, evidently ready to go to dine, lay Podarthes. Blood covered his body and the floor around him. And plunged into his throat was a golden dagger with an ivory handle, identical to the one that had been used to assassinate Leodegrance.

"Three," Merlin whispered to Brit. "We now have three of these knives. Of which there should only be two."

NINE

Over the next day the rain stopped almost completely, though there were still occasional showers. But the cloud cover did not break up; it seemed to everyone it actually got thicker and heavier. The day never grew brighter than twilight.

Across the countryside the floods began to subside. Rivers and streams began slowly to return to their accustomed levels. But the ground was soaked; more rain would inevitably lead to more flooding. Towns and villages were mired in thick mud. Animals drowned in it or were so deeply entrapped it was impossible to rescue them. And there were people lost to it, too.

At Camelot, on its prominent hilltop, everyone and everything was safe. But the old castle leaked water; servants were busy trying to swab it up. But it seemed to leak in faster than the household staff could cope. Sir Sagramore and Sir Accolon, who had been left in charge in the absence of Arthur and his chief advisors, gamely pitched in to help with the clean-up efforts. Only mad old King Pellenore seemed unaffected by the disastrous storm and its aftermath; he went on as usual, chasing phantom monsters and imaginary demons, cheerfully ignoring every suggestion that there might be a more immediate danger to be dealt with.

But even though the storm appeared to have passed, the countryside surrounding Camelot was quite effectively flooded. Huge pools of water covered the landscape. Roads were washed out; to travel any distance from the capital became virtually impossible. Sagramore sent word to Arthur at Corfe that a group of knights would join him there for the trial as soon as the roads were comfortably passable, but he did not hold out hope that it would happen in less than a week, and most probably longer. No one could imagine how long it would take the messenger to reach Corfe.

In the town of Corfe, in the shadow of Guenevere's castle, recovery efforts began almost as soon as the weather permitted, under the direction of Captain Dalley. Soldiers from the garrison helped clear the streets; thick inches of mud had accumulated. And a special team of military engineers worked to assess the damage to the harbor and plan ways to correct it.

The ship that had sunk and blocked off the harbor mouth was of course still there. Divers—men able to hold their breath for long periods without losing consciousness or experiencing vertigo—swam down to the wreck and inspected it. It turned out to be an Italian ship, the one that had brought Andrea of Salesi. Crews dove down to it with chains and hooks to attempt to secure it so that crews on shore could haul it out of the way of commerce.

Britomart came down from the castle on the day they did their work. Captain Dalley walked with her to a hill that overlooked the harbor's entrance, where they watched the progress through a pair of Merlin's "viewing lenses," and he explained the procedure. "If we had more time, we'd actually send men down to cut the ship to pieces. Dragging the parts out would be easier than moving the whole ship. But it would take time to prepare for that; the engineers work slowly and methodically. And you want this done as speedily as possible."

Brit watched the harbor and the men working. The ship's upper mast was protruding from the water; otherwise it was quite submerged. "The sooner we clear the harbor, the sooner we can send these damned diplomats on their way. Can't we dismantle the ship later?"

"They have been that much of a problem?"

"I would call two murders a problem, yes. Not to mention all the nonstop bickering and infighting. When I was a young girl in London I once saw a pack of widows ransack a dead man's house. They stole everything they could move—and some of them brought their daughters along to help. It was as ugly a spectacle as I've ever seen. And these diplomats were worse than that." She sighed and looked at Dalley. "How long will it take you to pull the ship far enough aside to permit commerce again?"

"Well, it's a question of main force. It will depend on how badly it is mired in the muck. And of course it would be almost impossible to pull it completely out of the water. Our best bet is simply to pull it as far to one side as we can, as you say, enough to open the harbor to its regular flow of traffic—or nearly so. It may be too much to hope that we can open it completely. If everything goes well, your diplomatic visitors should be able to start leaving within four or five days.."

"Good. Now I have to get back to the castle to give Andrea of Salesi the news that he'll have to swim home."

"Better you than me, Brit."

And so she gave the Salesian the news, and to her relief he was not very upset by it. "Well, then, I can send word to Salesi with one of the other delegates when they leave.

Several of them pass through the Strait of Messina. In the meantime, I am afraid I shall have to remain your guest."

"You'll have to discuss that with Merlin."

"Of course."

Still, though the country was soaked in muck and mire, though harbors were blocked and trade at a standstill, to most people the end of the rainstorm seemed like the dawn of a new day,

To all except Merlin that is. He had the murders of a king and an ambassador to unravel.

He was in an ill humor when Brit explained the situation to him. He listened patiently, then harrumphed. "Let us hope Andrea is the only one who wants to remain here. I can't tell you how deeply sick I am of them all."

"You're a minister of the crown, Merlin. You are not permitted to be sick of official visitors."

"That is what you think."

On the next afternoon sunlight finally broke through the clouds. The clouds did not dissipate; they only thinned. The sun's disc shone like a ghost of itself. Shafts of brilliant silver light poured down, not quite reaching the earth, it seemed, not illuminating it in any but a transitory way, but it was sunlight. To everyone who saw it, it seemed mildly miraculous.

In his cell Lancelot paced constantly, thinking—or trying to think—about the awful fact that he had been arrested for a second murder, of which he protested he was quite innocent, to no effect whatsoever. Then he saw the light coming from outside.

The only window in his cell, a narrow one, was high in the wall facing south, He scrambled to pile the room's scant furniture and climbed. He pressed his face to the barred window and watched the sky. The sun, in its weakened state, gave no warmth, only wan light. Before many minutes passed, the clouds closed again and the light was gone.

But he had seen a trace of the heavens' warmth, and it gave him hope. Somehow, someone would find the evidence needed to prove his innocence and free him. He and Guenevere would be king and queen one day; England would be theirs.

Like Lancelot, Petronus paced in his room. From the boy's perspective, the guards at his door seemed to have been there forever. But when he saw the sky lighten, weak as the light was, he became excited. He ran out of his room and shouted, "The sun is out! Quick, let's run and see it." But the soldiers pushed him back inside, and that was that.

His sister, Petronilla, sat by her window and studied that portrait of Lancelot. Candles burned. When the sunlight came, she did not bother to extinguish them. The daylight would be gone again soon enough.

Throughout the castle the various delegates and their attendants realized there was sunlight outside. They stopped what they were doing and moved to the windows like bees to clover. They would be out of this place yet. They would be home well before the midwinter holidays.

Guenevere's rooms faced north, so she did not see the sunlight, what there was of it. But from her windows she saw the sky lighten briefly. It was a sign; she told herself that. A new day. A new future, nowhere near as bleak as the one she had faced through the awful recent weeks.

And in her bedroom, alone among the castle's inhabitants and guests, Leonilla slept, lovingly watched over by Jean-Michel. She had become increasingly distracted and her behavior more and more erratic—aimlessly walking about the castle at all hours, muttering loudly to herself, seeming to recognize no one but her young man. It was more and more difficult for him and her other retainers to take care of her.

Britomart and her men found a place where the castle

ground was firmer, less yielding, less pervious to the rain-water; it was possible for them to exercise there. She joined the knights at their drill, and to work out seemed the most liberating thing she could imagine. When the sun came, that only made it better. For the first time since the conference began, her mood was buoyant.

Even Arthur, anxious for his numerous guests to leave, eager to return to Camelot, keen to find a village girl along the way and make love to her, saw the sun as giving promise. So when Merlin came to his rooms in his usual dark mood, the king did not want to hear him.

"Arthur, we are facing a difficult situation. All these days of darkness have depleted our supply of candles and oil."

"Look outside, for heaven's sake. That bright object in the sky is the sun. Don't you recognize it?"

"Even the sun will go down. Another few days—and nights—and Corfe Castle will be dark. And that's not to mention that food is running low. If these bloody delegates do not leave soon, we will be in real trouble. And I do not see how they *can* leave soon. The harbor—"

"Why are you bothering me with this? Tell Simon. He'll know what to do."

"Simon is the one who told me."

"Then what's the problem? I can't pull candles out of my crown."

"Arthur, I—"

"The delegates can't leave. Fine. Much as I'd like to see the back of them, you have the opportunity to ask questions about this latest murder. Let Simon worry about oil for the torches; I want you to draft a letter to Justinian informing him of Podarthes's death, apologizing and promising to bring the assassin to justice. If he decides we are somehow at fault, we could face an invasion come springtime."

"So much for the sun's promise."

"Stop it, will you, Merlin? The last thing I need now is one more person picking at me."

"One more, Arthur?"

"Morgan is whining about Gildas. Brit wants more men to help move that damned ship in the harbor, and I don't have any to give her. That squirrelly Lithuanian is complaining about—well, the gods only know what he's complaining about. But he's been showing up here every hour or two. And I've got the Byzantines to worry about. Just—just—just draft that letter, will you? Come up with something to mollify them, or at least stall them. You know perfectly well we could never stand up to their army for long."

"You know I will do what I can, Arthur. But—"

"Then do it. And don't give me any of your usual grief. The last thing I need now is someone else— I told you that already."

So Merlin left him and returned to his own study, grateful that at least Arthur was not drinking again.

One by one the delegates lined up for audiences with Arthur, Merlin or both. When would the harbor be open? When could they leave? Why were the portions at meals growing smaller? Bishop Gildas complained about drafts in his bedroom and announced that he wanted the cracks in the walls stopped up since he would be residing there permanently.

Merlin smiled. "Surely our 'bishop' should reside at Camelot, at the seat of power."

"I prefer Corfe."

"Nevertheless, this is Guenevere's castle, at least for the time being. Where she will reside in future has yet to be determined. We would not want you quartered here in a way that would be against your own best interest. No, if you are to remain in England, residence at Camelot is the thing."

Gildas bristled, and Merlin enjoyed it. He knew that Gildas was likely to side with Guenevere, given the opportunity, and Gildas knew that he knew it. "But King Arthur is not a Christian. I would hardly wish to embarrass him with my presence."

"No one in England is a Christian, with the exception of Guenevere and a few of her followers."

"Then I should reside with them, to minister to their spiritual needs."

"Gildas, you are here on King Arthur's sufferance. It would not be wise for you to cross his wishes. Not if you want to remain 'Bishop of England.' As I understand the protocols of the Christian Church, he should have been consulted before you were even sent here."

"We consulted with the queen."

"Precisely. You see the problem?"

Unsatisfied, Gildas left. But he made a point of promising further discussion on the matter.

A few hours later Merlin was in conference with Arthur when, amid a great deal of perplexing babble, the Lithuanian strode past Simon of York and into the king's chambers. Grandly he sat his squat body down and smiled; his reason was not clear.

Then, slowly, and in perfect, unaccented English, he said, "This chair is not comfortable at all, Your Majesty. You should have a better one for visitors."

Arthur registered surprise; Merlin did not. While the king collected himself, Merlin took charge of the exchange. "You speak English." It was an accusation.

"Yes, I'm afraid I do." The man looked vaguely shamefaced. "Since I am now in charge of the Byzantine delegation, due to the unfortunate demise of my colleague Podarthes, it seemed advisable to abandon my cover."

Merlin lowered his voice. "You realize this is tantamount to an admission that you are a spy."

"Have been. I have been a spy. Now I am the acting Ambassador Plenipotentiary of His Serene Majesty Justinian."

Arthur turned to a servant and asked for wine—for himself, not for his councilor or his guest. Then he turned to the Lithuanian. "So you admit it. We would be fully within our rights to arrest you on a charge of espionage."

"And face the wrath of my emperor? Belisarius and the army are on the border of France even as we speak. They could be here in a matter of days."

"International law—"

"With respect, Your Majesty, there is no such thing. International law corresponds to the will of the strongest nation."

There was a long moment of silence. Then Merlin asked, "May we know the name of the new ambassador, then?"

He made a slight bow to the king and then to Merlin. "My name is Eudathius of Ephesus."

"I believe I have heard of you." Merlin did not try to disguise his irritation. "An astrologer, are you not?"

"Among other things. At any rate, with the political situation in Europe changed as it has been by the deaths of Leodegrance and Podarthes—"

"Changed? Changed how?" Merlin was letting his annoyance show more and more clearly.

"With Leodegrance out of the picture, the political structure in France is, shall we say, in a state of flux. I mean, yes, it usually is, but even more so than usual now. I am afraid his grieving widow will soon find herself out of power."

It took a moment for the implications to register. "And Podarthes?"

"The late ambassador was to have cemented a relationship among King Leodegrance, Queen Guenevere and Byzantium. Obviously that is not longer feasible."

"Obviously."

"We wish to negotiate with . . ." He smiled like a shy schoolgirl. ". . . with you."

"With your army threatening us from across the channel." Arthur was deadpan.

Eudathius shrugged. "Diplomatic insurance."

The king leaned forward. "So the death of Podarthes has served to advance your own career."

"That would be a cynical way of looking at the matter, Your Majesty."

"Then tell us, is there some reason why we should not suspect you of his murder?"

It seemed to catch him off guard. "You are joking. Are you not?"

"You would hardly be the first Byzantine court official to advance his career by such means."

"But—but surely you have the culprit in custody. Lancelot did the murder and we all know it."

Merlin followed Arthur's lead. "The evidence, I am afraid, is inconclusive. Lancelot had no conceivable motive for killing Podarthes. You, on the other hand . . . How generous of you to explain your own motive to us just now."

Eudathius tried to sound forbidding. "I remind you, both of you, that you should not act rashly. You are dealing with Byzantium, not some minor French province. We are not so easily intimidated. Justinian would be most displeased to learn that his representative is being treated in this insolent way. And I urge you to remember that Belisarius is not far away."

"You may have an army in France," Arthur said in equally ominous tones, "but we most certainly have you. Call your army. Do you think they will hear you? Will they come? We could have you tried and executed for espionage before Belisarius could launch a single ship.

"I would advise you to return to your quarters. Merlin is investigating this second murder as well as the first one. You are hereby advised that you are under suspicion."

Incensed, his dignity affronted, muttering vague threats, Eudathius stood to go.

But Merlin could not resist a parting jab. "For a Byzantine 'ambassador plenipotentiary,' even an acting one, you are not very good at this, Eudathius. Justinian would be mortified."

Without a word Eudathius stomped out of the room.

Arthur turned to Merlin. "Well, well. What on earth are we to make of that?"

"So these murders may lead to war." Merlin frowned. "Guenevere may end up in charge here after all. May the gods help England."

"Not to mention us, ourselves, Merlin. If there should be a war, we would certainly be defeated. How could we withstand a force like the army of Byzantium under the most formidable general in Europe? A victorious Eudathius would surely want our heads."

"He can have mine. Death would be more of a relief than I can say."

"Provocative as philosophy. Worthless as a strategy. How certain are you that Lancelot killed Podarthes?"

Merlin shrugged. "He escaped his confinement. Podarthes was killed with his knife. I have inspected the murder weapon, and it is inscribed quite clearly *G to L*; it is Lancelot's. Until a few moments ago there was no reason to suspect anyone else. And I am still not certain . . . I mean, would even a Byzantine be quite so obvious about murder as career advancement?"

"The Byzantines and the French are in league in some way, or have been. I wish we could pin it down more precisely."

Merlin looked at him suspiciously. "You are suggesting that the French may have provided Eudathius with another of those knives?"

"We have three of the damned things already. Who knows how many more might exist?"

Deeply Merlin sighed. "Why is murder never simple and clear cut?"

"Why isn't diplomacy, for that matter? But it isn't. Find out what you can about those knives, will you? And ask Germanicus what he knows about Eudathius. They have obviously never met, but . . . our hope of untangling even the first assassination before the delegates leave is vanishing before our eyes. I still want everything solved, no matter now messy it becomes, and no matter how much time it takes."

"Yes, Arthur."

"Maybe you could use your magical powers."

"That is not funny."

"Smile, Merlin. You are always the one to be a wise-ass. Give me a turn, will you?"

"I suppose I deserve that. But what on earth are we to make of what we have just heard? How much of it can we believe?"

"As little as possible, without independent confirmation."

"One thing seems certain: His position among our Byzantine guests is not as secure as he would like us to believe. Otherwise, why would it have taken him two days before he revealed himself and came to us?"

Arthur leaned back and stretched. "I am not made for all this intrigue. I'm a soldier, a warrior."

"Unfortunately you may have to put those skills to the test before long."

A moment later Simon of York put his head in the doorway. "Excuse me, Your Majesty, but the French gentleman is requesting a moment of your time. Yours and Merlin's."

"French gentleman?" Arthur laughed. "Is there such a creature?"

Jean-Michel appeared in the doorway behind Simon. "Your Majesty, please. It is most important."

Arthur glanced at Merlin, who gave a slight nod. "Very

well. Come in. But I'm afraid we can't give you more than a few minutes. Merlin here has important work to do."

Jean-Michel stepped in, and Arthur gestured to a seat.

"Thank you, Your Majesty. I . . . I must ask a favor on behalf of the queen."

"You do mean Leonilla, don't you? Because if you're looking for a 'favor' for my wife, you can—"

Merlin, afraid Arthur might say too much, decided to interrupt. "What exactly does Her Majesty require, Jean-Luc?"

"Jean-Michel. Well, we have had . . . There has been news from France, and the situation there is not good."

"So it is good news for England, then?"

The young man seemed puzzled by this. "No, not at all. It appears the Byzantine army has crossed the border into France. Their advance agents are everywhere. They are threatening—"

Arthur leaned forward. "Where in France? Which part? After all, Gaul is divided into three parts." He turned slightly to Merlin. "You see? I have not completely ignored classical learning."

Merlin kept his attention on the young Frenchman. "Where are they?"

"Reports indicate Belisarius has entered the country through Alsace, sir."

"They are not really close to Camelliard, then."

"Not yet, sir, but they appear to be moving that way. Our intelligence was dated a week ago. And it seems they have been in secret contact with one of the queen's most bitter rivals, the Archduchess of Mendola."

"The—? I've not heard of her before. What do you know about her?"

"She is young, comparatively, only in her forties. And she is the most treacherous woman in France, if not in Europe."

Merlin wrinkled his nose. "What is more poisonous than

a French queen? But can she really be worse than
Leonilla?"

Jean-Michel ignored the dig. "She has poisoned three of
her own children who were gaining power and influence.
She has been envious of Queen Leonilla for years. And our
intelligence indicates the Byzantines plan to put her on the
throne of Camelliard. With our province as well as her own,
she would threaten the balance of power in all of Western
Europe."

Merlin wrinkled his brow and said softly, "Interesting."
Then he leaned close to Arthur and they had quick, whispered exchange. "But, Jean-Paul."

The young man rolled his eyes but said only, "Yes,
Merlin?"

"What is the source of this intelligence? How can we
know how reliable it is?"

"I'm afraid I cannot reveal that, sir."

"And how on earth did it reach you? Corfe has been cut
off from the rest of the world for—"

"You should never underestimate other nations, sir. Our
intelligence network—"

"Is frightfully efficient, yes. At any rate, we can discuss
that later. You are not to leave the castle without our express
permission, do you understand? What exactly can we do for
you now?"

He was not receiving the reception he had expected. Uncertainly he said, "Well, sir, it is the queen. You've surely
seen how terribly her mind has deteriorated over these last
awful weeks. Now, with this political situation at home . . .
I'm not at all certain she'll be able to hold her throne."

Arthur smiled and did not try to disguise it. "My poor
mother-in-law. So what do you want from us?"

Jean-Michel paused for a long moment, then said quietly, "Asylum."

"Asylum? For Leonilla or yourself?"

"For both of us, Your Majesty." He looked at Merlin. "I

told you, sir, I love her like a mother. That is what she has always been to me."

Merlin and Arthur huddled again. Jean-Michel watched them closely. Merlin asked him, "Do you know anything more concrete about this Archduchess of—?"

"Mendola. That Archduchess of Mendola."

"Exactly. Does she pose an immediate danger to England? Do her ambitions reach in our direction? Or will she have to spend time solidifying her position in France?"

Jean-Michel shrugged. "I've told you before, Merlin. I avoid politics."

"That is unfortunate, since your future seems to depend on all this political maneuvering."

"I know it, sir. I have been a poor servant to my queen."

"Yet you come here asking for political asylum."

Jean-Michel blushed exactly like a young lover. "Yes."

"I see." Arthur had not stopped smiling. "We will take your request under advisement. You may go."

"But . . . but . . . Your Majesty, she is your wife's mother."

"That is not something you should remind me of too often, not if you want her to reside here permanently. You are dismissed."

The young man stood to go. But Merlin put a hand on Arthur's arm. "If I may, Arthur." He turned to Jean-Michel. "We have been told that you are Queen Leonilla's court jeweler. Is that accurate?"

"Yes, sir. I am not much of one, though. She only appointed me to legitimize my presence at court. I was an apprentice to the actual court jeweler, Reynaud de Beliveau. Making jewelry has never been much more than a hobby of mine. I even—"

"But you made those knives? The ones used in the murders?"

He seemed surprised by the question. "Yes, sir."

"How many?"

"I beg your pardon, sir?"

"Knives. How many of them did you make?"

"There were prototypes. You know, tests before I made the final two, the ones that were sent to Guenevere and Lancelot."

"And where are the others?"

"In my workshop at home." Suddenly he seemed to realize where these questions were leading. "Oh, no, not even there. Beliveau told our servant to melt them down. I mean, they're gold. Not much use as knives, really, except ceremonially. Gold is too soft. But the metal and the ivory are valuable, So I—"

"How many? Three of them have surfaced here. The two for Lancelot and Guenevere's 'wedding gifts' plus one other. How many more exist?"

"I—I really couldn't say, I'm afraid. Beliveau is the real metalsmith. I—my appointment was more political."

Merlin smiled. "But you avoid politics." His voice oozed irony.

"I—I do. I am merely—"

"What? You are merely what? Is there a French term for it, or should we use the word the Greeks had?"

Clearly out of his depth, and obviously shaken, Jean-Michel fell silent. He folded his hands and stared down at the floor. "I thought you liked me."

Merlin decided it was time to soften his tone. "Jean-Pierre."

He looked up.

"You do understand why we must pursue this line of inquiry, do you not?"

"I suppose so. But I thought we were friends, At least on our way to becoming friends, To have you treat me like this, practically accusing me of—of—of I don't even know what . . . I didn't expect it from you."

"How congenial is this Beliveau? If you ask him for information, will he provide it?"

"I don't know. He was more Leodegrance's man than mine."

"Write him. At once. Ask how many knives he made and what became of them all."

"I will."

"And do it today. We will have it sent at once."

"Yes, Merlin."

"Go now."

He looked down again. "I will. Is there anything else you need me to do?"

Arthur decided to jump into the exchange. "It would help if you could convince us we can trust you. If you would tell us everything you know."

"Everything?"

"Who do you think killed Leodegrance?"

"I thought it was Lancelot. But you've confused me. I don't know anymore."

"If you think of anything else," Merlin told him sternly, "or if you learn anything else, you must tell us at once. Understand?"

"Yes, Merlin. I'm sorry you don't trust me."

"We want to, Jean-Paul. But you must help us. You must be as open as you can."

"I am. I will."

"Good. We will take your request for asylum for Leonilla and yourself under careful advisement. Go now, and write that letter to—what is his name?"

"Reynaud. Reynaud de Beliveau."

Jean-Michel left, looking rather badly shaken.

Merlin turned to Arthur. "Reynaud de Beliveau. I'll talk to Brit. She may be able to send a detachment of men to Camelliard to question him. Or better yet, to bring him here."

And so that evening Merlin had a word with Britomart. "Your men must be careful. The political situation there seems to be in, shall we say, a state of flux. Whatever contacts you have there may no longer be reliable."

"Of course," she said, looking more than slightly skeptical. "Things have been stable there till now, and Petronilla has proved so very reliable."

Merlin wrinkled his nose. "The French. They must be the most duplicitous race in the world."

"I thought that was the Byzantines."

"No wonder they are allies. But tell your men to act as swiftly as conditions permit. And make certain they understand they are to stay carefully undercover. The fluid politics may actually work in their favor. Even if some rat wants to report them, who would he report them to?"

"And you want them to bring this Beliveau back here with them?"

"Ideally, yes. But if that is not feasible, have them get a signed statement from him."

"You fascinate me, Merlin. On the one hand you want us to extract a statement from this man; on the other you want us not to use force or coercion. So does your aversion to torture or even the threat of it not extend to using it on the French?"

Merlin sighed like a man who was being questioned on a point he thought he'd already settled. "Camelot represents something new in the affairs of the world, Brit. I thought you agreed with the principles Arthur and I have tried to enact. If we abandon them because they become inconvenient sometimes, what we have built here counts for nothing."

"I do agree with them, and you know it. In what other place could a woman command the king's army? But, Merlin, you want us to extract a statement from this man, and to do it quickly, and not use force? That simply may not be possible. What do you know about him? Does he feel allegiance to Leonilla? Or to her late, lamented husband? Or to the Archduchess of Mendola, for that matter?"

"I see the difficulty; honestly, I do. All we know about

this man is what we were told by Jean-Pierre. *His* loyalties lie with Leonilla—as he does himself. But what form his loyalty takes . . . that, we have know way of knowing. Beliveau, he says, is the real court jeweler at Camelliard. Other than that, we know not a thing."

"You're sending us to France to get a statement from a man you know next to nothing about. And what little you do know, you've learned from someone you don't trust."

He smiled. "You have grasped it."

"Splendid. Merlin, you are the most infuriating man."

"I thought you might have noticed. Listen, Brit, I recognize the difficulties your men will face. But this man, this Beliveau, may hold the secret to solving these murders. It is vital that we get his statement. And you must send knights of more than average intelligence and resourcefulness. They will have to evaluate his truthfulness."

"Intelligent knights. While you're at it, why don't you ask for pigs with wings?" An idea struck her. "Better yet, why don't you go to France yourself?"

"Myself? I have considered it. In fact, I would like to. But Arthur disapproves of the idea. He says I am too valuable here. But at the same time he keeps pressing me to solve the murders."

"You want to get a good sense of what this Beliveau is like, don't you? And while you're at it, you might gain some insight into what the Byzantines are up to."

"I had not planned on going myself. But . . ."

"Give it some thought. Between the two of us, we can persuade Arthur. I'll send some soldiers with you of course. You *are* too valuable to put at unnecessary risk."

He turned thoughtful. "I have not been out of England in longer than I can remember."

"The change will do you good, then."

An idea suddenly hit him; he snapped his fingers. "There is someone I can take along, someone who knows that court and Camelliard better than any of us."

Brit looked at him skeptically. "You don't mean Petronilla?"

"No, of course not. I don't trust her as far as I could throw her horse. But . . ."

"What are you thinking? Who do you have in mind?"

"Her brother, Petronus."

Brit looked genuinely shocked. "The assassin. Oh yes, he'd make such a jolly traveling companion."

"He keeps trying to ingratiate himself, wanting to prove his loyalty. This would be as good a way to do that as any I can think of. And if he proves untrustworthy . . . Your soldiers will have knives, will they not?"

"You mean you'd execute him without a trial? Honestly, Merlin, I—"

"Only if he proves dangerous to our lives. Only if he really is treasonous, and only if there is no other way. I must think about this. And consult with Arthur, of course. But we shall have to leave soon—as soon as possible."

Her manner turned wry. "Perhaps you could disguise yourselves as Druid priests."

Oblivious to her irony, he mulled the idea and quickly rejected it. "No. We must find some hooded robes and pose as Christian monks. With our hoods up, we would be quite difficult to recognize. And the robes they wear are ideal for hiding our weapons."

She was not about to abandon her sarcasm. "You could pray the Rosary while you sharpen your knives."

"That, Brit, I will happily leave to the Byzantines." He paused for a moment. "It would be helpful if you could find some knights for me who understand several languages."

"Are you joking? These are knights we're talking about. Most of them are fine athletes, but what they're good for is physicality. Strength, force. Most of them have trouble enough speaking English. Aren't there orders of Christian priests who never talk, for some reason?"

"That is a good thought. Maybe we should encourage

Gildas to join one of them. But do your men have more discipline than you for keeping their mouths shut?"

"You're one to talk. Be quiet, Merlin."

"Petronus, I need you."

The boy looked first suspicious and then hopeful. "Me?"

Merlin nodded. "In France."

"You are sending me home?"

"No, I am *taking* you home."

The boy's confusion could not have been more evident. He stood at the window of his room, staring out at the blank sky and trying to make sense of what was happening. "You want me to spy?"

"Not exactly, no. And you will be under careful watch. I am afraid no one trusts you." He tried to put a kindly face on it; smiling, he added, "Yet. This is the chance you have been wanting to redeem yourself."

"Please, sir." He turned to face Merlin. "I don't understand this. Not at all."

"Let me sit down and I will explain, then."

"It has to do with the murders, doesn't it?"

He nodded and smiled. "Colin always says you have the quickest mind among the squires."

"He does?"

"I would not be quite so pleased if I were you. That only makes it easier to suspect you of evildoing. People are always suspicious of intelligence. Look at what happened to Socrates."

Petronus laughed at this. "People compare me to Socrates?"

"No, of course not. But being too smart or too clever always makes one supicious in the common mind. I often think that is what did in Athenian democracy. When a leader displayed too much cunning or resourcefulness, the people invariably turned on him. It was the fools, the panderers, the gulls who got embraced by the hoi polloi. But all of this is speculation. We can converse about it on our journey, if you like."

"It fascinates me. But where are we going?"

"As I said, to France." He paused, then added, "To Camelliard." He briefly explained the situation. "So, you see, a great deal depends on what we learn from this jeweler, this Beliveau. Do you know him, by chance."

Petronus nodded. "Yes, Master Beliveau. He's a nice man. Almost fatherly. He's a couple thousand years old. I never really had the inclination to socialize with him, but as a mentor and advisor he was always very nice to me. He is one of very few people I miss from Camelliard."

"I will need you to keep your eyes, ears and mind open while we are there. You must point out anyone you see behaving out of the ordinary, anyone who might be putting us in danger."

"You think there might be danger?" There was a tone of mild alarm in his voice. "I mean, I'm not much of a fighter. If anything happens—"

"We will be traveling with a dozen knights, and we will all be disguised as Christian monks."

"I'm too young to be a monk."

"You will be our novice, then. A devout, prayerful young man. Do you know much about Byzantium and its relations with Leodegrance?"

"I think it was Queen Leonilla who always managed our foreign affairs."

"Or mismanaged. Leonilla, for all her craftiness, is the kind of ruler the hoi polloi have always loved. Venomous creature that she has always been, she keeps tripping over her own intrigues. Look at all her botched attempts to make inroads in England. Venomous in small, she has never been in control of large events. I can only imagine what a mess she would have made of them. But at any rate, we will be attempting to gather intelligence on Justinian's activities. You will be a great help there, too."

"But—but suppose you can't learn what you want from Master Beliveau?"

"We must be clever. We must be devious and learn how many of those knives he made, and who he made them for. It is perfectly all right for a king's *advisors* to be clever, after all."

Arthur was uncomfortable at the thought of Merlin penetrating enemy territory, especially in company with Petronus; but he agreed, quite reluctantly, that Merlin was the person best suited to question and evaluate the jeweler. He gave his permission for Merlin to leave as quickly as the party could be readied. "And I suppose you should take the boy. If nothing else, I'll sleep easier with him in France."

"I am more and more inclined to believe he was an innocent pawn, Arthur. I do not believe he meant harm."

"We'll see, I suppose."

So on the third day Merlin, Petronus and a dozen soldiers, all wearing the robes of Christian monks, took ship at Corfe bound for France. There had been some discussion about a larger party, but there was concern that it would only make them more conspicuous, and a smaller ship could leave Corfe harbor more easily. The port was unusually busy, as various delegations readied their ships to leave England. Fortunately none of them paid the "monks" any attention.

The Channel was uncharacteristically calm when they crossed. Except for a stronger than usual south wind, the crossing was uneventful. The soldiers were commanded by Martin of Cokesbury. Merlin didn't know him well, so their conversation was limited to technical and logistical matters—the wind, the weather, what to expect when they got to France.

"I've never been to France before," Martin told him.

"No wonder Britomart chose you."

"She said she thought we'd get along. She always tells me I'm a smartass."

"The pot calling the kettle black."

"I once heard the king complain that if sarcasm were power, England could rule the world."

Petronus was excited by everything about the trip. "I can't tell you how grateful I am that you've trusted me to help on a mission this important."

"I need someone who knows Camelliard." Merlin was offhand.

"But . . . I'm still ashamed of the way I let them play me. When I think what might have happened to the king when I . . . when I . . . Thank you for trusting me, Merlin."

"That is all in the past, Let us leave it there."

"This is a chance to redeem myself, isn't it?" The boy looked anxious.

"I suppose that would be a reasonable way to look at it."

"I overheard some of the soldiers say that Britomart specially told them to keep a careful watch on me. If I do anything they find suspicious they will . . ."

"Just keep your wits about you, Petronus. Think before you say or do anything. Better still, say nothing. We're supposed to be an order of silent monks. Of all the squirrelly customs . . . But I suppose we can use it to our advantage."

"I'll try. Sometimes . . . sometimes I just get carried away."

"Do not let that happen."

They sailed south through the Pillars of Hercules, bound for Marseilles. As they passed Gibraltar a playful ape threw stones at the ship. Merlin commented that he hoped it was not a sign of things to come. One of the soldiers got his longbow and shot the offending ape; it plunged into the cold Mediterranean, struggled briefly, then disappeared under the waves.

"There," Martin said. "Let us hope that *is* a sign of what's to come."

"I would rather hope for an easy, nonviolent trip."

"If there is to be violence, you should hope it will be ours, Merlin. Otherwise, why bring us?"

The voyage took a day and a half. The port at Marseilles was crowded and busy and alive with activity. Merlin told Martin, "Instruct the men not to talk to anyone, not even to each other. They must leave that to either you or myself. I am the abbot; you are my lieutenant."

Petronus couldn't take his eyes off the city. He told Merlin, "I've never seen a place as large as this."

"Never? Have you not had the chance to travel?"

"When I came to England, it seemed the most thrilling place to me. But Corfe and Camelot aren't much bigger than Camelliard. And that's as much of the world as I've had the chance to see."

"You will see more, I am quite certain. But for now it is time to get into your monk's habit."

"I'm too young to be a monk."

"Novice, then, as we said before. Do it. I'm told priests are fond of them. But you must wear it. We cannot take the chance that someone might recognize you. This is a *secret* mission, remember?"

Martin's men rummaged through a pile of clerical robes and found ones that fit them reasonably well. There was a small robe that seemed tailor-made for Petronus. Merlin was the last to find his habit; the second one he examined fit him perfectly.

"Excellent. Let us all put up our hoods, make certain our weapons are well-concealed, and go forward. And we must all remember at all times that we are pious Christian clerics. Be humble and devout, with everyone, all the time. And keep your eyes and ears open for anyone who might be a Byzantine."

Martin laughed. "We're soldiers, Merlin. Humility does not come naturally to us."

"Nevertheless, our lives may depend on it, and we must all make the effort. We have a long way to go. It is time we enter Marseilles."

"Where is Merlin? I've been asking for him for two days now. One of the servants finally let slip that he's gone off on a trip to somewhere."

Guenevere had sent for Nimue/Colin, who had been ne-gotiating her way among all the delegates and all their de-mands. So far, only two had left. The rest were waiting for the harbor to be cleared completely, and they were feeling edgy and impatient. Food and other supplies were running lower and lower. The last thing she needed to deal with was Guenevere, who still seemed to think herself in charge.

"Merlin has gone off on a short holiday," she told the queen. "That is as much as I know."

"Rot. I've seen the two of you together. You're like his second self."

"I presume you mean that as a compliment? Thank you."

"Don't patronize me, young man. How can Merlin have gone off in the middle of his investigation?"

"I don't know a thing about his investigation, Your Maj-esty." She leaned on the final words ironically. "He said he needed a break. That is as much as I know."

"Break, break, break. If my mother had run Camelliard as loosely as Arthur runs England, it never would have amounted to a thing."

"It seems to be coming to nothing anyway. Or haven't you heard?"

Guenevere narrowed her eyes. "What do you mean?"

"Hasn't your mother been to see you?"

"Leonilla and I were not close even before she went off her head. Now . . . I want to know what Merlin has discovered about the murders. And I want to see Lancelot."

Nimue shrugged. "No one can think of a reason why Lancelot should have killed Podarthes. Not that it matters. Convicting him of one killing will be more than sufficient."

"But—but the two must have been committed by the same person."

"How can you know that, unless you had something to do with them?"

"Do not try to be foxy with me, young man. Neither Lancelot nor I had a thing to do with either killing. If Merlin was half the detective you all seem to think he is, he would know that by now."

"Yet people keep dying, and Lancelot always seems to be on the scene or nearby. Perhaps Merlin is trying to find evidence that you are involved. Have you thought about that?"

Guenevere glared. "Leave me. Now."

Nimue stood to go. "With pleasure, Your Majesty."

Guenevere turned to her mirror. But Nimue decided not to let her off so easily. "One more thing."

Without turning to look at her, Guenevere said, "Yes?"

"There is a court jeweler at Camelliard. A certain Reynaud de Beliveau. What do you know about him?"

"Beliveau? He is a fool. There were always rumors he had been one of mother's lovers. If that is true, he is the only one who managed to survive. Lucky for him she always liked pretty things. He must be the only lover she ever took who was older than herself." She turned suspicious; her eyes narrowed. "Why?"

"Pretty things? Do you mean him or his jewelry?"

"I told you to leave me. Leave me."

"Yes, of course." Making a showy mock-bow, Nimue turned to go.

"No, wait."

Nimue smiled to herself. "Yes?"

"You said there has been intelligence from France. What is it?"

"You mean your mother's . . . paramour has gotten word and you haven't? How interesting."

"Tell me. Please, young man."

"I have a name, you know. If you'll excuse me, I have duties to attend to."

Guenevere steamed, but Nimue left her and placed a guard prominently in the doorway.

Merlin had instructed her to keep a careful watch on Eudathius, who she still thought of as "the Lithuanian." So far he had done nothing suspicious. But on one of her mad walkabouts Leonilla had been found in his quarters, sitting on his bed and talking incoherently to herself.

And Andrea of Salesi had become increasingly strident, demanding special attention, demanding extra food for his retinue, demanding all sorts of things Nimue was hardpressed to provide. The last thing she needed was trouble from Guenevere, and she was grateful their audience had gone as well—and as briefly—as it had.

The harbor at Marseilles was crowded with people and bursting with activity. It did not take long for Merlin to learn that the same storm that had crippled England had also ravaged the French ports on the Channel and the North Sea. As a result, virtually all marine traffic had to pass through Marseilles; there was no other choice. Merlin had decided to land there because access to Camelliard, to the north, would be easier; and it proved to have been a fortunate choice. His soldiers tended to stay together, a short distance away from him. Petronus was his company.

The harbor was crowded with ships of every description, from small sloops to galleys to, ominously, the most imposing Byzantine war craft. There seemed to be ships from every part of the Mediterranean world.

Merlin relished everything he saw. "When I was a

younger man I traveled everywhere I could," he told Petronus. "Greece, Egypt, Byzantium, or Constantinople, as they call it now. I went everywhere I could. But I've never seen this city before."

"It must have been wonderful, Merlin. I'm jealous." Petronus talked in a whisper to help maintain the fiction that only Merlin was allowed to speak.

"I almost made the journey to India and Cathay. My wanderlust was that strong. Let us find an inn and eat something."

With hand signals he told Martin and his men to follow him. The streets were full of travelers of every kind. Merlin was delighted to notice Egyptians among the crowd. "When I lived there, Egyptians tended not to travel. They thought their country the center of everything. The great god Khnum fashioned mankind on his potter's wheel there, so why go to any other place? I'm pleased to see their world has widened."

"Or ours has."

"Look—those men. They look like Byzantines. Let us listen."

They were speaking Greek with a distinct Constantinopolitan accent. Merlin tried to pick up the sense of their conversation, but they interrupted it to suggest they take a meal in an inviting inn.

As unobtrusively as possible for a party of fourteen, Merlin and the others followed.

The place was crowded, mostly with more Byzantines. Either traveling to France was the rage among them or Constantine had sent hordes of spies and this inn was their meeting place. The restaurateur seated Merlin's party at a long table against a wall opposite the fireplace.

Merlin ordered roast beef and ale for everyone; when it was served his "monks" ate in silence. They all strained to hear what they could from the other patrons, but their presence seemed to inhibit the Byzantines.

The mere number of Greeks revealed a telling story. By the time the Englishmen finished eating, Merlin was quite convinced that Jean-Michel's intelligence had been accurate, at least the part about increased Byzantine activity in France.

They finished their meal in silence and left. Outside, they sky had become quite cloudy. Merlin paused to hope the last vestiges of the great storm were not about to strike. He got out a map and whispered to Petronus, "What is the quickest way for us to travel? I am quite disoriented, with no sun . . ."

"There is a great road heading along the eastern side of the Pyrenees from Marseilles. I'm not certain how to reach it from here."

"People will always give help and assistance to monks. I am certain we only need to ask."

But no one was as accommodating as he hoped. Everyone he stopped seemed to regard the monks and their leader, with his English accent, with considerable suspicion. The party headed away from the waterfront and hoped they would encounter someone more friendly.

After nearly an hour's walk through the city they came to a Christian church. Merlin and Petronus looked at one another as if to ask *why not?* And so they went inside.

An attendant, to appearances not a priest, was tending a rack of candles. Merlin interrupted him. "Excuse me. I am Father Methodius of the Abbey of St. Dymphna in England. Queen Leonilla has sent us on an errand to Camelliard, but I am afraid we have lost our bearings. Might you please direct us to the Pyrenees Road?"

The man turned to face him, and Merlin saw that he was a hunchback. "She is not queen here." He had a speech defect.

"We were planning to land at Brittany. But the storm— our map—we have quite lost our bearings. So you see, any assistance you can give us will be most helpful."

The hunchback wrinkled his brow, as if thought came hard for him. "You're not Greeks?"

"Good heavens, no."

"You want the Pyrenees Road?"

"Yes. We understand there is a good road along the eastern side of the mountains. If you could direct us there—"

"This is Marseilles."

"We are quite aware of that. We need to reach Camelliard. If you might—"

"That way." The man pointed to the church door.

Merlin looked at the threshold. "Is there someone else here?"

"That way," the hunchback repeated. "Go up that street and keep going. The mountains are that way."

"I see."

"First light a candle. The Virgin will protect you."

Obediently he lit not one but four candles. "For the Virgin and the Trinity," he explained.

The hunchback smiled, satisfied. A moment later the "monks" were back on the street and heading north. Merlin was pleased that his first attempt at a cover story had gone over fairly well. But not everyone they met would be as compliant as the hunchback in the church.

Outside, there were more clouds in the sky. Martin moved next to Merlin and whispered, "This is all too ominous."

"Do you mean the weather or the Byzantines?"

"Both."

"Relax, Martin. Tell everyone to be alert and to keep their ears open. But relax. We have the perfect cover. We are priests."

"I didn't notice the innkeeper or the hunchback to be very accommodating . . ."

At the northern end of the city, the Pyrenees Road was impossible to miss. It was Roman, one of the scores of ancient roads that crisscrossed Europe. A faded, almost illegible signpost at the entrance, carved into a rock, said it had been built at the behest of the emperor Hadrian. The paving was worn and cracked in places, but it was still quite serviceable. Despite that, traffic was surprisingly light.

"Perhaps people are staying indoors, sheltering from the approaching storm." Merlin produced one of his viewing devices and scanned the road as far as he could see. "Let us hope they are wrong. I saw enough rain in England to last me for a good, long time."

"My Roman history is not what it should be, Merlin." Martin walked beside him. "Is this the same Hadrian who built the wall between England and Scotland?"

Merlin nodded.

"Resourceful man."

"To say the least, Martin. And he is one of Arthur's personal heroes."

"His ambition keeps growing, doesn't it?"

Not in a mood to focus on anything but their journey, Merlin didn't answer. They set out, heading north. The clouds were dark and threatening, and the mountains to the west, on their left, looked equally so. Martin complained that they should find a dry, cozy inn and wait till the weather changed.

"The Pyrenees always look off-putting, Martin, even in bright sunlight." Merlin kept his eyes on the road, scanning the far horizon. "They are the gloomiest range in the world. But if we have trouble, it will more likely be from enemies than from nature."

"I wish I could be so confident."

"The French, the Byzantines, possibly even the Archduchess of Mendola . . . they are all active here. We have seen enough of the Greeks to know they are a strong presence. Treachery is everywhere around us."

A bolt of lightning flashed above the distant mountains. Martin noticed it from the corner of an eye and frowned at

Merlin. "And we are sitting ducks for all of them, even Mother Nature."

"I have always thought of Nature as more like a stern, unyielding father than a loving mother."

Martin smiled a deathly smile. "I'd like to be there sometime when you tell Morgan that. Her goddess is loving and benevolent."

"Morgan is not in the government. Do you suppose that might be why?"

Occasionally drops of rain fell, but they always vanished quickly and never turned into actual showers. After two hours of walking the party stopped for a light meal. Martin had taken a few of the men to a marketplace before they left the city walls, so they had supplies for a long journey. There were large packs of food, skins of water, blankets; everyone but Merlin was burdened.

Petronus's pack was as large as everyone else's; he struggled under it. Merlin asked if he was all right. "Are you certain you can manage all that?"

"Yes, sir."

"You should have something lighter."

"They don't like me," he whispered to Merlin. "They still think I tried to assassinate Arthur."

"You did." He smiled. "But perhaps they do not know the circumstances. I will have a word with Martin."

"Arthur has forgiven me. Why shouldn't they?"

"I'm not certain forgiven is the right word, Petronus. The king has taken my word for it that you did not do what you did voluntarily. But he is still skeptical. For instance he told me I would be foolish to bring you on this trip. Martin and the others are under strict orders to watch you carefully."

"Oh." The boy sounded glum. "I see."

"Just behave and be careful to report all that you see and hear, and everything will be fine. I want to believe in you. I do, in fact. Do not make me regret it. I brought you because

I think you will prove invaluable when we reach Camelliard. Please do so."

Petronus fell silent and walked apart from Merlin and the others for a long while. They passed occasional other travelers on the road now and then. Some were alone; most in groups. More rarely there was a minor lord or a wealthy merchant traveling on horseback, accompanied by servants. Some of them crossed themselves or nodded and smiled warmly at the supposed clerics.

When Petronus spoke again he sounded suspicious. "Why are we doing this, sir? I mean, next to Camelot or even Corfe, Camelliard is nothing."

"Beliveau. The court jeweler. I have a good idea who our murderer is. Beliveau is the one man who can give me the information I need to confirm my guess."

"Who do you suspect?"

"In good time, Petronus, in good time."

The journey to Camelliard took three days. Except for a constant cold, driving wind, it was uneventful. Rain squalls rode the wind; they would soak the wayfarers then vanish quickly. Their cloaks offered some protection; but the rain was so hard it soaked them. By the time they had dried out again, more rain would come.

The knights grumbled; they were finding this trip more miserable than they'd expected. It was with relief that Merlin noticed an inn on the road ahead. He handed his viewing glass to Martin and suggested they stop there for the night. Almost at once the men's spirits brightened.

There were other guests at the inn, several of them obviously from Byzantium. The knights arranged themselves at strategic points around the inn's common room to try to overhear what was being said. But the foreigners spoke their own various languages, and the knights were at a loss to understand them.

Merlin spoke Greek, but the interesting conversations always seemed to be taking place someplace other than where he had settled. Petronus tried his best—he knew a smattering of Greek—but all he could make out was a reference to the Archduchess of Mendola.

"Who will be in charge at Camelliard?" Merlin asked.

They were on the second day of their journey, walking on the Pyrenees Road. The knights walked in a group, led by Martin; Merlin and Petronus walked side by side. There were no other wayfarers in sight, so they talked freely among themselves.

"Leodegrance's majordomo, I think, Pierre of Autun." Petronus looked away. "My uncle."

"Good, that will give us an opening."

"Not likely, sir. He doesn't like me. He never has."

"What a turbulent family you have. But at least he knows you. That will give us a level of credibility."

"He'll be happy I'm a novice in a religious order. It will keep me out of his way while he chases various family legacies."

"One way or another," Merlin sighed, "all families have members like that, I suppose. Mine did."

"You never talk about your family, sir."

"No, I do not."

The conversation thus ended, Petronus moved off and walked alone. Merlin kept an eye on the sky to the west; so far there had been no severe weather. The knights were increasingly disgruntled but still compliant. Merlin also kept an eye out for another inn. The weather was growing colder; in wet cloaks it would be unbearable, and he needed the knights in a mood to obey, or at least co-operate.

It was after dark when they came to one. Unlike the first one, this was nearly empty. The only other guest was a young woman traveling with a manservant and a brace of hunting dogs. Her servant was large and burly enough to protect her. Merlin had the impression she was wealthy; it was odd for her to be traveling with just one man,

He made conversation with her. And it turned out she was leaving Camelliard. "Something is happening. I'm not certain what, but the mood in the castle is . . . peculiar. Everyone is on edge and distrustful of everything else."

"You are from the castle itself? Do you know a young woman named Petronilla, who was raised there?"

"We were friends. Well, not friends, exactly, but more than acquaintances. I can't say we were ever really intimate."

"I knew her in England. In fact, I was her confessor." He hoped he had the right tone to sound authentically clerical.

The woman smirked. "I imagine that took up a lot of your time. She always had a lot to confess."

"I may not say." He piously averted his eyes and crossed himself. "My novice, here, is her brother."

She looked at the boy, who had been listening in appropriate monklike silence. "Petronus? You must remember me. I'm Marie Philippeau."

He nodded but maintained his pietistic silence. Merlin was pleased. He steered the conversation gently back to the political situation.

Marie opened up. "Ever since word came that Leodegrance was dead, parties have been forming up. I mean at court. Leonilla's party is trying to maintain her position for her return. There are also agents from Justinian, from the Mendola region up in the mountains and even a few hangers-on who simply have to be Flemish. There's going to be trouble, I know it. I decided to take my servant and my dogs and get out while I could." She stroked one of the dogs affectionately.

Merlin pretended complete ignorance. "The situation is that bad?"

"You men of God have no idea how treacherous the world can be when there is power at stake."

"No, I suppose we are naïve in our piety."

"You should stay in your abbeys. They are the only truly safe places left in the world, and the only good places."

"We only leave when we must." He added helpfully, "On God's work, of course."

"But tell me, how is Petronilla? Does she like her life in England?"

"She never seems quite content. Shall I tell her you asked about her?"

"I'd rather you didn't. If she is at all unhappy, that is enough for me." She grinned. "As I said, we were friends."

He tried pumping her for more intelligence about what was going on at Camelliard, but she was too preoccupied for anything but gossip. He tried to learn something more about Petronilla's character and history, but Marie was too completely self-absorbed to say much about her. But he hoped the people at court would be too suspicious of each other to pay much attention to a group of traveling monks.

When they left the inn next morning there were signs that the sun was trying to penetrate the cloud cover. But the wind remained cold and damp. They could not have reached Camelliard too soon to please them.

On the road they passed more people who, like Marie, seemed to be leaving the region "while they could." It was not a promising sign. One young woman fleeing could be put down to fear or distrust. A mass exodus indicated there was something to be afraid of.

They were in the foothills of the Pyrenees now. The road topped a low hill. Then it descended gradually into a valley and then, in the far distance, rose again. At the top of that rise sat Camelliard Castle. Petronus made a point of telling everyone, and Merlin shushed him. "We must be extra careful not to give away our cover from now on. Remember, Petronus, you have taken a vow of silence."

"I'm sorry, sir," he whispered. "But it is home, and I haven't seen it since I left for England."

Instead of answering Merlin held a finger to his lips and made a show of crossing himself in mock-piety.

The English countryside was drying out, slowly and gradually. And Corfe harbor had been sufficiently cleared to permit about half of the legates—the ones with smaller ships—to leave. Andrea of Salesi was still in residence at the castle, as were the Byzantines, Merlin's friend Germanicus and assorted others. Morgan and Gildas had never stopped their bickering, most recently about who was to officiate at the funerals for Leodegrance and Podarthes, which were to take place as soon as the earth was sufficiently dry to permit the digging of proper graves.

Leonilla was of course still in residence, and her behavior was growing more and more strange. Her mad walkabouts were becoming increasingly frequent. Delegates, members of Arthur's staff, even servants would waken in the middle of the night to find her at their bedsides, talking incoherently or going through their things. Jean-Michel and the rest of her servants tried valiantly to control her, but a lifetime of cunning had taught her to elude them easily. People found her behavior and even her mere presence more and more alarming.

But the fact that guests remained did not make them any easier to deal with. Their unwillingly prolonged residence in England was making them more and more testy, more and more impatient. They seemed to have the attitude that they should be treated with all the honor and deference they would have received in their courts at home. Eudathius was growing especially demanding and arrogant.

Nimue had to deal with it all, backed by Arthur and supported by Simon. But she was finding it more and more wearisome. "I wish Merlin had not gone to France," she complained to Simon, "or that he'd get back soon. I can't tell you how happily I would be relieved of these duties. If that Eudathius makes one more demand—for snow with syrup, for candied hummingbird tongues or whatever—I swear I'll toss him into the harbor."

"I wouldn't do that. It is polluted enough already. You are not cut out for diplomacy, Colin."

"You're telling me?"

"And you are starting to sound like Merlin. He grumbles so memorably."

"Don't be rude."

Simon remained calm and cool through even the worst of the crises brought on by their guests' prolonged presence. "They are living here on our hospitality, not by their own choice. We invited them, remember? It is incumbent on us to do all we can to keep them happy."

"You're probably right, Simon. But I say the hell with them. And it won't take much more for me to say it to their faces."

"And how much of our work would that undermine?"

"Do you know I haven't read a book in weeks? Too many duties, too many people."

Simon smiled at her. "We have had no word yet from Merlin?"

Colin shook her head. "Nothing."

"He will be home soon enough."

"If he isn't in a dungeon or a torture chamber somewhere." She grinned. "The French know how to treat unwelcome guests."

On the day when the sun finally broke through the clouds and stayed out for the afternoon, a sentry went to Colin's office. "There are riders on the Camelot Road, sir."

"Our men?"

"They are still quite a way off. Even with Merlin's lenses we can't—"

"Keep a close eye out. If they are our knights, send out

riders with wine and mead. If not . . . I don't know, kill
them or ambush them or something. Check with Britomart.
The last thing we need is more unwelcome visitors."

"Yes, sir."

"Let's hope they are knights from Camelot. Arthur sent
word he needs two dozen of them to form the jury for Lancelot's trial."

Two hours later Sir Sagramore arrived with a contingent
of knights. They had ridden long and hard, and they were in
an unpleasant mood. Colin met them in the courtyard.
"Welcome. You made good time getting here. We didn't
think the roads would all be passable yet."

"They aren't." Sagramore snorted and looked around at
the castle. "This place is hideous."

"The castle isn't half as ugly as what's gone on inside,
believe me."

"Take me to Arthur. How is he, by the way? And where
is Merlin? I expected him to greet us."

She explained about Merlin's trip to France. "You've
heard about the two murders, I assume?"

"Two? We knew that Leodegrance was killed. Arthur
wants us to form the jury for the trial. Is Lancelot still the
only suspect?"

"More or less. There are other possibilities. But in Merlin's absence I'm preparing the prosecution—as if I didn't
have enough to trouble me—so we probably shouldn't discuss it. I wouldn't want to influence you."

"Believe me, Colin, the day a bookish boy like you can
influence the Knights of the Round Table is the day hell
turns to ice." He made a sour face. "Scholars. Real men
act."

She couldn't resist. "You'd rather deal with an actor?"

"Don't be sarcastic." He turned his back on her and adjusted his horse's bridle. "Where are the stables?"

"I'll have one of the pages show you."

With a cohort of his knights in residence, Arthur's mood

brightened for the first time since he'd arrived at Corfe. He exercised with them, wrestled with them, ate and drank with them. "This is the proper element for a king," he told Colin. "Action, not all this damned diplomatic palaver." He wrinkled his nose. "Talk, talk, talk. The politicians never do anything, and they never shut up about it."

"They keep the world functioning, Arthur."

"Poor world."

"You are not from Mendola?"

Pierre of Autun was every inch the careworn court official—pale, craggy, angular, with steel-gray hair. He stared at Merlin and his "monks" with undisguised suspicion. So far, Merlin had been unable to dispel it.

Merlin had introduced himself as Anselm of York, and no one had questioned his identity. He smiled like—he hoped—a benevolent abbot. "No. England, England. As I told you. We are from an abbey founded by Bishop Gildas in Londinium, or London, as the British are beginning to call it. We came originally from an abbey in Brittany and moved to England at Gildas's behest."

"Then what are you doing here?" Pierre scowled.

Merlin was the soul of clerical patience. "As I explained, Bishop Gildas gave us permission to return to the Continent, to make a pilgrimage to the shrine of St. James, at Compostela." He added helpfully, "It is just across the Pyrenees from here. There is a pass through the mountains that we—"

"I am quite familiar with Compostela," Pierre grumbled. "It is in Spain. Why are you in France?"

"We had planned to make landfall on the south coast of Spain. But the storm—"

"I see. Tell me something."

"Anything you need to know." He radiated goodwill and friendliness. "Only ask."

"A nephew of mine is in service at the court of King Arthur. Do you know him, by chance?"

"A nephew?" Merlin feigned ignorance. "What would his name be? There are so many Frenchmen at Arthur's court. I myself prefer to remain at the abbey in Londinium, but—"

"Petronus. He is a boy of about fourteen."

"Petronus?" Merlin played mock-surprise perfectly. "Why, I know him very well. He is one of our novices. He is traveling in our group, in fact."

"I see. Has he taken his vows yet?"

"Yes. Petronus is a splendid young man. He—"

"That is too bad. I would like to interview him, but if he is already pledged to a life of silence . . ." He left the thought unfinished. "Still, I think I would enjoy seeing him. Having one of my relatives silent will be more pleasant than you can imagine. We have scouts checking the condition of the mountain pass even as we speak. It is prone to flash floods. A great many people make the pilgrimage to Compostela, and most of them want to stay here with us before crossing the mountains. We have to turn most of them away. But you and your party may stay until out scouts return."

"Thank you very much. We—"

"You would be surprised at the number of travelers who make this journey, and as I said, they all seem to want to shelter here. We send most of them to inns. But of course, the clergy . . ." He waved a hand vaguely instead of finishing his sentence. "I'll have one of the servants show you to your rooms."

"We could not be more appreciative, believe me. But if I might ask one further indulgence, a small one."

Pierre turned suspicious again instantly. "Yes?"

"Petronus has a friend here. Or rather, a mentor. A jeweler named Reynaud de Beliveau. He would like to see the man once again. Might that be possible?"

"On theory, yes, of course." Pierre looked concerned. "But you will have to do it quickly. Reynaud is quite old, and I fear he is not in the best of health."

"I see. When may we see him, then?"

"Soon. Tomorrow. You will be accompanying Petronus?"

"I am afraid so, yes. As the only member of our party permitted to speak—"

"Of course. And I will want to interview Petronus myself. Will you be along as interlocutor?"

"It is quite necessary, I fear. Petronus, like all our clerics, has vowed never to speak, so that he may turn all his thoughts to the Lord, and so I—"

"I understand perfectly. Shall we plan to meet after the evening meal, then?"

"That would be most agreeable." Merlin made a slight bow.

"And needless to say, I will want whatever news you can provide about our queen."

Merlin nodded. "Naturally. Until then."

The castle showed signs of being fairly new but with a few wings that were clearly older; a great deal of it had been erected since Merlin's last visit, a decade earler. It was all in poor repair. Walls were cracked; water dripped from ceilings and walls; mold grew. Leodegrance and Leonilla's ambitions had outstripped their treasury; they must have been more hard-up for money than they ever let on; it made their various attempts to seize land in England that much more explicable.

"Anselm" and his monks were led through halls strewn with litter. Dogs ran wild in the castle, apparently underfed and ungroomed; hallways smelled of them.

As they neared the place Merlin had warned everyone that they would most likely be spied on; it was important that they all remember to maintain silence. If anything important came to light, they were to pass the information to Merlin in a note. As they moved through the castle halls, they got suspicious glances and even glares from nearly everyone who saw them.

Merlin and Petronus shared a room; Martin and his knights had three others. Once they were in their chambers, left to their own devices and untended by the French, he circulated a note reminding them of the importance of keeping under cover, which meant in essence maintaining silence and not prying too openly. *With so many suspicious eyes and ears,* he wrote, *our every move will be watched and probably reported. Remember that if we are taken to be spies, we will most likely be executed forthwith.*

Once they had stowed their packs in their room, Merlin found a servant to lead them to the chapel, where they made a show of praying in silence for an hour. At dinner they ate frugally. There was every reason for onlookers to believe that they were a poor religious order, humbly devoted to God's service.

When the prayers were done and the meal over, Petronus had his meeting with his uncle, chaperoned by Merlin. As they talked it became more and more apparent that Pierre was more concerned with chasing legacies than with security. Everything seemed to be to his satisfaction, which only served to convince Merlin more fully that they would be spied on.

Merlin told Pierre about the state of Leonilla's health and mental faculties, and Pierre's reaction to the news was impossible to gauge. Was he pleased or alarmed? Court official that he was, he gave nothing away.

Then, late at night by candlelight, Merlin conversed by note with Petronus. *I have seen no sign of Beliveau. I have not even heard anyone mention his name. I wish I could see him—at least catch a glimpse of him—before tomorrow.*

He is old. Very old. Older than you, even. Merlin scowled as he read it. *He usually keeps to his rooms.*

Where is his workshop?

On the top floor. It is usually guarded because of the gold, silver and gems kept there.

In the morning I will want you to take me there. I have told Pierre you and the man were friendly, so with luck no one will be suspicious.

What about the guards?

I shall have to play the gentle shepherd for their sake, benevolently concerned for his flock. That has not failed us yet.

That night people throughout Corfe Castle were wakened by screams. Everyone rushed to where they seemed to come from—the wing where Leonilla was quartered.

Jean-Michel, in his nightshirt, was clearly in charge; the other servants in Leonilla's retinue all looked to him for direction. Two maids, both crying hysterically, stood by the bed. The sheets were stained with blood. "It is the queen."

Nimue quickly took in everything and everyone in the bedroom. "Who was here? Who saw it happen?"

"The queen—murdered in her bed." Jean-Michel's voice broke off. For the first time Nimue took seriously the idea that he might genuinely have loved the old woman. He composed himself. "Leonilla liked to sleep with no one else in the room. I talked to her about it time and again, tried to convince her it put her at needless risk, but—" He spread his hands apart in a gesture of helplessness. "She was always a light sleeper. The least noise would awaken her."

"Pity she didn't hear the killer, then."

"She did. We all heard her scream."

"Has anyone examined the body?"

He shook his head.

Nimue slowly approached the bed. Blood was dripping

from the covers and onto the floor, and she was careful not
to step in it. She gingerly pulled the covers back.

In the bed was the body of a young woman. It was
Leonilla's maid, Marthe. Her throat had been slashed so
deeply that her head was nearly severed.

At that moment a figure wrapped in black robes appeared at the bedroom door. Leonilla stood there, wide-
eyed, trembling. "Where is my husband?" she cried.

Jean-Michel rushed to her side, put an arm around her
and hustled her to another room of her suite.

Nimue turned back to the body in the bed. The face was
contorted with fear and agony, but she recognized Marthe
clearly enough. Another servant confirmed it was her.

Impaled in her throat so deeply that only the end of the
handle showed was another of the ivory-handled gold
knives.

And so the next morning, well before breakfast, Merlin and
Petronus made their way to the top story of the castle to
Beliveau's workshop. A guard was posted there. Merlin had
a quick conversation with him, explaining that Pierre had
authorized their visit to the old jeweler. The man's suspicion was undisguised but he finally let them enter.

Beliveau's room was large and airless—not, Merlin told
himself, the healthiest environment for an old man who
worked with fire and chemicals. There were no windows;
no air circulated. Merlin remarked to himself that it was the
first time he had ever found a room in a castle with no
drafts. Only two candles lit the place, not nearly enough to
make it habitable, and neither flame flickered even slightly.
More frugality? Merlin wondered.

Against the far wall was a cot. Beliveau was asleep on it,
to the appearances. Petronus and Merlin approached silently,
not wanting to disturb the man. But when they were six feet
away from him, a dim reflection of candlelight flickered in

his half-opened eyes. In a surprisingly strong voice, he said, "Who are you and what are you doing here?"

Merlin introduced himself as Anselm, then had Petronus step forward so Beliveau could see and recognize him.

"Petronus. Little Petronus." The old man turned his head to them but made no attempt to sit up. He smiled feebly, but his voice remained strong. "My true apprentice. Not so little anymore. You will be tall and handsome soon. How are you, boy?"

Merlin explained about the vow of silence and that they were on their way to cross the mountains to Compostela. "But while we were passing near his home, Petronus expressed a wish to see his old master."

Beliveau smiled. "You always were a thoughtful, considerate boy. Are you visiting your family castle, as well?"

Petronus shook his head.

"I don't blame you. They are not the pleasantest people. But I am glad you have chosen a religious life. Cloistered, the world will not be able to corrupt you. Knowing that there is at least one good man left in the world, I may die in peace."

"Die?" Merlin interrupted.

Abruptly, as if he were explaining a minor annoyance, Believeau said, "I have a cancer."

In a low voice Merlin said, "I see. I am most sorry." He thought he saw tears forming in the corners of Petronus's eyes, and he looked discreetly away.

"May I impose on you to give me your blessing, Father Anselm?"

Merlin shifted uneasily. He had been vaguely aware that someone might make such a request. But from a dying man . . . He decided to change the topic and hope Beliveau would forget what he'd asked. "You say Petronus here was a good apprentice?"

"Yes, the best. Able, quick-witted, eager to learn. But you must know all that."

"Like all boys he has been a bit . . . problematic. But we are most happy to have him in our order."

Beliveau chuckled softly. "He is the best. Not like that other fool, the one Leonilla forced on me."

He was not about to lose this conversational thread. "Another apprentice?"

"A young villain named Jean-Michel. He was Leonilla's—what is the polite word?—her *favorite*. So he never did much work, and when I complained to the queen she simply laughed it off. It is the sign of a poor ruler to trust friends blindly. But she was wanting in so many ways. I assume you've noticed how badly the castle is crumbling, and parts of it are only a decade old. She was always too busy murdering supposed rivals to pay much attention to anything else. Queens."

"But what about this, er, 'favorite' you mentioned?" Merlin hoped his motive for asking was not too transparent.

"A horrible young man. A liar, a thief, a gigolo . . . He used to steal things all the time." Suddenly he winced with pain. Merlin grew alarmed, but the spasm seemed to pass quickly.

"You are an expert at your craft, Reynaud. I have seen the golden knives you fashioned for the wedding of Guenevere and Lancelot."

"Those knives. I wish Leonilla had never given me the job. It took forever to accomplish them. I made a dozen or more prototypes, and she rejected each one, wanting something fancier and more elaborate. All that gold, all that ivory—for nothing." He scowled, then coughed rather violently. Blood trickled down his chin. "You must excuse me, please."

"We understand quite well, I'm afraid."

"How anyone can believe this world is the work of a benign, intelligent Creator . . ." He burst out in another fit of coughing. Petronus rushed to his side and took his hand and stroked his forehead. He took a handkerchief and cleaned the man's face; there was blood. Finally the coughing passed.

Merlin pressed on. "I don't mean to impose on you at a time like this, but Petronus has described the excellence of your workmanship. Might I view some examples? You see, we are a new abbey, and we are still amassing our treasure. If we could . . ."

Beliveau feebly pointed to a wooden cabinet, then sat up and reached into the pocket of his garment and produced a key. "Security," he whispered, and chuckled. "As I said, even my apprentice was a thief. But go and look. I am flattered." Petronus put a hand behind the man's head.

Merlin took one of the candles and unlocked the cabinet with the key. On four shelves rested crowns and coronets, rings and necklaces, jeweled knives and swords. All of them were exquisitely worked, beautifully crafted. But there was no sign of the prototypes of the golden knives.

Merlin examined the cabinet and then, trying to sound casual, asked about the knives.

"Gone. Stolen." He coughed again, not so violently.

Merlin shook his head sadly. "It is such a pity. It is not possible to trust anyone anymore, certainly not this new generation. Who do you think took them?"

"Jean-Michel. I have given it a great deal of thought, and I don't believe anyone else had the opportunity to steal them. No one much came here. I have lived something of a cloistered life myself." Beliveau smiled weakly. "Leonilla came, now and then, to inspect the work, but no one else."

They talked for a while more. Merlin noticed that Petronus seemed genuinely fond of the man, and genuinely moved by his condition. When, finally, he said he wanted more sleep, they left him. Merlin was certain he had learned all he could from him.

When he got back to his own room, he scrawled a note to Martin. *When we leave here tomorrow*, it read, *have one of the men rush back to England ahead of us. Tell him to travel as rapidly as he can, and give this letter to my assistant, Colin.*

The letter to Colin was brief and to the point. *Delay the trial. Arrest Jean-Michel. M.*

TEN

At Corfe Castle the Great Hall was being stripped of the decorations from the birthday celebration and prepared for the murder trial of Lancelot. Simon oversaw the preparations with fussy efficiency. Meanwhile, Nimue was preparing the case for the prosecution.

Arthur was impatient; he wanted his wife's false husband out of the way, and he was anxious to do it according to the letter of the law, with all possible deference to fairness and justice. But time was dragging on. A warrior at heart, he wanted action.

"It shouldn't be hard to convict him, Colin," he complained. "He was caught with blood on his hands."

"Do you really want to trust me with the prosecution?" she asked. "I've never done anything like this before. Besides, I'm less and less certain Lancelot is guilty. Of Leodegrance's murder, perhaps, but what possible motive could he have had for murdering Podarthes? And poor Marthe?"

"Maybe she was another one of his mistresses. You know these damned Frenchmen. They screw everything that lets them."

"He was securely locked up when she was killed."

Arthur glared. "Then he put Guenevere up to it. Damn it, Colin, I want them found guilty."

"This is supposed to be about justice, not vengeance, remember?"

"Stop talking like Merlin."

"If what you want is the two of them out of the way—or even dead—then just do it. You're the king; no one can stop you."

This deflated him for a moment. "Merlin has taught you too well. I suppose . . . I suppose we can wait till he gets back. But . . ."

"Yes?"

"I hate this. I've told him so. Things were so much simpler before this 'new England' of his. No, of *ours*. Has he taught you this new game he calls chess?"

"Yes, of course."

"It's all the rage on the Continent, they say. The game pieces represent *us*—kings, queens, knights, castles." He laughed. "There is even a piece called a bishop, for that fool Gildas. And to win the game, it is necessary to keep as many pieces in play as possible. Even a murderous queen has her uses. Taking her—or her lover, for that matter—out of play could weaken me, eventually."

"Are you talking about a game or about life?"

"The two get confused." He sighed heavily. "I suppose we can delay the trial for a few more days. Let us hope Merlin gets back soon."

Most of the remaining delegates had left in the time since Merlin departed for France. A great many of them asked curious questions about where he had gone; the few members of Arthur's court who actually knew kept silent. Most pointedly, Eudathius and his Byzantines had lingered at

Corfe, claiming their boat needed a great many repairs but inquiring quite often about the state of the prosecution of the supposed killer of Podarthes, about Merlin's whereabouts and about anything else they could think of. There had been an incident involving one of their men. He had committed sexual assault on a servingwoman and was promptly arrested by two of Captain Dalley's guards. Eudathius had protested loudly that the man's diplomatic status gave him immunity from arrest under English law. But Arthur had had enough of them; his patience was too short for anything other than a speedy arrest and imprisonment. "We can deal with at least this one minor criminal, can't we? At least?" He told Dalley and Britomart, "I want him dealt with quickly."

"You may not do this, Your Majesty," Eudathius wrote in a formal complaint. And he followed up with a personal protest. "International law, Your Majesty—"

"International law hardly sanctions rape. At any rate, Eudathius, Merlin is my principal advisor on matters of diplomatic protocol, and he is unavailable at the moment."

"May I ask where he is and when he will return?"

"You may not. He will be here when he can. I can tell you nothing more. You may go." He smiled sweetly. "Oh, and one word of advice."

"Yes, Your Majesty?"

"Don't ever try to tell a king there is something he may not do. It never works."

Plainly vexed by this upstart king's impertinence, Eudathius made a slight bow and left. But the matter gave him a plausible excuse for remaining in England. He and his party settled in for what might prove a long stay.

Arthur worked out his frustrations with wrestling matches and footraces with his knights, who, like him, were feeling restless. Sagramore spoke for them when he complained one day after a vigorous bout of wrestling. "Arthur, we were summoned here to form a jury. So far there is not even a hint of a trial."

"Of course there are hints. Take a look in the Great Hall. You must have noticed it's being readied."

"That's housekeeping, not a trial. We—"

"Patience, Sag. The trial will happen soon enough. When Merlin gets back, I will lose no time—"

"Why on earth do you need Merlin? Lancelot was found over the body with his knife in the man's neck. My five-year-old son could present a case that would convict him."

"Said like an impartial juror. But are you offering to retire and give your post to your son, Sag?"

"No, of course not, but—"

"Good. Then you must learn patience. This new England we are building takes time. Believe me, I know how trying it is. Besides, you have no idea what a nag Merlin can be. If we start without him I'll never hear the end of it."

Sagramore made a face like he'd just drunk vinegar. "He's the next one you ought to clap in a dungeon. First Guenevere and Lancelot, then him."

"Don't think the thought hasn't occurred to me. But you know how valuable he is. Camelot—England itself—owes him so much. Now go and get yourself some soup. No, some wine."

Then, late that afternoon, the soldier Merlin had sent, still wearing his monk's robes in order to travel unrecognized, arrived with Merlin's note to Nimue. She read it at once and went directly to Arthur.

He scowled at it like a man who'd found a worm in his apple. "Delay. Delay. Doesn't he know I have a kingdom to run?"

"The soldier who brought this was sent on ahead. But Merlin is on his way."

"Splendid. No doubt he'll try to complicate matters even more. Why is everything such a tangle?"

"If I might make a suggestion, Your Majesty . . ."

"What?"

"The clearest case against Lancelot is for the assassination of Leodegrance. Even a prosecutor as inexperienced as myself could win that conviction. It's the other killings that complicate the matter. Is it possible for us to try Lancelot for that one crime alone, for the time being, and delay the others till Merlin arrives with whatever information he's learned?"

"Of course it's possible. I'm the king. I can do anything I like."

"But the law—"

"The law wants to see the guilty man punished. How quickly can you procced?"

"I can have everything ready by the day after tomorrow."

"Excellent, Colin. I will even give you an extra day, then. I will notify everyone involved that the trial of Lancelot for the murder of the French king will begin three days from now. My knights are getting restless; that should calm them down."

"The case will be ready for presentation to a jury, Your Majesty. I'm not at all certain we could convince a jury of his peers that he committed the other crimes. Not yet, that is; not till Merlin is here. But there is one more thing."

"Now what?"

She held out Merlin's note. "Shall I have Captain Dalley arrest Jean-Michel?"

Arthur rubbed his chin. "Merlin must have a good reason for instructing us to do that. So, yes, see to it." He folded his arms and laughed. "My mother-in-law's gigolo in irons. Every now and then, life offers up genuine pleasures."

"Yes, Your Majesty."

Captain Dalley handled the arrest himself. Nimue had warned him that even though Jean-Michel was a minor figure in the political scheme of things, there might be repercussions from the court at Camelliard. "I wish we could know for certain that Merlin is out of there."

"Leonilla won't be happy, Colin. She's certain to protest."

"Leonilla doesn't count for much. What with her kingdom slipping out of her hands, slowly but surely; with her growing madness . . ."

"There are people who think her madness is a sham. An act to cover up evil intent. She's been seen perfectly rational at times."

"Even so, her power is all but gone."

So first thing next morning Dalley and a half dozen guards went to the young man's chambers. They were located conveniently next to Leonilla's own rooms. The old queen was nowhere in sight, and Dalley was glad of it; the confrontation, if it came at all, would at least not be immediate.

Jean-Michel's bedroom faced east; bright sunlight poured in through the window. He was lying on his bed, reading, when Dalley and his men arrived. "Jean-Michel de Pelisard, you are under arrest."

He jumped to his feet. "Arrest? Me? On what charge?"

"You will be informed of that at the proper time."

He called out for help, and a moment later several servants appeared at the door. They smirked at him; one of them laughed openly. "The queen's favorite," one of them muttered and joined the laughter.

Protesting and struggling against his captors, he was led away. The dungeon chosen for him was immediately next to Lancelot's. A wit had scrawled *Gigolo's Row* on the wall.

"I want to know what I'm charged with," he complained to Dalley. "Don't I have that right?"

"You have the right," Dalley told him offhandedly, "to stay quietly in your cell. Be a good lover boy and behave yourself."

They left. Jean-Michel, clearly out of his depth, sat on the cold stone floor and sulked.

At Simon's instruction the Great Hall was decked in somber colors: grays, dull browns, with just a touch of navy blue. That, in his mind, was "dignified" and proper for a capital trial.

Nimue thought he had overdone it, and she said so. "Simon, it looks as if it's been prepared for a funeral." When she said as much to Arthur, as the two of them got into their judicial robes in the tiring-room, he shrugged and smiled, "Let us hope."

"Please, Your Majesty. This is the first important opportunity we have to show the world that English justice—the king's justice—is a model of fairness and impartiality. It would not do for you to be too keen on Lancelot's conviction."

"The bastard stole my wife. Well, no, I suppose I never really had her. But he cuckolded me. How can I not want to see him permanently in irons, or worse?"

"All I am suggesting is that you conduct the trial as fairly as you can. Justice will be done. There is no need for you to help it along."

"God, I'd love to set you on Justinian. But your point is taken. I will make every effort to dispense the king's justice most admirably."

"Excellent, Your Majesty."

"But make me one promise, will you?"

"Sir?"

"Stop talking like Merlin all the time."

"Sorry, Arthur."

A single trumpet sounded in the Great Hall, playing a low, mournful fanfare. It was time for the trial to begin.

Arthur entered the hall, turned and rushed back out again. "Damn it, I almost forgot to wear my crown."

Nimue adjusted it on his head to give him the most formidable look possible, and he hurried back out into the hall. At his waist he wore his sword, Excalibur, which had been polished to a brilliant sheen; it was the most impressive symbol of his majesty anyone could think of.

He nodded to the large crowd of onlookers assembled there, then mounted a dais where a throne had been set up for him. He was dressed in ermine robes dyed a brilliant red; he had insisted on fur for his judicial attire. "You know how cold and drafty that hall gets." Simon had the tailors work overtime to have the robes ready.

Just after Arthur, Nimue entered, likewise robed in fur. And she covered her head with a wig, partly for warmth and partly because this was the most important role she'd ever played, and she wanted to look the part. Besides, she had been passing as Colin for sufficiently long enough that presenting an ostentatiously male appearance felt right to her. A table had been set up; and all her assorted papers had been laid out for her there. Britomart and Captain Dalley sat there waiting for her.

Brit whispered, "Red robes. You've come a long way quickly, Colin."

"I am an agent of the king's justice. Besides, it was the only dye the tailors could find."

The hall was crowded with people. Guenevere sat on a low throne to one side of the king, far enough away so that he would not have to talk to her. She looked as unhappy as anyone could remember. The night before, she had sent for Colin. "Where is your master? Where is Merlin? He has broken his word to me."

Nimue was vague. "Lancelot is being tried for one murder instead of three. I should think you'd be pleased."

"He gave me his word."

"Merlin's word is always subject to the king's assent. Surely as a queen you understand that."

The entire Byzantine delegation was in the audience for the trial; one of them, at Eudathius's side, was evidently prepared to take notes on the proceedings. The remaining delegates—Germanicus, Andrea of Salcsi and the rest—surrounded them.

The household staff and even boys from the kitchen filled row after row of seats. In one corner stood Simon, smiling happily; his arrangements were perfect. This was to be the biggest event in years, more important even than the conference that had just ended.

A wooden box had been erected on a platform; it was to hold the jury. For the moment Sagramore and the others were arrayed on two benches. None of them looked happy to be there.

Sagramore stood and moved beside Nimue. "What is this about? Why have we not been seated in the box for the jury?"

"Be quiet. Arthur is about to begin."

"I askcd you a question."

She sighed. "I am to question you. All of you. We want a fair trial. If any of you seems to have made his mind up already, you will be dismissed from the jury. Arthur wants a panel of thirteen. The others will listen to the trial and stand by in case something happens to one of the actual jurors."

"What will you ask us? We know what Arthur wants us to do."

"He wants you to be fair. So do I. And I'm reasonably certain so does Lancelot."

"What does he have to do with it?"

She smiled sweetly. "He's on trial for his life. Haven't you heard?"

Sagramore stiffened. Being talked to this way by a clerk!

Then his eyes flashed and his jaw set. "Just a moment—are you saying that Lancelot will question us, too?"

"He has a right to defend himself. The king says so."

"King, my arse. This is Merlin's doing, to humiliate us."

"Relax, will you, Sagramore? Arthur knows how vital you are to his reign. But surely it wll not diminish you to see that justice is done, will it?"

Clearly unhappy, he resumed his seat. The other knights questioned him about what Colin had told him, but he simply sulked and wouldn't answer them.

Guenevere sat on her throne glaring at everyone and everything in the hall, guarded closely by four of Brit's soldiers. She squirmed uncomfortably and waved her guards away. Quite pointedly, they remained beside her.

No one had been able to find Leonilla that morning, so the throne that had been erected for her beside her daughter sat unoccupied. Simon joked that perhaps she had baked a file into a loaf of bread for her lover.

Everything was ready. It was time to begin.

"Oyez, oyez!" Simon intoned. "All rise for Arthur, King of England, Scotland and Wales, Lord of These Islands, Ruler of Us All." There had been a lively discussion about precisely how Arthur was to be styled. Arthur, impatient as usual with protocol, said it didn't matter and refused to take part. Simon and Nimue had worked out the formula.

Arthur entered and crossed to his throne; trumpets sounded; everyone in the hall bowed. Dressed in his best robes and wearing Excalibur at his side, he resumed his place on his throne and waved the musicians silent. The entire hall became hushed.

Ten guards led Lancelot into the hall, shackled hand and foot. He did not look good. His blond hair was unkempt;

his clothes were soiled and disheveled. He took his place in the prisoner's box and sat glowering at Nimue.

This was to be the first trial of its kind in all the years since Arthur had become king—the first under his new regime of justice and fairness for all. No one knew what to expect, and everyone was on edge. Nimue, prepared though she was, felt uncomfortable without a set of rules and precedents to guide her. Lancelot was working to contain his anger. Petronilla was in a seat near the back of the hall, not moving, beside herself with anxiety that her story might be called into doubt. The knights fidgeted. The atmosphere in the Great Hall fairly quivered with tension. Even the people not directly involved in the trial were on edge.

Arthur announced that Colin would make an opening statement, summarizing his case. Then Lancelot was to make a similar statement outlining his defense. Lancelot jumped to his feet. "Arthur—Your Majesty—I must protest. I am bound and guarded like a guilty man. No matter what I say to argue my innocence, my appearance cries out to everyone that I am guilty."

Arthur furrowed his brow. The trial had only just begun and already things were not going smoothly. Arthur and Nimue consulted quickly. Then Arthur announced that because of the gross, heinous nature of the crime—the murder of a king, no less—the prisoner must remain bound.

Guenevere jumped to her feet and protested. "Is this the fairness we have been promised? Is this King Arthur's justice?"

Arthur banged the edge of his throne with Excalibur. "May I remind you, Guenevere, that you are a prisoner, too? You have no standing in these proceedings; you are here merely as a courtesy, since you are so, er, closely connected to the accused. Please take your seat and remain silent, or you will be removed." Her guards moved to surround her closely, and, thus humiliated, she glumly sat down again.

At her table Nimue took Merlin's note out of her pocket. What could he know? What could he have found out in France? She looked around the Great Hall, wishing he would arrive. No one there looked happy, from Guenevere and Lancelot, to the knight/jurors, to the king himself. The trial had not gotten off to a promising start. There had already been breaches of decorum; it seemed likely there would be more. And even though every measure was being taken to ensure that the proceedings were as fair as could be—certainly more fair than any other king in Europe would have permitted—the scholar in her knew that things were arrayed against any possibility of Lancelot being found not guilty.

Arthur called on her to begin, and she rose and presented her case. It was all quite straightforward, and everyone already knew the salient facts. The murder weapon was his—or his lover's. He had been found standing over the body, soaked in the victim's blood. There was a witness who saw him do the murder. She indicated Petronilla in the crowd, and the young secretary squirmed in her seat, looking more than slightly uncomfortable.

Nimue laid it all out clearly, neatly and efficiently. When she finished, the people in the hall were mostly silent. Eyes were on the king or on Lancelot, anticipating his attempt to rebut what Colin had said.

Then, suddenly, a young woman rushed into the hall. "Your Majesty," she shouted in a strong French accent. "Your Majesty! The queen!" Four guards surrounded the woman and restrained her.

Everyone turned to look at Guenevere, who appeared as startled as everyone else.

But the woman was one of Leonilla's servants; Nimue recognized her at once.

Arthur, scowling, asked her what the problem was. "We are conducting a trial here, a capital trial. This interruption is most unwelcome. Take her away."

The guards began to do so, but she kept crying out. "The queen! The queen! Her life is in peril!"

Immediately Arthur got to his feet and called a recess. "We will resume in thirty minutes' time." Then he, his knights and most of the rest of the crowd followed the woman to the wing where Leonilla's rooms were. As they rushed through the halls the servingwoman explained. "The queen was asleep all morning. She had not slept much last night. When she woke, she called for Jean-Michel to come join her. When I explained that he had been arrested, she ran mad. She rushed through the corridors raving, trying to find the dungeons. When she finally did and the guards refused to admit her, she shrieked like a madwoman and ran off. Before I could catch up with her, she had vanished somewhere into the castle."

Arthur stopped walking and glared at her. "The queen has been more than half-mad for weeks now. Why haven't you been watching her more closely? And how does this put her life in danger?"

"I found her back in her bedchamber, sire. She was perched on the window ledge—and threatening to jump. And she kept crying, 'I want to see my young man. Let me see my boy.' When anyone makes a move to pull her back inside, she moves closer to the edge. Oh, Your Majesty, she will die."

They reached her chamber. A dozen servants were clustered around the window, all wearing looks of deep concern. Nimue wondered whether they were actually concerned about the old queen or were merely worried about what would happen to themselves should she die.

The servants parted to make way for Arthur. Nimue followed him to the window.

Leonilla stood on the very edge. Outside, the sky was overcast and a stiff wind blew. Nimue hoped the queen was strong enough to keep her balance in it. Her black robes billowed wildly. She was not holding on to the edge of the building. Over and over she repeated Jean-Michel's name, as if he might answer from the sky.

Arthur spoke to her in as soothing a tone as he could manage, given what was happening. Nimue joined him. With luck, one or both of them would find the right thing to say to calm her insane determination to end her life.

Leonilla was distracted by their talking. A gust of wind knocked her off balance. Just as she started to fall Arthur caught her by the arm and pulled her inside.

Guards carried her to the bed. She was oddly docile. She whispered softly, "Jean-Michel."

Arthur gave Captain Dalley orders for her to be closely guarded round the clock. "The last thing we want is another dead French royal." Then, slowly, the crowd dispersed back to the Great Hall.

But the incident had been too disruptive, too upsetting. After a brief conference with Nimue, Arthur announced that the trial would remain in recess until noon the following day.

Nimue remained restless all day long. That night she had trouble sleeping. Leonilla's increasing madness aside, she was concerned about Merlin, from whom no further word had been received. When, very late, the moon rose and shone into her eyes, she rolled onto her side and finally fell asleep.

Then, just before dawn, as the sky was beginning to lighten, she was wakened by the sound of someone in her room. Thinking it was an assassin, she gasped loudly and held her pillow in front of herself. But when she heard a familiar laugh in the shadows, she knew it was Merlin.

"What on earth are you doing here? Where have you been all this time?"

"Our channel crossing was slow—there were heavy winds."

"And what did you learn in France?"

Instead of answering he found a stool and asked her, "What has been happening here?"

She brought him up to date on everything: the trial, the knights anxious for action, the imprisonment of Jean-Michel per Merlin's orders. "Oh, and Leonilla is becoming more and more unhinged. When she found out we had arrested him, she tried to kill herself."

After a long moment's pause, Merlin chuckled and said, "Excellent."

Nimue sat up. "Do you mean to say you've solved the mystery?"

"I believe so, yes."

"Then tell me who killed Leodegrance and the others."

"In time, Nimue."

"Was it Jean-Michel? I half-suspected him."

"Jean-Michel," Merlin told her slowly and carefully, in precise measured tones, "is dead."

"Dead? But—"

"He is dead. I am telling you so. By mid-morning, the entire castle will know."

"Merlin, what on earth are you up to?"

"After breakfast we will have to confer with Arthur about what to do with the body. I think an unmarked grave would be appropriate. Do you agree?"

"For god's sake, Merlin, tell me what you found out. Who did these crimes?"

He buried his face in his hands. "I am afraid there is no one we can hold accountable."

"But—"

"Please, Nimue, I have not had any rest. I must go to my room and get at least a few hours' sleep. Things will become clear soon enough. Meet me in the refectory after breakfast."

By sunup the entire castle was buzzing with the news that the young Frenchman had died in his prison cell. One rumor held that some of Arthur's knights, anxious for some action, had forced their way into his dungeon and slaughtered him. Another version held that he had wrapped his chains around his throat and suffocated himself. Still again, there was a contention that some unknown assailant had somehow gained entry to his cell and done him in. The only thing everyone seemed to agree on was that he had died the previous day, under the noses of the guards. So, naturally, more theories sprang up, implicating them.

At breakfast no one talked about anything else. The diplomatic grapevine, whch had been operating more or less openly since the conference began, quivered and vibrated with the news. Someone claimed to have seen the ghost of Leodegrance stalking the halls of the Spider's House, so naturally he must have been killed somehow by Jean-Michel, who he now killed in turn.

As the morning passed, the theories grew more and more wild and improbable. Jean-Michel had been in league with the Byzantines, who murdered him to keep him silent. Suspicion even fell briefly on Germanicus, even though no one could suggest a possible reason why he of all people should have killed anyone; purportedly he had brought an array of poisonous spiders with him from Egypt and used one of them to do the deed.

Throughout breakfast Arthur and Britomart kept silent about it all. When they were questioned by this knight or that delegate, they claimed to know no more than anyone else and fell silent. They were unwilling even to confirm that the young man was dead.

Then, near the end of the meal, Merlin walked unassumingly into the hall and took his seat at the head table, beside Arthur. And he was immediately surrounded by the curious and plied with questions about Jean-Michel's death. But he ate a small breakfast and did his best to ignore it all. The only thing he was willing to say was that he had arrived back at Corfe only that morning; the lowest scullery maid must know more than he did.

Of all the castle's residents, only the French remained out of the buzz, presumably stunned by the death of still another of their number. Petronilla took a light breakfast alone in a far corner of the refectory, then left without talking to anyone. Neither Guenevere nor Leonilla appeared; they sent servants to fetch their breakfasts. The lesser French functionaries and the servants all maintained a reverential silence even though, to appearances at least, none of them had liked Jean-Michel much.

All day long the rumors circulated, each wilder and more unlikely than the one before. There were alleged conspiracies involving the Pope and Bishop Gildas, secret agents from China, and stories even more preposterous. Merlin went about his business, serenely ignoring it all. But he appeared pleased; about what, no one could say.

Just after the noonday meal Nimue confronted him. "I want to know what's going on."

He smiled. "I've had an idea about lens-grinding. If the technique I have in mind works properly, I should be able to make my viewing lenses even more powerful."

"That's not what I mean, and you know it perfectly well. What happened to Jean-Michel? Why all the secrecy about his death?"

"Honestly, Colin. One of the keys to wisdom is knowing where to direct your curiosity."

"There are times, Merlin, when I believe you became a state minister because it increases your opportunities to annoy everyone."

"You are not the first one to say so. But believe me, it is not true. What I do, I do for reasons that are sound, not frivolous—at least in my mind. Word of the poor boy's death has stirred up quite a little storm."

"And this storm is what you want?"

"Think. If you were the killer, and if you had been operating undetected all this time, how would you react to the presence of another killer? Something is bound to happen."

"If I were the killer, and if someone else was arrested for my crimes and then died—or was executed—I would hardly be able to contain my glee."

"That would depend on your motives for the killings, would it not? Besides, what makes you so certain there is only one killer? Can you think of any single individual who had motives for murdering all three—Leodegrance, Podarthes and Marthe?"

She was deflated. "No, I suppose not. But even so—"

"And yet I am fairly certain there was only one killer. And Jean-Michel's death may be the key to proving it."

"I could wish you didn't talk in riddles all the time."

He leaned back and stretched out. "The human race is a riddle. Humanity's willful evil is a riddle, to which I fear there is no solution. What do you think about life after death?"

The question caught her off guard. "I beg your pardon? What I think is that you're trying to change the subject."

"Not at all. Arthur believes in it. Do you?"

"You know the answer to that perfectly well."

"Do I?" He scratched his nose casually. "All of our suspects—everyone who might conceivably have done the killings—adheres to a religion that holds that death is not the end but the beginning. Morgan and her people have their Hall of Heroes rotating eternally at the north pole of the sky. The Christians have their heaven."

"Yes? Will you get to the point?"

"I think it is time to put the strength of their beliefs to the test. How would you like to become someone else?"

"I already have."

"How would you like to stop being Colin, then?"

"You've always encouraged this disguise. What are you suggesting?"

"Temporarily. For a short time."

"So help me, Merlin, if you don't get to the point, I'll tie your beard in knots and hang you from the top of Wizard's Tower."

"We are in the wrong castle for that."

"Even so. Tell me what you have in mind."

He rubbed temple thoughtfully. "Very well. But you must promise me you will not repeat this to anyone."

"What did you say? You want me to what?"

"It is a simple enough concept, Morgan. What do you not understand?"

The two of them were conferring in her chamber. Merlin had insisted she order everyone else away, so as to make sure their conversation was private. "Damn the fool who built this castle without proper doors."

Morgan was deeply suspicious but did as he requested. But she had her guard up. "I am the high priestess of England, as you know perfectly well. Our traditions are under attack by these upstarts—who you encourage. And now you want me to do this?"

"Relax, Morgan." He chuckled softly to himself. "It is not as if I were asking you to commit blasphemy of any sort."

"You and I have never been friends, Merlin; never even liked one another. You are much too committed to what you call rationality—as if anything human might be rational. If you are asking me to do this, now, you must have some irreligious motive. I will never participate in such a thing."

He folded his hands serenely. "Arthur wants it."

"You've had my brother in the palm of your hand for years."

"Even so. He is the king. His wish is your command, or should be. It is the will of the gods that he be king—that he should rule and we should follow. You said so yourself, at his coronation."

"If you think it behooves us to follow him," she smirked, "why do you lead him by the nose so blatantly?"

"Really, Morgan. No one is asking you to do a thing that might weaken your position as high priestess or that might cast any kind of doubt on your gods and goddesses."

Morgan was thinking. Merlin could almost see the wheels turning in her head. After a long moment she leaned back in her chair, folded her arms and smiled at him. "And suppose the gods tell me not to help you with this?"

It was the moment he had been waiting for. "How could they? They must know what else I have in mind."

She laughed at him. "And what would that be?"

Slowly, calmly, Merlin told her, "You want the Christians to make no inroads here. Presumably that is the will of your gods also."

"*Our* gods," she corrected him.

"Yes, of course. And what would please *our* gods in that respect?"

Still smirking at him she said, "I'm thirsty. Let me call a servant and have him bring us wine."

"I am not at all thirsty, myself. Answer my question."

She had been about to clap her hands to summon someone; she stopped and turned to face Merlin directly. "I want the Christians out of England. No bishops, no popes must impinge on the time-honored ways."

Merlin exhaled slowly. "Quite frankly, Morgan, I am not certain that can be done. You know perfectly well that most of Western Europe has been Christianized."

"Does that mean we must be, too?"

"Of course not. But what you are suggesting could easily have unfortunate consequences. If the Pope—I keep forgetting his name—"

"Honorius," she prompted.

"Yes. If Honorius were to plead for support from any of the monarchs . . . it might even lead to war. And we would almost certainly lose. Where would the time-honored ways be then? Do you want to see Christianity imposed on us at sword point?"

She froze momentarily. "Point taken. But this parvenu, Gildas—"

"Yes?"

"Confine him. Keep him here, or at Camelot. Give him no scope to spread his—let us be generous and not call it a superstition."

"Indeed, let us not. And if I agree to this?"

"Surely you mean if Arthur agrees."

He was beginning to feel impatient, "Yes, of course. If Arthur agrees to this . . . ?"

"Then I will do what you want tonight."

"Done."

Finally Morgan called a servant and had him bring wine. She and Merlin toasted their bargain. When she had finished her second cup she grinned at him. "Good heavens, I do enjoy being high priestess. But now you must tell me what you want me to say and do."

Merlin was feeling smug, too. "It will take place in private, so there is very little to rehearse. But we must spread

the word about what you are supposedly doing. Everyone
in the Spider's House must know."

"What?" Arthur glared. "You promised her what?"

Merlin's eyes twinkled. "Relax, Arthur. I need her help
tonight. That was the only way to get it."

"You had no authority to promise her such a thing,"

"Do you think I don't know that? Even she knows it, but
I managed to persuade her to overlook it."

"Honestly, Merlin." The king sighed, exasperated.

"You keep saying you want the assassin exposed. We
have suspects, we have motives, but no concrete evidence.
This has an excellent chance of providing it."

"You said that about your holiday in France."

"Holiday? You call traipsing around the Pyrenees in a rainstorm a holiday? Besides, I got some valuable information."

"Why don't you do this yourself? Why drag Morgan
into it?" The king paced; Merlin followed him, wishing he
would slow down.

"That is simple." He stopped following Arthur and sat in
a nearby chair. "I don't want anything convincing people I
am a wizard or that I traffic in the supernatural. I've spent a
lifetime attempting to build a reputation as a man of reason.
Morgan peddles her mumbo-jumbo everywhere she goes.
She is the logical choice."

Arthur stood face-to-face with him. "But will she do it
when she finds out I have no intention of confining Gildas?
The man is a tiresome nag, granted. A downright bore. Do
you know he tried to tell me drinking is wrong? Of course,
you always tell me the same thing, but . . . But if Morgan
thinks I might be willing to confine someone simply because he believes in a different pack of sins than she does,
she hasn't been paying attention."

"Your England is not hers, Arthur. But all you have to do
is not tell her so, and there will be peace."

He narrowed his eyes. "When she sees Gildas moving freely about the country, she just might guess."

"That will take months. By then we will have resolved this matter. Arthur, this will work."

"And what makes you so certain Jean-Michel didn't do the killings?"

"Well, primarily it is the fact that he had no conceivable motive. Leodegrance was the source of his 'lover's' power, so why kill him? And why would he kill Podarthes or Marthe at all? Besides, Beliveau told me he stole those knives but that it seemed out of character for him. Have you ever heard of a gigolo with enterprise?"

"Point taken. But the mere fact that we can't think of a motive for him doesn't mean he didn't have one."

"Arthur, this will work. Quite honestly, if it does not, I have no idea what will."

All day more and more rumors, carefully planted, circulated through the castle. Something was afoot. Morgan le Fay, High Priestess of England, was to conduct a séance that night, they said. She was to attempt to conjure up the ghost of Jean-Michel, the gossip claimed. When anyone asked Morgan, Merlin or Arthur, the rumors were denied. Yet they would not die; they gained more and more circulation.

At midnight the three of them, along with Britomart and Simon of York, gathered at the young man's room. They were attended by a dozen servants with candles and another dozen boys carrying incense burners. Sweet smoke filled the air. On a cue from Morgan the incense boys began to chant a Celtic hymn to the dead.

More and more curious bystanders gathered in the hall outside the room. Necks craned; noses intruded. Arthur summoned guards to keep them at a distance.

Morgan, in her customary black robes, intoned prayers that were echoed softly by the others. Then they all formed into a procession with Morgan at the head. Slowly, solemnly, accompanied by the incessant chanting of the attendants, they left the chamber and began to walk through the halls of Corfe. Boys chanted hymns; they filled the halls with incense. Guards cleared the way.

At the rear of the procession, Britomart whispered to Merlin, "This doesn't make sense. People will be suspicious."

"Let them be."

"The place to do the séance is his room."

"His room is too small, Brit. You saw how we were packed in there. Besides, a procession will get us noticed, which is precisely what we want. Keeping this secret would defeat the purpose."

And so the odd procession proceeded, followed by more and more curious gawkers. The guards had been carefully instructed to make token efforts to show disapproval but not to do anything that might actually scatter them.

Their route through the castle was the longest, most circuitous one possible. Morgan, her robes billowing in the castle's drafts, walked it slowly, permitting the hymns and the incense to attract more and more spectators. The general mood was more celebratory than solemn, despite the chanting and the grave demeanor of the principals. People who would normally have been in bed at that hour savored the diversion.

When, finally, they reached the Great Hall, dozens of people were following them, knights, diplomats, servants, people from every stratum of the castle's closed little society. The procession halted and Arthur stood at the door; he cleared his throat loudly and addressed the crowd. "Please, all of you, you must understand that we have embarked on a perilous undertaking. To disturb the dead carries danger. Once disturbed, the dead do not easily return to their rest. We are doing what we must in the one place with doors that close. Please respect that. We have no wish to put any of you at risk."

In the crowd Sir Sagramore shouted, "So it is that, then. You are raising the spirit of the dead French boy."

"I have said no such thing." To Morgan, he said, "Come, let us begin."

"Wait!" From among the onlookers Bishop Gildas stepped forward. "This is blasphemous. The sacred book clearly condemns divination through the agency of the dead."

Morgan sneered at him. "Does the sacred book condone the protection of their murderers then?"

She, Merlin and the rest of their party turned their backs on him and entered the Great Hall. Guards pushed the heavy doors shut behind them, barred them with thick wooden beams and suggested that everyone return to their business. But they made no move to actually drive anyone away. And when the crowd began to inch toward the door, the guards stood back and let them do so.

For what seemed an eternity nothing more happened. No voices were heard inside the hall. The smell of incense came from under the door, and candlelight could be seen flickering, but there was not the slightest sign of activity or even movement inside. Then at length Morgan's voice could be heard, intoning still more prayers.

From the hallway behind the crowd came a weak voice. "What is going on here?"

Some people turned to see Leonilla approaching them, walking heavily on a cane of blackthorn.

"What are they doing?" she demanded.

Sagramore stepped toward her. "We don't know for certain, Your Majesty. But word has it they are attempting to contact the spirit of your servant Jean-Michel."

She stopped walking; she virtually froze in place. Then, finally, she spoke one word. "Fools."

She turned and went on her way. After a moment everyone turned back to the huge wooden door. Suddenly Sagramore cried out, "What are we doing here? There are other doors!"

Followed by a dozen people, mostly knights and squires, he rushed off, only to find the other entrances to the Great Hall similarly closed, barred and guarded. Sagramore growled in frustration and struck the stone floor with his sword.

From inside the Great Hall came Morgan's voice, chanting more loudly and insistently, accompanied by her chorus of boys. Ears were pressed to doors, but no one could make out in a definite way what was happening inside. Sagramore's party went back to the main entrance of the hall.

This went on for long, long moments, and still it was impossible to tell for certain what Morgan and the rest were doing. The thick smell of incense began to make some people nauseated; others developed headaches. The crowd began to thin out. Sagramore, increasingly impatient, made a move to pound on the door; the guards sprang to action and stopped him.

Then, at length, everything inside became quiet. Someone tapped on the door and instructed to guards to open it and to disperse the crowd. Arthur emerged first, followed by Morgan, then Britomart, then all the rest. Merlin lingered behind.

Sagramore went inside to confront him. "What happened? What were you doing in here?"

Merlin appeared distracted, or perhaps disappointed. "Nothing."

"Don't be evasive. I want to know what the king was doing."

From the corner of his eye Merlin glanced at the knight. "A prayer service." He smiled, then added, "Of sorts."

"Don't make me laugh. What would you be doing at a

prayer service? Everyone knows you're the most irreligious man in England."

"Shouldn't you be off someplace with the other jurors?"

Sagramore snorted, turned his back and stormed away. Most of the crowd was gone. Merlin stood alone in the Great Hall, savoring the odor of the incense, and smiled to himself.

For the rest of the evening, predictably, gossip spread. No one knew for certain that the service Morgan had conducted had been a séance, but it gave every appearance of being that. But whose spirit had she tried to contact? Jean-Michel seemed the likeliest candidate, but there were people who argued that it must have been Leodegrance, Podarthes or even the maid Marthe.

Equally predictably, it was Sir Sagramore who repeated—and magnified—all the rumors and speculation most energetically. And he was eager to tell anyone who would listen that the séance appeared to have been a failure. Everyone emerging from the Great Hall had looked disappointed, not to say crestfallen. Whatever they had wanted to do had not been accomplished.

By late that night, well past midnight, despite all this activity, most of the castle's occupants were asleep as usual. It had been a long, eventful day. And once all the furor about the séance had begun to die down, the trial was on most everyone's mind as well. It was in recess but would resume soon enough. Following the conference, this new major event at Corfe was equally exciting, if not more so.

But the castle was asleep, along with most of its occupants, and these thoughts of trials and arcane rituals occurred in the minds of sleeping women and men. The ones still awake had more immediate things on their minds.

Guards worked not to fall asleep at their posts; conscientious cooks toiled in the refectory, beginning to prepare the next morning's breakfast; servants cleaned the castle's public spaces. Until—

Strange noises began to reverberate through the halls of Corfe Castle. Low howls echoed, The moans of someone in torment could be heard. People stirred in their sleep; half-awake, they covered their heads with blankets and pillows. Some were alarmed at what they heard; others tried to ignore it and go back to sleep. A particularly loud gasp of pain roused many of them completely; but when the air went silent again they quickly fell back to their dreams.

A guard at the door of the Great Hall was the first to see the apparition. A vague glow, as tall as a man, seeming to drift about the hall, stopping here and there and then moving again. It floated; it hovered. The guard watched, awestruck. And eventually he managed to make out more detail. It was the glowing figure of a knight in armor, his helmet tucked under one arm. The man's face was almost lost in the eerie glow.

Weakly the guard tried to challenge whoever or whatever it was he was seeing. "Stop! Identify yourself!" He felt foolish saying it—talking to a cloud of light. And as he expected, it did not answer but continued its slow progress around the Great Hall. When it finally moved through the door and out into the corridor, he was relieved. No one but he had seen it. Whatever it was, if he said it had not been there, no one could contradict him. When more people saw it—more than one at a time—it would become their problem.

He watched as the smoke or light or phantom moved along the corridor toward the wing where the guests were housed and disappeared around a corner.

There was a guard posted at the Byzantines' rooms; he was asleep, leaning against a wall. The cloud-knight moved past him without disturbing him. But the inhabitants of the rooms, or at least the light sleepers among them, stirred in their sleep and gasped at the sight.

One of the lesser members of their party rushed to awaken Eudathius. "Sir! Sir! You must waken and see this."

Eudathius opened his eyes and saw it at once; it had come to rest at the threshold of his room. He sat up in bed, immediately wide awake. "Podarthes? Podarthes, is that you?"

The specter did not answer him but seemed to quiver in the night air. Then it moved on down the hall.

Petronilla saw it next. She was sitting up, unable to sleep, doing needlework. The phantom light moved very slowly past her door. She froze then, shaking with anxiety, and she pricked her finger with the needle. Drops of blood stained the linen she had been working on. And then it was gone.

It moved on, groaning as it went, pausing at one doorway after another as if it were looking for someone or something. Next it came to Leonilla's suite. All of her servants were sound asleep, But the old queen was sitting up in her bed and drinking wine. When she saw the phantom she called to it. "Leodegrance? Is that you?"

The specter stood still and went silent.

"Leode—" Suddenly through the phantom mist she seemed to discern the ceremonial armor of someone other than her late husband. "Jean-Michel. It is you. I know it."

The light shimmered.

"Jean-Michel, I never meant for them to blame you. Please believe me."

No response came, not even a slight movement.

"Jean-Michel, you know I loved you, Of all my lovers, you were the one." She began to climb out of her bed and stumbled drunkenly.

Abruptly the light moved on along the corridor. Bishop Gildas saw it and, terrified, made the sign of the cross.

Petronus woke to find it looming over his bed; he shook with terror and, thinking it was an avenging angel, begged it not to harm him.

On and on it moved, crying softly in the night. And then at last its glow began to fade, and it vanished. No one who had seen it could shake off the memory. Very few of them managed to sleep again.

And in his room, Merlin sat and read an essay of Aristotle by the light of a single candle. Now and then, when the night's unexpected sounds came to him, he looked up from the manuscript, and he smiled.

A few moments later he began to nod off. But the sound of someone approaching awoke him. Standing in his doorway was Nimue, dressed in Jean-Michel's armor. She put the helmet down on a table and wiped her brow. "These things are hot. How do they do it? I mean, how do they manage all that exercise and all that warfare dressed like this?"

Merlin sat up. "The phosphorus makes it hotter."

"Even so. If I had to wear this nonsense all the time, I'd throw myself into the nearest moat."

"How did it go? Did you notice any reactions?"

"Nothing definite, but . . ."

"Anything at all?"

"No. Well . . . Leonilla said something odd." She told him about it. "But really, Merlin, do you think this will accomplish anything besides making me work up a sweat?"

"Think. If you had committed one—or all—of the murders, and if you knew Jean-Michel had been arrested for your crimes, and if you believed his spirit had returned from the grave, what would you be thinking and feeling?"

She wiped her forehead again. "That he was a nitwit to have worn this armor?"

"I am asking seriously. Even if no one reacted overtly tonight, it is only a matter of time. We simply have to sit back and let Sagramore and the other rumor-mongers do their worst."

"And if the killer or killers were not among the ones who 'saw' him?"

"Time will tell, Nimue. Time will tell."

The next morning the ghost was all anyone could talk about. Arthur announced that because of the disruption and agitation it had caused, Lancelot's trial would not resume for one additional day. Speculation about the ghost's identity ran rampant, but after a few hours a consensus developed that it must have been Jean-Michel. Despite the furor his appearance had caused initially, the morning meal was fairly calm and people were subdued. Merlin wondered if it was from lack of sleep; he himself had slept little enough.

People in the refectory talked in hushed tones, as if they had suddenly come to see Corfe Castle as a sacred place, or at least a very unusual one. Merlin was in a thoughtful mood; he sat beside Arthur, as usual, and kept a careful eye on everyone he suspected, hoping one of them might give something away.

Petronus, who neither Arthur nor Merlin really suspected might be at the bottom of the crimes, or at least one of them, appeared pale and shaken, but there was no way to tell if it was from guilt or simple fear. When they returned from France, Merlin had assigned him to watch Leonilla lest her mad ramblings lead to injury or worse. The boy was unhappy about it but obeyed. She had not come to the dining hall but sent a servant to fetch her breakfast. Petronus ate then went glumly to her rooms.

His sister moped and made idle conversation with the people around her, but not much of it; she ate very little and left. Eudathius and his people, with Gildas among them, talked softly among themselves; their general air was more of bafflement than of fright or nervousness. Guenevere was her usual imperious self; it was impossible to tell if her silence was the product of her usual aloofness or of something darker. Arthur watched her carefully; he still wanted her to be the killer.

Alone among the visitors, Germanicus seemed in a voluble mood; but he could find no one willing to converse with him. He moved from table to table, looking for amiable company. His aimless wandering about the refectory only served to remind several people of the previous night's apparition.

Merlin had instructed the kitchen staff to work at being especially convivial, hoping it might annoy someone to the point of indiscretion. "I want you to be jolly and carefree," he told them. "Nothing annoys a melancholy person more than seeing someone else in a buoyant mood."

"How can we be buoyant when there is a ghost roaming the castle?" one of the maids asked.

"Ghosts only stalk by night."

"That isn't exactly reassuring."

"I give you my word, the ghost will do no harm to any of you."

"How can you know that?"

"It is my job to know."

They found this more cryptic than reassuring, and so they grumbled more; they insisted that acting happy was more than they could do. But Merlin promised them extra pay, and their mood brightened considerably.

But despite close perusal, all the suspects' reactions proved inconclusive.

Even Arthur, who knew the truth of what had happened the previous night, was subdued. He ate his breakfast without much conversation. Then just as he was finishing, he whispered to Merlin, "Where is my sister?"

"Morgan complained that the strain of last night's performance gave her a headache."

"And you don't find that suspicious?"

"Morgan has a murderous nature, granted. But I simply

can't fathom what she might have gained by killing any of the victims. Now, if Gildas had been killed . . ."

"You think too much."

Merlin ran a finger around the edge of his plate. "I choose to take that as a compliment."

"I wish I knew whether I meant it as one." Arthur stood to go, then had another thought. "And I suppose Leonilla is off on another of those lunatic walks of hers?"

"Perhaps. I've sent Petronus to watch her; he will report on her doings. She has been teetering on the edge of madness for weeks. The sight of her dead lover may have pushed her past the brink."

"You do realize, don't you, that if this charade produces no results, you may have driven the poor woman mad for no good reason?"

"With all the killings, added to the loss of her kingdom, that would have happened anyway. She has been more than a little mad for years. We must hope it gets no worse. I do not think I can eat any more. Let me walk out with you."

The two of them moved toward the entrance. Various people tried to talk to them as they passed. Sagramore blustered and said they should all leave for Camelot as quickly as possible. "We can conclude the trial there. It will be safer."

Merlin smiled a sarcastic smile. "Is it possible to be safe from the supernatural?"

Sagramore grunted and went back to his breakfast.

As the two of them moved past Guenevere's table, she glared at them icily but said nothing. Arthur whispered to Merlin that it was a relief. "There is no one I want to talk to less than my sweet wife."

As Arthur drew near him Eudathius stood and said he wanted to lodge a formal diplomatic protest.

"About what, precisely?" Arthur asked.

"About . . . about . . . about all of this. About the delay in the trial. About this spirit we've all seen."

"Are you under the impression we have some influence

over the dead?" Arthur was abrupt. "Half the castles in Europe are haunted. Why should Corfe be an exception? Would you perhaps like to have Bishop Gildas conduct an exorcism?"

"No, sir, but—"

"Excellent. That settles it, then."

They moved quickly out of the hall. Merlin smiled approvingly. "You're getting better at this. In fact, you are handling it as well as I could myself."

"I wish you were the one who had to. And, for heaven's sake, don't remind me that I wanted to be king."

"I would not dream of it, Your Majesty." He leaned on the last two words with heavy irony. "But I find myself feeling fatigued. I need to get some rest now. Last night did not give me much chance to sleep."

Arthur grinned. "Perhaps if you drank some phosphorus . . ."

"That is not funny, Arthur. Sarcasm is not a style that comes naturally to you."

"Maybe not, but I'm being schooled by a master. How can you sleep with all this hubbub going on?"

"Relax, Arthur. The wheels are turning. We can count on human nature."

Merlin returned to his study, found his manuscript of Plotinus and read till he dozed off. When he finally woke the sun had wheeled round to the western sky; brilliant light poured in through the window.

Just as he was shaking off his sleep, he heard someone running down the hall. "Merlin! Merlin!" It was a boy's voice, a familiar one, though he was a bit too drowsy to recognize it. "Merlin! Come quickly! The queen!"

When the boy reached his room he realized it was Petronus. "Merlin, please, you must come at once. Queen Leonilla—"

"What about her? She has not been attacked has she?"

"You are the one expert doctor here. Come with me, please."

He was on the verge of hysteria. Merlin reached for his cane, got to his feet and followed him out into the hall.

Petronus rushed on ahead, pausing every few yards to look back and make certain Merlin was following him. Through the castle they hurried, past the refectory, past the Great Hall, to the visitors' wing. "Please, Merlin, you must believe that I had nothing to do with this."

"This? What exactly is the matter?"

"We're almost there. You will see."

And then they reached Leonilla's chamber. She sat there alone, in a wooden chair with a stiff, high back. She faced neither the door nor the window but stared at a blank stone wall. Black robes enfolded her, as if she were caught in a maelstrom of thick ink. A small table sat between her and the doorway where Merlin stood, and she rested her right arm on it. Her face in profile looked stark and angular; she resembled an aged bird of prey. Merlin found it appropriate. She did not look at him as he entered or acknowledge his presence in any way.

"What is the problem here, Leonilla?"

In a low voice she croaked, "There is none." She turned her head slightly and told Petronus to leave them.

Merlin was testy. "Then why on earth did you send for me? Petronus said you need a doctor."

"I do not. Believe me, medical assistance is the last thing I want."

"Then—?"

"The servants took it upon themselves to send him for you. I instructed them not to, but they ignored me. *Me*. If I live, they will pay dearly for their insolence."

"If you live? Be serious, Leonilla. You are made of iron. You will outlast all of us. Corfe Castle will be dust before you—"

She turned her head and looked directly at him. Her gaze was filled with malevolence; it put him off balance. Then slowly she raised her left arm, the one farther away from him. The billowing sleeve was wet; the fabric clung to her arm. A few drops of something dripped. They were red.

It took him a moment to realize what he was seeing. Then slowly she raised the hem of her robe and he could see on the floor beside her a metal basin; it was filled with blood. She peeled the damp sleeve back off of her left arm. And her wrist was slit open; blood flowed.

"Leonilla!"

Alarmed, he took a step toward her. She barked the word "Stop!"

"But Leonilla, I—"

"Do not move. Do not take another step." From her sleeve she produced a knife, still another of the gold and ivory ones, and held the point to her throat. "Stop, or I will end my life now, immediately."

He froze, And he gaped at her. "I knew, or rather suspected. But I never thought you would do a thing like this. Please, give me the knife. Let me bind up your wrist."

"They should have let me jump that night. Did I not make it sufficiently clear that I do not want to be alive? Why should *you* want me to live?"

Without moving, not wanting to startle her in any way, he said, "Beliveau told me that you and Jean-Michel were the only ones who had access to his workshop. I did not believe Jean-Michel was competent enough to have stolen all the knives without being caught. The thief had to be you."

"Jean-Michel was a bit of a fool. But I loved him. Loved him. Is it possible for the great man of reason to comprehend that?"

Merlin watched her blood trickle into the basin and said nothing.

"I was not about to die without knowing love. It had always seemed unnecessary, but the poets all suggested I was missing something. And he loved me, Merlin; he genuinely did. I have never known such a thing. I made him mine. I tried my best to love him in return. I never imagined he might die because of my crimes. So very, very young. So beautiful."

He spoke softly; he did not move. "So you did the murders. I suspected you must be behind them, somehow, but it seemed so unlikely you would have done them yourself. You *must* have been behind them; ultimately, I knew that. But in the past you have always used agents to do your foul deeds, to work your evil will. I thought that Jean-Michel . . ."

The flow of blood from her wrist strengthened, quickened, It splashed past the basin's rim and onto the floor. Unexpectedly she smiled, sighed and looked into Merlin's eyes. "If people knew how good this feels, a lot more of them would be doing it. Imagine how the world would be transformed if it were known that death brings pleasure, not suffering. This is the end I want. I will not die a useless old queen, stripped of power and majesty, an object of pity or amusement."

He wanted to keep her talking. "What a pity you did not allow Leodegrance that same choice."

"My husband was a complete fool. There has never been a greater ass. He actually told me he loved Guenevere."

His face froze. "She was his daughter. Surely such love is only natural."

"You have no idea the kind of world you are moving in, this world of kings and courtiers. Fool. I loathed Guenevere from the day she was conceived, Monarchs must of necessity hate their children. They replace us, they make us unnecessary. Looking into her face, I never saw anything but a death's head. Love a child? If someone were to show you your own burial shroud, could you love it?"

He groped for something to say. After a moment he

whispered, "She is your daughter. Your flesh. Every inch of her."

"If your Arthur had been a proper king, she would be dead now. I set her about treason against him often enough. Did he act like a king—like a *man*—and dispose of her? No, he did not. That was probably your doing."

"Leonilla, he loved her."

"Love. What does love have to do with rulership?"

"In theory, Leonilla, everything."

"It was so simple. She betrayed him. Often. Blatantly. If she lost, he would kill her, and that would be that. I would be rid of her. If she won, I would have England or a large part of it under my sway. How could I lose? I prodded her into this lunatic marriage with Lancelot, thinking that it, finally, must goad Arthur into destroying her. But I failed to reckon with my idiot son-in-law and his fanciful 'new kind of state.'" She turned to face Merlin again. "Or with the absurd advice you undoubtedly gave him. And now . . . my poor Jean-Michel. He is dead, and it is my doing. I want to be dead, too."

From the corner of his eye he saw Petronus reenter the room. He moved quite silently. Grateful that Leonilla was not facing him, Merlin made a slight gesture to indicate that Petronus was to restrain Leonilla at his signal.

There was a long silence. Merlin was all too aware that Leonilla's life was receding, that her blood was escaping on the far side of her, but he knew that if he made a move toward her, she would plunge the knife into her throat. He wanted to keep her talking till he saw a chance to move. Alive, she could be held to account for her crimes. "But then why kill Leodegrance? He had been your husband for, what, fifty years or more."

"He had been a fool for even longer. He opposed the marriage. But that gave Guenevere a plausible motive for killing him. I knew that if I killed him with one of the golden knives, suspicion would certainly fall on her and her jackass 'husband.' "

"And Podarthes?"

"Disposing of Leodegrance should have placed me firmly on the throne of Camelliard. It would be mine at long last. Then the Byzantines began to move in. Podarthes was Justinian's man in Western Europe. And that scheming slut Marthe was conspiring with him. She had to die as well. I thought feigning madness would keep you from suspecting me, but for once you were not a gull." She buried her face in her hands and wept. "My poor Jean-Michel. My poor, sweet boy. You'll never know how much I loved you, boy."

Softly, in a flat voice, he told her, "His supposed death was supposed to goad you into confessing. But not this. Leonilla, he is alive, in his cell. The ghost was a ruse, nothing more."

She gaped; her eyes widened. "Alive? No! No! That cannot be! I saw him."

"It was Colin. You must have noticed they resembled one another."

"Lies! I am going to join my sweet boy. Trouble me with no more of these lies."

Suddenly Merlin shouted, "Now!"

Petronus rushed Leonilla, caught her arm and wrestled the knife from it; it clattered to the stone floor. Leonilla fought, but Petronus was younger and stronger. Merlin got to his feet, tore a strip of cloth from the hem of his cloak and moved to bind the old queen's wrist.

But Leonilla reached into her robe with her free right hand. And in a flash she produced another knife, still another of the gold and ivory ones. She slashed at Petronus with surprising swiftness. The boy screamed and released her. His face and arm had gashes.

Then Leonilla turned to Merlin, smiled and pushed the

knife cleanly into her own throat. Blood spurted across the room. He was startled there was so much left in her. An instant later she fell to the floor and lay there twitching for a moment. Then she was still.

He checked for a pulse. He put his ear to her face and listened for signs of breathing. There were none. The old queen was dead.

Sadly he whispered, "You have redeemed yourself, Petronus. At least there is that."

EPILOGUE

"The boy will be all right?"

Arthur and Merlin rode side by side at the head of a column returning to Camelot. There was a stiff wind; snowflakes whirled around them.

Merlin pulled his cloak more tightly around himself. "Yes, I think so. Leonilla slashed him pretty horribly. I've treated the wounds to the best of my ability. I am afraid there will be scars. But he is feeling well enough to have insisted on returning to Camelot with us. He actually told me he was looking forward to getting home. Can you believe he thinks of Camelot as his home?"

"It seems he hasn't known any other; not really."

"Well, to make certain he knows what home feels like, I've arranged for him to ride between Morgan and Gildas." He gestured behind them. The two of them were bickering vigorously, as usual. And Petronus was looking perfectly miserable. "Before long, I imagine he will feel nostalgic for Leonilla."

"That's a horrible thing to do to him, Merlin." Arthur sent a soldier back to summon Petronus to join him. "Stay here, Petronus. Ride beside me."

The boy's smile beamed. "Thank you. But why, Your Majesty?"

"You have been through enough. I don't know why, Petronus, but amid all the death we've seen, I'd like to know you're feeling well." He turned to Merlin. "I feel like I'm being so ironic."

Nimue and Germanicus rode just behind them, not talking much. Germanicus was eavesdropping idly on their conversation. "There are so many ironies, Arthur. Do you know that people are saying it was Merlin who conjured up the ghost, not Morgan? He is the wizard, after all."

Merlin harrumphed at him. "Are you leaving for Egypt anytime soon?"

"I'm thinking of staying for an extended visit. If it is agreeable to King Arthur, that is."

Arthur nodded and grinned at him. "Anyone who annoys Merlin so expertly is always welcome. You may stay as long as you like. Your administrative experience should prove valuable."

"Thank you, Your Majesty."

Alone among Arthur's circle of advisors, Britomart was not in the party. She took personal charge of a special military mission to escort Lancelot and Guenevere to the north of the country, to be imprisoned in two separate castles. The castles were remote enough to make it unlikely they could find useful allies or hatch more schemes. Brit had argued that Arthur should execute them, but he resisted the idea, as always. "If I have them killed, Leonilla has won." That was all he said.

Jean-Michel really was still alive. He was released from his dungeon not long after Leonilla's self-slaughter. When Merlin explained to him what had happened, the young man went pale. "No. I loved her. She could not have done the killings. What does that say about me?"

"That you are still too young to be anything but stupid?" Merlin smiled.

Jean-Michel was put on a ship bound for France and ordered never to return to England. Later that day, at the next tide, Petronilla was sent home with a similar warning.

And the following morning the Byzantines, smirking in a superior manner, took ship for their home port. Merlin and Eudathius had one final exchange at the harbor. "You Byzantines. You came here expecting us to be pushovers. You outnumber us, to be certain. You can overwhelm us whenever you choose. But you will never grasp that strength is not the same thing as virtue."

"No, Merlin. Not strength. Power." Eudathius stepped onto the gangway and laughed at him. "Leonilla always said that you are all fools here. It seems she had a point."

Now, on the road back to Camelot, it seemed that all the evil had retreated into a distant background. Relief was quite easily visible on Arthur's face.

Nimue spoke up. "I find that I'm still quite shaken by everything that happened. A mother willing to sacrifice her own daughter to advance her schemes. It seems so . . . it seems so . . ."

Merlin turned back to answer her. "Unnatural? Leonilla was human, nothing more or less. And she was not the only villain. All of them—Guenevere, Lancelot, Petronilla— were quite fully as human as the old queen. It is as simple and disturbing as that."

"But nature, Merlin . . . I mean, even the lowest animals succor their young."

"You are young, Colin. Human nature is not only darker and more frightening than you imagine. It is darker and more frightening than you *can* imagine." He smiled, and Nimue was uncertain whether it was one of his ironic smiles or a genuine one, Then he added a single word: "Yet."

Nimue fell silent. But Germanicus leaned close to her and whispered, "Suddenly I'm not certain I want to stay here after all."

Merlin overheard. "You have seen enough of the world, Germanicus. Do you really believe that people are different anywhere else?"

"No. Of course not."

"Stay, then. Government isolates us. You know that. Friends, real friends, are so few . . ."

Arthur ignored this exchange. He reached over and ran a hand though Petronus's hair. Then he kissed the top of the boy's head. "England will suffer, but it will change and grow. You are the future."

Penguin Group (USA) Online

What will you be reading tomorrow?

Tom Clancy, Patricia Cornwell, W.E.B. Griffin,
Nora Roberts, William Gibson, Robin Cook,
Brian Jacques, Catherine Coulter, Stephen King,
Dean Koontz, Ken Follett, Clive Cussler,
Eric Jerome Dickey, John Sandford,
Terry McMillan, Sue Monk Kidd, Amy Tan,
John Berendt...

You'll find them all at
penguin.com

*Read excerpts and newsletters,
find tour schedules and reading group guides,
and enter contests.*

Subscribe to Penguin Group (USA) newsletters
and get an exclusive inside look
at exciting new titles and the authors you love
long before everyone else does.

PENGUIN GROUP (USA)
us.penguingroup.com